Unveiling SECRETS

Tennille Haig

Unveiling Secrets

Published by TJH Publishing

Rustenburg, South Africa

unveilingsecretsinfo23@gmail.com

ISBN 978-0-7961-4843-8

eISBN 978-0-7961-4844-5

2 4 6 8 10 9 7 5 3

Layout and cover design by Boutique Books

To my readers, may you enjoy this story as much as I enjoyed writing it. Thank you for your support.

Contents

Did you know that 1.3 million women are stalked each year in the United States? That means that one in every three women is a victim of stalking. An estimated 350 people per year get kidnapped. I was one of those unlucky victims. My story was going well, and then things changed.

Let me start from the beginning, where it all began.

Chapter 1

ARRIVAL

---

4 MONTHS EARLIER...

"There are seven more boxes in the trailer that have your name on, Amelia," Mother said, pointing towards the removal van.

We had just arrived yesterday and finally, early this morning, the van had come with all our boxes from Switzerland.

We had lived in Switzerland with my grandparents. My father is a journalist and he had been chasing a story, for two years. That's another reason why we stayed away that long. My parents just forgot to let me in on how long we would be staying and, before I knew it, we had spent two years overseas, but Dad's story was finally finished.

My mother had taken two years off from being a therapist and had decided to spend more family time with us in Switzerland.

We had lived in Lucerne, the biggest city in Switzerland. Our house was located by the edge of the Lucerne Lake. There was something about living right by the lake that brought tranquility to your soul. Gran would wake us up every morning with a cup of tea and breakfast out on the deck. The first thing you'd see in the mornings was the misty mountains ahead. Bliss. I was going to miss it. Gran and Grandpa just got used to us being a part of the furniture. The good thing, though, is that we know we will always have a home over there.

This year would be my year of decision making. North Carolina had been my home for sixteen years before we left. Now that we were back, everything was exactly the way I had pictured it. It made being back more comforting than I could have imagined.

"Amelia," my mother said. I snapped out of my reverie and looked back at her. She was standing above a box that she'd placed on the floor in the living room. Her dark brown hair was tied up in a ponytail and her glasses were resting on her lower nose, so that she could peer over at me with her green eyes. For the life of me, I couldn't remember what she was on about.

"Yes?" I asked cluelessly.

"The boxes, in the van. Outside." She pointed in the direction of the door. I looked and suddenly felt a weight of burden placed over me.

"Noo, Mom. Do I have to? Can't you just ask Marcus to take my boxes out?" Marcus was my older brother.

She placed both her hands on her hips and shook her head at me. "No, my dear. They're your boxes."

I folded my arms and couldn't disagree more. "But..." As I was about to protest, I heard a knock at the door.

"Good day, ladies. I heard someone needed a hand around here," a deep voice spoke.

We both turned and looked. I could barely recognize the familiar face. Alexander. His dark blond hair was pulled to the side in a combover. He wore a red V-neck shirt, black jeans and sneakers. His dimples showed and I couldn't help but squeal. I ran to him, and it wasn't even a second before he embraced me with his strong arms. Everything about him was different. I could feel it. He looked mature and handsome. I had to restrain myself from holding onto him longer than necessary. He put me down and I couldn't stop smiling.

"Wow, Alex, you look so different." I looked up into his blue eyes. In a whole crowd of people, the one thing that would single him out from the rest would be his ocean-blue eyes. He smirked at my comment and didn't break eye contact with me.

"So do you," he said. I looked away from him. He had a way of always making me shy. "You still have that shy streak in you; that's good to know," he said, not taking his eyes off me. I laughed and he pulled me in once more to give me another hug. When he rested his chin on my head, I didn't resist. I breathed in his cologne. He was a man now, not a young boy anymore, and I was struggling to wrap my head around it. Maybe it was the fact that I'd been gone for two years and had forgotten how gorgeous he was.

"I've missed you," I said softly.

"Me too," he replied.

We were both so in the moment that we forgot that my mom was standing there. "Good to see you again, Alex," she said, beaming.

I let go of him and he made his way over to my mom. "It's been a while, Mrs. Benson." He opened his arms and hugged her.

Alexander was my best friend. I'd met him at the house party that my brother threw when Mom and Dad were away for the weekend. I wasn't interested at all, and when I wanted to have Skylar over, she unfortunately couldn't make it. That's when I stumbled into Alex on my way to the fridge, minding my own business. He was probably the nicest person there. All I wanted to do was get out of there because my brother's friends were everywhere. They were having a gaming session. Some girls were there but I didn't take notice. I wasn't interested in impressing any of his friends, so I had gone down in my PJs, not knowing I'd bump into Alex.

He wanted to know my name and asked if I was Marcus's sister. He said that Marcus was clearly adopted because I was too beautiful to be his sister. He was flirting, which only made me more uncomfortable, even though I laughed. Long story short, we clicked, and he found himself coming over every day to "play video games", even though he spent most of it speaking to me. And then they graduated, and we moved away. So did Marcus. Marcus moved overseas as well, to enjoy his studies and the young adult life, although Mom had managed to convince him to fly here to see us for a week. Hence why Alexander was here, I supposed.

Seeing Alex in person made me nervous. We'd always chat over the phone when he wasn't busy with his studies, which helped us stay connected with each other's lives. But it was different now because he was standing right in front of me. He was studying to be in the medical field, which I could totally imagine. He seemed like he could be doctor, with his calm demeanor and his good social skills.

I couldn't take my eyes off him. I watched how he intently listened to my mother's conversation. His skin was tanned a nice golden brown. His eyes were moving from my mother to mine, as though he could feel me staring. He winked at me when he caught my gaze. I smiled and looked away. Before I knew it, he was at my side again and Mom was by the kettle making some coffee.

"Did Marcus invite you?" I asked, pretending to be occupied as I pulled out a cup from a box labeled "Kitchen." He towered over me, taking the cup gently from my hands, not breaking eye contact with me. Butterflies.

"No, he let me know earlier that he was available and that he was helping you guys move back and I just couldn't help myself," he said, holding the cup in his hand.

I chuckled. "Sorry. I guess I should have told you that we're back in town. It's just been hectic, you know," I said, shrugging my shoulders.

He waved me off. "Don't apologize; I understand. Right now, all I care about is that you guys got here safely and that you're here to stay." He beamed at me. Damn, I'd forgotten how perfect his teeth were. He sucked in his lip and took a step back. I looked away. He had me in a trance, and I didn't like it. "Looks as though you can't keep your eyes off of me," he smirked. I rolled my eyes and pushed him on the chest as I took two extra cups out.

"Stop. I just haven't seen you in a long time," I said, walking away from him. I walked over to my mom and gave her the cups.

"Thanks, hun," she said, while her eyes peered at the newspaper. "So, tell me Alex, how's medical school?" She set the newspaper down and poured us each a cup of coffee.

He stood by my side. "Good. Still got a couple more years to go, but I'm hanging in there."

Alex kept talking about his two years of studying and I politely excused myself. I went up the stairs and took a right. I pushed opened my bedroom door. My room was a mess. There were boxes everywhere. I hadn't even had the time this morning to really sit down and tidy everything up, before the removal van came with all our other boxes. We were told they'd come two days later, but I guess that was just an estimation, considering they had come today. I walked through my closet and opened the doors that led to the bathroom. How I'd missed my bathroom.

I looked to the left and saw myself in the mirror. I didn't even look nice. My hair was in a messy bun, and I had no makeup on. Not that I ever wore much, but I wanted to at least look appealing. I didn't really want to change my outfit because then it would have been too obvious that I had left Alex and my mom just to come upstairs to make myself look nice. I took my hair out of the bun and straightened it out. I applied a thin layer of lip gloss to my lips. I took out the mascara and put some on. Before I could even finish applying it to the second eye, I heard a knock. I jumped, almost smudging my left eye with mascara. I quickly hid the evidence.

"What are you doing?" I heard the voice coming from inside my bedroom. I turned around and left the bathroom.

"Nothing," I said quickly.

I walked through my closet and saw him standing outside on my balcony. I remembered the day when I'd told him we were moving to Switzerland, he'd stood in that exact spot outside on my deck, just thinking. He took it rough; so did I, though. It's not easy to just pack up and leave after living in one spot for sixteen years.

I walked up to the door frame and rested slightly against it and finally, for the first time that morning, I looked around at the scenery. Winter was here. The treetops were all white with snow and you could really feel the breeze push past your cheeks. I sucked my breath in and wanted to go inside the instant I walked out.

"You know," he said quietly as he turned around, and his eyes instantly locked onto mine. He'd always had this way of somehow making a deeper connection with me than anybody has ever done. I hated how he'd always catch me lying or catch me hiding my emotions because of how he used to watch me so intently. I know it sounds creepy, but after a while I got used to it. He never gave me the creep vibes; if anything, he gave me the opposite. No matter who came in our way, he always put it straight that I came first and that's one thing I loved about him.

"Yes?" I asked.

He stepped forward and brushed my hair behind my ear. Something I'd forgotten he always did. I couldn't help but break the eye contact. For some reason, I felt as though the room was getting smaller, or maybe it was because he was only inches away from me.

"You've changed, yet you haven't."

I couldn't help but fold my arms. Didn't expect that.

He saw my insecurity and immediately backed up his comment. "Don't get upset; you're absolutely beautiful. I'm just saying that the girl I once knew is now all grown and I almost don't recognize you. You can't imagine so much can change in two years," he said, and I blushed. He smirked when he saw how I reacted to his comment. I looked up at him.

"A lot can happen in two years," I said, inching back inside. He nodded and watched me.

"About that. I have someone I'd like you to meet," he said.

I watched as he grabbed my hand and tugged for us to leave the room. I could barely even grab my jacket before we exited. A little part of me already knew who it would be. My heart started slowly preparing for the crash landing.

Chapter 2

THE INTRODUCTION

We were deep inside the woods. Alex had made us walk all the way from home, till here. I was freezing. My breath made a white fog every time I exhaled. Eventually, I couldn't hide that my body was shivering. We were following a pathway through the trees.

"Are we going to the forbidden cottage?" I asked, wild eyed.

He chuckled. "Forbidden cottage?" he asked.

"Didn't your parents tell you about the place in the woods where all the teenagers and young adults would get away with murder?" I asked, taking slower steps as I heard the music in the distance. I looked out towards the direction of the music, but all I could see were trees, even though I knew that the cottage was close by. Mom would be so worried. Alex grabbed my hand to get my attention. We were standing completely still now.

He stood in front of me and looked me in the eyes. "Em, I don't know what your parents told you, but I know that the cottage that we're going to has no such thing as murder. There are only fun things that take place there. No one will hurt you or take advantage of you. I'll protect you," he reassured me.

I felt a warmth flow through me. I gave a small smile. "Thank you," I said, letting my bottom lip quiver.

He frowned and pulled me in. "You're cold," he said pulling me in for an embrace.

Even though he looked like he was wearing less clothing than me, he was surprisingly warmer. I gave a nervous laugh. I didn't want to ruin the moment, but I also didn't want to get too comfortable. I pulled away but he put his arm around my neck, pulling me to his side. I had forgotten what it felt like to be held so much by a man. It felt strange. I only allowed it because it was Alex.

"I promised your mother I would keep you warm," he said, and I rolled my eyes and couldn't stop myself from laughing.

"The gentlemanly thing to do," I mocked.

"You know me," he responded playfully.

We took another step together and as we got closer and closer, passing by the trees, I felt my stomach do a somersault. I started getting nervous. As we took some more steps, I heard voices in the distance. It sounded like a lot of people. My heart jumped.

"No, Alex." I pushed his arm off me, and I stopped dead. He could see the fear in my eyes, and he gave me a small smile, revealing his one dimple. "You know I don't like big crowds," I said, afraid of the unknown.

He shook his head and took a step towards me, and I took one back. "Don't be scared. I'll be with you. It'll be fun, I promise."

I shook my head and took another step back. I could see the cottage and hear the people more clearly. There were people everywhere in the distance. I immediately wanted to go back home.

"If it makes you feel better, Marcus, Skylar and everyone you know is here," he said, trying to reassure me. I nodded my head. It did make me feel better. I could see some people walking in this direction. I didn't like it. I turned around and quickly tried to run.

"Hey," I heard Alex say. Before I could even put down my second foot, his strong arms surrounded me, and he picked me off the ground. I couldn't help but laugh and in return so did he.

"Stop being so stubborn, Amelia," He teased.

I had forgotten how strong he was. He picked me up as though I weighed nothing. He put me down, while still holding me. My back was pressed against his chest, and I tried to get out from under his arms, but he was too strong. All I could hear was his snickering beside my ear.

"Alex, let go of me," I begged, although being so close to his body made my heart forget how to beat.

"Yeah, let go of her, Alex," a voice said from behind us.

We both stopped playing and looked in the direction of the voice. It was Marcus. My brother. Alex let go of me and I straightened myself out. Marcus wasn't the only one who had been standing there listening to Alex and me. There were about four of them in total. Three boys and one girl. I watched how my brother Marcus looked between Alex and me and gave us a suspicious look. Gosh, how humiliating. I rolled my eyes at him.

"Just having fun," Alex said, looking down at me and, in one smooth motion he gave me a wink. I shyly looked away. I didn't want to look so insecure, so instead I looked up at Marcus's friends.

"Amelia, this is Ivory." He pointed towards the girl, who had her arm around my brother. I didn't want to ask questions.

She had red hair and bright green eyes. She wore a red jacket with black jeans and brown boots. Her lips were coated with a beige lipstick, and I couldn't help but feel under-dressed. She smiled and waved at me. "Hey," her soft voice came out and I smiled back, returning the greeting.

"This is Blake." Alex pointed towards a guy who was standing beside my brother, taking a pull on his cigarette. He had sandy blond hair and his eyes were brown. I could see the color of his eyes, because he was looking at me and there was a light shining at them.

Unveiling Secrets

"Hey, beautiful." He nodded his head in my direction and I immediately got the chills. I smiled awkwardly.

"Shut up, dude," Marcus scolded him.

Blake shrugged, blowing out his last puff of smoke and throwing his cigarette on the floor, while stepping on it. "What? You didn't tell me your sister was so attractive," he said, putting his hands in his pockets and I couldn't have felt more exposed than I already did. Marcus shook his head at him.

"Now, that guy, you try and avoid," Alex said, pointing towards him. I burst out laughing and so did the others.

"Okay," I said, looking at how Blake rolled his eyes.

"Last but not least, this is Bas, aka Sebastian." He pointed to the guy standing next to Blake. He looked up and his eyes locked with mine. He gave a small nod and smile in my direction. He had chocolate brown hair and green eyes. He had a defined jaw line, and his hair was slightly spiked. His complexion was golden brown. He was attractive, and I got the impression he knew it. I waved and instantly felt stupid for doing so. He watched me.

Alex pulled me back beside him. "You should stay away from him too. He is also a creep," Alex said, and Sebastian laughed, looking away from us. Yet, I found this Sebastian guy very intriguing. I found myself staring too long at him. I could swear that in the sixteen years I had lived here, he hadn't been inhabiting this land. He tried to keep his eyes from catching mine and it instantly made me insecure.

I looked away from him and I heard Marcus say to Alex, "You shouldn't be getting so comfortable with my sister. You know how that would make Ingrid feel." I couldn't help but frown and I felt Alex tense a little. I looked up at him.

"Who is Ingrid?" I asked, confused. I heard them all scoff.

"Damn, you didn't tell her about Ingrid?" Blake said smirking. I pushed myself away from Alex and felt more clueless than ever. This was obviously the girl he wanted me to meet. Gosh, how I wish he wouldn't flirt with me the way he did.

"No, he didn't tell me about Ingrid. Who's Ingrid? Is she the surprise you told me about?" I looked at Alex and he had his sheepish smile on.

He nodded his head. "She was the one I wanted you to meet. I didn't want to tell you, I wanted to show you," he said. I felt so stupid. If I had known he had a girlfriend I wouldn't have let him hold me and pull me near like he was doing. I was sure that if his girlfriend found out how comfortable he was making himself with me, she'd be upset.

"Yeah, and Ingrid is the jealous type," Sebastian added. I looked to him and hated that he'd said that. I felt like I was left in the dark here.

Then I heard a soft voice. "Hey guys, why are you all huddled up here, when the fun is all back there?" It was Skylar. I would recognize her voice anywhere. It didn't take her long to step inside the circle and the moment we locked eyes, she screeched, "Amelia!" She let go of the other girl's arm that she was holding and leaped towards me. I opened my arms and gladly accepted the hug.

"Sky," I whispered, closing my eyes with joy.

"Ahh, I missed you. I'm glad Alex managed to convince you to come," she said, hugging me.

"She tried to get away," I heard him saying behind me.

I smiled and pulled away. "You look amazing," I said to her as she stood back and flipped her hair over her shoulder, accepting the compliment.

Her platinum blond hair was curled past her bum. She had some blue highlights in her hair. Her eyes were lightly touched up and she had on clear lip gloss. I always loved how naturally peachy they looked. Being around Sky made me feel so much better. I didn't feel under-dressed; other girls just wanted to over-impress the other guys. Her cheeks were lightly blushed, and her brown eyes glistened as she smiled. Her complexion was fair, but that was okay. She always looked like a beautiful porcelain doll.

I watched as Blake scooped his arm around her. "Yeah, you do look amazing," he said, planting a kiss on her cheek. I couldn't hide my disgust.

She bent down and pushed him away. "Get off me, Blake," she said, finally getting out of his grip. Some of the other boys chuckled. I just stood there, and I watched as she wiped her cheek. "Stop doing that. I'm not interested," she said, frowning at him. He gave her a wink and she scoffed. It must have been a recurring thing that happened. He seemed like the type that liked to pester people. I watched as he pulled out another cigarette and lit it. Gross.

"Sorry about that," she said, rolling her eyes, and I shook my head. There was so much I wanted to talk to her about. She stepped forward and brushed my hair back. "You look gorgeous too. Your hair has grown so much, and I don't know what you did over there in Switzerland, but the look suits you." I shyly smiled. She looked down at my outfit. "And damn, girl, your outfit!"

"Thanks. I picked it out for her," Alex said again.

I rolled my eyes and shook my head. "Ignore him," I said, and he laughed.

"I do, believe me," Skylar counteracted my comment. We both giggled. It wasn't long before the other girl joined the group.

Marcus smiled softly and I knew that there was something at play here.

"Hey, babe," she said and looked straight at Alex.

Jealousy enfolded me. She was a stunner. I now felt overdressed. Her hair was up in a messy bun. Her hair was black, and her eyes were an icy gray. She had a nose ring and these pretty tiny diamond studs in her ears. She wore nude lipstick and a black jacket with black jeans. Her boots had a slight heel to them. Wow, was all I could manage to think. Here I was, feeling confident about myself, looking all mature and everything, but she stole the show. My heart sank as I watched how he marveled at her beauty. So much for, *you look so gorgeous, Amelia.* There was no way I could compete with her.

I wanted to roll my eyes as I watched her place a kiss on his lips. I just wanted to get out of there. I felt so stupid about how I had been flirting with him and letting him hug me when all along he had this goddess right around the corner. I looked away from them, the moment their lips touched. Sky looked at me and gave me a sad smile. She knew how I'd felt about him all these years, even though we were just friends. Best friends never stay best friends just because they want to be friends. There's always some hidden kind of feelings.

"This is Ingrid, Em; she's the girl I wanted you to meet," Alex said, and I watched as he swiftly laced his arm around her hip. Just like he had done to me a minute ago. I looked at her as her icy eyes looked down on me. I felt like a child around her. She looked much older than us, to be frank with you. She gave me a small smile and all I could manage to do was wave.

"He's told me lots about you," I lied. She looked to him smiling.

"You did? That's sweet."

He smiled awkwardly. She was the only one in the room who believed me, and I liked it that way. She didn't even bother to ask what my name was.

"What took you so long?" she asked, watching his lips. She was the clingy type, I could see. I was already over the whole greet and meet thing.

"I told you where I was going," he said, sounding annoyed. I didn't blame him. She was acting like his mother. We all shifted uncomfortably.

"Alright, so can we go back to the cottage now?" Sebastian said, looking like I felt. Uncomfortable.

"Beats me," Blake said, flicking his finished cigarette on the floor. They both turned away from us and headed back with their hands in their pockets. Marcus and his girl were next. Skylar linked her arm with mine, pulling me away from Alex and Ingrid.

When we were far enough from them, she looked back at them and looked ahead of her.

"Sorry about that, babe. We didn't have a choice in the choosing," Skylar said.

"You said I looked good. *That* looks good," I said, looking back at them. I saw Alex looking up at me and Ingrid was gleefully talking away.

Sky tugged at my arm. "Don't be stupid. Looks can be deceiving. She's beautiful, yes, but she can be very nasty. You, on the other hand," she looked to me and smiled, "you are truly beautiful, inside and out."

I felt better already. "Thanks, Sky. I needed that," I said, and she smiled, resting her head on my shoulder.

"Now, forget about them and let's have some fun," she said with a skip and pulled me further towards the cottage.

My heart felt sad, but I wasn't going to let that get me down. I knew I probably shouldn't be upset, but I was or, should I say, I was more disappointed in how the matter had been handled, but I guess that was Alex for you. He'd always been a flirt. I shouldn't have let his flirting get to me. Now I knew.

The music only got louder as we edged closer to the walls of the cottage house. There were people making out in one corner, others dancing around the bonfire. Almost as though they were on drugs. Then again, that was likely the situation at hand. We took a slow stride through the crowd.

"That's like the make out corner." She pointed to the group of people feeling each other up. "That's where all the junkies hang out." She pointed at the bonfire, and I laughed. Just as I'd thought. She stopped walking and she looked at me. "Not to scare you, or anything, but there are many kinds of people here. You need to be careful where you leave your drink and who offers you a drink. Sometimes the nice guys are the ones you need to look out for," she said, breaking her eye contact with me and looking around her. It looked like a place of lust. My parents' darkest fear.

"What kind is he?" I asked, nodding towards Sebastian. He seemed mean and yet so mysterious. She looked at him. He'd joined Marcus and Blake as they stood amongst other people. Ivory wasn't with my brother.

Skylar smiled. "Sebastian?" She stood for a couple of seconds and looked at me. "He is the decent kind. Trust me."

I kept looking at him and watched as he smiled at some of the people. He was beautiful. "He's so mysterious," I murmured.

"He also doesn't date. He plays hard to get, and the list goes on. I think you should give him a hard pass," she said, smiling at him.

He started laughing and I kind of wished I were part of that conversation. He looked straight to where Sky and I were. His green eyes met mine and I immediately looked away. It's as though he'd heard us talking about him. Both Skylar and I laughed. Like we had been caught peeking through a door. I felt a rush flow through me.

I looked to the side and saw Alex standing by Ingrid. She had her arm tightly wrapped around his. They were also standing by a group of girls, and he was the only one who wasn't interested in the conversation. His eyes skimmed above the crowds and finally they fell on me. I wanted to look away, but I didn't. Skylar followed my gaze, and she shook her head at him. His look was everything but desire. I knew him; he didn't like to be hung on. He didn't like to be told what to do. He was very independent when it came to relationships. He liked his space, and *she* seemed all the opposite. He gave me a wink and I watched as Ingrid followed his gaze. Her eyes fell on me, and she smacked him on the chest. He looked at her and frowned. I could see her giving him an earful, and both Skylar and I laughed.

"Welcome home, my friend. Let me show you around," she said, and at that she linked her arm back in mine and we took a step forward. I was curious to see what I had missed in the past two years.

Chapter 3

PERSONAL SPACE

Skylar showed me around the cottage. Being so far in the woods made this cottage a nice hide-out point. The cottage was located right next to a waterfall. It was breathtaking. The perimeter was surrounded by a fence, which had been put there to protect the drunk people from falling off the edge. Walking along the fence made my stomach curdle. I wasn't a big fan of heights.

"That over there..." Sky shouted over the sound of the music. She pointed at an opening in the fencing. The opening led out onto a rocky pathway down to a little deck. "That opens up, and when you follow the pathway you find the deck, where everyone jumps off into the water."

"Bonkers," I said, shaking my head as we got to the opening. Skylar laughed. The ice had made the fence slippery to touch. That made me more cautious. "Have you tried it?" I asked as I looked down at the deck.

"I have, but it does seem intimidating until you're down there," she said, as she pointed by the deck.

No one was there, due to it being so cold. Everyone was either inside or around the fire. The sun was slowly starting to go down, and with it the temperature. I could feel my fingers aching from the cold. I hadn't brought gloves with me. Every time I wanted to open my hand to move my fingers, it was as though they were stuck in motion.

"Come on, I want to show you a safer way of getting down there," she said, pulling me along the fence towards the cottage.

The music got louder as we neared the house. The cottage was a double-story wooden cabin. It had a balcony on the second floor. We walked up three steps to the deck that was in front of the house. People were sitting outside with drinks in their hands. The music was blaring. Sky gave a quick wave at the people on her right, and I gave a small smile. She opened the door, and we stepped through.

She held onto my hand to guide me through the place. It was a big, open-plan house. There were fairy lights draped all over the ceiling, giving it a magical vibe. There were couches all along the wall. People were sitting around in huddled circles. Some were smoking together, which made the air a little foggy, and others were playing drinking games. There was laughter everywhere.

In the far left corner was a pool table. Alexander and Sebastian and two other men I didn't recognize were playing a round of pool. They didn't see us, due to the over-crowded area. To the right was a ping-pong table. In the center of the room was a big, round table where some people were sitting around, playing spin the bottle. Ahh, my heart jumped. I hated that game. Everyone always took advantage of each other in that game. Usually, whenever my friends played it, I always chose truth, until they made a rule that you could only chose truth twice, for the whole game. Imagine that!

I looked at Skylar as she turned around to face me. "Upstairs," she shouted, pointing to the staircase that was right next to us.

I nodded. She let go of my hand and I followed up the stairs. The stairs felt weak under my weight. I didn't trust them one bit. I held onto the railing and decided to shoot one more look at the boys, while they played their game. The one man noticed I was staring and smiled at me. I smiled back, being polite. The man said something to them, and they all turned to look. I looked away, hating the attention.

We made our way upstairs. It opened into three sections. The first section was like the living area. There were couches against the walls and there was a table in the center. There were three windows at the end of the wall, but no curtains. There wasn't anyone up here, which I preferred. It was much quieter than downstairs.

"This is where I like to come sometimes to relax, if the noise downstairs gets too much," she said, looking around. "And then this…" she turned left and walked up to a closed door. "This is where people sleep." She opened the door, not worried that anyone would be inside. The door made a creaking noise. "And where they sleep with each other," she said, and she giggled. I smiled, pulling my face.

"Remind me later where not to sleep when I need a place to stay," I said.

"I know, right? Like you'll get a STD just looking at it," she joked and we both shivered.

The room inside was dark. There wasn't really any space in it because the bed took up most of it. It smelt musky and it wasn't properly ventilated. The bed was a mess, almost as though someone had just used it. You could see they only used it for one thing. I hated it. I just wanted to get out of the room, so that I wouldn't give anyone ideas. As I looked to the side, I saw a door that was basically hidden.

"What's in there?" I asked, pointing to the door.

"It's the bathroom, but I'm not going to show you that now," Skylar said, turning around and walking to another door. I closed the door on my way out. She tried to push that bedroom door open, but it was locked. She giggled again and I felt oddly amused.

"Occupied," we heard someone shouting from inside the room. Skylar put her finger on her mouth and started giggling again. She grabbed my hand and pulled me towards the stairs. "Enough of that. Let's go outside on the deck so that you can see the best feature of this house."

"Gladly!" I laughed.

This would be the last place I would come if I wanted some space. I'd be too afraid to come up here all by myself, just in case a man's like, "Hey, you want to join me in the room?" No thank you.

We walked down the stairs again. I held tightly onto the railing and followed Skylar down. I felt like I was being watched. At the bottom of the staircase there were three guys who were smoking cigarettes and talking. My stomach immediately churned.

Skylar turned to me and whispered, "Stay close."

At that, she grabbed my hand and continued downstairs. I was hoping that maybe Alex was around just in case something bad happened. They looked like they were in their late twenties. One had a red cap on, and he had a trimmed beard. He wore a red hooded jacket and blue jeans. He stood by the railing of the staircase. The other two men were against the wall. They both wore dark jeans. One man had two earrings in his ears, and he wore a dark blue jersey, which was slung over his shoulders, and the other one had on a white jacket. They looked like they hit the gym two times a day and that just made me worry more. I shot my gaze across the room, to see if Alex was around. I couldn't see him. We reached the bottom of the stairs and one of the guys sucked in his breath.

"Skylar, aren't you going to introduce your new friend to us?" red cap said. I didn't want to look up in case that led him on.

"No, sorry Lincoln. We're busy," she said, pulling my hand, getting ready to move forward. I felt the guy in the red cap touch my hair as I moved past him. On instinct, I smacked his hand. Bad move.

"Ahh, she's feisty," he said, looking at his friends. Immediately I regretted it. He grabbed my hand and pulled me in. I had no choice but to look up at him.

"Can I help you?" I asked, trying to pull my hand away from him.

"You can have a drink with me," he said looking down at me with his black eyes. They were so cold. He looked down at my lips and I could hear how his friends started snickering.

"Leave her alone, Lincoln," Skylar shouted over the music. I could see in my peripheral vision that the guy in the white jacket had pulled Skylar against him.

"No, thank you," I said boldly. He started laughing and pulled me in close, making it hard for me to breathe. I looked to the side but didn't want to cause a scene.

"I have a better idea. Why don't we go upstairs?" His eyes filled with lust as he brushed my hair away from my face. I pulled my face from his touch.

"I also want a turn," I heard the guy in the blue saying behind me.

"I don't think so," I heard a voice say. Sebastian grabbed my arm, pulling me behind him and, in one swift motion, Sebastian hit Lincoln between the eyes, causing him to pass out instantly. The other two saw what had happened and tried to jump at Seb, but they were too slow. Alexander and Marcus quickly showed up. They grabbed the men and somehow managed to restrain them from swinging their arms.

"Didn't your parents teach you any manners?" Sebastian said, looking at them and shaking his head. I could feel his body tense. Everyone was looking. So much for not causing a scene.

"We just wanted to have some fun with the girls. No harm in that," the guy in the blue said. Alex was restraining him, and I watched how his jawline tensed at the man's comment. He threw him down so hard against the stairs that even I was afraid.

I felt Skylar grab my hand and she pulled me away from the situation. She headed in the opposite direction from the front door. I heard Alex say some more words, but they weren't audible over the loud music.

I could feel a knot in my throat. My eyes started burning and all I wanted to do was go home. I kept my eyes down as we pushed past everyone, to get to the other side of the house. We reached a sliding door that led out onto the deck. I watched as Skylar slid it open and stepped outside. I followed, sliding the door closed behind me. I felt the cold hit me like a ton of bricks. I sucked in my breath and folded my arms. She turned around and looked at me.

"I'm so sorry that that happened to you. You might think I'm lying, but that doesn't usually happen here," she said, stepping closer to me. She saw how vulnerable I was, and she pulled me closer to give me a hug.

"Thanks, Sky, but I'm okay. I'm glad nothing else happened and that the guys came fast enough," I said, resting my chin on her shoulder.

She nodded her head. All I kept seeing was Lincoln's cold eyes practically undressing me. I pinched my eyes shut and wanted to push the thought away. The sliding door opened, and we both pulled away, looking up at the door. It was Marcus and Alex. Alex closed the sliding door behind him, and I couldn't stop thinking about where Bas had gone. Marcus looked upset. He took a step towards us and pulled both Sky and me in for a hug.

"Sorry that we didn't come anytime sooner," he said, squeezing us. "But you guys are alright? They didn't do anything to you guys?" he asked, and I shook my head and so did Sky. Her hands were around Marcus's waist. She had a crush on my brother, and he was just too stupid to see it.

"No, it was a close call. But there were too many people around. I'm sure they wouldn't have done anything," Skylar replied, letting my brother go when she saw I did it first. He pulled a face and shrugged his shoulders in disbelief.

"I don't know, hey, Sky. They are bad men. It's not the first time we've run into them..."

"It will be the last time they'll ever come here again, that's for sure," Alex said, interrupting my brother. His back was against the railing, and he was watching us. His hands were folded across his chest, and his eyes were dark. He looked at me and tensed his jaw and then looked away. I kind of felt as though I had done something wrong.

"Yeah, we managed to get rid of them. We spoke to Ramon, and he said he'd make it a priority to not let them back onto the premises. Sebastian warned them that he'd take them down to the station if they even stepped a foot near this place or you girls again. So, they won't be coming back," Marcus said, folding his arms.

"Is Ramon the guy who owns this place?" I asked, confused by the name. Marcus nodded his head. "Is Sebastian a cop?" I asked and Marcus nodded his head again. Wow, now he stands even higher in my books.

"I'm kind of beat. Would you mind taking me home?" Skylar looked up at Marcus and he gave her a small smile.

"Not at all. Em, are you coming with?" he asked, and turned to look at Alex, who was still looking away. I didn't want to bother him. Besides, his girlfriend was probably somewhere inside. I looked back at Marcus and nodded my head.

"Yeah…"

"No, don't worry, dude, I'll take her home," Alex interrupted me.

Marcus put his hands in his pockets and nodded his head. "Alright, see you two later," he said, giving me a concerned look before stepping back. "Be careful, okay?" he said, giving me a stern look. I nodded my head and folded my arms while looking down. Sky came over to give me a hug goodbye and whispered sorry again, and I waved her off. I watched them both walk towards the sliding door and then they were gone. Alex and I were alone outside and, when I turned around to face him, he was staring at me. I felt like a little child who had done something wrong.

"How are you holding up?" he asked as he scanned my body. I shifted uncomfortably under his gaze.

"I'm fine. I feel a bit violated, but I'll be okay," I said. He pushed himself away from the railing and started walking towards me. His eyes never left mine and I couldn't help but break the eye contact.

"How are _you_ feeling," I asked looking at the snow that was resting on my boots. He was right in front of me by now. I looked up at him as he spoke.

"I'm upset that this happened, and I wish I'd got there sooner." His eyes held so much turmoil.

"Where were you? I thought you were playing pool and when I looked again you weren't there. None of you were."

He broke the eye contact this time and ran his fingers through his hair. I watched as his jaw tensed and I felt bad that I asked him that question. "I was saying goodbye to Ingrid. She wanted to go home, and I told her I had to stay to make sure you'd be okay, and little did I know what was happening at that moment." He sounded so frustrated. "I'm sorry," he said, looking back at me.

"How did you know?" I asked, curiously. If he hadn't been inside, then how did he know to come to the rescue.

"Sebastian," he said, looking away.

"Oh," I said, looking down. I looked up at him one more time and he seemed so worn down. Not the guy that I knew. "Hey," I said, taking a step forward. "Thank you for saving me. I appreciate it." He shook his head in disbelief and still didn't want to look at me. I grabbed his chin with my hand and pulled it down so that he could face me.

"Stop it now," I said, giving him a small smile. "I'm okay; it's going to be okay," I added quietly, trying to reassure him. He gave a forced smile and he put his arms around me. He picked me off the ground and I held on tighter. "You must put me down, otherwise people are going to start saying things about us, and you don't want Ingrid to get upset again," I said.

"I don't care what people say," he whispered in my ear.

I smiled into his neck. "Thanks," I whispered back.

He put me down and instantly the warmth was gone. He looked down at me and his eyes were back to normal. Ocean blue. It made me happy to see him happy.

"Come on, let's go home," he said, grabbing my hands and taking me towards the door. I didn't want to go back inside there. I tugged at his arm, and he stopped and turned to look at me.

"If it's okay with you, can we go the other way? I don't want to go back in there."

He nodded his head and immediately redirected our steps towards the rocky pathway up to the open fence, which Skylar had showed me earlier. His grip was strong, and I was grateful for that because the last thing I wanted was to fall off of the edge.

"Please don't let go of me," I warned him.

He chuckled. "Still afraid of heights?" he asked.

He made me go first and I put my foot on the rocks. Damn, were they slippery. The snow had made them difficult to step on. He placed his hands on my hips when he saw I was having trouble balancing and I couldn't have been more grateful. I looked down at his hands and I know he noticed. A warmth ran through me. I pushed the thought out of my head. He had a beautiful girlfriend, and I was his best friend. There was no in between.

"So, Ingrid's lovely," I said sarcastically.

He laughed. "I was waiting for you to say something. Sorry I never told you about her and sorry for the way she reacted. She is actually a nice person." We were halfway up, and I couldn't wait to get home and have a nice warm cup of cocoa.

"That's fine, don't worry about it. It's just if I had known she was a goddess I would have dressed better, you know?" I said, looking slightly to the side.

He burst out laughing. "Oh, come on. She's not a goddess," he said.

I stopped walking and turned around to face him. "Stop lying. She is gorgeous and you know it. She's like the perfect definition of *the perfect girl*," I said, making inverted commas for *the perfect girl*. He was so amused that he couldn't stop laughing, and he loved that I was fussing over her. I smacked him on his shoulder, and he shifted back a bit, making me feel as though I was going to fall. My heart jumped. I gaped and grabbed him. "Don't do that!" I shouted at him, and he opened his mouth and gave me a small disbelieving smile.

"You're the one hitting me," he said, putting his hands up in the air.

I rolled my eyes at him and turned around. "Whatever. Stop talking. I don't want to die today, so can we please just make it up there without anyone falling down the edge?" I moaned.

"Do you really think your little smack will push me down the edge?" he teased, and I couldn't help but scoff at him. He grabbed my waist again. Butterflies. I didn't want to feel anything like that for him. I didn't want to get my hopes up. We had been friends for six years and he'd never made his feelings clear, so maybe I just had to stop thinking that one day he was going to confess these unknown feelings for me. I was so upset by the thought that I pushed his hands off my hips.

"I don't need your help," I said and realized it came out more rudely than I'd wanted.

"Fine, suit yourself, bossy boots," he said. He sounded offended and I instantly felt bad.

We reached the top and I grabbed the fence to pull myself up. Alex gave me a small push, by touching my ass. I gave a little laugh. "You must love this," I said sarcastically as I reached the top.

"Not as much as you do," he wittily rejoined.

"Please," I mocked.

I watched him pull himself up. I watched as he made his way over to me, with such ease. I looked to the side of the cottage and thought about the incident again. He saw me looking and I knew he knew I was thinking about it.

"Come on," he said, draping his arm around me. He walked and I stopped before we were about to exit the premises.

"Where is Sebastian? I'd at least like to say thank you to him," I said as Alex looked down on me and shook his head.

"He left straight after. He said he wasn't in the mood to hang around and that he'd maybe see us later," Alex replied. I looked away and felt bad.

"Was it because of us?" I asked as we continued to walk.

He frowned and I looked ahead as his arm still rested on my shoulder. "It's not your fault. Bas just hates getting into fights but, if he has to, he will," Alex replied. I felt kind of special. He'd saved me from the guy and there was no kind of way I could repay him.

"Should I get him something to say thank you?" I asked, looking up at him. I saw him roll his eyes and I couldn't help feeling offended. "What?"

"Look, I guess if you want you can, but you don't have too. Sebastian might take it up the wrong way."

"You are probably right," I said, looking down as our feet crushed through the snow. I thought that he was upset because he hadn't been the one to pull the guy from me. He was jealous, or maybe I was just over analyzing the situation.

There were still people around the bonfire and more around the lawn. But not as many as there had been when we had just got there. I watched how people were watching us. It made me uncomfortable. I didn't want to be labeled.

I pushed his arm off my shoulder. "You shouldn't put your arm around me, Alex. You have a girlfriend," I said, walking beside him as we exited the premises. He stopped walking and pulled my hand so that I would also stop walking. We weren't in sight of anyone anymore, but I didn't care.

"Where is this coming from?" he said frowning. He let go of my hand and I looked at him.

"Alex, you know that it doesn't look right for you to do stuff like that. Ingrid gets upset when she sees you giving me winks, even if it's just innocent. I don't want to be labeled as a boyfriend stealer and you know that," I said. He laughed when I said, "boyfriend stealer."

"Everyone knows we're friends," he said. I looked down and put my hair behind my ear.

"I get it, Alex, but when you have a girlfriend there are boundaries. You can't go holding other girls' hands and giving away winks whenever you please. Especially if Ingrid is the jealous kind," I told him, crossing my arms over my chest as I felt the cold breeze working its way up my back. He stiffened his jaw. I was making him upset, but it was the truth.

"The thing is, I don't just do it to other girls. I only do it with you because we have a connection," he said, stepping forward towards me. His eyes looked vulnerable. He was right, we did have connection.

"Alex, as long as you're in a relationship with another girl, you can't hold my hand or pull me in for hugs. Anything you would do in a relationship, you can't do to me," I said, taking a step away from him. He looked hurt and I felt so bad about what I'd said.

Unveiling Secrets

"Okay, if that's what you want, then it's okay," he said coldly. I already felt so far away from him and the day that had turned out great just started to feel a whole lot worse.

"Will you still take me home?" I asked, looking at the pathway that disappeared into the forest. I didn't want to walk home all by myself, especially not with what had happened earlier.

"Of course, I will. What kind of question is that?" he answered, taking a step forward. "Come on, better get back before it gets dark."

He walked past me, and I followed. I already regretted saying the things I'd said. I loved our connection. It was the closest bond I had ever had with any man. He was like my person. The only thing was, I hadn't been here for the past two years, and it felt like I was the new girl again. I didn't want to start bad vibes. I wanted it to be a good year and if I had to lay some ground rules down then I was going to.

We walked until the music disappeared and I felt oddly safe, knowing it was just me and him.

"You know you have nothing to be insecure about, right?" he murmured.

"What do you mean?" I asked, watching him walk ahead of me.

"I saw the way you looked at Ingrid. She's beautiful, but so are you," he said quietly, not looking back. I felt that warmth again in the pit of my stomach. I couldn't help but smile.

"Thanks," I whispered.

We walked quietly back home. I was so happy to be back in my house, where no weirdos would invade my personal space. Alex didn't mention anything to my parents about what had happened. Marcus wasn't home yet, and I could only imagine why. Alex stayed for some hot cocoa, which made me feel better.

I was afraid he would stop being my friend because of what I'd said. But he was more mature than that.

Before I could even ask Alex if he wanted a second cup of cocoa, the doorbell rang. My father got up and we all watched to see who it could be. He looked outside and picked something up from the ground.

"Who is it, Dad?" I asked as he walked back inside with an envelope.

"I don't know, but they left a letter." He paused looking at it and then he looked up at me. "It has your name on it, Amelia," he said.

I frowned and pushed myself off the couch. I took the letter from my father. My name was written in cursive: *Amelia*.

I opened the letter and started reading.

Chapter 4

THE LETTER

"So, do you know who it is?" Sky asked, folding the letter back up.

I shook my head. "To be honest with you, I don't know. Could be anyone but then again it has to be someone who would know my address," I whispered.

She handed the letter back to me. Her hair was pulled into a pony. She still had some mascara on. She looked at me and I could see she was lost in thought. "Maybe it's Bas?" she said, still thinking. I shrugged my shoulders. "Really, I mean think about it. The person said, *'I'm sorry for what happened to you earlier. I'll make sure it never happens again.'* And I mean, he was the one to pull you away from Lincoln, wasn't he?"

"Look, if it is him, how am I going to ask him? We don't know each other at all and now I'm going to ask him if he wrote a letter to me? How awkward that's going to be," I said, and she chuckled and looked back in the mirror.

"You know what?" she said, looking back at me. "Just ask Alex to ask him."

It was a good idea. "Okay, I'll ask him," I responded, standing beside her looking at myself in the mirror. Sky had lent me some of her clear lip gloss. I applied it and ran my fingers through my hair once more.

Alex had invited me and some people to his house for a gaming night. When I'd lived in North Carolina previously, Alex had lived with his parents. He didn't have his own place. So, this was the very first time that I was getting to see his house.

I looked around his place and marveled at it. It was beautiful. It was perfect for one's first apartment. We were standing inside his bathroom. Everyone was downstairs. I had texted Skylar earlier about the letter, so she'd pulled me aside and we had come to the bathroom.

The music was playing outside, but at a moderate level. The bathroom was nice and big. He only had a shower, which I understood because his whole apartment wasn't built for a family. It was perfect for two. The shower was big enough for five people. It was very spacious and all I wanted to do was try it out. He had plants on the wall of the shower, giving it a mystical feel. There was a shower head against the wall and the shower glass was see-through. His sink was on a brown wooden cabinet, which was attached to the wall. It was beside the shower, on the right. There was a big, beautiful mirror above it and the cabinet had four draws attached to it. We were standing on a nice memory foam, gray carpet. His toilet was just to the left of the shower. He had a fern in a white pot, which was in the corner of the bathroom, right next to the sink. It was breathtaking, and that wasn't even the best part of his place.

"You good?" Skylar asked as she waited at the bathroom door.

I hadn't even realized that I had been daydreaming, looking at myself in the mirror. I nodded my head and turned around. "Yes, let's go," I said.

We both exited the bathroom, and we could hear all the happy chatter downstairs. Right outside the bathroom was Alex's bedroom. Being up here in his bedroom, you could see everyone downstairs. He was a very neat man. His bed was right in the corner to our left. He had white sheets on his bed. Right next to his bed was a built-in bookshelf and there was a painting on the wall above his bed. Fancy. To our right, across from the bed was a flat screen TV against the wall, and that was as big as his room got.

We walked past the TV and headed down the dark-colored stairs. I placed my hand on the wooden railing as I took a step down the staircase. There were family photos up on the wall as you walked down the steps. I slowed my steps and admired it. There was a picture of him with his mom and dad when he graduated from high school and there were some pictures of his friends. He and Marcus with a bunch of other people. There was a picture with him at the coast, with his parents' dog, Red.

My heart warmed as I thought of his golden retriever. He was the friendliest dog I'd ever met, and he never said no to a walk outside. I remember how Alex and I always use to take him for walks when Marcus was busy. I loved Alex's dog. I wondered if he were still alive. My eyes landed on the last picture. I couldn't help but smile. It was Alex and me. It was a picture of him holding me around my neck and I was hugging him back. Marcus had taken the picture. We were snow-boarding that day. He wanted a picture with me because it was the first day that I'd got over my fear of going down a slope. I couldn't help but touch the picture. It felt so special knowing I was on his wall of fame.

"I can't believe he put this up here," I said as Sky was looking at the pictures with me. She came closer to look at the picture.

"Why can't you believe that? You've been a big part in his life for so long, Em. You really need to start giving yourself a break. You should be happy. I'm sure Miss Queen B back there can't stand it," she said snickering, and I couldn't help but laugh as well.

"I know, right? I love that I know him so well," I whispered as we made our way downstairs.

Alex had a gray L-couch that stood in front of a fireplace. His floors were wooden and polished. To our far left, close to the entrance, was his kitchen and dining room table. His kitchen was small, and he had three black lights that hung above the dining room table. He had another bookshelf built into the wall that was close to the fireplace. To the right of the staircase was his garden. He had tall glass windows, which went all the way up to the second floor. If you were wondering if he had curtains, he didn't. He did, however, have this button he would press to close the window, and make it matted so that no one could see in. The one glass door was open and everyone was outside.

Sebastian, Blake, Marcus, Ingrid, Alex, Sky and I were here for the gaming night. I didn't want Ingrid to be here, but I didn't have a choice. All of them were standing outside, around the bonfire. There was another girl standing next to Ingrid. She must have been her friend, considering how close they were standing and how they were laughing together the whole time. Sky looked to the right and saw Sebastian sitting by the bench. He was sitting by himself, and he had a drink in his hand. He was watching the others while they gleefully spoke around the bonfire.

Sky looked at me, almost as if to say, "Here's your chance". "I'll catch you later," she said, leaving me to stand by the doorway all by myself. The thought of being alone with Bas made my stomach curdle. I watched her join the crowd by the bonfire. She joined my brother's side, and he wrapped his arm around her.

"So, tell me," I heard Bas say. I turned to looked at him. Intrigued. I folded my arms to try to keep warm. "Do you miss Switzerland?" he asked, looking from his drink to the people by the bonfire. I smiled at his effort to try to make conversation.

I took a couple of steps closer and rested my hands on top of the chair. I noticed he moved uncomfortably when I got closer.

"I do, but this has been my home since I was a kid. So, there are things I miss over there in Switzerland, but I've missed this place more than you can imagine," I said looking past the people at the bonfire, towards the view. It was beautiful. The kind of place where I would sit and read. I loved it. The trees were dressed in white, and they look scenic. Nightfall was on its way.

"How long have you known Alex?" I asked curiously. I looked to him and watched him think while he looked away from me.

"About two years now," he said, turning his head to look at me. His green eyes fell on me. A warmth ran through my body. I couldn't break the connection and, before I knew it, he'd turned away.

"Listen, I just wanted to say thank you for what you did yesterday. I don't know what would have happened if you hadn't pulled me away from him," I said awkwardly, thinking back to the moment.

"Don't mention it. I'm just glad I could help," he said, and I couldn't help but look back at him. His jaw stiffened and I could see it was making him upset.

I tried to change the subject. "So, Sebastian, I hear you're a cop. What made you decide to become a cop?" I asked him curiously. I decided to sit down in the chair that was one chair away from him.

He looked almost hesitant to answer. "What do you want to be, Amelia?" he asked, avoiding my question. He turned his head and looked at me. I liked the way he said my name.

I looked down at the table and folded my arms, thinking. I could feel him watch me and I loved it. "I don't know. I'm kind of stuck on that one. I don't know what I want to be."

I looked to the side and looked at him. His hair wasn't as spiked up as it had been the day before. It still looked good on him. I noticed he had a black earring on the top of his left ear. My eyes trailed down to his lips. They looked so inviting I almost felt guilty for even staring at them. He looked up and he gave me a smirk. He hadn't taken his eyes off me. A small part of me couldn't help but think he liked the attention I was giving him.

"I'm sorry," I whispered, looking away and placing my hand to my mouth.

"Don't be sorry," he said. I looked back at him, and he was staring straight ahead. I couldn't place my thoughts around him. He was so mysterious. It made me want to get to know him.

"Can I ask you a question?" I asked, looking at him as he thoughtfully looked at the sun disappearing.

"Only one," he said. I laughed, feeling immediately pressured,

"Well, now I'm not so sure about my question, since I can only ask you one," I said enthusiastically. He laughed and instantly I got butterflies in my stomach. I was just happy I'd got him to laugh. "The question is nothing special, I just wanted to know why you were sitting here all by yourself instead of going over there to them?" I said, pointing at the group.

I noticed Alex occasionally shooting glances our way. In the past, he was always so concerned when any man came close to me, let alone spoke to me. He would always swoop in and pretend to be my boyfriend, just to scare them off. Sometimes, if he could see I was having a miserable time, he'd be there to help me out. There were times I appreciated it and other times I didn't. I'm so grateful that Bas knew that Alex was my best friend, and that Alex had Ingrid by his side because, if he were to come over here and break up this conversation I was having with Bas, I'd be upset. I looked to the side, and I watched Sebastian.

"Sometimes you have to break away from the noise and just sit down and think for a while," he said thoughtfully.

I felt instantly guilty as I had interrupted his me time. "I'm sorry, did I interrupt your quiet time?" I asked and he chuckled at my question.

"You did not. Thank you for being so concerned about my mental health," he said, looking at me and smiling. He was playing with me, and I liked it. He had such a warm smile. It was very inviting. I could feel someone stare and I broke my gaze from Bas and I looked to the side. Ingrid's friend was staring. I watched how she looked from Sebastian to me, and back again. Jealousy. The moment she saw me look up she looked away slowly, almost as though to show me that she was keeping an eye on us. Sebastian looked where I was looking.

"Who is she?" I asked, looking at her as she pushed her brown hair over her shoulder. I heard him sigh.

"Her name is Maggie," he said, looking away from her.

I looked to him and frowned. "Are you two together?" I asked curiously.

He immediately shook his head. He kept staring at the table. "We hooked up one night and she won't get it into her head that I'm not interested," he said, looking back up at her and he frowned slightly. I felt the burn in my chest. So, he was that kind of guy. I didn't blame the poor girl. After sleeping with a gorgeous guy like him, who wouldn't want to take things further? I felt so out of my game here. Probably everyone at this party had slept with someone. I didn't want to dare say that I was still a virgin. Knowing that he had probably done it multiple times made me feel like he was totally out of my league. I looked away from him and immediately felt demotivated by the conversation. There was no point in trying to connect with someone who seemed as though they were just using girls and who also seemed like a hot shot.

"I see. Well. I'm not going to give her any more reason to look over here. I'm going to go over there, to where all the noise is," I said, pointing to the group. I stood up from the chair and I knew he could sense that I had been put off by his comment. I didn't want it to be awkward so, instead of just walking away I said, "Are you coming to join us?" I asked and he looked ahead at the group and stood up. Wow, I couldn't believe that actually worked. I smiled a little because I was chuffed with my success.

We walked beside each other, and I couldn't help but love the attention it brought. As we got to the group, I left his side and joined Skylar.

"I love it," she shouted over the music. I laughed and didn't want to give the matter too much attention.

"Okay, everybody, let's play a game," Marcus shouted over everyone else. I froze and immediately knew what we were going to play. Simultaneously Marcus and I both said, "Truth or dare." I looked down and covered my hands over my eyes. No, not this stupid game!

Chapter 5

TRUTH OR DARE

Alex knew how I felt about the game and before we walked in he told me he would ask me simple and easy questions. I felt better knowing that he remembered how I felt about it. I had asked if I could skip the game, but everyone said no. We all walked inside, and the boys put out the fire outside. I overheard Maggie saying to Ingrid that she had to dare Sebastian to make out with her. Skylar and I moved the coffee table off the carpet, so that we could all fit on the carpet.

"Don't worry, Sky. We'll dare Marcus to kiss you," Maggie whispered playfully as we joined them on the carpet.

She shook her head suspiciously, as the boys came inside. I felt so out of place, knowing I didn't know the girls so well and that Skylar was friends with them before I came back. It wasn't long before Blake forced himself between Sky and me. I laughed awkwardly as I didn't know how to handle the situation.

"Between these two beautiful ladies, I will kiss Skylar first and then it will be Amelia," he said proudly, as he was about to put his arm around my neck. I laughed, putting my hand over my mouth. I shook my head, pushing his arm off my shoulder.

"You wish," I heard Alex mutter as he got a bottle out of the cupboard. I couldn't help but smile.

"What was that babe?" Ingrid said cluelessly as she looked to the left where Alex was.

"Nothing. I was just saying I need to find the right bottle so that it can spin right," he said, taking an empty wine bottle out the cupboard. "Found it," he said and made his way over to us. I smiled, looking down at my crossed legs. He'd lied to her because he knew she would flip out if she realized he was getting upset that Blake was giving me attention.

Marcus sat between Skylar and Ingrid. Alex sat between Ingrid and Maggie and Sebastian made his way between Maggie and me. I felt nervous about the situation. Knowing that Sebastian was sitting so close to me made me feel uncomfortable just breathing.

"Good luck," Bas whispered, and I looked to him, stunned that he had even tried to communicate with me again. I could sense the jealousy as I saw Maggie look at us.

"Okay, so rules are rules. You aren't allowed to pick one option the whole time. You have to do both options," Ingrid said, looking around the circle. I hated it. I didn't want to play.

"Okay, but then the dare mustn't be too gross." The words fell out of my mouth, and they all looked at me and laughed.

"Don't worry, princess, we'll go easy on you," Blake said, still sitting next to me. I felt so stupid. I watched as Sebastian leaned forward, giving me a scent of his cologne. I wanted nothing more than to grab him and breathe his cologne in. I pushed the thought out my head and felt guilty for even thinking something like that. Thank God no one could read my thoughts. He spun the bottle and we all watched in anticipation as it moved its way around the group. The bottle moved past me and started slowing. I couldn't help but smile. It slowed and landed on Maggie. She giggled and looked over at Ingrid. They gave each other a look. Bas looked at her and I could see his body was tense.

"Truth or dare," he asked, waiting for her to respond. She looked up thinking. She bit her lip and looked back at Bas.

"Dare."

Alex looked to Sebastian and smiled. Bas looked at him and nodded towards the kitchen counter.

"Alright, I dare you to drink ten liquids in one cup."

She laughed at his comment. "I was expecting something difficult. No problem, bring it on," she said smirking as she sat with her back up straight.

"I didn't say alcohol. It's ten different liquids of anything, in one drink," Sebastian said, and we all laughed as we watched her smirk disappear. Alex stood up and walked over to the kitchen.

"That's disgusting!" she said, pulling her nose up.

I watched how the stud above her lip sparkled in the light. She had dark eyes and dyed black hair, just like Ingrid. She was pale. She had some freckles on her nose and under her eyes. She looked more like a goth princess to me. She was pretty and I couldn't imagine why Sebastian didn't like her. Although maybe she was darker than she looked.

"Here you go," Alex said, handing the concoction to her. She scoffed taking the small glass from him. "I would suggest not to look at it," Alex added, as she peered into the glass. It looked like mustard. I wrinkled my nose.

"What the hell is in here?" she asked and Sebastian laughed. She wasn't impressed.

"It's best if you don't know," Bas said sarcastically. Damn it, I wish I could only choose truth the whole time. I was glad I wasn't her.

"Hold your nose, babe, then it will go down faster," Ingrid said as Alex joined her side again, placing his arm around Ingrid's neck.

We all watched how Maggie held her nose and closed her eyes. She took the glass, and she drank the liquid. She gagged, making us all jump and laugh out of nervousness. I pulled my legs up against my chest, getting ready to jump up. She put the cup down and held her hand to her mouth, closing her eyes.

"What was in there, Alex?" she murmured.

"I can't say; bro code," he said chuckling, and shot Sebastian a look.

She waved her hands and opened her eyes. She stood up and went and poured herself a glass of water. She stood there for a while, and then poured herself another cup. We all waited for her to finish, and eventually she put the glass down and walked over, sitting down in her place.

"Okay, it's on," she said, leaning forward and turning the bottle. It landed on Skylar and I smiled.

"Truth or dare," Maggie said, looking at Sky.

Skylar smiled. "Truth," she said, also holding her legs to her chest.

"Boo! Why are you being so boring, Sky?" Ingrid shouted at her. She would probably think I was completely lame, because if I could I'd always choose truth.

"Okay. Who in this room would you sleep with?" Maggie immediately shook her head and covered her eyes with her hands and started laughing. "Or should I rather say, who in this room haven't you slept with?" she said, smirking.

I gaped and couldn't believe she had assumed that Skylar was loose.

"No!" Skylar said under her breath. We were all watching her. She looked up from her hands and looked across the room at everyone. If she had to choose someone to sleep with, it would probably be my brother. The thought made me cringe. I just didn't know if she would confess it. She looked at Marcus and then she gracefully looked past him and continued down the line. "It would definitely be," she said, stopping at that, and we all waited curiously, "Amelia," she said, giving me a wink.

I laughed, knowing she'd used me as an escape. I would have done the same thing to avoid the question. The men in the room whooed. I hugged my legs tighter because I'd started getting nervous, as I knew my chance to go was probably near.

"Alright, ladies, go ahead," Blake said, leaning back. I laughed and I couldn't help but hide my head between my knees. I could feel my cheeks flush. I didn't like to be the center of attention.

"That's not fair. You're not allowed to choose a girl," Maggie said, getting upset.

Skylar shrugged her shoulders. "Next time, be specific, Mags," she said, leaning forward.

We watched the bottle spin, and it went once around the room and then it started to slow as it passed Sky. Immediately my heart started to slow. It landed on Blake. I smiled and held my chest, mentally shouting, Yes!

"Truth or dare," she asked him, and he immediately responded, "Dare."

"I dare you to pole dance on an imaginary pole," she said, giggling.

He jumped up, smiling. We watched as he placed his hand on his chest and moved them down his body. He started wiggling his ass and pointed it at Skylar and she started laughing. He held his hand in the air, holding the imaginary pole and then he went around and around in circles.

"Alright, enough of that; my eyes are sore," Marcus said, laughing.

Blake stopped what he was doing and had a big smile on his face. Clearly satisfied with himself, he leaned forward and spun the bottle. It fell on Alex.

"Dare or Truth," he asked, giving him a wicked smile.

Alex casually said, "Dare." He looked around the room and I didn't feel so good about his suggestion. Blake, the instigator.

"I dare you to kiss any girl here in this room, except for your girlfriend," he said in a sly tone. I hadn't expected that dare.

Alex shook his head and Ingrid folded her arms, glaring at Blake. "What the hell, man, you always do this. I won't do that," he said, clearly upset.

I hugged my legs and placed my chin slightly on my knees. I watched as Blake shook his head. "When the game started you didn't say that girlfriends and boyfriends were excluded from kissing other people. If you didn't want anything like that to happen, you should have said no kissing anyone in a relationship. Sorry bud," Blake said shrugging his shoulders. Alex looked anxious and he looked next to him, to where Ingrid was sitting. She didn't look at him.

"Dude, it's fine. Choose something else," Marcus said, defending Alex who was clearly upset.

Blake shook his head. "Rules are rules."

I watched how Ingrid kept her eyes on the bottle. If she could have set it alight with her mind, she probably would have. They weren't all snuggled up in each other's arms anymore. She could see him waiting for her permission.

"Ingrid, I won't do anything you're not comfortable with," Alex whispered to her as we all watched them.

She didn't look at him, she just kept staring at the bottle. "Just do it, Alex, it's fine," she said coldly.

The air was so thick you could cut it with a knife. Alex looked to me, and I shook my head slightly so that I wouldn't draw too much attention. Sebastian noticed as he had followed Alex's gaze. Alex kept his eyes on me for a second longer and I knew

I was going to regret the decision later. He turned his head and looked to the side at Skylar. Relief. Skylar shook her head as well and that meant Maggie was the last one to choose. Alex turned to give her a kiss on the cheek. It was so fast that, if you'd blinked you'd have missed it.

"No, on the mouth," Blake protested. I shot him a look. I was waiting for someone to hit him.

"You should have specified where, Blake," Ingrid spat the words out. Her eyes were so white I could swear she was going to cut him with them. Blake just sat there, smirking. I'm sure she was going to give Alex a big speech later. I was flattered to know I was his first option, although I didn't want to think too much about it.

"Alright, Alex, go," Bas said, to break the silence in the room. Alex leaned forward and spun the bottle. It spun around the group, then slowed as it got to Blake, and I already knew it was going to land on me. Alex locked eyes on me, and I could see his blue eyes were a darker shade than normal. He wasn't happy and all I wanted to do was hug him.

"Truth or dare, Em," he asked, searching my face. I trusted him, so I knew whatever I was going to choose, he wouldn't embarrass me.

"Dare," I said quietly.

He pointed to Sebastian. "I dare you to make out with Sebastian," he said, and I gaped at his command. So much for don't worry I have your back. It was strange that he would make a suggestion like that, because he usually hated seeing me around other guys, let alone seeing me kiss one of them. My heart skipped a beat and I looked at him and shook my head. He looked away from me and looked at Sebastian.

"Nice," I heard Blake comment.

I watched as Ingrid gave a small smile. I think she'd had a small part to play in this. It was the last time I was going to trust Alex with this game. All eyes were on us, and I looked to Bas. He was quiet the whole time. I wondered if he was okay with the dare. He turned to look at me and instantly I wanted to back out. His eyes were a deep green and I couldn't help but feel so nervous about the dare.

"Let's get it over with," he said.

I immediately felt annoyed by his comment. I'm sure it was the line he always used with the girls he slept with. I didn't want it to be like that. If anything, I wanted to leave him guessing after the kiss, so that he'd know I wasn't just like any other girl he'd been with. I sat on my knees and brushed my hair past my shoulders and I made the first move.

"Wow, I can feel the chemistry already," Blake commented, and everyone laughed.

I placed my hand on his neck and I edged closer to him. I could feel the warmth of his neck, and I felt as I edged closer how his breath softly passed by my cheeks. My heart was pounding in my chest. He placed his hand on my hip and instantly I felt a warmth flow through me. I looked at his lips and moved in. Our lips brushed together, and I could feel the butterflies in my stomach going crazy. He parted his lips and our tongues touched. His lips felt so comfortable and familiar, even though I could count on my hands the number of guys I'd made out with in my lifetime.

The warmth turned into a fire, and I didn't want to stop. At that moment I remembered that we were still in a room filled with people staring at us. I could hear Sky whooing for us. Blake and Marcus made comments about how uncomfortable they were getting. I used the opportunity to be the first to break the connection. I could feel my cheeks were burning and I didn't dare look at Sebastian. I was too shy. I held my hand over my lips and sat back down. That was definitely the best kiss I had ever had in my life. I couldn't stop smiling.

"Thank goodness. I almost thought I'd have to break you guys apart," Blake said, and I couldn't look up. I didn't like public affection, so that was a big step for me.

"Alright, Amelia, spin the bottle," Alex said, and I knew something was off because he never called me by my full name unless he was being serious.

I looked to him, and he didn't look at me. I didn't understand because he was the one who'd suggested that I kiss Sebastian. I felt as though I was being punished. I guess we both had our ways of getting jealous over one another. Sebastian was quiet and I thought he'd be a fool to not admit the chemistry that flowed through us when we kissed. It was amazing. It was going to be so hard to ignore the feeling that I was feeling. Yet, I was probably just another girl that he had kissed. Not to mention, probably all the girls felt like this with him. I tried to push the thought out of my head. I leaned forward and spun the bottle. It landed on Sebastian. I looked at the bottle and he looked to me.

Chapter 6

MYSTERIOUS KNOCK

"Amelia?" I awoke to Alex's voice.

I cringed at the bright light that was shining through the glass window. I rubbed my eyes and tried to remember where I was. Alex's apartment. I'd had one too many last night, so he'd told me to crash here. I groaned as I lifted myself up from the bed. I slightly opened my eyes and looked beside me. Alex was lying next to me without a shirt on. I immediately pulled the covers over me.

"Why are we sleeping next to each other, Alex?" I groaned as I closed my eyes again. I didn't have a headache and I was very grateful for that, considering how many glasses of wine I'd actually drunk.

"I wanted to make sure you were okay," he said, giving me a small smile.

I shot my eyes open as I thought of Ingrid. "Where's Ingrid?" I panicked, and he looked down, as though he were ashamed of himself.

"She left yesterday already. Don't you remember?" he asked, looking up to me with his dark blue eyes.

I held my hand to my head and tried to think. I remembered that after spin the bottle she wasn't really speaking to anyone. I remembered we ate and had some drinks, and some parts were fuzzy. "I'll be honest with you: I don't quite remember when she left," I said, looking to the side.

He was lying down in bed with the covers over his chest. The thought of us being in a bed together like this made me feel guilty, as though I were doing something wrong. It was partially because he had Ingrid, and it wasn't just him alone anymore. I watched as he stretched his arms behind his head, and he looked up to the ceiling thinking.

"She pulled me to the side last night and told me that she wasn't going to sleep over anymore and that she needed time to think," he softly uttered.

"About what exactly?" I asked, curious.

He removed his hands from behind his head and he shrugged his shoulders while he crossed his hands over his chest. I watched as the blanket pulled slightly down his chest and revealed that across his chest was dark ink.

"Is that a tattoo?" I asked, moving closer to him.

"Oh yeah," he said looking down at his chest and I watched as he pulled the blanket down.

I gasped. He had tribal symbols spread across his chest like a breastplate. It looked so good on him. I pulled my hands out from under the blanket and I turned towards him so I could be more comfortable.

"Can I touch it?" I asked without thinking.

He gave a small smile and he nodded. I leaned all my weight on my left hand, and I gently glided my fingers across his chest. His skin was warm under my touch, and I could feel him tense. He focused his eyes on me as I marveled at his beauty.

"When did you get it?"

"About a year ago," he whispered, not taking his eyes off me.

I could feel the desire to continue touching him, but I pulled away and looked away from him. I had to keep reminding myself that he wasn't a free man anymore. Someone else had his heart, and I didn't want to be the downfall of that.

"Sorry," I said as I looked across his apartment. The sun was beaming through the glass windows, and it hit the floor in the softest way.

"Don't be sorry; you did nothing wrong." He gave a small laugh.

"I know. Anyways, it's very nice. It suits you well," I said, looking away.

His place was even better in the morning light. It felt homey. All I wanted to do was kick my shoes off and stay here for as long as I could. "I'm sorry about you and Ingrid," I said again, thinking of the night before and how he was going to choose me to be the one to kiss. I'm sure Ingrid could see it. Everyone in the building could.

"Don't worry about it. She has her mood swings," he said, sounding defeated. I moved forward and lay back down again next to him, holding tightly onto the covers and making sure I kept my distance. His cologne brushed past me, releasing butterflies in my stomach.

"Does she know that I slept over?" I asked, looking up at his wooden ceiling. He had a beautiful green plant in a white pot hanging from the ceiling. I heard him sigh and I knew the answer.

"No, but it's fine. She's not my mother. I don't have to ask for her permission. It's my house and I can ask anyone to sleep over if I want," he said, annoyed.

I started laughing. "Alright, tough guy," I said, chuckling. I knew how he felt. He hated being controlled. That's why he got his own place; his parents were always controlling. Never wanted him to stay out too late. So, I can only imagine how he hated being controlled by her.

He turned to me. I watched as his dimples showed and his blue eyes had a lighter glow to them. "What are you laughing at," he teased.

At that, he reached his hands under the blanket and he grabbed my hips. This bubble of laughter came out of my mouth. I arched my back away from him and I tried to push him away, but he was strong. He moved his hands all around my waist and up my back. I couldn't help but scream and he laughed.

"Stop it, Alex!" I struggled to get the words out.

"Ahh, but I love your laugh," he said.

I tried to turn away, but he grabbed my hand, pulling me closer. I started losing my breath. He placed his hand on my leg and instantly my heart skipped a beat. I got such a fright I leaped forward, not realizing the bed wasn't long enough and I fell off. I hit the floor and I groaned. The floor was freezing and all I wanted was to climb back into the bed. I watched as Alex popped his head out. He smiled at me, and I could see he was holding back a laugh. I pulled myself off the ground and stood up.

"I told you to stop," I said, smacking him on his chest as he leaned back.

"I know where your weak spot is now," he said, smirking.

I instantly rolled my eyes at his comment. "Shut up, you don't know anything," I said, smiling. I watched as he scanned my body. I folded my arms over my chest and felt uncomfortable. "Stop it, Alex," and at that I turned around and headed for the bathroom.

I shut the door behind me and locked it. You can never be too safe. I walked over to the mirror and saw my reflection. I wore one of Alex's shirts. I didn't have pants on, and I only realized how bad it looked now. My hair was a mess, and my makeup was smudged. I looked terrible and here I'd thought I looked beautiful. I was wearing his shirt, we'd slept in the same bed together and his girlfriend didn't know about it. I felt guilty and I knew it was wrong. I made my way to the shower. I turned the water on and climbed in. The hot water burnt my cold skin. Goosebumps rushed all over my body and I couldn't think of a better shower than this one. It was amazing. It felt like a waterfall.

I finished showering and I ran my fingers through my wet hair. I looked around the room and sighed. I'd left my clothes outside with Alex. I tied the towel around my body and crossed my arms over my chest. I slowly walked towards the door and opened the door slowly.

"Alex?" I asked, not opening the door too much.

"Yes?" he replied.

"Can you please bring me my clothes?" I asked softly.

He sniggered and I hated that I had to ask him. "Come outside and get them yourself," he teased, and I rolled my eyes.

"Stop it, Alex," I insisted.

I heard two voices laughing and I froze. I popped my head around the corner out of curiosity. Sebastian was sitting on the bed, looking through his phone, and Alex's back was resting against the wall. He looked my way the moment I revealed my head.

"Ahh, there she is!" he said, a bit too loudly, and beaming.

Sebastian looked up and looked my way. I closed the door immediately. I could hear Alex laughing even more. I wanted to hit him. I leaned my body against the wall and waited.

"Alex." I heard the two voices speaking outside. It wasn't even a minute, and I heard a knock at the door. I opened it slightly and I watched a hand pop around the corner to hand my clothes to me. His wrist had dark ink on it. It was another tattoo. I took my clothes gratefully. "Thanks," I whispered.

"No problem," Bas replied, and I immediately closed the door gently after I'd received my clothes.

Gosh, if I had known he was downstairs I never would have been as loud as I had been. I could only imagine how it sounded. I felt embarrassed, knowing that he was there, and he'd heard all the commotion. I wondered what he thought of me. I wondered why he'd stayed the night. I'll be honest, I didn't remember everything towards the end of the night. I didn't even remember putting on Alex's shirt. I wanted to take the whole night back. Except the part where I got to kiss Sebastian on the lips.

I caught myself fantasizing about the kiss. I shook my head and pushed my smile away. He'd probably had many sessions like that. I put my clothes on and looked once more in the mirror and I pulled my hair into a bun. I didn't have makeup on anymore after the shower. Honestly, I didn't need to impress any of them. Sebastian didn't like dating and for that reason he was a no-go zone and Alex was taken. They were friends.

I opened the door and saw the bed was empty and messy. I heard them downstairs. I made my way downstairs, and I could hear soft music playing on the stereo. I glided my hand down the staircase railing and when I got to the bottom of the stairs I saw both boys in the kitchen. Sebastian was leaning against the counter with his back towards me and Alex was making something by the stove. Alex had a white, long-sleeved shirt on. His hair was a mess, but he looked cute. Sebastian wore a gray, long-sleeved shirt with two white stripes on the sleeves, like a jock. I was sure that he was one when he was in high school. He certainly suited the profile.

I walked over to the island and made my presence known. "Hey," I softly said, and Sebastian turned around.

He gave me a small smile. "Hey," he replied.

I sat down and looked away from him. He was holding a juice box in his hand. He leaned his body against the counter on the other side and Alex looked up to me from the pan. He was frying eggs. "Sebastian and I were just speaking about going for a nice hike. Do you want to tag along?"

I looked from Alex to Bas and they both had their eyes on me. I couldn't handle the attention. I looked down and shrugged my shoulders. "Sure. Where would we go?" I asked as I played with a piece of paper that was on the table.

"We were thinking about Mount Brent's. The one where the waterfall is on the edge," Bas said, looking from Alex to me.

"Is it the one where the cottage is?" I asked, thinking back to the waterfall that was on the edge of the house. They both shook their heads.

"This waterfall is better, much better," Alex said, smiling as he took the toast out the toaster.

"Have you never been there?" Bas asked, and I liked that he was engaging in conversation with me.

I shook my head. "I can't recall," I said thinking about it, as I looked at him.

"I'm sure you have. You'll remember once you've seen it," Alex said, as he put the eggs beside the toast.

"Will it just be us three?" I asked, looking between the two of them.

Sebastian shrugged his shoulders as he looked at Alex. There was something about Sebastian when he acted like a jerk that made me like him more. It was that bad boy, I don't care act.

"Why not. Ingrid doesn't really like to hike. Marcus said he was doing something today," Alex said as he pushed one plate over to me. I couldn't help but raise my eyebrows at his comment about Ingrid. Terrible match they were.

"Thanks, Alex. You didn't have to make breakfast," I said, taking the plate from him.

"It was Bas's suggestion," he replied.

I looked at Sebastian and he gave me a small smile. "You're welcome," Sebastian said and immediately I smiled back.

I couldn't handle the two of them in one place. Alex grabbed a seat across from me and sat down with his plate of food. Bas grabbed three glasses and poured the remaining juice that was left in the box for us. After handing it to us, he grabbed a seat beside me.

"It will be fun, just the three of us," Alex said, before he took a bite.

"Okay, that's fine. I just want to get a different set of clothing, if you don't mind," I said looking at both of them.

Sebastian had rolled up his sleeves and his tattoos were revealed. He also had tribal symbols around his wrists. I watched as his veins branched all the way up his arms. By the fold of his elbow, he had numbers in roman numerals.

"You're like a kid who's never tasted candy before," Alex said, watching me as I admired Sebastian's ink. Sebastian laughed because he knew I was staring.

"I like them. Tattoos fascinate me," I said, feeling caught out. I took a bit of my food and looked to Bas. "Did you guys get them at the same time?" I asked, looking from him to Alex.

Alex smiled, revealing his dimple. He didn't look up at me.

"We only got the tribal symbols together, not the others," Sebastian, said looking at Alex, thinking.

"Why tribal?"

"Why not?" Sebastian replied.

I smiled and looked away from his green eyes. I thought about the fact that they had others. Where on earth was Alex's other tattoo?

"Can I see your other tattoos?" I asked Bas. He gave a small smile and looked down at his food. I could see he felt uncomfortable.

"Geez, Em, you got one kiss out of the guy and now you want to undress him?" Alex teased and I rolled my eyes. Sebastian chuckled and I felt embarrassed.

"Stop it Alex." I glared at him. He was making everything uncomfortable between the two of us. I didn't want to think about the fact that our lips had touched last night, but he wouldn't stop bringing it up.

"How about this?" He looked up from his food and placed his one hand on his side and the other rested on the table. I nodded my head, listening intently. "You make it through the day with the hike, and I'll maybe consider showing you one more tattoo," he said, challenging me.

I smirked. I felt a burst of excitement.

"Dude, do you honestly think she won't be able to hike Mount Brent?" Alex said, clearly annoyed by the silly challenge.

"We'll find out, won't we?" Bas said, shrugging his shoulders.

We ate the breakfast that Alex had prepared for us. I watched the two of them talk. Sebastian and Alex were long done, but I was still nibbling on my toast. I watched as they spoke about something that had happened to Blake when he'd tried to make a move on one girl and they both broke out in laughter as they'd watched how it turned sour. They were both so beautiful in every way. I honestly felt like the luckiest girl to be sitting between them. One of them was my best friend and the other one a new friend. They both lit up when they were talking. I couldn't help but lose myself in my secret thoughts.

We heard a knock at the door, and I snapped out of my thoughts. Alex got up and went to the door. He opened the door and he was silent, which only made me more curious.

"Who is it, Alex?" I asked, finishing off my piece of toast. I watched as he picked up something from the ground. A letter. I watched as he looked at the envelope and folded it into two and placed it in his back pocket.

"It's just the mailman dropping off my letter to confirm my next study books and dates," he said, forcing a smile.

I squinted my eyes at him. I knew when he was lying. "Are you sure?" I asked, looking at his pants with the hidden letter.

He took the plates from the table and put them in the sink. "Uh-huh," he said.

I looked over to Sebastian, who seemed to have read Alex's mind. Gosh, the curiosity was killing me. Sebastian fell quiet and I could see he was thinking. I wasn't going to sit there and be the fool. I walked around the island and placed my cup in the sink while Alex placed the plates in soapy water. In one swift motion, I reached into Alex's back pocket and stole the letter. I turned around and tried to run, but he was always a step ahead. He placed his arms around me and grabbed the letter out of my hands. He held me tight so I couldn't escape. He signaled for Bas to take the letter from his hand. I couldn't help but laugh and also get annoyed at the same time as I watched them work together to hide the letter from me.

"You don't need to know everything, Amelia," Alex said as he let go of me and watched Bas go upstairs with the letter.

I turned around and I already felt a burst of frustration welling inside me. "What's up with the secrecy?" I asked, folding my arms over my body. He looked away from me. He looked worried. "I know you're lying, Alex," I said once more as I watched his jawline tighten.

"Just trust me when I say that some things you don't need to know." The words came out of his mouth and I instantly grew angry.

"Stop treating me like a child." I rolled my eyes after I said it and headed for the door. I didn't want to be around him at that very moment. I wanted to breathe.

"Amelia, wait," I heard him say and I could see he was following me. I placed my hand on the door and opened it. The cold air rushed in, and I felt all the goosebumps on my back rising.

"Don't go out there by yourself," Sebastian said. I turned and faced them both. He looked so serious that it made me worried. Honestly, I felt as though I was being reprimanded for doing something wrong. I felt small.

"Why not?" I asked Sebastian and he hesitated before he spoke the next sentence.

"Because," he said slowly, and he shot one look at Alex and Alex shook his head.

"No, tell me, Sebastian," I said and at the mention of his name he locked his eyes on me.

"Don't, dude," Alex warned him.

"What could honestly be so bad?" I asked, confused. The breeze slowly blew past me, numbing my back.

"The letter was addressed to *you.* Considering it's the second letter now, I would say you have yourself a little stalker," Sebastian said, holding the letter in his hand. How did Sebastian know that I had gotten another letter before this one? Alex must have told him. I looked at both men, who looked straight back at me. Oh, how my life had just taken an interesting turn.

Chapter 7

THE STALKER

The letter was written in the same handwriting as the previous letter. Sebastian suggested that he take it with him to the police station so they could run the handwriting for any clues. I didn't want any more attention on the matter than there already was. Alex and Sebastian drove me home, so that I could get a clean set of clothes. I grabbed the first letter on my way out, so that I could compare the two letters.

Sebastian said that it was fine if we didn't take the matter further. If I got a third letter, I would be able to hand the letters in and they would be able to make a case out of it. Sebastian told me that it was safer if we reported it and that it would only help protect me in the long run. I took all his advice in and just asked them to keep it secret and that said I would tell them if I got a third letter. He also suggested we told my parents, but there was no way. For all we knew, this person could have had a crush on me and was just speaking his mind, instead of planning to actually do anything about it. I didn't want to make a big thing of the matter.

"Amelia, we don't have to go on the hike anymore," Alexander said as Sebastian glanced over at me through the rear-view mirror. I looked away immediately. The car slowed and I watched as Sebastian pulled off on the side of the road. I frowned and looked at them.

"No, what are you guys doing? It's okay," I said, looking as Sebastian and Alex turned around to face me. "It's a stupid crush. Who knows, maybe it's a little kid or maybe it's nothing.

Whatever the matter, I don't want to worry about stepping outside my door because of this person. And I definitely don't want my parents to know. Knowing them, they might make us move again," I said, looking down at my hands. "So, to be honest with you, I think going for this hike would be the best thing to take the letter off my mind."

I looked up to both of them and they both were concerned. Alex was tensing his jaw, and his eyes were dark. He sat back in his seat and gave a big sigh. I looked over at Sebastian, who was still analyzing me. His dark hair was pulled to the side. I hadn't even known him for long, but I could see that his green eyes weren't glowing. He was worried.

I watched as Bas mouthed the words "Are you sure?" I gave him a small smile and a nod. He turned and looked to Alex. "Dude, it's fine. We will be going with, and we'll keep an eye out. Besides, if she wants to go, let's take her. I'll just take my gun with for protection."

Alex looked over to him and he gave him a telepathic look. Gun? I felt nervous about the situation, although I must be honest that I really wanted to see Sebastian in uniform.

"If you want, we can invite Sky. Maybe that will ease up the tension," I said, leaning forward to fit between the two seats. I watched as Alex put on his safety belt again and Bas started the engine.

"Okay, off to Skylar we go," Alex said. Bas turned back onto the road, and we headed off to Skylar's house.

...

We reached a viewpoint while we were climbing up the mountain. We were surrounded by trees and nothing but more mountains. The waterfall was right beneath us as we sat on the ledge. We were standing on a ledge, and it was the perfect place to take a break. Sky stood beside me and took a deep breath. I took some sips of my water and admired the view. I could see the big lake beneath us. The sky was clear, for the first time in days. The snow stopped falling and thank God for the snow, because it was a whole lot safer to hike in winter because the bears were in hibernation. The treetops were white with snow and there was a calming silence, except for the sound of the water gushing out beneath the rock we were sitting on.

Alex stood next to me and Sebastian next to him and I could hear us all breathe in unison. The boys weren't so chatty, and I knew why. We hadn't told Sky about the letter, probably because I hadn't mentioned it and the boys probably didn't want me to think about it. Although the whole way up, even though Skylar was talking the whole way, I kept thinking about the second letter. It was more detailed than the first and creepier.

"Makes you forget about all your problems," Alex said as he looked over the horizon.

We all stood there in silence. I looked over to Alex and analyzed him. His face had relaxed a bit, which made me happy. I didn't want them to worry about it. His nose was pink from the cold weather, it made me smile. I reached for his hand and softly placed mine in his. He closed his hand over mine and I could see a slight smile. He didn't look my way but that was okay. I was just glad I could make him feel better.

"So, tell me, why is everyone so quiet today?" Skylar asked, looking at the three of us. She looked at my hand in Alex's, but she didn't say anything. Her hair was held back in a ponytail, the same as mine. She didn't wear much makeup today and I hadn't even bothered putting any on either. I just wanted to get out of my house and save myself all the questions my mom and father would have about the previous night. I let go of Alex's hand and felt the warmth leave my hand.

"Nothing much; just in thought, that's all," I said, looking to her and away to the view again. I could see she was scanning me.

"You're hiding something," she said.

"Who's hungry?" Sebastian said as he walked over to the wall, which was made from a giant rock. He pulled his backpack off his back and laid a blanket out on the floor. After it was made, he sat down on the ground.

"I am," Alex said and joined him.

As he walked away, I took the moment to speak to her about the new letter. I looked over at Alex and Sebastian. They both leaned their backs against the rock, and I watched as Sebastian passed a sandwich over to Alex. Bas glanced over at me once he was comfortable, and I didn't even realize I had looked at them for so long. I broke the gaze and looked over at Sky, who was also looking at them.

"Well, there is something that happened this morning," I said, looking down at the ground. I tried to speak quietly, even though they knew exactly what we were speaking about. She frowned when she saw how serious I was.

She stepped closer to me. "What do you mean? Did you and… you know?" she said nodding over her shoulder, asking the only question everyone is always so secretive about.

I shook my head and couldn't help but smile. "No, Sky. No one did anything," I said awkwardly, hoping they hadn't heard what she'd said.

"Then what is it?" she asked, looking down at my lips.

I looked out at the view again. "Alex found another letter," I said, not looking over at her.

"What? Where?" she said, raising her voice a little too loud.

I looked back at her. Her eyes were wide, and I had all her attention. "It was earlier at Alex's house, when we all three were there," I replied.

"So, do you think it's from the same person?" she asked.

I nodded. "The handwriting was exactly the same," I said slowly, and I watched as she placed her hand over her mouth.

"So, you have a stalker?" she asked.

"Seems that way, but I'm sure it's nothing to be worried about," I said, looking away.

"You don't know that," she said, and I couldn't help but feel offended. "Look, don't get me wrong. I understand what you're saying, but I also want you to be okay. Yeah, maybe this person isn't all that bad, but what if they are?" she asked, and I didn't want to look at her.

"Yeah, I just don't want it to be a big thing. I mean, they're just letters," I said.

"Do you have the letter here?" she asked, and I looked over at her and nodded my head. "Ahh, can I please see it?"

I turned and looked over at Alex. "It's in Alex's bag," I said.

She turned and walked over to the boys. She asked Alex to see the letter and he handed it over to her. She sat down opposite Bas, and I joined them all on the blanket. I watched as she read over the lines, and she turned to me.

"I don't think this is minor, Amelia," she said, looking over to me, and instantly I felt a cold breeze blow over me. I looked into the distance towards the trees, and I felt as though the stalker was already here with us. I could see nothing but branches and trees. The further the woods stretched out, the darker it became. To be frank, anyone could hide in there and watch us and we wouldn't know about it.

"Don't say that," I said, still looking around and hoping the stalker wasn't going to come running out of the woods.

"The fact that he dropped the letter off at my house tells you that he knows where I live, and he knows that Amelia was with us at that moment," Alex said, and I looked at him and he looked at me. His eyes were dark again and I hated that we had to bring the topic up again, but it was better to get it out of the way. I sighed, rubbing my eyes out of frustration. He was looking at me and I couldn't really read him.

"I wonder what this character wants from me. I've done nothing. I haven't even gone out of my way to go to foreign places, nor have I gone to many clubs. I don't understand how this person has found me and why the fascination?" I said, looking at the mat that Sebastian had laid out for us. It was a green and white blanket, and it had a waterproof seal on at the bottom, perfect for if you wanted to lay it onto snow or wet ground.

"There's so much more to stalker cases really. We've dealt with a couple of cases in the past. Nothing too serious. Small fascinations that the stalker grows as time goes on. I guess it depends how long the stalking goes on for us to really know how serious the matter is. The longer the stalking, the crazier and more obsessed the person becomes," Sebastian said as he held onto his sandwich. His expression was stern and serious.

I still couldn't wrap my head around the fact that he was an officer. I was all eyes, though. It was interesting to hear it from the professional side.

"Luckily, it's just recent. So, I don't think this has been going on for long," I said hopefully. I looked at Skylar and she was quiet and concerned.

"It depends, Amelia. They are called stalkers for reasons. Some stalk the victim long before they eventually initiate any form of contact with the victim," Sebastian said, looking at me. I felt defeated and, quite frankly, I was afraid. I looked away and frowned. It was a bad idea to talk about this. It just made me feel more afraid.

"Look, you have us on your side. Everything should be okay. Like you said, he might be a pushover. Let's treat the situation as though it's nothing serious and just a plain old crush and then, if you get another letter, which let's hope you don't, but if you do, we will give everything to Bas, and he can take the matter further. Okay?" Alex said, trying to cheer me up. I nodded my head at him. Both men were looking at me and I felt insecure, so I looked down again.

"Well, I can tell you something, this person does think you're real special," Sky said, handing the letter over to me. I took the letter and looked over the words again.

It read:

Dearest Amelia,

I hope you don't mind me writing. I can't manage to think of anything other than you. I try to keep myself occupied but I find myself pondering over you the whole time. All I want to do is be close to you and hold you tight. I envy the people in your life. They have no idea how special you are. It makes me angry when I see people mishandle you or even when you're kissed by boys, who don't know how lucky they are to touch your beautiful lips. Please know that you are one of a kind and when we meet I'll make sure to show you how special you really are.

Yours sincerely.

Unveiling Secrets

I closed the letter, cringing.

"He's a sicko, if you ask me," Alex said, looking over at Sebastian, and they both exchanged looks.

"I hope I never meet this person," I said, handing the letter back over to Alex. Re-reading the letter just made me realize how serious this person was about their feelings for me. "The stalker must have seen us last night, playing the game," I said, fiddling with my fingers, too insecure to look up.

"Yeah, what a comforting thought," Alex said.

"I'm sorry," I said, looking up at him once more.

He shook his head.

"Don't be sorry, silly. It's not your fault," Skylar said, rubbing my back in a comforting way. I gave her a small smile, to say thank you.

"Yeah, he will be sorry when we find out who he is," Alex said, defending me. I felt strange with all the help and protection they were giving me.

"Out of curiosity, because of what the stalker said. Was that kiss last night the first kiss you've had in a long time?" Sebastian asked, and I looked down already regretting my answer.

I placed my hands over my eyes. "Uhm, you're the only guy I've kissed in years, to be honest," I said softly, and I could feel my cheeks flush. Skylar gasped and I thought I heard Alex chuckle.

"Wow, Em, you don't get out much," Skylar said, giving me a sympathetic smile.

"You're really innocent, aren't you?" Sebastian said looking at me in a whole different light. His expression had changed from serious to intrigued in a second. Bad idea for me, great idea for players.

I rolled my eyes and looked the other way so I could somehow stop them from overthinking the situation. "Yeah, don't make a big thing of it, though. I don't really like to get involved with kissing games, let alone men. It's just trouble and drama," and I looked away from them all. I looked back at Alex, who was smiling at me.

"That's why you're special. Because you're not like every other woman," Alex said.

"Gee, thanks Alex," Skylar said sarcastically.

We all burst out laughing and she smiled. Luckily, she wasn't the kind to get offended quickly.

"No offence, Skylar," Alex said, smiling at Skylar.

He looked inside his bag and passed both Sky and me a sandwich, and I was grateful that he'd changed the topic. I turned my back to them, and I looked towards the view. Alex was right. Looking at the view made you forget about the problems in your life.

I looked over at Sebastian as I remembered his promise to me. I smiled at him, and he frowned slightly, as he could see I was up to something. "You promised me if I came with you guys and hiked up here, you'd show me your other tattoo."

He chuckled and looked down.

"You haven't seen it?" Skylar asked surprised, and that just made me more curious and jealous in a way.

"Ahh, c'mon. Skylar's seen it. Now you have to show me," I said, upset at the fact that she'd seen it and I hadn't.

"We haven't completed the hike yet," he said, looking back at me and smiling.

I shook my head at him, but I held his gaze. I liked that we were at least getting along. He had seemed so cold to me in the beginning but now it was much better. I looked away from him and looked over at Skylar, who smirked at me.

"I just want to say one more thing: promise me that, if you get another letter, you won't shut us out? That you'll let us know, right?" Alex said from behind me as I was facing the view.

I turned and looked at him and he was serious. I gave him a reassuring smile and nodded my head. "I promise."

The view and their company helped me to think about better days. Maybe with them by my side we could fight this stalker together. Hopefully, I would not get another letter.

Chapter 8

DEPARTURE

It was late at night. I decided to go for a run. For some reason, the dark woods didn't frighten me as much as they should have. With each tree I passed, I jogged faster. I just so happened to look down at my shoelaces, which were untied. I stopped running and I bent down to tie my shoes. The process took much longer than I would have liked. I heard a noise to the left of me, in the darkness. A rustling of leaves. I cocked my head up in the direction and my anxiety levels began to rise. At that moment, I realized how vulnerable I was, being all by myself in the woods at night. I finished tying my shoe and I jumped up and ran faster than I had before.

I came around a bend and didn't see the branch that was hanging lower than the rest of the branches and I hit my head. I fell down instantly and groaned as the pain throbbed at my forehead. I wiped moisture from my forehead. It was blood. I heard a few more twigs break to my right and for the life of me I couldn't understand why I would be so foolish to run all by myself at night in the woods. I looked to the right and everything inside me froze. In the darkness, I could see a figure standing there. The fear engulfed me. I didn't even think to scream. I slowly pushed myself up from the floor and rose to my feet.

"Amelia," I heard the voice say.

At the mention of my name, I turned and ran in the opposite direction. I ran so fast that my mind blanked about where I was headed to. When I felt a stitch in my abdomen, I slowed my pace and looked behind me. There was no one that I could see. I looked in front of me and saw a tree. I hid behind it and tried to slow my breathing. I wanted to hear the stalker's footsteps. My heart was hammering against my chest. The darkness enfolded me. I couldn't see anything because it was so dark. The emotions rushed through me and all I could think of was how I wished I had stayed at home.

I felt a lump in my throat as I looked slightly around the tree to my left. There was no one to be seen. The forest was quiet, except for my breathing. I tried to shallow my breathing, but it only got worse when the tears began to sting my eyes. I frantically looked in front of me. A hand was placed firmly over my lips. I screamed. My body felt lame, and I felt my head start to fizz. The person was drugging me with something. I held the person's hand and tried to fight it, but they were too strong for me. I started to cry.

"Shhh, it's going to be alright. Don't worry. I'm going to keep you safe," the voice said, letting go of my mouth. I frantically started kicking as I felt the energy draining from me.

"Please," I cried.

"I promised you that I'd come and get you. I love you, Amelia." The man's voice echoed in my ears as I felt myself fall unconscious. My body shook.

"Amelia, wake up," I heard a voice echoing to me.

"Amelia." At the second cry of my name, I opened my eyes.

I gasped. I sat up immediately and wiped my eyes. They were wet from tears. I looked around the room and I almost started to cry again but I managed to contain the urge to. I could feel my heart rapidly beating against my chest. It had just been a dream. I sighed out of relief and rubbed my eyes. My mother sat beside me on the bed. Her expression was filled with worry and concern.

"It's okay, sweetie, you just had a bad dream," she said, looking deep into my eyes. I nodded my head.

"What did you dream of, sweetie?" my father said, coming to my mother's side. His hair was a mess, and I could only imagine I had woken them up. I looked down at my white sheets and thought back on how the man had placed his hands over my mouth. I was dreaming of my stalker, or at least what I thought he was like. I shook my head.

"It was just a normal nightmare; I was running in the woods and things got out of hand," I said, not looking into their eyes.

"Why were you running in the woods?" mom asked, concerned.

"Because I like to run there, and somehow the dream twisted and someone was chasing me. Nothing else happened," I said quickly, pulling the blanket higher up so I could cover my shoulders.

"It sounded quite serious, Amelia. Is everything okay?" Dad questioned.

I looked up to him and saw his dark brown eyes glued to mine. I felt so stupid that they had heard all of that. I looked away and rubbed my head. "Yeah, everything is okay, I promise. It was just a bad dream," I said, looking down at my covers again.

"You haven't had one of these dreams since we were kids," Marcus said, and I cocked my head up to look at him. He was leaning against my door frame and his arms were crossed over his chest. I hadn't even noticed that he was standing there. I looked away, insecure.

"Your brother's right. Is everything okay? Is it because of the big move again?" my mother asked, touching my shoulder out of sympathy.

I frowned, shaking my head. "No, don't worry, it's okay. I'm fine. Don't worry about me," I replied.

"You know that we are always here for you if something's wrong," my father said.

I looked up at him and gave a small smile. "Yes, I know. Thank you. I'll keep it in mind when there's something wrong."

"Promise?" My mom said, looking at my emotions carefully.

I nodded my head and looked away. "I promise."

My father and mother told me to freshen up and meet them downstairs for a nice family breakfast. Marcus lingered a bit and finally he left when he realized I was fine. I exhaled with relief. I can only imagine how concerned Alex would be if he had heard me scream like that. I placed my head between my legs and thought of the next couple of hours. I wasn't really prepared for my brother's departure. I didn't like saying goodbye to anyone.

I jumped out of bed and walked to the bathroom. I climbed into the shower when the water was warm enough. The warmth of the water brought goosebumps to my skin. I rinsed my hair and thought of the stalker. The stalker knew where I lived, and the person also knew where Alex lived. The stalker knew when I was having fun or when I was spending time with "people who didn't deserve me", as the person would put it. I wondered if the stalker was watching me right now. I wiped my face and looked to the side. My glass windows had misted up, but I didn't see any figures in the background.

I switched the shower off and let my hair drip dry. I pulled a light pair of jeans on and my nice white jacket. I wasn't planning on putting on any shoes just yet, so I slipped my slippers on as I made my way out of my closet. When I had finished making my bed I walked on over to my door, and when I had opened up my curtains I passed down the hallway and past Marcus's room. I saw how his suitcase was already packed on his bed. Everything in his room was neat and tidy and a sad wave came over me. I turned left and headed down the wooden stairs. I could smell mom's yummy bacon. Marcus was sitting on the couch across from the fireplace and Mom and Dad were by the kitchen island. I passed Marcus and walked over to mom. She looked up to me and smiled when she saw me approaching.

"Ready for some yummy breakfast?" she said, looking down at what was lying in front of her. Mom had made scrambled eggs, toast, bacon, mushrooms, pancakes, and some strawberries with chocolate dip for a treat. She'd made a big feast, and I nodded my head eagerly.

"Definitely."

"Alright, Marcus. Come and dish up, my boy," Mother said, raising her voice a little so he would hear her. I joined my father and sat next to him. Marcus came over and sat next to my mother as he placed a jug of juice on the table. I smiled and so did everyone else.

"A special meal for your last day," Mother said, smiling at Marcus.

We all dived in and dished up as Marcus thanked my mother. We ate gleefully as we spoke about funny childhood memories. Marcus spoke about how excited he was to get back to his campus and dive back into his studies. He wanted to be a lawyer. It seemed that everyone had their careers all figured out.

Before we knew it, we were all finished, and Dad and Marcus went and got his things so they could put his luggage in the car. My heart still ached, and I could see my mom was fighting the urge to tear up.

"Mom, I don't want to come with to the airport. I can't handle another goodbye. I'd rather just do it here."

My mother turned around from the dish washer. She was frowning. "Why on earth would you not want to come with?" she asked, and I looked away.

"Because I just feel comfortable staying home and saying goodbye here. I don't want to drive anywhere, and I don't want to say goodbye at the airport. It's much better for me to say goodbye here, Mom," I said, standing beside the island. Mom folded her arms across her chest and she gave a big sigh. I heard my brother and father pass as they opened the front door and headed out.

"Alright, Amelia, but I want you to at least call Alex, or someone to come stay over so you don't have to be by yourself here," she said turning around. She closed the dish washer and switched it on.

"Alright, I'll give him a call," I said, looking down at my phone. I typed in Alex's number, and I moved away from the island. I walked over to the couch and sat down. The line rang for a long time and I almost ended it when I heard his voice on the other end.

"Hello, Em," he said, out of breath. I frowned.

"Hey, Alex. Sorry, are you busy?" I asked, confused.

"No, don't worry. What's up?" he asked. I shook my head.

"Uhm, I was wondering if you'd like to come over. Mom and Dad are taking Marcus to the airport, and I don't want to go with them. Would you like to join me at my house?" I asked.

"Uhm, I..." I heard him hesitate.

"Who's that, Alex?" I heard a female voice in the background. Ingrid. I instantly felt annoyed.

"Em, listen, today is a little bit tight. Maybe later, or what about tomorrow?" he asked, sounding vulnerable.

"Sure, Alex," I replied blankly. What did I expect? He had other responsibilities.

"Will you at least tell me if someone is there so that I know you're not alone," he asked, and I nodded as though I thought he could hear me.

"Yes, I will. See you around," I said and before I knew it the call ended.

I sighed as I thought of how everything had changed since I came back. A part of me wished I'd never left to start with. The last night I was here in North Carolina, before we left to my grandparents, Alexander had shared a kiss with me when he'd sneaked his way into my room late at night. I had fallen asleep next to him, lying in his arms, and I was certain things were going to change between us, in a more romantic way. But, as you know, time and distance aren't the greatest things to build relationships, although we tried to always send messages to each other. But a lot can happen in two years. Especially his line of studying. He wanted to be a doctor, so that meant a lot of hard work and studying, not to mention the practicals, and we had only spoken or phoned twice a month.

I remembered how it had made me feel, just being so close to him and knowing that finally all the years of friendship had paid off. I sighed again as I thought of how foolish I'd felt when I found out that all of his flirting when I had returned wasn't to reel me in, but only to play games with me. How silly of me to think that he would have waited for me to come back. He was gorgeous and he deserved to have a beautiful girl. It just hurt, knowing that we weren't as close as we use to be.

"What did he say?" my mother asked, interrupting my thoughts.

"He's busy, but I'll phone Sky," I replied. She nodded her head and turned away from me.

I dialed Skylar's number and she answered.

"Hey, Em, what's up?" she said, and I fiddled with the fabric on my jeans.

"Hey, would you like to come over? My parents are taking Marcus to the airport and I'm staying behind."

"Ahh, thanks for the invite, hun, but I'm actually on a date at the moment," she said, chuckling nervously.

"Oh! Sorry. Okay, no it's fine," I said, holding my hand to my mouth. "You must enjoy it and tell me all about it later, okay?" She laughed. We said our goodbyes and I didn't have anyone else to call.

I didn't want to go with them, but maybe I could convince my mom that one of my friends was going to meet me at a restaurant in town. "So, Mom, one of my friends will meet me at a restaurant. If you guys can just drop me off on your way, that would be great," I said, turning around on the couch to look at her.

She looked at me skeptically and slowly nodded her head. "Okay, but I'm trusting you, Amelia," she said, and I looked away from her at the fire.

"I know. I promise I'm not lying," I said quickly as she looked at me.

"Alright. Get your stuff. We're about to head out," she said, turning around and finishing up with what she was busy with.

I smiled and felt the guilt all over my body. I didn't like lying, but I also didn't want to go with them. The drive would be tiring and also the emotions would be exhausting. I grabbed my handbag from the chair and before I knew it my father was at the door.

"Okay, you all ready?" he said, looking at my mother and me. I nodded and so did she.

"Yes, let's go," my mother said looking at me.

We left the house and walked outside into the cold. A part of me didn't want to go to the restaurant all by myself, but I also didn't want to tell my mom I was lying. We climbed into the car and Marcus was already in the back seat. I explained to my father and him that I wasn't going with them. Marcus understood but I could tell my parents were unimpressed. I wanted to go to the Read In Café. We drove out onto the road and Marcus put his headphones in and I looked out the window. We passed different neighborhood homes and my father turned left at the T-junction and it opened up into our pretty little shopping center. The café that I wanted to go to was to the right, at the end of the shopping center. My father pulled up in front of the double-story building. My nerves gripped me, and I looked over to my brother. He looked back at me and smiled. I leaned over to him and gave him a big warm hug as the car came to a halt.

"Good luck with your studies and don't work too hard. Please know that I love you lots," I said into his shoulder and both my mom and dad were looking at us. He pulled away first and he looked at me with his hazelnut eyes.

"Listen, I can't be here to protect you all the time, but I trust that you will make wise decisions. Please be careful out there. There are a lot of strange characters. I'm trusting Alex to look after you. I know he will; he's like your second brother," he said smirking, and I rolled my eyes at his comment.

"I wouldn't say he's like my second brother, but okay, I understand your concept. Thank you," I said, and we both laughed. I looked forward and my mother handed me money.

"Whose meeting you here?" my father asked, looking at me from the driver seat.

"It's a boy. His name is Sebastian. Don't worry, Alex knows him. He's decent and I'll let you know when he gets there," I said quickly, and I reached for the door.

Marcus gave me a look and he could see I was up to something. "Sebastian, hey? Is that right?" he said, giving me a wicked smile. I rolled my eyes and smiled. He didn't have to know anything.

"Okay, well, we'll wait until he meets you by the door," my mother said. She was too smart for me. She knew all about my wicked plan. I shook my head at her.

"No, he will be meeting me here. I told him that I'll find a table inside. Don't worry, I'll let you know the moment he gets here," I said nervously. She squinted her eyes at me skeptically. I gave a weak smile. "I'll even take a photo if you want," I replied, feeling stupid for even suggesting that. She nodded her head, and I knew I was off the hook.

"Just be safe, alright?" my father said again, looking at me in the review mirror.

I nodded and opened the door. "I love you guys," I said, before I climbed out, and they all smiled and Marcus waved at me.

"We love you too," Dad said.

I closed the door behind me and walked towards the doorstep. I turned around once more and waved to them, and my father turned back onto the road. I watched them leave and a small part of me regretted not going with them, although I thought that it was a better idea to have come here instead. At least it was nothing like my dream, isolated in the dark woods. Here it was populated. I took a deep breath and turned around and pushed the door and observed the sign that said "Open".

The doorbell jingled as I walked in, announcing my arrival. There were stands of donuts in the windowsill and cakes on display. I walked in and looked around. There was a self-service area to my left, with many different assorted treats and savory foods. There was a coffee machine on the shelf. The coffee scent filled the air. I looked to my right and saw lime green couches, on which people were sitting and socializing. There were bookshelves everywhere. At the far back of the restaurant were open tables. The light shone on all the tables, giving it an airy vibe. The windows were wide and tall, giving it a glass house feeling.

I walked over to the back and chose the corner table. I sat in a way that allowed me to see the view outside the window, and that also enabled me to see the people to my right, who were sitting chatting away. Some were reading a book from the bookshelves in the café, and others were on their laptops. I looked outside the window and looked out onto the deck. A little past the deck was the beautiful scenery of a stream flowing by peacefully. The trees made their way all along the side of the stream. Calm acoustic music was playing over on the speaker, making this place the best place to sit and just escape from your thoughts. That's why it was called the Read In, because the place had originally been a bookstore that they had turned into a bakery and restaurant.

There was a fire burning in the corner to my right where the couches were. It helped give everyone that homey and comfortable feeling. I gave a deep sigh and took my phone out. I saw I had a text from Alex; he was checking up on me. He had asked if I had found someone to come over. I looked past the message and sent my mother a message to let her know I was okay and that I was sitting down at the table. I looked out at the stream and observed how peaceful everything looked. I heard the front door jingle. I couldn't help but look out of curiosity. I smiled at the stranger I saw at the door.

Chapter 9

HELLO, STRANGER

It was late in the morning, around eleven thirty, when a man walked through the doors of the Read In Café. I didn't think anything of it but just gave a polite smile when he looked my way. Our eyes met for only a second before I looked away because I didn't want to give the wrong impression, knowing I was all by myself. A waiter had come by and had brought me a cappuccino. Before sipping it, I stood up and walked to the bookshelf behind me. Nothing like getting lost in a nice book, I thought. I looked at all the colorful labels and finally decided to pick a romantic novel. *Our last touch.* The title seemed captivating enough and on the front page were two hands parting. I didn't even bother reading the blurb. I just took the book and found my seat.

How the café worked was that, even if you liked a book you weren't allowed to take it home, but you were allowed to hand it in and write your name on it. When you returned to the store, you just had to say your name and they would hand it back to you so that you could continue reading. I sat down and opened to the first page of the book and started reading.

...

I was on page thirty-five when I heard a voice beside me.

"Interesting book?" the voice said from next to me.

I stopped reading and looked up at the stranger speaking to me. The young man had a light stubble on his cheeks. His hair was brown and cut short on the sides and combed over on top.

His eyes were dark brown, almost black, and he wore black-framed glasses that fit his face nicely. He wore a black shirt, which was tucked into his dark jeans. He wore a black blazer with the outfit, making himself look like a professor. His eyes were looking from my book to my face. Quite intrigued, I would have said. He had a calm demeanor to him.

I gave a polite smile and looked to the book. "It's interesting, yes," I said, looking back up at him, not knowing what else to add to the topic. I saw that he was holding a book in his right hand. I pointed to his book. "Any good?" I asked politely, just trying to make conversation.

He looked down at the book and gave a smile. "Yeah, I guess the little bit that I did read," he said as I looked at him and he smiled down at me, making me feel a little uncomfortable. His teeth were too white and perfect. I could definitely see him standing in front of his mirror, brushing them for hours. He looked as though he could be a neat freak, considering how neatly his hair was combed back. But then again, I could be wrong. Maybe he was just like me and wanted a friend to talk to.

"Are you from around here?" I asked, and he shook his head slightly.

"No, I've actually just moved here. I heard that this place had a high rating because of the books, and the nice environment it has. So, I decided to make it the first place to visit," he said, smiling and looking outside at the stream. I watched as he studied the stream outside, and I felt oddly fascinated at how strange he was. He looked smart, like he was good with math or problem solving. Maybe it was the glasses that gave him that effect. He seemed kind, considering that he just walked up to me and started a conversation.

"Ahh well, welcome to our little town. I'm sure you'll learn to love it here," I said, giving him a small smile, and his dark eyes fell on me again. I looked away because I couldn't handle his gaze. I heard the doorbell sound. Either someone had just come in or someone had left. I couldn't see who it was because the man was standing in the way of the door. To be decent, I offered for him to stay.

"No, I'm fine, thank you. I have to run, anyways. I'll be coming more often. Thank you for being so kind, though. It's not often that you stumble upon kind strangers like you," he said, smirking at me, and he folded his hands over his chest.

I shrugged my shoulders. "It's my pleasure. I hope you come right," I said, and he smiled.

"Thank you. If I may ask, what might your name be?" I forced a smile when he asked the question and I looked away. I didn't know who he was, and I was all by myself. I looked at him and decided to lie instead.

"My name is Jennifer." The moment the words came out my mouth, I felt the guilt spread all over my body. I couldn't even look at him.

"Nice to meet you, Jennifer. My name is Tyron," he said politely, and I looked down and smiled at my book.

"Nice to meet you, Tyron." I finally looked up and our eyes met. There was something about him I couldn't place. His whole demeanor. He seemed too nice. I looked away and before I knew it, he greeted me.

"Well then, thank you, and I'll see you around. Hope you have a lovely afternoon further," he said, and he gave me a small wave.

"Thank you, same to you," and at that he turned around and I watched him leave.

He handed his book in at the front desk, and he shot me one more look. I quickly looked away, already giving away the fact that I was staring, and then I heard the doorbell jingle. Maybe it was the way he acted like a gentleman? Nowadays, it isn't so common to see something like that or maybe it was something else. I'm just glad he didn't agree to be seated with me. I didn't want any company right then.

I picked my book up again and continued reading where I left off.

"Excuse me, miss," I heard someone say and I looked up from my book. Not another weirdo, I thought. I looked to my right, and I didn't see anyone. So, I looked back at my book and tried to continue reading.

"Sorry, miss, can you please stop reading. It's considered to be rude to ignore people." I heard the familiar voice again and I looked up from my book and turned around. There, in the seat behind me, was Sebastian. He gave me a smirk and my smile instantly grew. How had he known where to find me? He had been summoned.

"Hello, stranger," I said, beaming, and he sat back in his chair. He had a cup of coffee in front of him and his green eyes were glowing. "What's the odds that you and I end up in the same store together?" I asked, and he shrugged his shoulders.

"Some people call it fate," he said smoothly, and he kept his eyes on me. He was flirting with me. I looked away from him and turned around, smiling.

"Well, I think fate can hold on, because I'm quite busy at the moment." At that I opened my book again and pretended to read. I heard him get up from his chair and I thought that maybe I'd offended him. I watched as he appeared to my right, and he pulled the chair that was next to me out. I smiled, and he knew

I liked it. I looked up at him and he had placed a book in front of him. There was a bookmark inside it, and he seemed almost at the end.

I frowned. "Really? You read books now?" I said, holding onto mine.

He looked at his book and shrugged his shoulders. "What's the matter, you don't think I read?" he asked, offended, holding his hand to his chest in a playful gesture. I smiled at him and shook my head.

"No offense, pretty boy, but you definitely don't seem like the book type," I said rolling my eyes at him and he smirked at my comment.

He shook his head in the same motion. "Alright, to give you some insight into me. Believe it or not, I actually like reading. I took this book out two days ago when I came in here. The Read In is my favorite café to come to. And it turns out it's actually a great book," he said squinting his eyes from the light that was coming from the view.

I couldn't help but analyze him. There was so much about him that I thought I would get wrong if I had to profile him. On that day, he wore a red jacket with dark jeans. His hair was spiked up in a lazy way, although it didn't look like he used any products in it. The red jacket made his eyes stand out more. I could smell his cologne as I sat next to him, and I was taking in all of him, bit by bit.

"You honestly surprise every time," I said, scanning his face. He looked from the window and his eyes fell on me. For the first time ever, I was able to see his green eyes properly. There was a tiny splash of yellow with the green. He didn't break eye contact and for some reason neither did I.

"Never judge a book by its cover," he said, and then he looked away. I looked down at my book. I guess we do that don't we? Judge books by how colorful they are and how nicely displayed the font is.

"It's easier said than done," I said. "Besides, aren't you supposed to be locking guys up?" I asked, watching him take a sip of his coffee. Oh, how a small part of me envied the cup for touching his lips. I frowned and looked away, trying to not think about him like that.

"Officers need breaks too," he said as he looked over at me with a polite smile. Fair enough. I smiled back and looked at my half-empty cup of coffee.

"Do you enjoy it?" I asked him and he nodded his head.

"Every job has its challenges. But yes, I enjoy the physical fitness and helping people," he said, playing with the corner of his book while he spoke.

I put my book to the side and folded my arms over my chest. "Can I ask you a question though? How did you know I was here?" I looked at him.

He shrugged his shoulders. "I didn't know, honestly. I usually sit in this spot because it's closest to the view and also furthest away from all the people, and when I walked in today, there you were, in my seat," he said, looking back at me with a smile. I frowned a little.

"So, Alex didn't tip you off? He didn't mention me or anything?" I asked, confused.

He shook his head lightly while staring at me. "No, he didn't. Why would Alex find the need to mention to me where you are?" he asked, and I looked down, feeling silly for asking.

"No, I was just asking because I actually told my parents I was meeting you here, because everyone I called couldn't come out today. And I didn't want to go to the airport to say goodbye to my brother, so I lied and said that you were going to meet me here," I said, looking down.

"What would you have done if I hadn't shown up?" he asked, and I shrugged my shoulders.

"I didn't think that far, I guess," I said looking up at him.

He looked amused, his eyes scanning my face lightly. "Don't like goodbyes?" he asked softly. I looked up at him and shook my head. He then looked back at the view. "Yeah, they suck," he said looking out ahead. His face went from calm to very cloudy in a matter of seconds. I wondered what monsters he had dealt with in his life.

"Can I ask you a question?" I asked, still scanning him. He looked over to me and gave me a small nod. "Are your parents still around?" and he nodded his head and looked away again.

"Yes, they are. They live in a different town than us, though. Why do you ask?" he asked, looking down, and then he managed to find my eyes again.

I shook my head lightly. "No reason. I was just curious."

I watched as a waiter walked up to us and she looked between Bas and me. "Sorry to bother. I was just wondering, since your drinks are finished, if you'd like a refill?" she asked, giving us a genuine smile.

Sebastian looked at me and then back at the waitress. "No, that's alright. I'm going to head out," he said, giving her a small smile. "But thanks anyways."

I watched as she pulled her eyes off of him and looked over to me. "And you, mam?" She waited patiently.

I shook my head slightly. "No thank you, I'm fine for now," I said, and she nodded her head and gave us her greetings and then she was gone. I gave an uncomfortable chuckle as she left.

Bas looked down at his hand and a part of me was sad that he wanted to leave. That meant I was going to be alone again. A part of me wanted to ask him to stay a while longer, but I didn't want to sound strange.

He looked up at me and grabbed his book. His green eyes were soft and very enchanting. "Would you like to come over to my place and wait there for your parents to get back?" he offered, and I was shocked as I hadn't expected it. I gave him a smile and said three words which set it all in place.

"Sure, let's go."

The excitement pumped through me as I stood up and knew exactly where I was headed, to his house, alone.

Chapter 10

HIS SECRETS

I drove with Sebastian in his car. He didn't seem to live far from town. He had a small cottage in the woods up on the hilltop. Thank goodness, he had neighbors all around him, otherwise I'd have felt a bit unsafe since I didn't really know him that well.

He walked around the car and opened the door for me. I smiled politely at his kind gesture. I'd have sworn this wasn't the same guy I'd met that first night. He seemed more relaxed now and open.

"So, this is my place," he said as we came around the car. He pointed to this pretty little wooden house. There were wooden stairs that led all the way up to the deck on the house. It was beautiful. I could feel him staring and I knew he was judging my emotions.

"Wow, Bas, this place is beautiful," I said, not taking my eyes off the house.

The house was a double-story. He had these old vintage lamps on the outside of his door. Outside on the deck was a small wooden chair and beside the chair was a perfect small coffee table. You could see he didn't often have guests over as he had only one chair outside for him, and no one else.

"Thank you," he said, satisfied with my answer.

He held out his hand and gestured for me to take the steps first. I gladly went ahead. I placed my hand on the railing and started stepping. There were about ten steps before it opened up into the deck. He had a pot plant outside the door. His door mat read "Welcome", and I honestly felt nothing but welcome, just from seeing the outside view. The house was surrounded by trees, and we were on a higher level after we climbed the steps.

"How is your place in bear season?" I asked, looking at all the trees. I saw someone sitting outside with their partner. They were drinking something out on their deck. Their house was a fraction bigger than Sebastian's. The other houses were quiet, even though there were cars parked outside.

He placed the keys into his door and unlocked it. "So, we do get bears in the area, quite often. I'm happy that my house is a little elevated from the rest. When it's bear season, we put out the spikes at night and sometimes during the day. I do have bear spray as well inside." He finished his sentence off by looking around the deck. His hand was still on the front door handle. I nodded my head as I could only image all the bears up there.

"Have you had any encounters with the bears?" I asked curiously.

He smiled and shook his head. "Not yet, thank goodness for that. I've had this place a year and a half and I must say it's as safe as it gets out in the woods," he said, meeting my eyes. I nodded my head, and I watched as he turned the door handle to open the front door. He pushed it open and gestured for me to step inside.

"Thank you," I politely said as I took a step inside.

I stood aside as I wanted him to guide me through the place. He had a small L-couch in his living room. In front of the couch was a fireplace. He had cute small coffee tables beside the ends of the couch. He had a green carpet just in front of the couch. To the right was his little kitchen. It was neat. He had a small island and two chairs in front of it. His stove was a gas stove. He had another pot plant on the counter and some utensils in a container. He had a wine bottle holder, in which six wine bottles were placed. His counters were against the wall and the counter doors were made of glass, so that you could see what was inside. A little to the right of the kitchen was a glass door that I presumed led out into the backyard. Dividing the kitchen and living room was a small staircase, which spiraled up into the ceiling.

"This is the living room, and the kitchen and up there is the bedroom and bathroom," he said, pointing at each place and lastly at the ceiling. "Would you like to see upstairs?" he asked, looking at me.

I smiled and nodded my head eagerly. It intrigued me to actually see what kind of space he lived in. He took a step forward and gestured for me to walk up the stairs again. I started stepping and, before I knew it, the staircase opened up into this beautiful, open plan room. He had wide windows that allowed one to see far out in the distance above the trees. His bedroom windows were pointed out to the back of the house, so they caught the view of the trees moving all the way down the slope. You could see the whole valley.

I found myself walking towards the window without even noticing. He had a small couch alongside the window, and I could only imagine what a nice place it was to read books. I touched the glass and marveled at the scenery. He joined my side a couple seconds after I stood still.

"Wow, Sebastian. I have no words. You must have paid a fortune for this place, especially with this view."

"I was very lucky to have got the offer when I did," he said, stepping away from the window.

I turned around and looked at the bed. He had a beautiful white and green theme. His bed was opposite the window, and he had two bedside tables. He had a green carpet on the floor beside his bed and, a little to the left of the big window, he had a big bookshelf filled with books. I couldn't help but walk over to see what kind of books he was interested in. There were all sorts of books, many non-fiction. He seemed to be into crime and science fiction as well. I looked over to him. He stood looking over the books as well.

"It makes sense that you like the crime books, considering your profession," I said looking over the books. He gave me a smile.

"It's always good to get lost in a book," he said, touching one of the crime books with his index finger.

"Very true," I observed, looking away from the books. I watched as he walked over to a closet.

He opened it up and it was a walk-in bathroom. Just like mine. "Here is the bathroom if you ever need it," he said, looking inside, almost to make sure it was neat and tidy.

I smiled and nodded my head. I didn't go inside as I felt I had already seen a lot. I felt my phone vibrate. I looked down and saw there was a text message from Alex. He was wondering if I was okay. I didn't want to respond.

"Okay, would you like something to drink?" he asked, walking towards the staircase.

I nodded my head. "Yes, please, anything would be okay," I told him, following him towards the stairs.

"Okay. Since you say anything, would you like some wine?" he asked, as he spiraled down the staircase.

"Why not? Wine is always a good idea," I replied playfully. I heard him chuckle.

"It's red wine," he said, stepping off the last step. He walked over to the kitchen island and took one of the wine bottles out of the wine holders.

"I love your wine bottle holder," I said, feeling satisfied that I'd mentioned it. It looked fancy. He took two wine glasses out his cupboard and placed them down on the counter. He looked up from the glasses as he opened the bottle, and he gave me a smirk. I gave an uncomfortable smile back. "Why are you smiling?" I asked curiously.

He looked down at the bottle. "No, nothing," he said, and I watched as he poured the wine into the glasses.

I looked down. A small part of me wanted to know if this was such a good idea. We were both alone and no one knew where I was yet. A small part of me thought of my dream. When I had gone out for a run and I'd told no one about it. Who knew? Maybe this was my dream just playing out in a different manner.

He handed me the glass and I smiled politely. "Thank you," I said, and I swirled the wine around in the glass. "So, you're a wine drinker?" I asked, and he held the glass in his hand and nodded his head.

"I am, yes," he said simply as he smiled at me.

He had filled the glass to the top. Alarm bells. I was going to make sure not to drink everything as I didn't want anything to get out of hand, and I wanted to make sure I was in control of my emotions. I watched as he walked over to his stereo and played some calming acoustics. He then walked over to the fireplace and started the fire. There was nothing that was taking place in his house at that moment that made me feel uncomfortable. He had a strange way of making me feel at ease. Especially now that I knew what his house was like. He seemed neat and organized. He liked books and there was still so much more I could see he had inside him.

I sat down on the couch as the fire started up. I took a sip of the red wine. It was dry and sweet at the same time. I watched him put the logs on and I watched how he knelt calmly in front of the fire. He watched it grow and I marveled in his peacefulness. He had a jersey shirt on. He had pulled his sleeves up to his elbows and I watched how his muscles tensed as he pushed himself up. He was very attractive and being alone with him was making it harder for me to deny the fact that I was starting to fall for him.

I pushed the thought out my head, as I didn't want to make this year about men. I needed this gap year more than anything. He walked over to me, and I felt the tension in the room rise. His green eyes fell on me, and I couldn't have felt more vulnerable than I did in that moment. I didn't break eye contact.

I heard my phone ring and I looked over to the kitchen counter. "Sorry, let me get that". I jumped up and checked caller ID. Alexander. I answered. "Hey, Alex, what's up?" I said softly into the phone as I could feel Bas staring.

"You didn't tell me if you were safe or not. So, I drove to your house, and no one answered. I figured maybe you were just ignoring me, so I snuck around the house and climbed up your balcony and realized you weren't there. So, where are you? Are you okay?" His voice was flat, and I could hear he was annoyed. I looked over at Sebastian, who had turned his back to me and was looking at the fire.

"Sorry that I didn't let you know. I was just busy. I'm fine now. I still didn't go with my mom and them. Everyone was busy, so I told mom that I was going to meet up with some friends at the Read In Café,"

"And did you?" he asked.

"No, I lied," I said softly.

"Why would you do that, Amelia? You know it's not safe for you, with you having a stalker running around." I turned around and tried to walk towards the glass doors, which led out back. I saw a wooden staircase leading into the forest, something that grabbed my attention immediately.

"I know. I just didn't want to go to the airport,"

"Why didn't you tell me?" he said frustrated.

"Because I didn't want to bother you. You're with Ingrid anyways. You sounded pretty busy with her when I called." I swear I could practically feel him roll his eyes at my comment.

"Stop it. You know I told you I'd be here for you. Where are you now? Are you still at the Read In Café? I'll come and get you," he asked.

"What about Ingrid?" I asked, wondering how she'd be okay with this conversation and also the fact that he'd left her to see me.

"I told her I had a family emergency," he said softly.

"So, you lied as well," I said, feeling childish. Hearing him call me family didn't quite sit well with my heart. I was just another annoying little sister to him. I couldn't help but feel a little hurt.

"Stop playing games, Amelia. I'm driving to the Read In Café and I'm coming to fetch you," he said, and I swear I could hear his car start.

I shook my head. "No don't. I'm fine now. Sebastian walked into the café, and we spoke, and he invited me over to his house. So, I'm here now. Don't worry about me. We're going to wait until my mother and father are finished at the airport and then he'll take me home," I said, and I could swear at the mention of his name, he was staring at me. There was silence on the other side of the phone. "Alex?"

"I'm here. Listen, I don't like the idea. I can still come pick you up. I can take you home. I mean, you don't even know him very well, and I know him. I know what he's done with girls." I turned around when Alex mentioned all these things about him.

Sebastian had pulled out his phone by now and I couldn't help but watch him. He seemed harmless and gentle. The way he'd treated me this morning had made me feel as though he was nothing but nice. I turned around and reached for the door handle. I didn't want Sebastian to hear our whole conversation. So, I pushed open the door and closed it behind me as I stood outside on the open deck.

"Alex, I'm fine. Stop being so overprotective. Sebastian is just a friend. He was being nice and didn't want me to sit there all by myself, so he offered for me to come over to his place," I said, folding my arms over my chest.

"Listen, I'm just saying there's red flags everywhere. Do your parents know you're with him?" he asked.

"Yes," I said softly.

"You're lying again." He raised his voice.

"Okay, Alex. I'm done talking about this. You wanted to know if I was fine and I am. You know where I am. I'm okay. Go and entertain your girlfriend. I shouldn't be the first of your worries."

At that I didn't even wait for him to answer. I ended the call. I couldn't help but feel a burn in my chest. It was the first time in a very long time that our conversation had gotten so heated. We always just went with the flow. A small part of me just wanted everything to be okay and for everything to go back to the way it had been before his girlfriend and before he became such an ass. I felt bad about how I'd handled the conversation, but he was starting to act like my father. All I wanted to do now was to prove him wrong. I walked over to the edge and wanted to walk down the staircase. I watched it disappear around some trees. My curiosity grew and actually all I wanted to do was run and clear my head. I was about to take a step when I heard the door open.

"Amelia?" Sebastian said my name and I gave a small sigh.

I turned around and looked at him. "I'm sorry. I didn't mean for you to hear all of that. Alex is just worried about me, that's all," I said, looking at him as he leaned his body against the door frame.

"Don't explain yourself. I know why he'd be overprotective. He's known you for so long and he is only looking out for your best interests," he said, and I couldn't read the emotion on his face.

I looked down and decided to change the subject. I turned around and pointed to the staircase. "Where does this go?"

"To the small stream we have here in the neighborhood. It's something else in summer. For now, it's just snow and mostly the stream is frozen over. So, we can't swim in it around this time. There's even a rope down there that you can use to jump into the water with," he said, sounding uplifted. I smiled at the thought.

"Can we go see it. If the stream is frozen over, it means that we can ski on it?" I asked, excited.

"Can we go later?" he asked, and I turned around and nodded my head. I didn't want to overstep.

"Of course. It's your place after all," I said politely, and I gave him a small smile and he gave me one back.

"Let's go inside. It's warmer there," he said softly, and I nodded my head.

I walked towards him, and he stepped aside only a fraction so that I would slightly rub past him. A small part of me knew what he was doing. His cologne brushed past me and all I wanted to do was devour every bit of it.

...

I looked at my glass of wine. I had one last sip left. Call me irresponsible, if you wish. All I knew was that I was having such a nice time there with him. He was such a comfortable soul. His glass had been finished long ago. We were sitting closer together than when we'd started drinking. We had gotten to the comfortable level of deep conversation. He had put logs on the fire three times, and it was long past five o'clock. I had called my mother and told her the situation. She said it was fine, as long as I came home at a reasonable hour.

"Would you like a refill?" he asked as he watched me take my last sip.

I smiled at him. "I don't know if I should," I said softly, looking at the glass. I could feel my head was already fuzzy.

"Okay, that's fine. Would you like something else, like water or a hot beverage?" he said, standing up in front of me. I smiled because him not forcing me made me feel even more comfortable being around him.

"Tea please," I responded.

He smiled and took my glass and nodded his head. "Alright. Tea coming up." He turned and walked over to the kitchen.

I watched the fire and couldn't stop watching how each flame changed from orange to purple and red. It was very mesmerizing. I felt relaxed. I didn't drink much, so the wine was hitting me a lot faster than it did Sebastian.

"Can I ask you a question?" I said, turning to look at him. I was still trying to behave and act like a lady, despite my condition.

He waited for the kettle to finish boiling. He crossed his arms over his chest and he leaned against the cupboard and looked over at me, amused. "Go ahead," he said.

"If I may ask, how many girls have been here before? Like what number am I?" I asked, resting my arms on the arm rest and putting my chin on my arms.

He chuckled and looked down. "Damn, so are we getting to these questions now?" he said. The kettle boiled, and he made himself busy by pouring the water into my cup.

"Sorry. You don't have to answer," I said, pushing myself off the couch. I looked back into the fire and there was silence between us for the couple of seconds he took to make the tea.

He handed me the tea and sat down beside me and looked into the fire. "If I must be honest with you, only three girls, and that includes you."

I cocked my head as he said it. He didn't look at me and I could tell he felt vulnerable.

"What? But you're known as a player," I said, without even thinking about the words. I watched him frown at the word "player".

"The thing is, I don't like girls coming here. It's a very personal thing and girls get clingy once they see your place. I don't know why, but it's like that," he said, still looking into the fire. "I don't mean to play around with their feelings; it's just I have my reasons and, at the end of the day, it's better for the both of us if there's no emotions attached."

I watched him look down at his cup of tea. He'd also made himself some. I smiled at him. "If I can be completely honest with you, I wish I knew what it is like to have that kind of lifestyle. When you guys speak about it, I always feel so left out. I always feel like the child in the group because I've never dealt with anything like that before," I softly said, and I felt more vulnerable that I'd ever felt in front of a guy. I could feel him look at me and I knew I probably sounded like a loser. He lifted my chin with his finger and immediately I was drawn to him. His green eyes were soft and understanding. The orange glow from the fire reflected in his eyes.

"There is nothing more beautiful than someone who hasn't been around the block. Don't ever want that kind of lifestyle, Amelia. It's very lonely and sad. There's nothing that's nice about it," he said, letting my chin go. I could still feel where his finger had rested, and my heart warmed at the thought.

I nodded my head. "So, can I ask, why did you show me your place?" I asked, and I watched as he gave a small smile.

"I don't know. There's something about you that feels comfortable. I feel like I can trust you," he said softly, without looking at me.

Knowing he had given me so much validation made my heart burst. I hadn't realized that I meant so much to him. I felt honored, in fact, to have been only the third girl to have seen this amazing place. "Thank you for trusting me," I said softly, resting my hand on his leg. It felt intimate and a small part of me didn't want to remove my hand because it felt right. He looked at my hand, but he didn't move his leg.

"Can I ask you another question?" I asked, and he smiled, nodding his head as he looked into the fire. I took my hand off his leg.

"Yes, you may," he said, and he looked over to me this time.

"Who were the other girls?" I asked.

He looked away from me as I asked the question, and he gave a small sigh. I must have asked a big question. "Wow, you know how to get in deep, hey?" he observed, putting his cup down and turning his body towards me. I did the same, as I thought the conversation was about to get very serious.

"So, the second girl I brought here," he said, rubbing his chin a little and then looking up to me, "her name was Payton. I thought she seemed okay, but after I'd let her in she became crazy. Very demanding and wanting to know my every move. Even when I was here all by myself and she wasn't, she'd flip out because she wanted to be around me. It got so bad that she started contacting my friends to know where I was and why I wasn't answering her texts," he told me, looking away and frowning.

I shook my head. "She sounds like a stalker, almost," I couldn't help but add that into the conversation.

He looked at me and nodded his head. "Exactly. So, when it got out of hand, I told her that she couldn't see me anymore. It took her a while to get it into her head, but eventually she got the picture."

"Have you seen her since?"

He nodded his head. "The places we go to hang out at, she's sometimes there. I keep clear of her when I see her, but I've seen her with another guy, so that's good at least."

"So, after her you never let girls over again?" I asked, and he nodded his head.

"Until you."

"And the first girl?" I asked, playing with the scatter cushion in my hand.

He turned away from me and, when I looked up to him, I could see the peace he'd had when he looked over at me was now replaced with pain. I frowned, but I didn't reach out to him because I felt that the moment wasn't right.

"So, remember you wanted to see my tattoos?" he asked, and I nodded my head.

Confused by the diversion. I watched him reach for his shirt and I sat up straight. I watched as his shirt gracefully slipped off his back. His chest was cushioned to the right size. His arms were built. He had a tattoo running across his chest. One on his bicep and another around his wrist. He was so beautiful. All I wanted to do was run my fingers over his body. He pointed to the armor symbols that were around his arm. I had already seen that one.

"You already know about this one, but this one was the one you asked about," he said, pointing to the roman numerals on his bicep. I nodded my head, so captivated by what was in front of me. "Her name was Victoria. She was beautiful and everything I always wanted. We had been dating for four years and she found out she had cancer," he said, and I could hear the pain still in his voice. I couldn't help but gasp. "We planned to get married and have a long life together. She didn't see this place for too long. She wanted it, actually. Everything about it she loved. So, I gave them a good price and the buyers sold it to us. Before I knew it, she got to stage four cancer and it wasn't even a week and she was dead," he said, looking into the fire.

I felt a lump in my throat, and I didn't mean to make the situation about me but I couldn't help the tears from burning my eyes. I saw the pain in his eyes.

I watched as he took a breath and he continued. "She died in my arms in hospital, and I've never felt such pain before. Everything was just ripped away from me, from us. I couldn't even get married to her." I heard his voice break a bit and the tears streamed down my face. I honestly hadn't expected the visit to turn out like that.

"After her, everything changed. I got the tattoo as a reminder to never forget the day she died and, honestly, I think that's also when my morals changed about love. I didn't want another girl to love me. I didn't want to love another, and Payton came after her. I was stupid and thought that maybe it would work but, like every rebound relationship, it ended horribly. Ever since I've only been keeping it plain and simple. I didn't want to be in a relationship and the girls knew that. I always went to their houses as it was easier to leave the next morning," he said, and I could sense the anger in his voice. I honestly felt so sorry for him because he had to deal with such pain. I wiped the tears away and looked down at my hand.

"I'm so sorry you had to go through that. I don't think anyone deserves that kind of pain," I said softly. My heart felt so sad and there was nothing I could do to help him. "So, you never thought of moving after she left?" I asked, and he shook his head.

"It crossed my mind once, but I knew she didn't just choose the place because she loved it. She chose it because she knew I would find peace here," he said, and he looked at me for the first time since he had started talking about her.

"I completely understand why you didn't want anyone else over here," I said quietly, and he nodded his head. I looked at his other tattoos. The one across his chest said *Create your own reality*. "What does that one mean?" I asked, pointing to his chest, trying to change the topic.

He looked at it and looked back up at me. "After getting the tattoo of Victoria, I got this one as well. I didn't want to live in the pain, so I wanted to pretend like it wasn't there. I wanted to create a better reality than what I was in."

"It's beautiful," I said, and he looked at me and smiled.

"Thank you," he responded, turning around and grabbing his cup of tea.

I did the same. I decided to look at my phone and my heart froze. It was already seven thirty and my mom had already given me three missed calls. After Alex had tried to phone back, I had put my phone on silent and I'd forgotten to put it back on.

"Is everything okay?" he inquired, concerned.

"I forgot to turn my phone on loud, and my mother has tried to call me three times already," I said, looking up at him. I dialed her number and put the phone to my ear. It didn't take long, and she answered.

"Amelia! Why on earth haven't you answered your phone? I called Alex and he said that he was sorry that you weren't answering your phone but that you were outside, and you'd forgotten your phone inside the house. Is this true?" A small part of me got annoyed at how Alex was standing up for me.

"Yes, I'm sorry."

"You need to be more responsible Amelia, you made me worried" she said and I looked down.

"I know. I'm sorry, Mom," I said, feeling bad.

"If you're going to stay there tonight, I at least want you to keep your phone on loud so that I can call you any time. Is that clear?"

I was very confused by her suggestion for me to sleep over at his house. "Wait a minute. What did he organize with you?" I asked and frowned.

"He said that you were going to stay there for the night and that he'd bring you back tomorrow morning."

"Okay, makes sense now. Thanks, Mom. So, I'll see you tomorrow morning."

"Yes, but if you keep your phone on silent you'll never sleep over again," she commanded, and I looked up to Bas, whose eyes had been on me the whole time.

"Okay, I promise. I'll keep it on loud. Love you, Mom."

"Love you too, and stay safe." At that she ended the call, and I put my phone down.

"What did she say?"

"Alex saved me and said that I was going to crash at his place for the night."

Sebastian frowned and finished his tea in one big gulp. "So, should I go drop you off at his house?" he asked, and I looked at my phone and back at him.

"I don't know. I'm enjoying myself so much. I'm not in the mood for all of his questions right now." I watched him smirk.

"So, what do you want to do then?" he asked, and I looked to the kitchen and then back at him.

"Maybe let's eat something and then we can go," I suggested, and he nodded his head.

"Okay, I'll put a pizza in the oven. Is that okay?" he asked, and I smiled, nodding my head.

"Sounds great."

I watched him push himself off the couch and he walked over to the fridge to get a pizza out the freezer. He didn't put his shirt on again and I liked it that way. Every muscle on his back tensed as he moved the pizza out of the freezer and into the oven. I was never the confident type when it came to situations like this, but something about him made me want to come out of my comfort zone.

"Thank you for having me over. You have no idea how much I appreciate it," I said, smiling at him.

"Of course. I enjoyed the time. You're more than welcome to come over any time you want," he said, placing the pizza into the oven when the light went off.

"I'll definitely hold you too it. Especially since I haven't seen that amazing frozen-over stream you were telling me about," I said, and I heard him chuckle as he closed the oven.

I finished my tea and placed the teacup beside me on the table. He sat down beside me, and I felt butterflies rush through me as his arm brushed past mine. I didn't move my arm and I let the warmth flow through us for a little longer. The slightest touch from him felt so intimate. I looked up to him as I saw him relax into the chair.

"Aren't you getting cold?" I asked, looking at his bare chest. He smiled and shook his head.

"I'm not, but if you're getting uncomfortable, I'll put my shirt on," he said, reaching for his shirt. I could feel myself blushing at his comment.

Before he could even put it over his head, I stopped him by placing my hand on his arm. "It isn't; don't worry. I actually like it," I said and almost regretted it the moment the words left my lips.

He seemed puzzled at first and then he smiled. We were frozen in a gaze for a moment, and I could feel the chemistry between us. "Alright, if you say so," he said, placing his shirt down on the arm rest beside him.

"Sorry, I don't know why I said that," I said, looking away and feeling insecure about being so forward and honest.

I could have sworn I saw him smile. I tried to speak some more but I felt him place his hand on my cheek. He turned my face towards his. His eyes were filled with warmth, and I could feel his breath brush past my lips. It was a moment frozen in time and, in one swift motion, he pulled my face gently forward and closed his lips over mine. I was so stunned by the moment that I forgot to move. I placed my arms around his neck and kissed further into his lips. When our tongues touched there was fire that burnt inside me. I couldn't quite explain it. It felt so electric. I felt elated as he pulled me so easily onto his lap and I didn't deny it. His hands fell to my hips and his grip tightened. I pulled away and looked at him. His eyes had changed color and he seemed vulnerable. I smiled as his hands moved their way behind my neck. He smiled, brushing my hair back.

Everything was moving so fast in the moment that I just had to get a breather. He leaned forward and placed a kiss on my cheek. I closed my eyes from the sweet gesture, and he tilted my head back slightly and moved his lips lightly down to my neck. I giggled as he got to the ticklish part. He chuckled when he made me laugh. His laugh was like music to my ears. He placed another kiss on my collarbone, and he gave me a soft tug. I pushed him away slightly. I looked into his eyes and then looked down at his chest. The moment I had been waiting for was finally here.

I moved my hands slowly across his chest and his skin felt so soft under my touch. The desire for more of him started growing inside of me. He was watching me as I glided my fingers over his arms. I looked up to him and smiled and he did the same thing. I leaned forward, placing my lips over his. Our tongues touched again and this time our kiss grew. His lips brushed past my lips harder than before. He lifted me and lay me down on the couch and then he moved his way between my legs.

A small voice inside me started shouting, *Get out now, Amelia!* But I didn't want to listen to the voice. I heard the alarm bell ring for the pizza. I moved my lips off his but that didn't stop him. He kissed my neck so tenderly that I almost forgot that the pizza was going to burn.

"Sebastian, the buzzer," I said, giggling as he got to the sensitive part in my neck.

"I like burnt pizza," he said, and I started laughing. "I love your laugh," he said into my ear, and I moved my face back in front of his. His eyes were filled with so much love and warmth. I placed my hand on his chest and moved him a little off me.

"C'mon. As much as I love this, I don't want to go too fast," I said, and he gave me a small smile. He leaned down and kissed my nose and then placed one last kiss on my lips. It was so soft and so loving that I didn't want him to pull away. I even closed my eyes a little longer than I wanted just because I was savoring the moment.

"Sebastian, open up." We heard a raised voice from outside his door. He jumped up off me to look over the couch and I pushed myself up as well.

"Who is it?" I asked, and he frowned.

"I think it's Alex," he said and as he said it the oven's buzzer went off and we realized that the first buzzer hadn't been warning us that the pizza was done. It had been Alex ringing the doorbell.

Bas climbed off me and I straightened myself up. He stood up and walked over to the door. He rested his head on the door and asked a question, "Alex, is that you?"

"Yes, now open up," Alex replied.

Sebastian grabbed his shirt quickly and placed it over his head. I could feel the tension rising in the room as I watched him open the door. The moment it was open, Alex's eyes fell on me and it was as though he knew exactly what had happened. His blue eyes were dark, and I knew things were about to go down.

Chapter 11

THE UNRAVELING

I didn't think I would have any affectionate feelings towards Sebastian, but I did. Luckily, he'd put his shirt on before he opened the door to Alex, otherwise he would have thought we were trying to do other things.

Alex had stayed for the pizza. We ate it in awkward silence. Sebastian tried to make conversation with Alex, but he wasn't open to conversation. I caught myself glancing over at Sebastian a couple of times and I tried to stop but, somehow, I always found my way to him. So did he to me.

Alex asked what we had done for the day, and we told him we'd mostly just spoken about everything. He was one sour lemon. Alex had come to fetch me because he'd promised my mother that he'd let me stay with him and he didn't want to lie to her. He offered for Sebastian to sleep over, but Sebastian got the vibe that Alex didn't want him there, so he declined. We didn't stay long and, before I knew it, Alex said he'd meet me at the car. I was grateful that he'd at least let me say goodbye.

Sebastian was leaning against the door frame as he watched Alex walk down the steps. Sebastian had a smirk on his face, and I couldn't help but smile back.

"Why are you smiling?" I asked, and he shook his head and looked down to me.

"Ahh, nothing. Good luck with him tonight. Thank you for coming over, and for the talk. It felt good to share it with someone," he said, and I looked up at him as he took a step closer to me.

I felt so small around him. He brushed a strand of hair out of my face and his pupils were dilated due to the low lighting. For some reason, it only attracted me to him more.

I nodded my head at him and smiled. "It's a pleasure. Thank you for rescuing me at the café from complete loneliness," I said playfully, and we both chuckled. He leaned in and brushed his lips past my ear. I laughed as it was very ticklish, and he whispered something.

"You're beautiful." His words nestled themselves nicely into my heart, making me smile and feel in love at the same time.

He pulled away and only left goosebumps running down my neck. He didn't take his eyes off mine. I watched as he rubbed his thumb softly over my bottom lip, which only tempted me to kiss him. His eyes burned with desire and this time I didn't wait for him to kiss me. I took the first step. I stood up on my tiptoes and wrapped my hands around the back of his neck and I placed my lips onto his. They were soft and warm. I didn't want to let go, but I could feel Alex staring at us from the car, so I didn't quite feel as comfortable doing it as I had before. I pulled away and I smiled at him.

"Good night," I said, and he smiled at me, still holding me close to him.

"Sweet dreams," he whispered as he looked from my eyes to my lips again. He leaned down to give me one last kiss, but Alex blew the horn and we both jumped. I started to laugh and that only seemed to amuse Sebastian.

"His so jelly," I said as I pulled away from Sebastian.

He looked out towards Alex, and he shook his head. "You should go before he comes back," Sebastian said, and I nodded. At that I squeezed his hand, and I turned around and started walking down the steps. "I'll call you," I heard him say as I walked down the steps and I turned and nodded my head, smiling back at him.

"Okay," I said hopefully.

Alex was being so annoying and, honestly, I didn't want to go home with him. For the first time in my life, I wanted to choose someone else other than him, and I was sure that was what was driving him so mad. I walked over to the car and opened the passenger door and climbed in, closing it behind me. Alex sat inside and he said nothing. As Sebastian saw the car reverse out the parking lot, he turned and walked into his house.

"Childish much?" I said, feeling upset that he'd behaved that way. In fact, I was disappointed at his behavior. I'd expected better from him. He didn't want to look over at me. His jawline was tense, and I could see his eyes were fixed on the road. The car was quiet.

"Sorry, I must have fallen asleep on the horn. You two were taking so long," he responded flatly.

"I'm disappointed in the way you've handled this situation," I said, looking at him.

He brought the car to a halt. I jerked forward in my seat. Thank goodness for my safety belt. There were no cars on the road. We were the only ones. He cocked his head around and looked at me.

"You're disappointed with how I handled the situation?" He spat the question out sarcastically. I folded my arms over my chest. I wasn't interested in his horrible attitude. "I have had a shit day because I've been chasing after you," he raised his voice. His eyes were dark, and I think it was the first time I had ever seen him this mad at me.

"I didn't ask you to." I spat the words back at him.

I reached for the safety belt and unclipped it. I didn't want to sit here and be shouted at like a child. I wanted to go home, one way or another. I reached for the door handle and, as I opened it, Alex leaned quickly over and shut it. I felt so small, especially when he was this mad.

"Let me go Alex!" I shouted, but he locked the door through central locking.

"No. Ingrid doesn't want to talk to me because I'm sure she found out I lied to her. You didn't answer me the whole day and ended our call on a rude note. Don't you think I care about you? I had to lie to your mother about your whereabouts to save your ass. Now don't tell me that you're disappointed in my actions, because quite frankly your actions were very questionable today!" he said, more loudly than I liked.

I looked out the window and only felt vulnerable. I didn't like to be shouted at and a part of me wanted to hide away. I felt the lump in my throat and the more I tried to stop the tears from falling the more the tears stung my eyes. I looked up, but that only helped the tears stream down my face faster. I was a big mess. I didn't want to be in this situation and he of all people should have known that.

"Don't cry, Amelia," he said, a little softer than before, and I heard him sigh. I wiped my tears as they came, and I didn't look at him once.

"Let's just go home," I said and at that he started the car and we drove in silence.

He put the radio on to drown out the quiet. My tears dried and it actually helped to not speak. I was able to think clearly. The journey felt a lot shorter than I had hoped. He pulled up in front of his house. He climbed out and I didn't allow him to open the door for me, and I climbed out at the same time he did.

He opened the house, and I walked in first. He switched on the lights and locked the door behind us. His home felt so familiar, and the feeling helped me ease up a bit. I walked over to the couch and placed my bag down on the ground. I sat down and folded my arms. He put the car keys down on the kitchen island and I could feel him stare at me.

"I'm sorry for shouting at you," he whispered, but I didn't want to hear it. "I've just had a horrible day and you're the first one I've seen since everything happened," he said, sounding exhausted.

"Alex, I wanted you today. The moment I heard her voice, I didn't anymore. Ingrid has become more a part of your life than you can imagine. You don't do anything anymore and the old Alex I used to know would have told me that he would never let a women own him the way that she owns you right now," I said, and I didn't care if the words hurt.

"What do you want me to do, Amelia? It's not easy for me. Since you've been back, all I want to do is spend time with you, but because of Ingrid I can't." He almost sounded as though he were pleading with me.

I looked at him and I shook my head. "You have a choice, Alex. She is poisonous. I can't even imagine why you'd stay with her."

"It's easier said than done. She can be nice," he said softly.

"Yeah, in bed, I'm sure," I spat the words out and they felt good.

"Hey, that's not nice," he said, defending her, which only made me more upset.

I looked over to him and I felt as though this conversation was going nowhere. "Admit it! The main reason why you're still with her is because she rocks your world like no one else can." I felt so sick after saying it I even stood up and put more distance between us.

"Stop it, Amelia," Alex warned.

"Alexander, as long as you're with her this friendship will not work out. She doesn't want me in your life and, honestly, I don't want to always fight for your attention," I said, raising my voice a bit. I could feel my heart aching as I did the one thing I'd never thought I'd do. I watched as his expression went from serious to hurt in one motion.

He shook his head. "You don't fight for my attention, Amelia. You get more of my attention," he said, sympathizing with me.

I shook my head. "The main thing is that she doesn't want me around and I can never see us being friends, so maybe we should just stop being friends altogether." The words hurt worse than I expected.

He shook his head slowly and I could see the pain in his eyes. I didn't want to hurt him because I loved him. All I wanted to do now was hug him and say I was sorry, but I couldn't stop the words that had been spoken. I looked away from him because I felt as though I couldn't face him anymore.

"Amelia, no, I won't let that happen," he said, walking towards me and it only caused me to step back further. "Every day of my life, I wake up wondering if you're okay. Since you got back, I have been sleeping better. I look forward to every day with you and now you're telling me that you want to take it all away?" His voice almost sounded as though it was about to crack. I stopped walking when he started talking and, before I knew it, he was in front of me. His eyes were so vulnerable and so were mine.

"I'm not going to make you choose. I'll just make it easy for you and leave," I said, looking at him and I could feel the lump in my throat again. He shook his head.

"If you think it's going to make my life easier because you're not in it. Then you're wrong," he protested, and I looked down.

I felt so defeated. I had no idea what to say anymore. He placed his hand on my hip and I looked up at him, immediately confused by what was happening. He pulled me in, and his arms embraced me. I almost gasped at what was happening.

"I'll always choose you, Amelia. You are the one thing I want in this life. Don't ever doubt it. I've always known it was you," his breath tickled my cheeks, and I had no words. I was stunned by him. This was the moment I had been waiting for my whole life. He leaned down and brushed his lips gently against mine, as though he were savoring the moment.

I pulled away and looked at him. "Alex what are you doing? You have a girlfriend, remember?" I said, trying to push him away from me, but it only made him hold me closer. He shook his head.

"I don't care about her. I don't care what she thinks. I care about you and about what you think and right now all I want is you."

His words burned deep inside me. I felt so confused by all the emotions inside me. I looked into his eyes and watched how he looked down at my lips, greedily. I didn't think twice. I leaned forward and grabbed the opportunity. Our lips crashed upon each other, and I had forgotten what it felt like to be kissed by him. He lips tasted sweet and also bad because I knew it wasn't allowed. Every sensation in my body was on fire. I felt him move his hands down from my hips to my legs. He gracefully pulled me up and I wrapped my legs around him. He pulled away, holding firmly onto my back.

"Hold on," he said, and he started climbing the steps up to his bedroom. As he climbed, he planted kisses down my neck, making me giggle in bliss. We made it into his bedroom and he softly placed me down onto the bed. I was well aware of what was about to happen. He smiled as he looked down at me and I leaned up and held onto his shirt, bringing him down. He moved his way between my legs, and he placed his hand softly against my face. The thought of this happening made me feel as though I were dreaming. I had never thought it would get this intense. Even the last night we were together it was only one kiss and then it was nothing. This was different. It was the end of the long wait of secret glances and hidden desires.

"You have no idea how long I've been wanting to do this," he whispered.

I gave him a small smile. I didn't want to confess the same thing back. He leaned down and placed his lips over mine and I allowed it. Our tongues touched and everything inside me felt weak. Our tongues intertwined with one another, and I wrapped my legs around him. I moved my hands swiftly under his shirt and he allowed me to glide them along his skin. I had never wanted anything more than I wanted him in this moment. If my first time were to be with him, there was no one else I would trust more than I trusted him.

I moved his shirt up and he got the message. He pulled away and moved his shirt over his head. I ran my fingers along his chest and, as he came in close, I moved my hands along his back. Exploring him. I felt his hand move slowly under my shirt and he placed his hand softly over my chest. I could feel my cheeks burn. With my eyes closed, I felt his lips open against mine. I shivered under his touch.

He stopped kissing me and looked into my eyes. His pupils were dilated. "Amelia, are you comfortable with what's happening?" he asked softly, and I nodded my head. He leaned down and planted a kiss on my neck. In the moment I thought of Ingrid and how she'd feel if she knew what was happening. I thought of how he'd just earlier had sex with her and here I was, giving in to him. Giving something so special to him. I closed my eyes and tried to fight the thoughts.

His lips found mine again and I let him tug on them hungrily. If I was going to stop this, I wanted to just savor it for a little while longer. I felt him tug at my shirt and, I don't know why, I let him take my shirt off. A part of me felt as though I needed him to see me, or I wanted him to maybe see me in a different light. His eyes never left mine and I silently watched as his lips moved down to my neck and then to my breast. He unclipped my bra and I felt exposed. He softly placed his lips over my nipple, and I closed my eyes in pleasure. I felt like I was on fire. I felt his hands move down my stomach and his hands stopped to unbutton my pants. As much as I wanted this to go on, I just had a bad feeling. He was still in a relationship, and I was scared.

I breathlessly grabbed his hand and stopped him from going any further. He looked up at me and I shook my head. "Wait, Alex," I said, trying to catch my breath. I closed my eyes and I could feel him watching me.

"Is everything alright?" he asked. I nodded my head. I just kept thinking of how Ingrid would feel, or if he had done this many times with women other than Ingrid.

"I'm sorry. I thought I was ready, but I'm not," I said quietly.

I looked the other way and he lifted himself off me. I lay there and felt nothing but empty. He looked over to me as I looked at the ceiling. I sat up and grabbed my shirt and quickly pulled it over my head. I felt so vulnerable.

"Amelia, it's okay. I'm not mad. I understand," Alex said softly, touching my back.

I wanted to continue but I couldn't give him that sacred part of me knowing he was still with Ingrid. Especially knowing he'd just had sex with her that same day. I felt so stupid that I had fallen so deep into his seductions. I turned and looked at him. He was resting against the headboard, just watching me.

"I'm sorry. I'm just not comfortable with it yet," I said, looking down. He nodded his head softly and his eyes were so understanding, despite the situation.

"That's okay with me," he said softly, He held out his hand to me "Will you at least let me hold you," he asked politely, and I gave him a small smile.

I moved over to him. I lay down a bit and rested my head on his chest and he placed his arm comfortably around me. This felt better. A moment ago, I hadn't been thinking clearly, and I'd almost given him all of me. A small part of me was upset with myself, but another part of me knew it was the right decision. His heartbeat started slowing down and I felt bad for him.

"I'm sorry I led you on," I said once more. I felt like the more I said it, the better I would feel about myself.

"Don't be sorry, Em. I'm happy the way it turned out," he said running his finger up and down my arm. "Everything in good time," he whispered.

"I'm sure not many girls have rejected you," I said with a smile on my face, and he snickered.

"Wow, already starting with your comments," he said humorously. "And no, I am proud to say, no girls reject me," he said confidently, and I couldn't help but push myself off him.

"Except me," I proudly said. I looked over at him and he gave a small sigh, despite the smile on his face. His blue eyes were on me.

"Except you," he whispered, and I could only imagine what he thought. "You are really different." I looked away from him and looked down at my jeans. Sometimes I felt like an outsider when he called me different. "Hey, it's a good thing," he said, touching my arm slightly. "If anything, it makes you more desirable."

At that, I looked up to him and smiled. I could feel my cheeks burn and I looked away again. Despite him having a girlfriend and him cheating on her, he had made me more confused now than I had ever been in my life. I was confused by the fact that our friendship had been altered and I had no idea how it was all going to play out now. I was confused because I had just started feeling things for Sebastian and he had completely opened up to me tonight about his past. I didn't know how to handle all of this. I wanted to think about it, in my own time, because sitting next to him was clouding my vision. He was beginning to unravel me, and I felt like a big mess.

"Alex, could you maybe sleep downstairs tonight?" I asked, looking over to him, and he frowned.

"Why?" he asked softly.

"Because you are making it hard for me to think at the moment and I need to clear my head," I said, watching as he pushed himself off from the headboard.

"Alright, if that's what you want, but I promise you the bed will feel warmer if I'm in it," he said, teasing me. I gave a small laugh.

"I can imagine, but you forget: I'm used to sleeping alone."

I watched him shake his head at me and I couldn't help but laugh. He climbed out of bed and started murmuring things.

"Stop being childish," I said, amused.

At that he started descending the stairs and I felt so much better. I could breathe.

Chapter 12

MY HALF-BROTHER

I was sitting on the edge of the bed. I felt Sebastian touch my back and I turned around, smiling. I lay beside him, and he lifted himself up and he moved his body over mine and he planted his kiss down on my lips. I let him. He moved his hand down my shirt and he slipped his hand under it. I allowed him to kiss my neck. I closed my eyes in pleasure as his hand moved higher and touched the brim of my bra. I opened my eyes. Sebastian had disappeared but Alex was on top of me.

"I love you, Em," he whispered, before he moved down and kissed me. The emotions rushed through me, and I didn't know what to do. Alex's hand reached behind my back, and he unclipped my bra. I gasped and he started moving his hands slowly over towards my chest.

"Hey, lovebirds," a voice said from beside the bed. We both stopped and looked up to the figure, who had a black hoodie on. The face was completely blacked out. Sebastian reappeared and Alex had left. He sat in front of me and was guarding me.

"Who are you?" Sebastian asked, and the figure didn't reply.

"This will be the last time you every feel or touch her again," the dark hooded figure said. Right in front of my eyes I watched as the figure raised a gun to Sebastian's head and it didn't even take a second. Before I'd finished gasping, the figure had pulled the trigger. I screamed as I felt moisture splatter against my face. The fear engulfed me and all I wanted to do was run, but I was paralyzed. I watched how Alex's body lay there dead. The tears streamed down my face.

"No, no, no! Please, I'm sorry," I said touching the lifeless body.

"Amelia," the voice said to me, and I jumped up and curled in a ball, placing my hands over my ears and screaming for help. I was all alone.

"Amelia!" I felt someone shake me and I woke up. I shot my eyes open and in front of me, kneeling beside the bed, was Alex. His face was full of concern. I sat up in bed and wiped tears from my eyes. It took me a second to gather myself and realize it had just been a dream. I could feel my heart hammering in my chest. I looked next to me and looked at Alex. I felt scared.

"Sorry, I didn't mean to wake you," I said, and I glanced around the room, just to make sure there was no figure waiting for us.

He shook his head and stood up. He sat in front of me. His hair was a mess, and you could see he had just woken up from his sleep. His shirt was off, and I looked at his tattoo. His blue eyes were dark, and he didn't take his eyes off of me.

"What did you dream of? You were screaming and then you started crying," he said. I looked down and sighed. I rubbed my eyes and didn't really want to think about the dream. I pulled the blanket up a little higher so it could cover my arms.

"I've been having night terrors about the stalker," I said softly, almost as though I was afraid the stalker would hear, if he were listening.

Alex sighed and I could see from the corner of my eye that he scratched his head in frustration. "What dreams?" he asked seriously.

"Well, I haven't had many. They actually started two nights ago," I replied, and I looked up to him.

"Is it because of the second letter?" he asked, and I nodded my head.

"I guess," I said, shrugging my shoulders. He pulled his legs up onto the bed and he folded them, he crossed his arms over his chest, and he looked at me.

"So, can you tell me about these dreams? What was the first one about?" he asked, and I looked at him. I was so grateful it was a dream and that he was alive.

"The first one took place in the forest. I ran all by myself and I didn't tell anyone where I was going. I kept hearing noises in the woods, which only made me run faster until I hit my head on a branch and fell. When I looked up, I saw a figure in the distance, and I ran. I tried to hide behind a tree and, when I thought the figure was gone, I turned around, only to have the figure in front of me. The man placed a cloth over my mouth. He was drugging me, and he told me he wouldn't hurt me. That he was going to take care of me.

"I wanted to scream, but it didn't work. He told me that he'd warned me he would come and find me. I couldn't really do anything as I could feel my body losing strength." I replayed the scene in my head. I looked at him and he was frowning. He was obviously taking it more seriously than I would have liked him to take it. Thank God it was just a dream.

"And the other dream?" he asked.

I looked down and didn't want to tell him because it involved him and Sebastian. To be honest, I didn't know how he was going to take this one. "Well, the other one is a bit different," I said, looking back up at him. He didn't break eye contact once. "Sebastian was in it." At the mention of Bas's name, he looked away and then he looked back to me. He didn't like it, I could tell.

"Then Bas changed to you." He frowned, and I couldn't handle all his expressions, so I looked down.

"What were we doing?" he asked.

I rubbed my forehead in shame. I even gave a small smile because I was embarrassed. "Okay, so I was sitting on the edge of the bed and Bas was there and we started kissing." I made sure not to look up to Alex. "Then, when it got heated and I opened my eyes, Bas had disappeared, and you were the one kissing me." I heard him chuckle.

"Having dirty dreams about me, are you," he said, and I looked up as he lay his body down and leaned against his arm. His muscles were tensing as he held his body in one position. He had a smirk on his face, and I rolled my eyes because he only cared about himself. "What did I do to you?" he asked, amused.

I looked down and shook my head, pulling the blanket in a bit more. He was making me feel so embarrassed and uncomfortable. "Stop it, Alex. You didn't do much because the stalker stopped us"

"What do you mean?" he asked, clearly frustrated.

"Well, before you even reached my chest, the stalker was there, and he said 'Hello, lovebirds,' and then you disappeared, and Bas appeared. He was protecting me from the stalker," I said, looking up at Alex. He had rolled his eyes and he looked the other way. "The stalker said to Sebastian that it would be the last time he ever touched me again and then, before I knew it, he took out a gun and he shot him in the head."

I looked down at the bed and remembered what it felt like when all the blood was on my face. Fear. "There was so much blood on my face, I screamed and, when I looked at Bas, he had changed to you again and I knew that I had lost you. The stalker said my name and I curled into a ball. I was afraid and I didn't want him to hurt me."

"Look, Em, at least you know it's just a dream and it won't happen," he said in a serious tone again.

I looked at him and he was upset, but I didn't want to think too much about it. "I know. I just don't want to lose anyone because of some stupid person who has an obsession about me," I said, looking down at the blanket again. He sat up again and looked at me. He reached over and grabbed my hand, squeezing it.

"Don't worry, Amelia. I'll do everything in my power to make sure nothing ever happens to you," he said, and I shook my head at him.

"I appreciate that, but the thing is, I don't want anything to happen to *you*," I whispered, looking into his eyes. "You are too much a part of my life, and I would hate myself if something had to happen to you," I sternly said and I looked down. He gave a small chuckle and, by holding onto my hand, he pulled me forward and I was embraced by his arms.

"It's going to be okay, Em," he said, giving me a small kiss on my head. The warmth of his chest was lovely and I closed my eyes as I listened to his heartbeat.

"Maybe it's better if we just don't..."

"Don't start with that bull. I'm not worried about this guy. We'll be okay," Alex interrupted me. "I would, however, like you to maybe talk to your parents about it," he said.

I instantly pushed myself off him. "No, there is no discussion about this. They will never let me go out, or they will make us go to the cops because I have someone interested in me," I said frowning.

He watched me and I knew he was thinking of the right things to say. He looked down and shook his head. "Alright, enough about this. Let's go get something to eat." He pushed himself off the bed and he walked over to his cupboard.

I watched as he scrabbled through his clothes and he picked out a dark green hoodie. He slipped it over his head and, when he was about to put his pants on, I looked away and decided to walk over to the bathroom. I didn't want to think of this stalker. I didn't want to read any more letters he had to write to me. I was done being worried and paranoid. I closed the door behind me and walked over to the shower. I put the water on and, when it got hot, I took all my clothes off. I stood under the warm water, and let it clear my thoughts.

...

After we had eaten, we were on our way back to my house. He came around the corner and I saw my house. I could only imagine my parents lecturing me about my irresponsible behavior. I looked over to Alex and from the corner of my eyes I saw his phone light up. Ingrid was calling and I watched as he quickly shut his screen off. He was ignoring her, and I felt so guilty for it. I knew it was because of me and I knew she was only going to hate me more once she found out what had almost gone down last night between Alex and me. Not only would Ingrid hate it, but Sebastian would too. I felt like such a cheap girl.

My heart felt heavy, and I looked down. I wanted to tell Alex none of this could happen again until he broke up with Ingrid, but I also didn't want to force him to make that decision. I wanted him to come to that conclusion on his own. I just hoped

Sebastian would forgive me, and understand how difficult it was for me to say no.

"Who's this?" Alex said, frowning as we pulled up in front of my house. I looked to where he was looking and parked in front of our lawn was a big blue car.

"I don't know, I don't recognize the car," I said frowning.

Alex put the ignition off and then he climbed out the car. The car looked new, as it didn't even have a number plate. My door opened and I climbed out as Alex shut it behind me. He placed his arm around me, and I didn't resist, even though I knew it was probably wrong. We walked up our pathway and, as I got to the front door, Alex opened it again for me and gestured for me to walk inside. I smiled and thanked him. Alex followed behind me.

"Hey, Mom," I said quietly, as I saw her at the kitchen counter looking down at her cup. She was drinking something. She looked worried and I frowned, as I had never seen her in this state. She looked up at me and I knew she wasn't happy.

"Hey, guys. Glad to see you are okay." Her voice was quiet, and I knew immediately something was wrong.

I walked over to her. "Is everything okay, Mom?" I asked and sat down in front of her at the table. She looked down at her cup. She played with the ear of the cup, and she looked almost defeated.

"Whose car is that out front?" Alex asked. My mother looked up and blankly looked out past the wall, as if she could see the car.

"Oh that, yes, the car," she said, and she looked back at her cup again. "So, we have a visitor. He is in the bathroom at the moment." Alex and I looked at each other with concern.

"Who's the person, Mom?" I insisted. She shrugged her shoulders.

"He said his name is Tyron, and he claims to be your father's son," she said, not looking up from her cup. I shook my head.

"What do you mean? Dad doesn't have any other children," I said, offended by the accusation. My mother looked up at me and you could see she wasn't in the mood for this conversation.

"Let's just wait for your father to come from his office. He'll be home soon. I called him," she said, and then she took a sip of her coffee.

"Why on earth does that name sound so familiar?" I said, thinking about it.

"Hi, Jennifer," I heard a voice say, and we all looked in that direction. I was stunned to see it was the man I'd met at the Read In Café yesterday. He had his black-framed glasses on.

"Tyron," I whispered softly, remembering the name. He smiled when he saw me, and I couldn't return the smile.

"Wow, what a small world, hey? I didn't know your father was Benjamin." He was so pumped and full of energy. I shook my head at him.

"How do you know my father?" I asked, confused.

He gave a small smile and then he looked down and wiped the smile off his face. "I don't really feel comfortable speaking about it in front of him," he said, pointing towards Alex. I looked over at Alex and I watched his jawline stiffen.

"You must be kidding me if you think I'm going to leave you alone with these two women." He practically spat the words out at Tyron. I felt quite intimidated by him. Tyron and Alex didn't take their eyes off one another, and I felt the air in the room start to grow thick.

"Alex is like family, son. It's okay," my mother said to Tyron. I couldn't take my eyes off him.

He shook his head and looked away. "Let's just wait for your father to get home," he said and, before I knew it, I heard a car door open and shut and it didn't take my father long before he walked through the front door. He watched as we all three stood there and my father's eyes instantly fell on Tyron. I didn't want to be there anymore. I felt like something bad was going to happen.

"I'm going to go. I'll see you later," Alex said, and he grabbed my hand and squeezed it softly. I nodded my head. A small part of me didn't want him to leave, but I knew it would be so awkward for him. He greeted my parents and I watched as he opened the door, gave me one more glance, and then closed it behind him.

"Hello, Benjamin," Tyron said, and I instantly grew mad. My father nodded his head in Tyron's direction as a greeting.

"I'm going to my room," I said and, before anyone could protest, I walked past them and went straight to the stairs. I could feel them look at me. I reached the top of the stairs and shut my door without walking inside my room so that I could eavesdrop. I sat down against the wall and listened to them speak.

"Sit down, son," I heard my mother say.

"So, I hear you claim to be my son," my father said.

"Well, my mother, Alison Watts, said that you guys got together and had a one-night stand. She fell pregnant, and she never told you about it because she said you got back together with Evelyn," he said, and there was silence between them. "I wanted to meet you. I'm sorry it had to turn out this way. I didn't mean to make anyone upset," he said softly.

"No, don't worry. It's not your fault. It's just a shock to us all," my mother said softly.

"I'm sorry that Alison never told me," my father said, and it only made me mad.

Had my father cheated on my mother? They had been high school sweethearts. They loved each other. I couldn't imagine them doing that to each other. I wanted to get out of here. I stood up and opened my door and shut it again. I knew they could hear it, but I didn't care. I sat down on my bed and called Skylar.

"Hey babe, what's up?" she said, all cheerful.

"Hey, listen, I really need a saving moment. Can you maybe come pick me up? Maybe tonight we can go to a club, only us two girls. No boys?" I asked.

"I'm on my way," she said.

"Thank you. I'll see you now," I replied.

At that, she ended the call, and I gathered my bag with some clothes. I wasn't planning on coming home that night, and I wanted to be prepared. After packing my bag, I quickly got a notepad and wrote down on it that I needed space and that I was crashing at Skylar's for the night. I left the note on my bed, and I walked to the balcony and climbed over the railing. I jumped off and landed on the ground. I groaned and sucked up all the pain. Once I'd gathered myself, I ran around the corner and waited for Sky outside. I didn't want to see my family fall apart. This year seemed to be spiraling in completely the opposite way I wanted it to.

I sat down on the grass and pulled my legs up and hugged my knees, resting my head on them. I couldn't wait to get this information off my chest. I sat there and thought about all my actions in the past couple of hours. I didn't know how I was going to tell Sebastian about what I had done to Alex. I felt so guilty. I hid my head in my arms as I waited for Skylar to pitch up. I couldn't believe that I had a half-brother.

After ten minutes, I heard a car on the road. I looked up and saw Skylar pull up in front of our lawn. I got up and ran over to her car, hoping that no one saw me. I climbed in as she opened the door, from the inside. She looked over at me and frowned as she saw my whole face drop.

"What's the matter, babe, tell me all about it," she said, and I gestured for her to drive.

She pulled onto the road, and I began telling her about what had happened in the past couple of hours.

Chapter 13

COLORFUL LIGHTS

I told Skylar everything about the day before. She devoured every juicy bit, and she couldn't believe how much she had missed in basically two days. She asked which one I was going to choose and, quite frankly, I didn't want to choose. I didn't want to tell Sebastian about Alex, and I know Alex didn't want me to be with Sebastian. It was one sticky mess. I had phoned my mother and told her I was sorry that I had left but that I wanted to give her and my father some space and that I would be crashing by Skylar's place that night. She said it was fine and that she was sorry about everything. I told her it was fine.

Anyways, I wasn't the only one with juicy news. Skylar had met a guy named Cole and she said that he was a gentleman and she really liked him. They'd spent the whole day together the day before. He had already called her and asked her what she was doing for the day, but she'd explained to him that I needed some time with her today and that she'd be with him tomorrow.

Sky and I were getting ready to go to the Hot Shack. I had never been there before. It was a little out of town, but she said it was the best place to get loose and just have fun. It was already dusk by the time I finished putting on the pair of closed high heel boots that Skylar had lent me. I didn't like heels, but she insisted I take a pair there. So, I didn't protest. We wore jeans and both of us wore jerseys. Her jersey had lots of glitter on it, but I didn't want to stand out so much. My jersey was black, and I loved it because it was cozy, and it didn't draw too much attention. I straightened my hair and she curled hers. We both put makeup on. I applied a smoky eye look and she went for a cat eye liner look. We looked great, and I couldn't wait to go.

We grabbed our essentials and placed them in a small bag. We left her house and climbed into her car, and we got onto the road. Skylar had already started playing music in the car to get our vibes pumped for the evening.

"Don't think about anything tonight, okay? Just enjoy yourself. You never do this, so do it and have fun. Don't let weird guys talk to you and, number one rule: never take a drink from a man. It's probably spiked," she said, holding her index finger out at me while keeping her eyes on the road.

I shook my head. "Wow, this place sounds super safe," I said sarcastically. She laughed and so did I.

"Don't worry, man, just make sure that if you get a drink from a man it's from a bottle that's closed, and you open it yourself, so that you can see it hasn't been spiked," she said.

I nodded my head. "Alright, I'll make sure I won't take any drinks from anyone," I said.

It took us ten minutes of chatting in the car, and then we reached a building. She drove into the parking lot. It was packed and I started getting butterflies in my stomach. You could hear the music pumping inside and there was a long queue of people waiting outside. I shook my head when she stopped the car.

"I don't want to go inside," I said, and she shook her head.

"I didn't do all of this for nothing. C'mon, man. I know you're going to love it, okay. Let's go," she said, grabbing her bag and climbing out her car.

"Okay," I said nervously. I stopped and looked at her once I was outside. "Do you think this is a good idea, you know with the stalker running lose and all?" I asked and she shook her head at me.

"This is your night. Forget about the stalker and just enjoy yourself" she said smiling at me. I nodded my head and looked ahead.

Sebastian didn't contact me and that was probably for the best. Alex asked if I was okay, and I told him I was fine and that I had gone to Sky's house. I told him I was going out, but I didn't tell him to where. He wanted to know, but I ignored the messages. I wanted to stop talking to everyone, so I decided to turn my phone off. Probably not the wisest thing to do, but I didn't feel like talking. I put it in my back pocket. We walked over the road, and I could feel eyes on us as we made it to the line.

Skylar looked at the line and sighed. "Hold on, I know the bouncer," she said, and I followed her up the line as she got to the front. The bouncer instantly smiled when he saw Skylar.

"Buddy, how are you?" she said enthusiastically to the bouncer. He was so big. He towered over her and me, even though we had heels on.

"It's good to see you, Skylar. There's always space for you," he said, basically flirting with her. She smiled, and I watched how he lifted the rope and let us pass.

"Thank you, Buddy, I owe you one," she said and confidently stepped inside. I followed her in and smiled at him. He smiled back down at me, and I just wanted to get inside.

"Anything for you, Skylar," he said and at that we walked inside the club and it was dark. There were colorful lights flashing all over the club. I leaned in closer to her.

"How did you do that?" I asked stunned by what had just taken place. She shrugged her shoulders,

"I have my ways" she said, smiling and looking into the crowd.

The place was packed, and Sky hooked her arm through mine. "Stay by my side!" she shouted over the music, and I nodded my head.

We walked past so many people, and I could feel so many heads turn as we walked past them. I liked the attention for once. We walked over to the bar, and she ordered drinks for both her and me. I didn't know what to drink so she just ordered anything. The barman tapped Skylar on the shoulder, and she looked over at him as he pointed at the group of men that was to our right. He put down two shots in front of her and me and he said, "Those men bought these for you." We looked at them and I smiled and so did she.

"Thanks," she mouthed, picking up the shots and I looked at her.

"Is it safe?" I asked, picking it up.

"Yes," she nodded her head, "because it was made by the bartender."

We took the shots and I cringed at the burn. Tequila shots. We took our drinks, and she grabbed my hand and we headed down to the dance floor. There was a song playing over the stereo, which made me think of both Sebastian and Alex. The songs moved through my body, and I could feel the bass vibrate its way inside my chest. I moved my hips and closed my eyes when the song reached the peak and it dropped. I felt so high. The whole place was buzzing, and I actually loved the vibe. It was my first club.

I let the music flow through me and my movements. I swayed around and around and for the first time in my life I felt so free and light. It was such a drug, to be honest. If this was what it felt like to be free and young, then I wanted to do it more often. Skylar started dancing against me and I couldn't help but laugh.

So, I followed her vibe and I was sure that if Alex could have seen me, he would have wanted to eat me up. I thought of Sebastian as Skylar and I placed our backs against each other, and we slid seductively down and back up again. I wanted him to see me. I wanted him to run his hands against me just like I knew he wanted to do. I downed my drink because it only annoyed me to have to hold it when I was dancing. I watched Skylar laugh as she saw me drinking it all.

"Slow down, girl. You can't be on another level than me," she shouted over the music. So, I watched her start to down her drink as well.

After the song was done, we walked over to the bar and I told her I wanted the bathroom. She nodded her head and we threw our bottles away on our way to it. We entered the bright light and Sky and I squinted our eyes. I used the rest room and then we looked in the mirror. I could feel I was perspiring from the dancing.

"It's nice, hey?" Sky asked enthusiastically.

I smiled and nodded my head. "Yes, I love it. Thank you for this, by the way," I said, squeezing her hand.

She smiled at me. "Of course, babe, anything for a girls' night out," she said, and we both left the bathroom. The lights hit us again. Something about this room made me feel so high. My head started fizzing and it felt good.

"Let's get another round of shots," she said, and I slowly nodded my head. I didn't know if it was such a good idea, but I didn't care.

"Okay, but just this one for now," I shouted back, and she laughed.

As we reached the bar, she saw someone in the distance. She pointed there, and I turned to look. It was Ingrid, and she was standing with Alexander. Everything inside me burned and I wanted to throw a drink at her. She clung to his side like some poor baby. She pulled his head down and she whispered something into his ear and he smiled. Then I watched as he planted a kiss on her lips. Jealousy spread through me. Why on earth had I thought it was going to be different between him and me? Of course he hadn't broken up with her because he still loved her.

I wondered if he hadn't just said all that stupid stuff just to get me into bed. Luckily, I'd denied him. It was as though he heard us talking because he just so happened to look in our direction, and his eyes fell on both Skylar and me. I could see he had regret on his face and all I did was turn around. I didn't want to see him anymore. Skylar looked at me, concern on her face.

She looked over at the bartender and she smiled. "Give us the strongest cocktail you have," she said, and he smiled back, nodding his head. Before he brought us the cocktails, he pointed at two different men.

"It's your lucky night, ladies. Here's two more shots on those men," he said, and we looked at the men and they also held two shots in their hands and lifted them in the air as we took ours. We did the same.

"Bottoms up," she said, and I downed it, trying to hide the burning sensation in my heart. I knew Alex was watching and I enjoyed every moment of it because I wanted him to know that he'd laid hands on me for the last time.

The bartender came back and handed us our cocktails. They were colorful and I was excited to taste mine. I placed my lips on the straw and took a few sips. It was sweet. Bad thing. I could see this drink going quickly. I couldn't even really taste the alcohol.

"Heads up: we have company," she shouted over the music.

She looked past me, and I knew who it was going to be. I turned around and watched as Alex made his way over to us. He looked good and it only made me more sour. I didn't stop sipping my cocktail as he approached. I could see he had a serious expression on his face.

He got to my side, and he stood in front of me. "Hey, Em," he said, almost as though he was depressed about seeing me there.

"Fancy meeting you here," I said sarcastically. He just kept looking at me. I watched him watch me. He was frowning by now. I took a step back and stumbled a bit. I giggled.

"I think you've had enough," he said, stepping forward and catching me.

I pushed him away. "You have no say over me. Why don't you go and give your girlfriend orders," I said, stepping back from him. I placed my drink on the table. It was basically finished. I glared at him and I could see that he was getting angry.

"Don't start your shit now, Amelia. Let me take you home. Before the wrong person does," he demanded as he took a step forward.

"Is that your pick-up line for girls, right before you take them home and sleep with them," I said, and I watched as his jaw tensed. "Or is it just me you declare your undying love to, and then go back to your girlfriend like nothing we shared the previous night was special?" I spat the words out and I could see he was hurt.

He looked away from me and then back again. "Look, it isn't as easy as you think it is," he said, and I felt a flame burst inside me. I took a step towards him and shook my head.

"You are so pathetic! You're just like every other man, making promises you can't keep," I shouted over the music.

"Alex, what's going on here?" Ingrid appeared beside him.

"Oh snap! Things are about to go down." I could hear Skylar saying the words behind me. I didn't know what to do in this situation. My head was spinning and I was sure I was going to regret everything later. I watched as Alex looked between me and Ingrid. He was ridiculous and, quite frankly, at this point I wanted nothing to do with him. I looked at Ingrid and she looked at me and I could see she knew something was up.

"Nothing serious, just how I'm done being his friend. You two should enjoy each other." I said the words and they stung really badly.

I watched how his face changed from being stern to being hurt. I frowned and I watched as Ingrid looked from him and then back at me again. I turned around and didn't want to be a part of that conversation anymore. Luckily, Skylar was there to hold me. She linked her arm in mine and she pulled me away. She asked me if I wanted to go to the bathroom and I shook my head, gesturing to the dance floor. If anything, I wanted to dance my sorrows away. I heard her say she was sorry, and I waved it off. I wanted to deal with this the next day, not then.

When we thought the coast was clear, we moved our way through the crowd. The room went completely dark and I grabbed her hand and she laughed. The whole crowd cheered. Some lights flashed to the right as the next song started and then lights flashed to the left and it started climbing and everyone started cheering. I felt my head get a lot lighter and it felt so good. The beat dropped and all the lights came on and went off and then started flashing everywhere. The whole crowd jumped up and down and so did I.

I opened my eyes and twirled around, making myself more drunk than I already was. I stopped myself and felt off balance. I looked out into the crowd, and I marveled at everyone who was so lost in their own worlds. My eyes skimmed over the crowd, and shot past a figure who had on a black hoodie. I instantly shot my eyes back in that direction. The figure was standing some distance away, and it didn't look like it was dancing. I blinked and tried to look again, and I think the figure realized I had noticed, because suddenly it was gone. I looked around the area and I saw a black hooded figure walking deeper into the crowd.

My curiosity got the better of me. I followed it, leaving Skylar behind. I could see the figure moving faster and faster into the crowd, only making me push past people faster as well. Was this my stalker? Was he here with me in this crowd. There was only one way that I was going to find out.

"Hey, where are you going?" A man grabbed my hand and pulled me in his direction. He had brown hair and blue eyes.

I looked away from him, frowning. I tried to look in the direction of the figure, but he was long gone. I pulled my hand away from the man and shook my head. "I have a boyfriend. Mind your own business!" I shouted at the man over the music, and he smiled at me.

He put his hands up in the air. "Alright, miss, no need to get feisty," he said, and I rolled my eyes at him.

I walked back the way I had come, but I only felt more lost. I was searching the crowd for Skylar, but I couldn't find her. I walked more and more and something must have been on the floor as I tripped and fell. I groaned, as I had hurt my knees. I felt everything tingle as I tried to push myself up and I could see everyone was looking at me. I felt so stupid and embarrassed. I looked over the floor and figured if I just broke through the crowd then I could get into the hallway and to the bathroom. I pushed past many people and eventually the crowd ended.

I saw the sign for the bathroom in the distance. Maybe Skylar would be in there.

I started to panic as I knew I was alone and intoxicated. I knew that I was prey to any sick man. My stalker might be there, and it would be the perfect time to kidnap me as well.

I managed to reach the bathroom and I pushed the door open. "Skylar?" I yelled over the loud music. There was no reply. I decided to walk over to one of the bathroom stalls anyway and I locked myself inside, just in case something happened, because I honestly feel like that man wasn't going to let me go.

After locking the bathroom stall, I sat down against the door. I looked at my hands, which felt tingly. I pulled my legs up against my chest and rested my head between my legs.. Being here felt a lot safer than being outside there. I heard someone burst through the door and open the stall next to mine. The girl threw up. I closed my eyes and groaned, as this was the last thing I wanted my night to be like. I wanted to go outside and continue searching for Skylar, but I was too out of it to defend myself if a man was going to approach me.

I heard the door open. "Hey, pretty girl," a man said.

I instantly felt ice cold. I slowly moved my hands against the walls and leaned harder against the door. I never should have come inside here. That man had obviously followed me. I heard his footsteps coming closer.

"I didn't see your boyfriend anywhere, so I thought I'd wait with you until he gets back. Are you inside here?" he asked again.

I closed my eyes and my heartbeat started climbing. His footsteps were nearing and I even wanted to climb onto the toilet to hide away. I heard a knock on the door two stalls away. The girl answered him, and I heard him knock on the stall next to me and my heart was hammering in my chest as the girl next to me denied him. I could hear his footsteps in front of my stall and there was a silence. The knock on the door made me jump forward. I shook my head, and I didn't know what to say. I placed my hand over my mouth and didn't reply.

"Pretty girl, are you in here?" he asked again. I shook my head.

I took the chance and tried to fake an accent. "No," I said.

There was silence and I heard his footsteps moving down further to the other stalls. I let go my breath silently. I heard the door open again I heard how the music from the outside started pouring in.

"Hey, man, what are you doing in here?" It was Skylar's voice, yelling over the music.

"Ahh, sorry. I guess I'm in the wrong room," I heard the guy say. My heart swelled at the sound of her voice. I guessed she'd waited for him to leave because I heard the door open again and only then did she call out my name.

"Amelia?" she called out desperately.

I gleefully replied, "I'm here," and I stood up and instantly felt lightheaded. I unlocked the door and stumbled back a bit. She opened it and she was so worried and concerned at the same time.

She knelt beside me and hugged me. "I'm so happy I found you! Was that guy in here for you?" she asked, frowning and looking outside the stall at the door.

I nodded my head and closed my eyes. "Yes. He's so hungry, you know," I said, not too aware of my words.

"So sorry that had to happen. Look, you might not like this, but I called Sebastian," she said, looking at me.

I looked up and shook my head. "No, not him. I don't want him to see me like this," I said, placing my hands over my eyes. A small hiccup left my body. I smiled at her.

She shook her head at me, and she couldn't hide her smile. "He's outside at the moment, waiting for me to call him in if I need his help. How are you feeling? Can you walk?" she asked, analyzing my body.

I nodded my head. I stood up and took a step forward. She gave me a weary look and then she grabbed my hand and we tried to walk through the front door, but I stumbled before we even reached it. Skylar gasped and I slipped and knocked my head on the wall closest to the door. Everything in my body felt fizzy. I sat up and she let go of me.

"Listen, I'm going to call Sebastian. He'll help you," she said, nodding her head at me.

Her expression was stern. She turned away and she headed straight out the door. Before I knew it, I heard the door open again. I turned to see who it was, and Sebastian walked through the door. I smiled at the sight of him because he was the only thing I wanted at this moment. He looked so damn fine when he was so serious. I must have looked like such a loser sitting on the floor, but I didn't care.

He looked worried when he saw me seated on the floor. "How much did she drink?" he asked Skylar while he knelt beside me. His cologne smelt so good and all I wanted was to breathe all of him in. I looked down and held my hand to my head and shook it.

"Enough to want to eat you up," I slurred and giggled at the same time. I heard him sigh and then he asked Skylar something. "There was a guy who wanted to come into my bathroom stall. I scared him away," I slurred some more.

He picked me up and held his hand to my back to steady me. His hold on me was so strong. I couldn't have thought of any other way I would have wanted this night to turn out. I leaned forward and rested my head on his chest. "You smell so nice," I slurred, and I felt him hold me tightly.

"Alright, Amelia, let's get you out of here," he said to me and then I watched as he looked at Skylar. "I'm glad you contacted me," he said, seeming concerned. His green eyes were staring down at me. I liked that he was so interested in looking after me.

"You're very beautiful, you know that, especially when you're acting strong and bossy," I said and giggled again. It felt so good to get it out.

"Stop talking, Amelia," I heard Skylar say as she giggled at me. I liked that she laughed, and I just felt laughter bubbling inside me too. Sebastian smiled.

"Whoo-hoo," I shouted as Sebastian left the bathroom, with Skylar following him. I heard Skylar giggle, and I couldn't help but join her.

I rested my head against his soft chest, and I felt so secure there. Sebastian walked past a group of men, and they all called out his name. He greeted them back, but he didn't go to them. He stayed on the path. We walked a little while longer, and then he pushed open the door for the exit, and we were in the open air. I felt the cold burn my skin and I was grateful for Bas's warmth. Skylar and Sebastian said some things, but I wasn't listening. Sky headed to her car and Bas took me to his. He opened the back door and carefully placed me on the back seat.

"I'll take you home," he said softly, looking down on me with his beautiful green eyes.

"I don't want to go home. I want to stay with you," I said, sitting with my legs out the car. He was still standing in front of me. I watched him chuckle at my comment.

"I'm sure you don't want to go home," he mocked, and I looked from his eyes, down to his body. He looked alluring and I just wanted to feel him again. I placed my hands on his torso and slowly moved them down to his lower waist. He smiled and grabbed my hand in the progress.

"Don't, Amelia. You aren't fully aware of what you're doing," he said, looking at me. His green eyes had darkened.

I moved a little off the seat and smiled at him. "I know what I'm doing, and I know what I want," I said, moving my free hand up his leg.

He stepped back and chuckled. His teeth were so white, and even in the dark he looked so gorgeous when he was smiling. I felt lucky that he was around me and that I could kiss him.

"Amelia. You're making this very difficult for me. I don't want to do anything right now, especially when you're like this," he said, and his smile disappeared when he said the last sentence.

I sighed and moved back onto the seat. "Alright, suit yourself," I said, and I moved completely back onto the seat and turned away from him. He was being so boring. He smiled and closed the door. I lay down on the back seat and I watched him climb into the car and the last thing I remember was his eyes looking at me in the review mirror. I entered quickly into Lala Land as he pulled onto the road.

Chapter 14

THIRD TIME, NOT A CHARM

Sebastian woke both Skylar and me up with tea this morning. His hair was a mess, and he had a big smile on his face. He sat on the edge of the bed when I sat up. He asked me if I was okay. I nodded my head. I felt a little nauseous, but it wasn't too bad.

"I'm so sorry you had to see all of that last night. Honestly, that's not me at all," I said, looking down at my cup, ashamed of how many drinks I'd had.

"I know. It's okay. I'm just glad you were fine and that you didn't get hurt or anything," he said, holding his cup. He looked at me with his green eyes and I looked away.

"There was a man who followed me into the bathroom. He found me as I was passing by the crowd," I said, and I thought back to the figure I had seen. The whole reason why I had trailed off. "I think I saw my stalker yesterday, but then again I could be wrong," I said, confused.

"What do you mean, you saw your stalker?" Skylar said, sipping her tea.

I shook my head. "I was dancing and then I saw a man in a dark hoodie staring at me, I think, and eventually, when I continued staring at him, I think he got spooked and he tried to disappear into the crowd," I said, shaking my head, feeling as though it was a dream and that everything seemed fuzzy when I thought back on it.

"That's why you disappeared?" Skylar said.

I looked at her and nodded my head. "Yes, I'm sorry. I should have told you, but I was so in the moment. I just want to see who

Unveiling Secrets

the person was, and I guess I didn't realize how dangerous the situation was," I said quietly.

Sebastian's face was serious. "Did you see his face?" Sebastian asked, and I shook my head.

"No, I was getting close to him and then that creep pulled my hand and asked me where I was going. Eventually, when I looked again, the figure had disappeared into the crowd," I said, and Sebastian folded his hands over his chest.

"That's obviously when the guy saw you all by yourself," Sebastian said, and I nodded my head.

"Yes, I told him I had a boyfriend and that he should leave me alone. But I don't think it takes a fool to see how drunk I was. He was obviously a predator," I said, thinking back on how I remembered him breaking into the bathroom.

Sebastian shook his head. "Look, I'm just glad I came when I did. Otherwise, it could have been bad. Next time you ladies mustn't go alone," he said, and he looked from Skylar to me. I nodded my head.

"I wonder if that really was your stalker, or just some random person," Skylar said, her eyes glued to mine.

I shrugged my shoulders. "It's just an uncomfortable thought, that he was there, just staring at me, if it was him," I said, thinking about it while shaking my head.

"That's what stalkers do," Sebastian said, and I looked at him. His green eyes were bright this morning and he wore a long-sleeved white shirt with dark jeans. He must have already gotten dressed when we were sleeping. I couldn't believe that I'd got the chance to kiss this good-looking guy. Just thinking of it made butterflies tickle my tummy.

"The reason why we went alone was because we wanted a girls' night only. I didn't think we would have needed any men with us, but clearly we did." Sky replied to Sebastian's earlier comment about us not going to the club alone.

"Well, now you know. Next time take us with," Sebastian said, and I looked away from him.

"Do you know how quickly they'd eat you up if you told them you are a virgin?" Skylar asked, looking at me.

I looked at her and I could only imagine that creep stealing my virginity. I shook my head, closing my eyes. The night I'd had with Alex flashed in front of me. I had been so close and that was the same night I kissed Bas. Guilt engulfed me. I didn't think I could ever tell him.

We heard a ring and we all looked to Skylar's phone. She put down her cup of tea and picked up her phone and mouthed the words *It's Alex* before answering it. I watched Sebastian stand up and he told me he'd be back in a moment. I watched as he walked away. I looked at him and observed his broad shoulders. I remembered how I had run my fingers over them. His tattoos were so alluring to me; it was definitely something that brought out his features much more. His eyes found mine before he disappeared, and I smiled at him.

"Don't worry, we're fine. We're at Sebastian's. I was able to get a hold of him. So, everything's fine," Sky said, looking at me. "Okay, bye," she said again and at that she ended the call. I shrugged my shoulders at her, and she shook her head.

"He phoned to make sure you were okay. He asked that I tell you that he's sorry about how it all went down yesterday. He says he knows you probably still don't want to talk to him, but he just wanted to make sure you're okay. He said he wanted to talk to you while you were sober," she said, and I shook my head as I thought back to the night before, when I'd seen him with Ingrid.

Sebastian's doorbell rang and both Skylar and I frowned. We heard Sebastian open the front door and we heard the familiar voice. Alex. Both Skylar and I looked at each other.

"You'd better run, girl. Both the men you kissed are in the same house," she teased, and I couldn't help but laugh.

"Why did he even phone if he was going to walk through the door now?" I asked. I couldn't face Alex while being in the same house with Sebastian. I wished he'd never come. I put down my tea and placed the covers over my head. I could feel Skylar snicker. A couple of seconds passed, and Skylar joined me under the duvet. Alex was going to ruin everything. If anything, him coming was only going to reveal that things had gone down between the two of us and Sebastian was going to figure it out.

I looked at her and smiled. "I love his bedding," I whispered to Skylar, and she laughed. I could smell his cologne on the sheets. I could have lain there all day.

"Girls, can we come up?" Sebastian asked and Skylar yelled yes.

We both sat up quickly. I could feel my stomach churn. I was very nervous to see Alex. I wasn't ready to see him so soon after yesterday. I picked my teacup up and held it close to me as I heard them climb the staircase. I could feel my heartbeat climbing and I kept my eyes down. Skylar had pulled her legs up to her chest. She had already finished her drink. I looked over at her and she smirked, and I couldn't help but smile back and shake my head. I heard the voices stop as they reached the top of the stairs, and I looked back down at my cup.

"Good morning," Skylar said, smiling ahead, looking at them.

"Morning, ladies," Alex said smoothly. I looked up and saw him. His hair was brushed to the side. He wore a dark green hoodie with a jersey number on it. He wore dark jeans and his sneakers. He looked so good. "How are you guys feeling?" he asked, and his eyes fell on me. His blue eyes were bright, and I couldn't help but look down. I shrugged my shoulders.

"I'm fine. This one, on the other hand, I'm not so sure about," Skylar said, looking to me. I looked at her and smiled.

"I feel fine, actually," I said, defending myself. I looked up and both Sebastian and Alex had their eyes on me. I looked from Sebastian to Alex and then looked down, feeling ashamed. Both of them watched me intently. My heart skipped a beat when I realized that both the men I liked were watching me. I had to really try my best not to let my cheeks flush.

"How are you?" Skylar asked Alex, trying to change the subject. I looked up at him carefully and watched how his eyes moved from Skylar's face to Sebastian's. Sebastian had his arms folded and he was watching Alex. I watched as his jaw line tensed as he focused on Alex. He looked like he wanted to say something, but he didn't. I wished I knew what he was thinking. Alex had his hands in his back pocket, making himself look attractive in the position.

"I'm okay. Ingrid doesn't want to talk to me," he said, shrugging his shoulders. Serves him right. I also wouldn't want to talk to him.

"What did you do this time?" Sebastian asked, and I wished he hadn't. If only he knew, he would have kicked us out a long time ago. Guilt rushed all over my body. I looked over at Skylar and she looked back at me. We both knew this wasn't a good conversation to get into. Alex looked up at me and I looked away from him immediately. I didn't want him to give Sebastian any hints.

"It's complicated. You know how she gets," he said annoyed at the question.

Unveiling Secrets

I watched how Skylar smiled and I couldn't help but look down at my hands. Gosh, I just wanted the subject to change. Sebastian looked at me and he looked back at Alex, who was also looking at me. I could see he was piecing things together. I could see Alex trying to ruin my and Sebastian's chances of even starting a relationship. I could see that Sebastian was about to ask something. Here we go.

"Alright, so do you guys want to go out for breakfast?" Sebastian asked, and looked at us, trying to get the attention away from Alex. I was quite surprised. I wanted to do anything that would change the subject, so I nodded my head.

"Yeah, why not," Alex said, and both the boys looked at each other, nodding their heads.

"Where, though?" Skylar asked curiously.

"Maybe Starlings?" Sebastian offered and I looked at Skylar, who shrugged her shoulders.

"Okay," I said quietly. I didn't want to talk much, especially knowing that Alex was in the same room. I couldn't think with both the men there.

Sebastian looked at me and nodded his head. "Okay, so we'll drive in my car to save gas?" We all nodded our heads. Beats me. I didn't even have a car.

Skylar slipped out of bed. I pulled the covers off and I pushed my legs out of the bed. I was wearing my long-sleeved crimson pajamas and Sky was wearing her long-sleeved silk pajamas. I took my hair out of the bun that it was in, and I ran my fingers through it. I watched as Skylar walked to the bathroom door, smiling, and I frowned at her.

"Your bathroom's in here?" Skylar asked looking back at the boys.

"Eh, yes. Just pull the door open," Sebastian said, and I looked at him as he pointed to the cupboard door. I smiled as both Alex and Sebastian looked guilty, as though they had just been caught out.

"Alright, so we'll see you two downstairs," Skylar said, gesturing for them to leave.

Both boys nodded their heads and turned around and headed towards the steps. I watched as Sebastian went down the stairs first and then Alex. Before Sebastian disappeared, he glanced up and smiled at me. Alex looked at Sebastian and followed his gaze. Alex's glance was different than Sebastian's, though. Alex's glance held pain in them.

I looked away and waited before I continued to get undressed. I wondered if he'd even told Ingrid about us. Maybe that was why she didn't want to speak to him. I walked over to Skylar, who was brushing her hair while looking in the mirror. Sebastian had a triangular bath in the right corner.

My heart was saddened as I thought of the baths he must have shared with Victoria. It must have crushed him to have to return to a house where she wasn't anymore. To have to look at the things they used to do and know that they couldn't do them anymore. Just the very fact that they had chosen this house together. In a way I could feel her here. I could feel her in the choosing of the themed colors. Maybe she was the OCD person in the relationship and Sebastian just wanted to keep everything all neat and in place, just out of respect for her.

"Hey babe, what's up?" Skylar interrupted my thoughts. She looked at me in the mirror as I stared at the bath.

I turned away and smiled, shaking my head. "Just daydreaming, that's all," I said, shrugging my shoulders.

She was applying her mascara when I joined her side. My hair fell past my breasts and curled so beautifully from being up in the bun the whole night. I was so grateful it looked so nice, since both the boys were here.

"You know, they were watching you like teenagers. When you let your hair down, they couldn't take their eyes off you, and it made me smile," she said, handing me the mascara.

I was drawn to her conversation. I felt my heart leap and I couldn't help but giggle. "Really? Wow. I figured the reason why they went so quiet was because they were either looking outside at the view or they just had nothing to talk about," I said, shrugging my shoulders.

She laughed and shook her head. "No, honey, they were watching you like you were some goddess. Like it or not, they both have their hearts set on you, and I have a feeling this is going to be a very confusing time for you; more so than what you can imagine," she said. I was so captivated by what she'd said that I forgot to apply the makeup.

"But that's the thing, Sky. Why is it now that I care for Sebastian that Alex finally wants to step up?" I asked.

She looked down and shrugged her shoulders. "I don't know, hun, but you have to think carefully about this. Don't give either of them false hope. But damn, I wish I were you. They both are gorgeous. I would do anything to have them both on *my* back," she said, smirking, and I couldn't help but giggle while pushing her shoulder playfully.

"To be honest, Alex has really shown his true colors and he clearly doesn't want to leave Ingrid, so I definitely think I'm going to go for Sebastian," I told her, looking back into the mirror.

She smiled and walked off. "Best decision you ever could have made," she said, standing by her bag. She opened the bag and pulled out her clean clothes.

I sighed as I thought of the two men. Knowing my decision only made me more uncertain about it. I still loved Alex, but maybe it was a good thing to try to see where things would go with Sebastian. If he didn't find out I had kissed Alex two nights ago.

...

We had finished our breakfast at the Starlings Restaurant. Skylar had invited her new boyfriend Cole with us to breakfast. He seemed nice, if very reserved. The boys hit it off well with him. They even invited him over for a game night on Wednesday. It was Sunday today. Alex didn't make much conversation with me; he mostly just spoke to Sebastian and Cole. Skylar sat next to Cole and clung to him like he was her air to breathe. I sat next to her, while Alex and Sebastian sat across from me. Maybe it was for the best. I did notice that Sebastian stole a couple of glances at me. I didn't speak much. Instead, I thought about what I had to deal with when I got home.

Mom and Dad had had to deal with a new son in the family. I didn't even know how Mom was taking it so lightly. Dad had practically cheated on her. How on earth was that okay? I wondered if Marcus even knew about it. After breakfast, Skylar drove home with Cole, who had come in his own car. I thanked her for everything, and I told her that I was sorry about how things had turned out at the club. I was left to drive with both Bas and Alex in the car. I mostly stared out the window as we drove. I didn't have much to say, and I didn't really know what to say, to be honest.

"So, what are you going to do for the rest of the day?" Sebastian asked. I looked to his seat, which was in front of me. I watched how Alex's blue eyes fell on me as he looked into the rear-view mirror. He was driving.

"Well, considering I have a new brother, who just pitched up yesterday, I guess I'm going to be talking to my parents about that," I said softly back to him. "Besides, after last night I feel quite partied out. So, I think I'm just going to rest." I thought back to how Sebastian had saved me last night and how I'd had that silly fight with Alex.

"Good luck with all that family drama," Alex said, staring straight ahead. I didn't know how to respond to his comment, so I said nothing at all. I thought back on how that weirdo had followed me into the bathroom and wondered if it had ever happened to the boys.

"Do girls ever follow you guys into the bathroom?" I asked innocently, not realizing what I'd asked. Both boys snickered.

"I don't think you want to know that answer," Alex said, amused.

He was right, it wasn't the answer I was looking for and I didn't want to know about it. It actually just put me off of both of them. I frowned and looked out the window again. I didn't want to talk anymore. Both boys kept quiet and when we pulled up in front of my house I unclipped my seatbelt and leaned forward.

"Thanks again for saving me last night and I'm sorry you had to see me like that," I said, leaning forward and looking at Sebastian.

He smiled and nodded his head. "Don't mention it. It's my pleasure," he said looking at me with his beautiful green eyes. I looked down and I then looked over to Alex.

"Why did you need saving?" Alex asked out of curiosity, and I looked away from him. The emotions were still very fresh.

"Because I was way too intoxicated and there was this creep who followed me into the bathroom," I said softly. I watched as Alex sighed and looked out the window without saying anything. "It's over now and I'm fine. Sebastian helped and I'm grateful for that," I said quietly.

He took a while before he turned to look at me. He gave me a fake smile and he nodded his head and that was it. He was mad at me, and I didn't blame him. But I was mad at him too. I looked at him a little while longer before I turned away from him. Then I scooched over to open the door and my heart pained a little.

"Thanks for the ride," I said, looking at Alex.

"Not a problem," he said and at that I opened the door. I'm glad Sebastian didn't do it, because I'm sure it would have just made Alex more upset.

"Bye, guys," I said smiling and looking back at them and Sebastian winked at me as both of them said "Bye" in unison.

I got out and pulled my backpack onto my back. I shut the car door behind me, and I watched how Alex didn't look my way. I took a few steps forward and I opened the picket fence gate. I closed it and followed the pathway up to my front door. I could feel them both watching me, and I didn't dare look back. I looked to the right and saw the carport was empty. My parents were probably out somewhere. I looked over at my front door and I stopped in front of it. A flash of white caught my eye. I looked to the left and looked carefully into the bush. There was a hidden letter. My heart skipped a beat, as I knew who it was from. I stepped closer to the bush and pulled the letter out. The word *Amelia* was written on the front. I held my chest as fear rushed over me. This was the third letter. I promised Alex I would go to the police if another pitched up.

I looked up and their car was still there. The boys were talking about something in the car. They hadn't noticed that I had found the letter. I could feel my hands shake. The envelope felt thick. I turned the letter around and opened it slowly. My heartbeat started hammering in my chest. Inside was a small letter. I took the letter out and read it.

Amelia.

You seemed to have misbehaved quite a bit these past days. You've made me so angry so many times, I wish you would just behave!

You almost lost your virginity to Alex. I almost did something I didn't want to do, but I stopped myself. Thank God you came to your senses and realized that he wasn't so special. I hope you know that your virginity isn't something to be taken lightly. It shouldn't be anyone else but me who gets to make that decision for you. You deserve a guy who will respect you, like I will.

Not only did you break my heart when you almost had sex with Alex, but you kissed Sebastian on the same day. Your behavior is extremely unacceptable. I'm not going to lie: I expected better from you!

I hate it when you underestimate your beauty! No man should get to touch you when I can't!

I have no choice but to tell you that I no longer want to see you with these boys. They can't respect you or love you like you deserve. In time, you will see what I mean. I forbid you to kiss them or even visit them. It will be my last commandment to you. Please don't disobey me. Know that I'm doing it for your own safety and good.

Please don't do that again to me. Know that I'm writing this because I care about and love you. I'm not trying to scare you. Believe me, that's not my intention. I'm here to look out for you. Trust me.

Yours sincerely.

I didn't realize my hand was placed over my mouth in shock. This was the worst letter yet. He had knowledge of every situation. He had seen everything and now he was threatening me. I looked inside the letter and found pictures. I could feel my eyes burning as the tears threatened to fall. I shook my head as I took the pictures out of the envelope. The one picture showed me sitting on top of Sebastian, and rubbing my hands down his chest. There was another as we were kissing while I was on top of him. All the pictures had a big X over Sebastian's face. I shook my head in disbelief. The next picture was of Alex on top of me. He was shirtless and so was I. I watched how his hand cupped around my breast and his lips covered my nipple. Alex's face also had a big X on it.

I closed my eyes and shook my head. "Oh no!" I said, a little too loudly.

I couldn't believe this person had got all these pictures of us. Everything inside me wanted to shrivel up and hide away. I'd never thought we were being watched.

I looked at the next picture, where I had taken Alex's shirt off. If anyone got hold of these pictures, they would never believe me if I told them I hadn't slept with Alex. I felt moisture run down my cheeks as I looked at the next picture of me on the dance floor, dancing away. This person was so close to me. The person was everywhere where I thought I was alone. So, I had been right, the stalker had been there on the dance floor with me. The stalker had taken such personal pictures of me.

This was serious and I didn't think the stalker was playing games anymore. The stalker had gotten into my personal life and taken pictures of me practically naked.

I felt so violated. I looked to the right of me and looked around to see if I could see the stalker, because I knew he or she was probably watching me right then. I frantically looked to the left and didn't see anyone. I started feeling dizzy and I held my hand to my head as I could feel my vision fading. I closed my eyes and tilted my head downwards. I tried to breathe calmly but I felt like I was only getting worse.

"Amelia," I heard both Alex and Sebastian say.

I opened my eyes to look at them, but I could only see white. Before I knew it, I had collapsed someone grabbed me and that was the last thing I remember.

Chapter 15

ISOLATION

Nine days had passed since I'd found the third letter. My parents had me on strict lockdown rules. They had seen the pictures and so had Alex and Sebastian. After I'd collapsed from the shock, I awoke in my bed and my parents were home. Alex and Sebastian weren't anywhere to be seen. My parents said that as soon as they'd arrived, they'd sent the boys home.

My parents sat me down and asked me a bunch of questions. I was so ashamed of my behavior. I couldn't even look at my parents. You could see my father was disappointed. He didn't say anything to me, but you could see he was holding back. My mother said she'd expected better from Alex. Gosh, the last thing I would have wanted was for them to see those pictures of Alex and me. I can only imagine how Sebastian felt. The thought made me cringe in my seat.

I'd stayed inside the house ever since the incident and I'd turned off my phone because I couldn't bear to face Sebastian and Alex, especially Sebastian. I wondered if he would forgive me or believe me when I told him that I had never slept with Alex. Every time I thought of him, I thought of how he'd opened up to me. And to think I was going to choose Sebastian after all, and now my chances with him were probably zero. It made me angry with myself and my decisions. I could have handled everything better, but I hadn't. He would now forever think that I'd led him on, and I was sure he would never open up to me again.

I thought of Alex a couple of nights, especially when I felt really alone. I thought of all the nights we had shared all our secrets with one another, and even though we weren't dating we could hold each other at night and not feel uncomfortable. I cried those nights as I lay in my bed alone. I wondered if he missed me like I missed him.

Skylar told me that Alex was different. She told me that, even though he was going out and everything, he seemed sad. She told me it was either because he'd broken up with Ingrid or because of what happened between him and me. She said he wasn't as chatty as he usually was, and I could totally understand. A part of me felt so sorry for him. I was glad that he wasn't with Ingrid anymore; she was bad for him. Skylar told me that, even if Sebastian and Alex were in the same room, they didn't talk to each other much. So now I had that on my conscience too. I had broken up their friendship and they had seemed close, considering they'd gotten tribal tattoos together.

I wondered what had happened when they'd both seen the pictures. I wondered if they'd fought. I wondered who'd caught me. I was sure it had been a very quiet ride home for the two of them. I shook my head as I thought of all the things that could have played out between the two of them. The last thing I wanted to do was separate them. It was all because of me.

Skylar came over a couple of times just to check up on me. One day, I invited her and Cole over for lunch. It was nice. She seemed happy with Cole and I was glad. He spoke about all the shoots he'd had in the past few weeks and said that he loved capturing moments between people. Cole was a photographer, although it was more like a hobby than a job.

Skylar had asked him to show me his portfolio and he definitely had a talent for capturing moments. I found myself captivated by his portfolio. So many different pictures of couples kissing or smiling at the camera. Some pictures were of them looking into one another's eyes, some pictures were wedding pictures. Some had different themes, where there was a woman at a well and there were kids playing around her. There were landscape pictures and pictures of animals. So many natural photos. I was definitely captivated. He was excellent. He had apparently traveled the world, taking pictures. He told me he had more pictures and that he'd show me his studio, where he would develop the pictures. I looked forward to seeing that. He seemed like a decent guy for Skylar. Seeing them so happy made me want that kind of company. Despite me not wanting Alex close to me, I really missed him in times when I was surrounded by other male company.

I'd stayed inside the whole week and a bit and it was day nine since the incident. I didn't trust going outside by myself, or even going with anyone. I didn't want to get anyone else involved with this whole stalker obsession. Who knew? Maybe the stalker would say I couldn't see my parents either. I rolled my eyes thinking the stupid thought. I didn't want to go outside because it would just give the stalker more of an opportunity to obsess.

I didn't feel unsafe only when I walked outside onto my balcony; I also felt unsafe when I slept at night or even when I showered. Everything I did, I thought twice about doing it. I always felt as though I was being watched. A couple of times at night I'd wake up sweating, and some nights I'd have my night terrors of the stalker. Some nights it would be better than others. My mother and father knew exactly why I was having them, and my mother wanted me to get help to talk about everything. She said I was mentally traumatized. I mean, do you blame me? I felt more violated than anything.

During the week, Mom and Dad got the police to check our place for bugs or any hidden cameras, not that this stalker really seemed to be that serious. Although he *was* stalking me, and he was always there when I thought he wouldn't be. In that time, they gave us a place to stay for three days. I felt better at night, knowing that there wasn't maybe a camera watching me in my room. I was glad that they suggested it. I'm sure Sebastian had heard all about my case at his work. So sad how I'd missed out on an opportunity to be with a cop.

They had found two cameras. One in my room, close to my bed and another in my bathroom. It was disgusting to say the least. I didn't want to go back home. The police told my parents that I had to stay strictly aware of my surroundings and that they were aware of my case. They said that I had to try to limit how many times I went out and if I did go out I should never go out alone, for my own safety. They did take the letters and they said they were going to run some tests on DNA and also some handwriting tests to see if they could find any matches anywhere. They did want to deploy extra protection and have a police officer follow me around, but I told my parents that I didn't want to feel smothered. At least the police had the letters, and they knew what they were doing, so I did feel as though I were sleeping a little better than I had before. Especially knowing that they had removed all possible ways of any camera's or bugs being inside the house.

I shook my head as I thought of how quickly this year had spiraled. Between drama with Alex and Sebastian, me finding out I had another brother and me also having a stalker. Why on earth did it all have to come at once? I thought that I needed a distraction. I looked at my phone and decided to turn it back on again. I thought that a nine-day rest from social media was a good thing.

My phone binged as the messages came in. Some were from Alex, and some were from Skylar. She had given up after she realized that I wasn't answering my phone. She got hold of me through my mother. I was grateful that she did. I was also grateful that she didn't judge me and wasn't upset that I didn't want to communicate with anyone. But I didn't think she would really be fast to judge. She was the understanding type.

I read the messages from Alex.

Hey Em, how are you? On the 18th. This was the first day after the incident. I went into the next one that was three days old.

I'm sorry how everything turned out. I figured you put your phone off. Skylar says you're on house arrest. I can only imagine how frustrated you must be feeling. Let me know if you need company. Alex.

That was the last message from him. There was none from Sebastian and it only pulled at my heart. I had really hurt him and he looked like the kind to completely close a chapter on you if you did him wrong. I jumped as someone knocked on my door. I looked up, holding my chest.

"Yes?" I asked and watched as the door opened.

My mother popped her head around the corner. She smiled. "Sorry, didn't mean to scare you. We have a visitor. Tyron is here. I would like it if you came downstairs and accompany us while he is here."

I looked at her and shook my head.

"No, I'm fine thanks, Mom. He's weird and I don't want to see anyone who has basically ruined our family," I said, looking down at my phone.

I looked up and watched as she folded her arms over her chest. "Now, don't say that. He didn't do anything. I think you should give him a chance. He is actually a really sweet young man," she said, frowning at me.

I looked away and looked outside as I watched the trees swaying in the wind outside. It was a cold day today. Nothing better to do than to sit in bed and read books. Having a nice cup of soup and enjoying my own company.

"I'm not asking you, Amelia, I'm telling you. Get dressed and come downstairs," she demanded. At that she turned around and closed my door.

I sighed and rested my head against the wall, closing my eyes in the process.

I guessed Alex had given up on me when he realized I wasn't speaking to him. I felt regret. I opened up the chat and started typing him a message. I told him I was sorry and that I had put my phone off, and that I didn't mean to be so distant. That it was hard for me to just reach out and speak after everything that had happened. After typing everything down, I re-read everything twice and I deleted the message. Maybe it was better if I didn't send him a message at all.

I put my phone down and stood up. I didn't want to spend time with my so-called half-brother, but I had no other choice. I walked over to my closet and picked out an outfit. I put on my tights and hoodie. I didn't care about what he would think of my outfit. I pulled my socks on and slipped my feet into my slippers and, without looking in the mirror, I pulled my hair up in a messy bun. I wasn't going to even try to put effort into my look. I opened my door and headed down the hallway. I took a left at the staircase and headed down the steps.

Dad was at work and Mom was still off for a while before she went back to work. So, she was mostly home. The fire was on, and I frowned at the sight as I knew Mom didn't know how to do it, so obviously it was Tyron who had got it going. I could feel someone staring at me as I walked down the staircase with no care in the world. I looked up as I reached the bottom and there he was. Sitting on the couch, in front of the fire with his coffee in his hands. His eyes were on me. He smiled when he saw I was looking, and I gave an awkward smile and looked away.

"Hey, Amelia, it's nice to see you again," he said, holding his cup neatly on his lap. My mother was in the seat next to him and I could see her expression wasn't pleased with the way I was dressed. She looked at my attire. I didn't care.

I looked back at him and nodded my head. "Hi, Tyron," I said flatly. I walked over to the kitchen and boiled the kettle. I hadn't yet eaten that day, so I was starved. I heard footsteps behind me as I opened up the fridge door.

"So, how have you been lately? I heard about what happened. Your mother told me about the stalker," Tyron said as I turned around with a loaf of bread in my hand. I looked at him and narrowed my eyes. Then I looked past him at my mother.

"Gee, Mom, why don't you tell the whole world about the creep who's sending me love letters?" I said sarcastically, looking at her. She looked down at her tea as she was caught red-handed. I shook my head. "Did you show him the photos as well?" I asked, annoyed.

She looked up at me and frowned shaking her head. "Come, Amelia, stop being so dramatic. Of course, I didn't show him. Now be respectful and don't speak to me like that," she said, looking at me with her big hazel eyes.

I looked down and bit my tongue. Not only had she raised her voice at me, but she'd also made me look like a fool in front of Tyron. Not that I cared what he thought, but honestly, I think if anything I needed to get out of the house. I was starting to go stir-crazy.

"I didn't mean to pry. I was just trying to make conversation," he said softly.

I looked up at him. His eyes were dark brown. He had a beauty mark right under his left eye; his glasses almost hid it. He wore a gray jersey, with dark jeans. He didn't look bad.

I sighed after he finished his sentence. "I know. I'm just not in the mood to speak to you, or anyone for that matter, about the stalker. I don't want to be reminded of him," I said, looking up at him, and he nodded his head sternly, his arms crossed over his chest.

"No need to explain. I understand," he said. He sat in the chair that was across from me and he watched how I prepared my sandwich. I looked up at him again, annoyed because he was being weird.

"Do you want one?" I asked. Maybe he was hungry. He gave me a small smile and shook his head. I looked down and finished making my sandwich. I didn't like the awkward silence, so I decided to ask him a question. "Did you finish that book you were reading?" I asked, cutting my sandwich into a perfect triangle. My favorite.

"Uh, yes, as a matter of fact, I did. It was quite interesting," he said. I nodded my head. "Did you finish your book?" he counteracted.

I shook my head and took a small bite of my sandwich. I looked up at him when I felt him looking. His dark eyes watched how my lips chewed. I shifted uncomfortably. He was strange.

I jumped at the sound of a knock at the door. I watched as my mother walked to the door, frowning. "I wonder who this could be?" she said, pulling the handle down. She opened the door and in came a cold breeze. I sat as I watched my mom smile. Curious, I moved a little more to the right to view who she was smiling at. "What a surprise. I haven't seen you in a while. How are you? Come on in," my mother said, stepping aside.

"I was in the neighborhood and thought to stop by. I also brought you some flowers to say I'm sorry for everything." Alex's voice came through, and my heart leaped. I watched as he made his way through the door with a bunch of yellow roses. I watched how he handed the bunch to my mother, and she gleefully smiled.

"You didn't have to, son," she said, greedily smelling the flowers. She looked up at him and she smiled. "Would you like something to drink?" She gestured towards the kitchen, where I was sitting and eating my sandwich like a hungry lion. He nodded his head. I looked terrible and remembered how I hadn't even put any effort into my look. I wanted to run away.

"That would be great, thank you," Alex said.

In slow motion, he looked towards the kitchen and his eyes fell on me and my heart skipped a beat. I smiled and so did he. I watched as his dimples showed and it made me forget why I had put my phone off for so long in the first place. Despite everything and how he'd treated me with Ingrid, I did miss him. His hair was spiked up, highlighting his facial features. He looked stronger, more muscular since the last time I had seen him. He walked up to me slowly and I placed my bread down without even thinking. Seeing him was probably the best feeling I'd had since everything had happened. His eyes were glowing and before I knew it we were standing in front of each other, and he looked down to me and I looked up to him. His cologne nestled its way into my heart. I forgot how irresistible he smelt.

"Hey, Em." His words sounded sweet to my ears, and I couldn't help but smile.

"Hey," I whispered back nervously.

His eyes burnt into mine and I watched as he wrapped his arms around me. I disappeared. I closed my arms around his waist. I closed my eyes as I felt as though everything was falling away. I felt him rest his chin on my head. We both pulled away and I had forgotten that my mother and Tyron were in the same room. I could feel my cheeks flush. I looked to my mother whose back was towards us. I was grateful for that. Tyron was looking down at the table and tapping his finger. Gosh, how I wished it were only my mother and Alex there.

I walked back around the island and looked at Tyron before sitting down. "Do you remember Alex, Tyron?" I asked, pointing to Alex who stood beside me.

I watched as Tyron looked up at me and then looked at Alex and forced a smile. "Yes, I remember him very well," Tyron said, holding out his hand. "Hey, man, how is it going?" he asked Alex, not breaking any eye contact. I could swear, Tyron looked mad in a way. Alex took his hand and shook it. I couldn't believe he would actually do that, considering how those two had met the first day.

"I'm fine, and you?" Alex said back plainly.

"Can't complain," Tyron responded with a smile that I couldn't describe.

I watched as he broke the eye contact with Alex and his eyes fell on me. I looked away immediately. I looked down at my sandwich, which I wasn't in the mood for anymore. I looked up at Alex. His eyes immediately fell on me.

"Would you like to go upstairs?" I asked, looking into his eyes. I found my eyes moving all the way down to his lips. A part of me craved his soft lips. He smiled when he saw where my eyes were, and I looked away, ashamed.

"I don't think so, my girl," my mother said behind me, and I cocked my head.

I folded my arms over my chest and frowned. "Really, Mom, you don't trust us?" I asked, annoyed.

She glared at me, and I could feel her getting upset. "Don't start, Amelia. You know my reasons." I rolled my eyes, looking away from her as she said the words.

"It's fine, Em. We can sit here," Alex said, trying to ease the tension. I looked at him and felt annoyed, but the irritation left when I saw his smile. I hadn't seen him in so long that the last thing I wanted was to be rude to him or make it uncomfortable for him.

"Okay," I said, moving to the chair beside me. He placed himself down in the seat beside Me.

"So, Alex," my mother said, putting the coffee down in front of him. I saw how pink his nose was from the cold outside. His skin was smooth and flawless. I watched how he thanked my mother. His strong hands gripped the cup and I watched how he placed it against his lips.

"Amelia," Tyron said, and I broke out of the daydream I was in. I looked to Tyron.

"Yes?" I asked, confused.

He smiled looking down. He was always too happy for my liking. "Would you like to go out for lunch tomorrow? Do some brother, sister bonding?" he asked me.

I heard my mother speaking to Alex about something else. I looked down, uncomfortable about the fact that he'd called me his sister. We were anything but family. "Ahh, I don't know, hey. Ever since the stalker I'm afraid to really go out," I said, looking back up at him.

He shook his head at me. "I don't think you need to worry when you're with me. We'll go somewhere quiet," he said, and his dark eyes looked into mine and I didn't feel comfortable with the situation. I looked to my mother, who was seated beside Tyron, and she had stopped talking for a couple of seconds.

She looked at me and she frowned. "How about this? Why don't you come over tomorrow. I'll make sure I'm not in the way and you guys can have some lunch here?" my mother said, looking to Tyron.

He didn't look like he liked the idea, but he started nodding his head. "Alright, I'll take it," he said, smiling at my mother. "What do you think, Em?" he said and instantly I cringed at his words. Only Alex called me that. I looked down and took a breath. I nodded my head slowly because I felt like if I had to say anything then I was going to explode.

"Then it's settled," Tyron said cheerfully.

I looked at him and I didn't like him. I didn't like anything about him. He was so annoying in everything he did. I hated that he was in our family. Everything felt different and I felt like he was an intruder.

I shook my head. "Tyron, don't call me Em, please. My name is Amelia. That's how you should address me," I said coldly. I didn't want to make friends with him.

His eyes flinched a second and then he hid his emotions with a small serious expression. "I'm sorry. I didn't mean to upset you. I'll call you by your name," he said sincerely. My mother touched his arm, and I could feel her glare at me.

"Sorry about her, Tyron. Her manners have slacked a lot ever since we moved back," Mother said, looking at him and he gave her a small head shake.

"No, don't worry. I understand," he said, looking away.

I looked at Alex. His coffee was finished. "Do you think maybe it's time that we go outside?" I asked him. He looked at me and nodded his head nervously. "We'll be outside if you need us," I said to my mother.

She nodded her head and gave Alex a small smile. "It was nice seeing you again, son. You should come more often," she said, and he beamed at her. His dimples showed and I missed them so much.

"Thank you for having me, and for the coffee. With such cold weather, it's the best thing," he said, standing up with his cup.

"You can just leave it on the counter. I'll put it in the dishwasher," my mother said, pointing to the sink.

"Okay, thank you," he said quietly, and he gave one look to Tyron and nodded his head. "Cheers man, see you around," and Tyron smiled, nodding his head softly too.

"See you around."

At that we both walked to the door and Alex turned to me before opening it. "Don't you need a jacket? It's freezing outside," he said, scanning my small figure. I looked down and forgot I hadn't worn anything pretty or appealing.

"I'll be okay," I said softly.

He gave me a sympathetic smile and opened the door. "I have a jacket in the car for you if you want," he said softly, and I smiled.

"Sure."

He opened the door and the cold breeze hit me like a ton of bricks. It was a very cold day. He let me step outside first and he closed the door behind me. He grabbed my hand and we walked hastily towards the car. He opened the door for me and when I climbed in I could see the fog from my breath as I breathed in and out. He climbed into the car and closed the door. It was just us two now, in the car. I smiled at him as he reached to the backseat and got his jacket out. He handed me the jacket.

"Here you go," he said. I took the black jacket and slipped it on over my head. I heard as Alex switched the heater on and he put the radio on as well. I had forgotten what it was like to be alone with him.

This time it was different though, because he didn't have Ingrid anymore. So, if anything had to happen it was serious. I knew that we both had feelings for each other, but I didn't know how to act on my emotions.

I sat quietly in the seat and smiled at him. "You know, it's good to see you," I said, looking at each of his features. His eyes were glowing, and his lips were a little purple, especially because they were cold. His jawline was defined and all I wanted to do was place my lips softly on it. He even looked more built.

His eyes softened at my comment. "I'm glad you're okay, after everything, you know," he said softly, and I shrugged my shoulders. I thought back to the photos that the stalker had taken of us. I felt ashamed and looked away from him.

"Yeah, can't tell you how it's been," I said softly, playing with my fingers. I watched as Alex grabbed my hand, making me look up to him.

"It's going to get better now, don't worry. I really mean it this time. I'm sorry about everything. I promise that I'll be here for you all the way," Alex said softly, reassuring me. I looked into his eyes, and I didn't know how to handle the comment. His eyes were soft and readable. I couldn't help but feel as though it wasn't going to get better.

I looked away from him and looked out of the window. "Thank you, Alex, but I feel like this guy isn't going to stop until he removes everyone I love out of the equation," I said softly, watching the trees sway in the distance. The windows had started covering over from the heat inside the car compared to the cold outside.

"Did your parents take the letters to the police?" Alex asked, and I couldn't help but turn to look at him.

I nodded my head. "Yes, that very day when the letter came in. My parents waited for me to wake up and settle down and then they asked all the questions. They also asked for the other letters so that the detectives could have a better idea about the stalker's handwriting and everything," I quietly said, watching his blue eyes slightly darken.

"And? Have they found anything yet?" he asked curiously, and I shook my head, looking down at my lap. I heard him sigh.

"Okay. Well, the fact that they have all the information they need is a start. Before you know it, they'll call you up and say they found a match for the person, and they'll catch them. Okay?"Alex said, reassuring me. I watched him smile and I watched how each one of his dimples formed and I couldn't resist smiling back at him.

"There's one more thing; they found two camera's, one above my bed and one in my bathroom." Just saying it sent shivers down my spine.

Alex's face went from smile to disgust in a second. "What? Are serious?" he asked, disbelieving, and I nodded my head sadly. "What the fuck? This guy is so messed up! Who does that? Why are there no cops here then, Amelia? This guy seems pretty serious about you. When do you think he put it in place?" he asked.

I shrugged my shoulders. "I don't want cops. Everyone will know something is down. I will be the talk of the town. Besides that, I don't think it's that serious yet that a cop needs to be following my every move. The police say they think the person must have put the cameras in place when we weren't here yet, so when we were still in Switzerland," I said, looking down.

I heard him sigh. "Look, the best thing now is that they have everything they need. They removed all cameras and everything. The stalker can't get to you. You're going to be okay," he said smiling, grabbing my hand and squeezing it.

He was trying to be hopeful, and I appreciated it. Every minute alone in my room I'd spent fantasizing over how this stalker was able to know my every move and if the stalker would ever be identified or even get caught. Being with Alex right now made me forget about all of that.

"Would you like to go somewhere fun?" he asked, placing his one arm on the steering wheel and the other on his lap. I looked back at the front door and thought about what my mother would say.

I looked back at Alex and shrugged my shoulders. "I don't know, Alex. I'm scared to go anywhere," I said softly, in case the stalker had bugged the car. He reached forward and grabbed my hand.

He lightly squeezed it and his dark blue eyes were burning into mine. "Amelia, as long as you're with me, I'll keep you safe. I can assure you that nobody will come near you," he said sternly.

I nodded my head. I didn't want to be the person who crossed Alex's bad side. I looked over at the front door again, still with my hand in his. "What about Tyron? He wanted to go out with me just a short while ago. Don't you think he'll be angry when he finds out I went out anyways, just not with him?" I asked, slowly turning my head around to look at Alex.

Alex shook his head and let go of my hand, leaving the cold to rush back through my fingertips. He looked ahead and started his car engine. "I don't give a rat's ass what that guy thinks. He is a stranger, and I quite frankly don't care if he gets jealous or upset. I have every right to take you out. He, on the other hand…" He snorted as he said his last sentence. I even think I saw him roll his eyes. I couldn't help but laugh.

"Okay, Alex, let's go somewhere fun," I said and at that he pulled onto the road, and I watched as his smile grew.

"That's my girl," he said confidently, and I couldn't wipe the smile off my face.

A sense of rebellion fell over me as I knew my mother wouldn't be impressed with the idea and I also knew the stalker was probably screaming with frustration because he or she didn't want me to see Alex anymore. I looked into the side mirror and watched as my house became smaller and smaller until I couldn't see it anymore. I felt Alex grab my hand as he drove.

"Where are we going?" I asked curiously.

He gave a small smile and looked ahead. "My hideout," he said, and at that I watched how the cars drove by. I watched how quiet the streets were because of the weather. I couldn't wait to spend the next hours with him.

"I missed you," I said softly, looking straight ahead.

He squeezed my hand a little and smiled. "I missed you too, Em, more than you can imagine." His words moved their way into my heart.

The rest of the trip was lovely. We spoke about a lot of things and before I knew it Alex had stopped his car and turned off the engine. I looked ahead and gasped. We were at the hideout.

Chapter 16

HIDEOUT

We stopped the car in the parking zone. We were deep inside the forest and there were tree houses everywhere. I watched as Alex got out the car and opened the door for me. I climbed out and he closed it behind me. The houses were lovely. There were wooden bridges linking one tree house to the next. There were fairy lights all along the railing of the wooden steps. It looked magical.

"Do you like it?" Alex asked curiously.

I looked at him and smiled. "I hate it," I said sarcastically. We both laughed.

There were other people also parked in the parking lot, which made me feel a little safer, knowing we weren't the only ones so deep inside the forest. I felt Alex grab my hand and tug softly forward. I followed.

"Come on, I'll show you my hideout place," he said, and I let him lead me in the direction. We walked onto a wooden pathway. It moved in between the different trees as we walked through it. I looked up and heard how the people mumbled on their balconies up in the trees. It was tranquil and unique.

"How did you find this place?" I asked, marveling at all the connected bridges.

The further we moved past the houses, the more I started to hear a stream. As we got to the edge of the forest I could see that it opened up into a wide space. The big lake was in front of us. I gave a small laugh of excitement as I couldn't believe that this place even existed. I smiled at him as we walked, hand in hand, on the pebbles, close to the water.

"I found it on the internet. I've had it for a while now; I just haven't said anything to anyone about it," he said quietly as he looked out to the waters. There were other people taking walks along the water. Many couples were here; you could see it by the way everyone held hands and snuggled up close. It was freezing here, due to being so close to the water.

"Come on, my little hideaway is this way," he said.

He took a left and I saw there was a staircase leading its way up to a fork in the air, going in four different directions to four different houses. I let go of Alex's hand to hold onto the railing while I climbed the staircase. The fairy lights lit the way, and it made me feel as though I had escaped a nightmare and entered into a dream world. We took another left as we reached the fork and we were right in front of the lake. We had the perfect view.

We walked along the railing until I saw Alex stop in front of a door. We had arrived. He placed a key into the lock, and I watched as he unlocked it. He opened the door and stepped inside. He held out his hand once he was inside and gestured for me to walk in. I eagerly stepped inside.

There was a bed to the far left and above the white-sheeted bed hung a big mosquito net. Beside the bed was a sliding door that I presumed led out onto the balcony. To the right was a small kitchen, just fit for one person to cook in. There was an island table with two chairs by it. There was a door next to the kitchen. I assumed it was the toilet.

To my right, nearer to the door, was a bath, which was hidden by blinds. I didn't know how comfortable I'd be bathing here, but it was beautiful. I walked up to the sliding door and opened it. I walked out onto the balcony and saw the lovely fairy lights which were on the railings of the different pathways, leading to all the tree houses. There was a small couch, which looked over the lake. Thank goodness that, if you sat down on the couch, no one could see you from below because every balcony fence was covered. There was a small table next to the couch and a barbecue stand was out in the far-left corner, at the edge of the fence. The deck was big enough to hold up to eight people. I turned and looked to the right and in the right corner was a hidden shower. I frowned and walked up to it. This place really had a way of taking something private and making it public.

"Why is there a shower here?" I asked as I approached it. The inside was covered and, as far as I could see, no one would be able to see you, if you showered here. But I still didn't feel comfortable with the idea of being outside and showering.

I heard Alex step outside onto the deck and he chuckled. "One of the coolest things they installed in this little flat was that shower. In summer, when it gets really hot, the shower helps, especially after you've taken a dip in the lake. The shower really helps you feel like you're in nature," he said, leaning against the door frame and pointing up. "Especially with this view as you look up while you're showering," he said, and I followed his gaze. He was probably right, but with my stalker running around there was no way I was going to make myself vulnerable outside, just to get a view like this in.

I shook my head. "I don't like it. I don't think I would ever use an outside shower. Especially knowing I have a stalker," I said, thinking of my stalker who would love the idea.

He gave a small chuckle and I loved that he thought I was funny. I loved hearing him laugh. Just to think that the last time we saw each other it was uncomfortable, and we didn't have much to say to each other; now all he was doing was looking at me.

"I think you will, just in summer though. It's a horrible idea to do it when there's snow outside," he said looking around. So did I.

"So, this is where you come to clear your head?" I asked, looking out at the lake. I watched as each little wave overlapped the other. It was very peaceful and, honestly, I thought I could move there permanently. It was stunning. He came to join my side. I looked at him and I saw how he had folded his arms over his chest.

"Yeah, this is definitely the place to come when you need to clear your head from reality," he said softly, still looking out at the lake. I thought he'd spent some days there when I was in isolation and when he'd broken up with Ingrid. I guessed the past couple of days had been rough on all of us. I watched as he turned his face and his eyes fell gracefully on me. They were blue, and not as dark as they usually were, when he was worried. I watched as his jawline tensed and his lips pursed slightly.

"I'm sorry that I acted like a dick the last time I saw you," he said, watching my every move.

I looked down and shook my head. No need for the language, Alex. "Don't worry about it. I'm sorry I was mean to you as well," I said, looking back up at him.

He shook his head. "Don't be. I could understand why you didn't want to talk to me anymore," he said, pushing himself off from the frame. I shook my head as he turned around to walk inside. I followed him.

"So, are you and Ingrid officially over?" I said as I watched him walk over to the kitchen. I was nervous to ask him the question, but it had to be asked. He didn't want to say much. I watched as he nodded his head and switched the kettle on. I could imagine that in a way he must have loved her. I felt sad for him. "Are you okay though?" I asked, and he looked over at me when he took the cups out the cupboard.

"I'm better now," he said with a smile. I smiled back at him. I knew how it felt to be alone, so I was glad I could make him feel better in a way. "I knew where you were going," Alex said, his back still towards me.

I frowned. "What do you mean, you knew where I was going?" I asked curiously.

After the kettle had boiled, he poured some water into our cups. He added the rest of the ingredients and placed my cup down on the counter in front of me and looked up at me. "You went to the only club in town. The only place where everyone goes when they want to party. So, I took Ingrid as well the day you and Skylar went. I didn't want to spy on you, I just wanted to make sure you were safe. Then obviously you saw us together and it set everything off," he said. I could sense he felt guilty for telling me this.

I thought back to the night and I remembered how jealous I had gotten. "You can imagine how I felt. I felt really jealous, seeing you with her," I said. I felt the anger build up inside me when I thought of how we had almost had sex the previous night and then the next day he was there with her at that club, the same time I was. I watched as he nodded his head.

"I know. I'm sorry. But I did care about her. I just wanted the right time to tell her about us, that's why I hadn't broken up with her yet," he said, and I looked down. He broke up with her because of me. It gave me a whole new look on things.

"I'm sorry that you did that. The last thing I wanted was to pull you away from her," I said, lying a little just to make him feel better.

He shook his head and smiled at me " You're lying" he said and it only made me laugh. He looked down at the cups. "It's fine. She was dark anyways," he said, and I nodded my head. "Sebastian told me that you saw the stalker that night on the dance floor?" he added, watching me, and I nodded my head. It all felt quite blurry, to be honest.

"I did, and I tried to follow him, but another man found me in the crowd and then the stalker got away," I told him, shaking my head, remembering his black hoodie.

"Gosh, Amelia, it could have been much worse than it was," he said. I saw his eyes grow dark.

I nodded my head. The night was meant to be good, and then it had just spiraled. "I know. We just wanted to have fun. It wasn't meant to get so dark," I said, and he didn't take his eyes off of me.

"Darkness seems to like you. So, If I were you, I would assume that everything will go wrong," he said, and I felt quite offended by what he'd said. I'm sure he could see it. "Em, in a good way. I don't mean to offend you. I think it's because you're beautiful and people are attracted to anything that's pretty," he said, and he definitely lightened the mood.

I gave him a small smile. "What a curse I have," I said.

He gave a small chuckle. "Okay, let's change the topic," he said, waving his hand. I nodded my head gladly. After he had given me the cup of tea, we walked over to the bed and sat down on it. I sat opposite him, and he rested his back against the headboard of the bed.

"What happened the day I passed out? How did Sebastian react to the photos?" I asked curiously, and he looked away from my face to the outside.

"Ahh, well, I can't say he was happy. He hasn't really spoken to me since. I guess I can understand why," Alex said, and I could only imagine how awkward it must have been.

"We never should have done it," I said, letting the words slip out of my mouth.

He looked at me and shook his head. "I'm glad we did. I had been wanting to kiss you for so long and then he pitched up trying to steal you away. I'm glad I did it," he said, looking away from me and I gave a small smile because he was being protective.

"You saw what the stalker said, right? That I should stop seeing you guys, otherwise there will be consequences?"

He nodded his head. I watched how he frowned. "There's no ways in hell I'm letting that person dictate who I get to see and who I don't. I think this person is all big talk and no play," he said, placing his cup down next to him on the small desk, and folding his arms over his chest.

"What if he is not, Alex? What if he really hurts someone," I said nervously, as I could feel Alex was angry.

"I guess we won't know until we try, hey. But, in all honesty I felt as though I had lost you the day of the club. And quite frankly I'd rather know I tried everything inside me to see you, than step back because I was afraid of some wimp," Alex said, defending me.

"I wonder who on earth it could be," I said and then I thought back on Tyron, who was with my mother. "I wonder if Tyron is upset because we left?" I asked, and Alex shrugged his shoulders.

"I'm sure he is, but I really don't care," Alex said, looking so attractive when he looked mad. I looked away from him and took a sip of my tea.

"Why don't you like him?" I asked, and he shook his head.

"There's something about him. I can't put my finger on it," he said. He looked away and I nodded my head.

"Maybe it's because his so weird and introverted?" I asked, and Alex shrugged his shoulder.

"I don't know, but I know it's something."

I was about to ask him something else when I heard my phone ring. I pulled it out my pocket and knew immediately who it was. Mom, the caller ID read. I sighed and looked up to Alex. "Hey, Mom," I said nervously.

"Amelia! You know that you're not allowed to leave the house without our permission. You don't know if it's safe or not, especially since you have a stalker running around," she said, shouting through the phone.

"Mom, I'm fine. Alex wanted to show me something, so we left. I'll be back," I said.

"Amelia, that's not the point. You left without saying goodbye and I had to make an excuse on your behalf to explain why you wouldn't go out with Tyron a couple of minutes ago, but you so eagerly went out with Alex," she said

"Do I really have to explain why I went out with Alex and not with Tyron?" At the mention of his name, Alex lifted his head and he watched me. I looked away. I think it's a pretty understandable situation. Of course I'm rather going to leave with Alex instead of Tyron.

"Amelia, you have a stalker on the loose and I don't think you should be outside the house until the cops find him and capture him." She sounded worried and tired.

I felt frustrated. Everything I had done this week was because of this stalker. The stalker had started to become an obsession in my life, and I was tired of hiding away. I wanted to see Alex and everyone I loved. I didn't want to be stuck inside the house, away from socializing.

"I get it, Mom, but how long will I have to stop living until they find this person? This year is meant to be fun. It's meant to be my year where I can find what I want in life and what I want to study. I don't want to be controlled by a stalker, who might not even be a potential threat."

"Amelia, I love you and I don't want anything to happen to you," my mother said, and I nodded my head.

"I know, Mom. I'll be careful, I promise. If we see any suspicious activity, then what we'll do is just report to the cops and then yes, I will never leave the house again," I said hoping to convince her a little.

"Just this once, Amelia. It isn't safe, and I want to know when you leave the house and where you are going at all times. Is that clear?" she commanded, and I nodded my head.

We said a last couple of words and then we said our goodbyes. Alex had gotten off the bed and had walked over to the sink by the time I had put the phone down. Alex turned around and leaned against the counter with his arms outstretched. It made me want to walk up to him and run my fingers along his body. I didn't think I would feel like this, seeing him again, but I did. He was gorgeous and I didn't know if it was because he didn't have Ingrid as his girlfriend anymore or if it was because he just seemed different since the last time I'd seen him, but something was attracting me to him.

"Is everything okay?" he asked, and I nodded my head, putting my phone down on the bed. I finished off my tea and then I walked over to him.

"Thanks for the cup of tea." He took my cup and our fingers brushed slightly passed each other. The warmth flowed through me, and I watched as he gave a small smile.

"No problem," he said placing the cup in the sink.

He turned his back on me and washed both cups. There was a peaceful silence between us as he put the clean cups on the drying rack. Despite his history with girls and being a player and all, I thought the best thing to see was his true side. Not the person he portrayed in front of other people, but the person he was when he was alone. I was very lucky to get to see that side of him. I watched as he turned around and he saw that I was looking. He smiled and I looked away quickly.

"Like what you see?" he asked confidently, and I couldn't help but giggle.

"Stop it, Alex," I said, feeling my cheeks flush.

"What must I stop? You're the one pining over me," he said, giving a small chuckle. There was the old Alex I knew. He was back.

I rolled my eyes at him. "I was just looking and then you turned around," I said, looking away from him.

"It's okay. You don't have to lie," Alex said, amused. I laughed and walked away from the kitchen table. I walked out towards the sliding door and smiled. He was teasing me, and I wasn't having it. I stepped out and looked at the water.

"When last did you go sailing?" I asked him, as I watched the waves lap over each other.

"Long ago," he said as he joined my side.

His arm brushed against mine gently and I let it. I looked up to him and I watched how the light danced on his face. His blue eyes glowed in the light, and I loved how his iris had a slight darker blue twirl around his pupil. His eyes were beautiful.

"We should go some time. It will be fun," I said, and he looked down at me, making me feel smaller than I was.

He smiled and nodded his head. "Let's go today," he said, giving me a small smirk.

He was always more clued up on where the best places to go sailing were. I was looking forward to the fun experience. I gave him a smile back and nodded my head.

"Okay, let's go."

Chapter 17

TRANQUILITY

I watched as Alex walked over to the receptionist. Alex had told me to wait outside as he explained to the receptionist that he knew someone who had a boat here. I turned away from him and looked out at the view and walked to stand on the open deck. There were many boats out on the water, and some where still tied to the wooden bridge. I walked over to the edge of the deck and held onto the railing. I let go the instant I felt how cold the railing was against my hands. I looked out at the water and felt a feeling of peace. The soft breeze brushed past me, and I closed my eyes and listened to the water softly hitting the edge of the deck. I loved everything about this place. It was so tranquil.

"Amelia! Babe!" I heard a familiar screech from the distance. I opened my eyes and looked to my left. My eyes fell on Skylar, and I instantly smiled.

"Skylar?" I asked, surprised, taking a step away from the railing in her direction. She had her hair pulled up in two ponies. She wore a long-sleeved jersey dress, with thick winter leggings and her black boots.

"What are you doing here? Aren't you like isolating?" she asked as she came closer. I saw how Cole followed behind her. He wore a gray jacket and black jeans, a scarf and brown mountain boots. I looked at Skylar as she wrapped her arms around me. I returned the hug.

"Alex managed to get me out," I said as she pulled away. "What are you doing here?" I asked, looking at her eyes. They were glowing. She smiled and turned to look at Cole, who was only a few feet away from us. He had a black cap on, making him look very mysterious. What were the odds of us finding them here?

"You know, you would think that with your short legs you'd walk slowly, but you always manage to out-walk me," Cole said in his husky voice. He was looking at Skylar with a smile and I could see his playful nature coming through. I couldn't help but smile at them.

She looked up to him and she pushed him playfully away. "Sorry, babe, just got so excited when I saw Amelia out of hibernation." At that she looked from him to me, and I rolled my eyes at her. I watched as Cole smiled and then his eyes fell on me. I gave a small smile.

"Hey, Cole, how are you doing?" I asked, folding my arms over my chest for comfort.

He nodded his head. "Hey, Amelia, I'm doing quite well. And you?" he asked, and I shrugged my shoulders.

I broke eye contact and I looked out at the water. "It feels good to be out, that's all I can say," I said, looking back at them.

"We can imagine." Skylar's voice filled the air. I smiled and looked down and at that moment I felt Alex lightly brush my arm with his as he joined my side.

"Hey guys, what's the odds of meeting you guys here?" he asked, and I could see he couldn't believe it. Almost as if I had told Skylar that I was here and I had planned this. He looked at me, to check if I had had something to do with it and I shook my head.

"Hey, Alex." I watched as Cole stretched out his hand. Alex accepted the handshake and shook his hand back.

"We actually thought, strangely enough, that today would be a good day to go out on the waters. They said after nine the wind would subside and there might be a rare occasion of the sun peeking its way through the clouds," Skylar said excitedly. I looked up at the sky and couldn't imagine the clouds parting as they seemed pretty thick to me.

"Sounds about right," Alex said, also looking out at the clouds.

"Whose boat are you going on?" Cole asked, interrupting the silence as we all looked around. I looked to Alex, and I watched as he stood up straight and crossed his arms over his chest.

"I know a guy who has a boat out here, so I managed to convince the people at reception that the guy knows me and that I'd take care of the boat," he said, looking at Cole.

"If you want, you can join us on our boat. That way we can catch up," Cole said, smiling and pointing to the boat out of the water, at the end of the bridge. His boat was white and brown. The name, *The Sparrow*, was written across it.

"Ahh, that's a great idea!" Skylar said, excited by the idea. I smiled, looking up to Alex, who turned to look down at me. He shrugged his shoulders, and I could see that he had other ideas in mind.

He looked away from me and nodded his head at Cole. "Sounds like a great idea," Alex said, giving a small smile.

Skylar jumped up and curled her arm in mine. "Just one thing," Skylar said, holding up her finger. I frowned looking at her. "Sebastian is on the boat, as well as his plus one."

My heart felt a knock and I didn't know how to react to the news. I looked down at the deck and bit my lip to hide the hurt I felt. I guessed he didn't stop and wait for anyone. What had I expected? He wasn't going to wait for me, or even tolerate what I did to him. I felt a sore burn in my heart. I didn't know if I was ready to see him yet, after everything.

"Good to know," Alex said, taking a step forward as Cole stepped forward. Both Skylar and I watched them walk ahead of us and they started a conversation.

I felt Sky tug at my arm as we followed the boys. "Are you okay with Sebastian being there?" she asked, looking to me and I forced a smile.

"I guess I couldn't avoid him my whole life," I said, looking ahead, watching how Alex walked beside Cole and they both looked at each other and smiled. I watched as his dimple showed and I could only imagine how this whole scenario was going to play out.

"Sorry that he has another girl here," she said sympathetically, and I looked out towards the water. It stung but I didn't blame him for moving on. To be quite frank, he had every right to do so. We weren't dating, and I had kissed another man on the same night that he and I had been together. So, I deserved it.

"Don't be sorry, Sky, I don't own him. We weren't dating – we just had a fling – so I guess he has every right to move on," I said, watching the birds flying in the distance. I felt her rest her head gently on my shoulder as we walked.

"Alright, hun," she said, and we came to stop.

She let go of my arm and both Cole and Alex let her and me pass. I could feel Alex stare at me. Skylar walked up the step first, taking Cole's hand, and then Alex held out his hand almost immediately. I took his hand and a small warmth flowed through me. I softly said thank you and I let go of his hand once I'd climbed into the boat. Once the boys had climbed in, Cole gestured for us to walk though the other side. I could hear Sebastian speaking. My heart was beating fast. Skylar asked Cole to rather lead the way and I was grateful for that. I followed her and I was last to walk through the entrance. I heard Cole announce our arrival and I could only imagine how Sebastian must have felt.

"Hey man," I heard Alex saying to Sebastian, and they both greeted each other.

The moment I walked through the door, I could feel all eyes were on me. I gave a small smile towards where the two of them were sitting. Sebastian's hair was spiked, and he wore his diamond earrings. He had a white hoodie on and dark jeans with his black sneakers. He had his arm around the beautiful girl he was sitting next to. I had forgotten how beautiful he looked and when my eyes met his all I wanted to do was cave. His green eyes stared into mine and he gave a small nod. I could see he was putting up a cold front. I didn't know how to handle the emotions that were running through me. I was sure that he wanted me to see him with someone else, just so that I would know what he felt like. I could see he felt awkward. I'm sure I was the last person he wanted to see. He kept his arm around the pretty girl. A small part of me wished it were me that he had his arm around. I felt bitter as I thought that I had, for sure, lost his trust forever.

"This is Ruby," Cole said pointing towards the red head. Of course her name would be Ruby.

Her eyes shone a smoky blue. She had a few freckles over her nose and her lips were a pretty, deep pink. She must have dyed her hair because it was a shocking red. Her hair was curled all the way down, past her breasts. She wore a thick black dress, with black leggings and brown boots. Ruby was a beautiful name. She waved at me and smiled politely. She didn't give off any nasty, catty vibes. She seemed nice and polite and I'm sure she had no idea that I had kissed Bas or even wanted to start a relationship with him.

"Hey," I said softly. I saw how her hand rested gently on his thigh. I was sure that they had already slept together. I looked away because I was sure that if I looked anymore I'd give it away that I was jealous that his arm was around her and not me. In all fairness, I had come here with the guy I'd "cheated" on him with.

"Alright, so this is us," Sky said, and I watched Cole standing next to Alex. They were both standing outside by the railing. I was guessing Cole had already offered him a drink because he was holding one in his hand and so was Cole.

"Come on, let me show you outside," Sky said, gesturing for me to follow her. I think we could all feel the tension in the room. I gladly left.

"Why do I feel like I'm missing something," Ruby whispered to Sebastian as I left the room. I could only imagine what he was going to say.

I stepped outside with Sky and the wind had slowed down a lot. There was barely a breeze. I watched Alex and how he listened attentively to Cole. They were speaking about the yacht and how long Cole had had the boat. Alex had always been very interested in sailing. He loved the water. In summer, he would often hire or rent a boat and go sailing for a weekend. That was in the past, though. I was not too sure if he still did it. He looked fascinated as Cole showed him all the ropes and Alex nodded his head, giving his knowledge back on what he learned from his father. They seemed to be two peas in a pod.

"They seem to like each other," I whispered to Sky, who'd walked over to the opposite side of the boat.

She turned with her back against the railing and looked at the two boys. "Yeah, it's sweet. I think this is the first time Alex is actually getting to know Cole," she said, smiling. I stood beside her, and I exhaled.

"She's beautiful; so, so beautiful," I whispered softly to Skylar. She turned to look at me and she frowned, trying to understand who I was speaking about. She shrugged her shoulders lightly and pointed towards the door we'd just come through. I nodded my head, and she gave a small smile and nodded her head.

"She is, but that doesn't make you unbeautiful," she whispered back.

I looked down at my feet and thought for a moment. "When did he meet her?" I asked curiously.

She looked out ahead of her to the boat that was stationed next to us. "Yesterday, actually. We all went to a house party, and I don't know how it happened but somehow they found each other and it seems like they really hit it off," she whispered back to me. I frowned and looked down. "Come on, let's move a bit closer to the water so that we can talk more about this," she said, once more pointing towards the front of the boat.

There were seats on either side of the boat, where you could sit and enjoy the water. There was a small platform that you could climb onto and lie down right by the nose of the boat. I was sure many women had tanned in this spot. I watched Skylar climb onto the platform and she sat on the edge, letting her feet over the side, close to the water. I copied her and sat beside her, leaning back with my arms outstretched.

The water slapped softly against the boat and, because the wind had slowed down completely, it wasn't as cold anymore. I looked out into the distance and tried to imagine what it would have been like to see orcas in the water. Thrilling. I looked over my shoulder to make sure that Alex and Cole weren't close. I didn't want them to overhear our conversation. They must have gone inside. I heard the engine start up and both Sky and I looked at each other.

"Fancy having a boyfriend who owns a boat, hey?" I observed, smirking at her.

She squealed and gave a small giggle. "I know. I love every moment of it," she said, smiling at me. I watched as she bit her lip. "I'm so happy with him. Everything about him is just so alluring," she said, looking down beaming. She was glowing.

I reached over and grabbed her hand and lightly squeezed it. "I'm so happy to hear that, hun."

She looked over at me and smiled. "I don't want to dampen the mood, but have you gotten anymore letters from you know who?" she said, looking around. I shook my head and took a small string off my pants.

"The stalker's been quiet. I don't know if that's a good thing or a bad thing, but I certainly don't want to read any more from him," I said, frowning.

I watched as the boat moved forward and I brought my feet up from the side. Skylar left her feet hanging off the boat. I felt my phone buzz as we exited the small harbor, and we entered the open water. I heard muffled speaking behind me. I guessed that Sebastian and Ruby had decided to come outside. The buzzing continued and I pulled my phone out my pocket, holding on tight to ensure it didn't fall overboard. Someone was calling and I didn't recognize the number. In my peripheral vision I could see Skylar was frowning at me. I answered the call.

"Hello," I said slowly.

A voice came through on the other end. "Hey, Amelia, it's Tyron. I hope I'm not disturbing you," he said back cheerfully. I looked over at Skylar and she shrugged her shoulders, wondering who it was. I looked away again.

"No, it's fine. What's up?" I replied.

"I was wondering if you'd like to join us tonight for some supper at my place. I've invited your mother and our father, and I was wondering if you were going to join us. I'd really appreciate it if you could make it," he asked, and I could only imagine how he would have a smile on his face when doing so. I shook my head and grimaced at the thought of us all being in the same place. Not to mention that he kept saying that our fathers were the same man. For all I knew, he could have been lying.

"Look, Tyron. Thanks for the invite but I'm going to have to do a rain check. I'm having supper with my friends tonight. Sorry. I hope you can understand," I said a little too abruptly. I heard him scoff in the background and I squinted.

"Alright, that's okay," he said, clearly offended by the refusal. "I guess I'll see you for lunch tomorrow late morning then, at your house?" he asked. And I rolled my eyes, annoyed that he just wouldn't take no as a signal.

"Yeah, I'll see you tomorrow," I replied and at that he told me goodbye, and I ended the call. I looked at Skylar and shook my head. "Tyron. He wanted me to go out with my parents to his house tonight. I declined and said I was having supper with my friends," I said, frowning at her.

She shook her head. "Have you gotten a DNA test of this man yet?" Skylar asked, and I shook my head slowly. The boat came to a stop when we had gotten to the middle of the lake.

"I don't know why I haven't thought of that yet," I said, looking out at the water. It was dark and it reminded me of all the dreams I'd had of falling in and struggling to get to the surface.

"Ladies..." we heard someone say behind us and we both turned to look. Cole was standing there with a tray of shooters, and I looked away and gave a small laugh. It was never a good idea to have shooters so early in the day. "Would you care to join us," he said again, and Sky snickered and stood up. I followed.

"So early in the day, babe?" Skylar asked, taking one glass from him and they exchanged a look which looked playful from where I was standing.

I took a glass and stood next to Alex. He smiled at me, and I returned the smile.

"What is this?" Ruby asked curiously, looking at the brown liquid.

"Jackies," Cole said, smirking at all of us as we stood in a circle. The music was playing, and the vibe was comfortable.

She frowned at him. "What's Jackies?" she asked, confused. She sounded like me, inexperienced.

"Jack Daniels," all three boys said at the same time, and we all looked around the circle and burst out laughing.

"Alright, cheers everyone," Cole said, holding up his shooter, and he drank it the moment he was finished with his speech. So did everyone else. I did the same and grimaced as the bitter and sweet liquid went down.

"Yum," Alex said, and I shook my head, placing the cup down on the tray. It was disgusting. I didn't like the taste.

"Alright, here is a sweet taste to help with the after taste of Jackies," Cole said, placing the one tray down and taking out another tray with pink shooters. I shook my head and gave a nervous laugh. Last time I had done this, I'd got way too out of hand.

"Everyone take one," Cole said, once the tray was out in front of everyone. I didn't like the idea of this.

"Oh, anything pink usually tastes great," Ruby said enthusiastically. I looked at her and smiled and she did the same. She didn't seem like the horrible type.

"You're right about that one," Alex said smirking, and didn't know if he was speaking about the same thing that she was. I rolled my eyes at him. I was the last to take a shooter.

"Bottoms up," Skylar said, smiling.

I watched as everyone threw their heads back and took the shooter like they did it every day. I placed it to my lips and gulped it down. It was sweet, but the aftertaste was strong. You could definitely taste the alcohol. I placed my cup down and looked over at Sky. It didn't look like it even affected her. I didn't want to have any more shooters. If I continued, I would probably make a big fool of myself.

"Alright everyone, if you want anything to drink you can find drinks in the container outside. Just help yourselves," Cole said, looking at each of us.

"Thanks man," Sebastian said as he walked with Ruby, past Cole and into the boat. I wanted to puke on them. If it wasn't Alex with a partner, then Sebastian had someone. I could never win. Sky walked up to Cole, and he held his arm out and she snuggled herself under it.

"Would you like anything to drink?" Alex asked from beside me.

I looked up to him and his eyes were a dark blue. "Just something plain. No alcohol, please," I said, smiling at him, and he smiled back at the reply.

"Okay. I'll be right out."

At that he walked inside, and I was the only one left outside. I turned around and walked back to the spot where Sky and I had been sitting. I sat there and looked out at the view. I loved the peace. The air was cool, and the sky was cloudy. Most people would think this was a miserable day, but there was nothing miserable about it. The birds flew in the distance and in a split moment the clouds parted a tiny bit and, for the first time in a long time, the sun shone on the lake, sending warmth through my skin. The tranquility was breathtaking. I closed my eyes and lifted my face to the warmth.

I heard footsteps behind me and figured it was Alex. The next thing I heard was a "click" and then another. The sound of a camera capturing a moment. I frowned and opened my eyes, turning in the direction of the camera. Another click went off and I could see who was taking the pictures. It was Cole, and he was taking pictures of me.

Chapter 18

THE GAME

I turned around and frowned at Cole.

"What are you doing?" I asked, shifting away from him. His face appeared from behind the camera, and he gave me a small smile. I frowned and felt uncomfortable. Why on earth was he taking pictures of me? He held up his one hand and looked at me with a serious face.

"Don't worry, I didn't mean to alarm you. I wanted to capture how beautiful the sun rays looked on your face when you were closing your eyes," he said, sounding normal, even though what he had done only made me feel more uncomfortable. I thought back to the letters from the stalker and how I had been captured in my moments of lust. I frowned at him.

"Don't take pictures of me, I don't appreciate it," I spat out.

He held up his hand in surrender. "I'm sorry. I just wanted to capture a beautiful moment," he said apologetically.

"What's going on?" Skylar said from behind him, and he turned to show her the camera.

"Cole took pictures of me," I said, offended, and Skylar turned to him and frowned.

"Why would you do that, Cole? You know about her situation and that stalker of hers," she said, frowning and folding her arms over her chest. He looked defeated and I looked away from them I just wanted to get out of the situation.

"I completely forgot about that. I'm really sorry, Amelia. Look, I'll delete them right now." He looked down at his camera and I rolled my eyes at him. "There, they're gone," he said, showing me the camera. I looked away and nodded my head. "I really didn't mean any harm, I swear. I won't do it again," he pleaded with me.

"It's fine, Cole. I was just spooked, that's all," I said, looking at him and then away again. "Can we just forget about it?" I said, turning away from them. I looked out towards the water.

"Sure thing," he said, sounding relieved. I heard footsteps and then I felt a small soft touch on my back. I jerked and looked to the side. It was Alex.

"Hey, Em, here is your drink," he said softly. I presumed he heard the commotion.

I leaned to the side and took the drink from him. "Thank you," I said softly. He poured me some punch. "It's clean, hey?" I asked looking at it skeptically.

He chuckled. "Thanks for the lack of confidence you have in me. Yes, it's clean. You didn't want alcohol, so I gave you clean punch," I smiled at him as he looked at me with defeat. His blue eyes were dark, and they were looking at me. I looked away from him.

"What is it, Alex?" I asked, smiling and looking at my drink. I looked to the side and watched as he drank a sip of beer. He had plumped himself down beside me. Despite what had happened a couple of moments ago, Alex made me feel better in a way.

"Nothing. Just happy to have you out and socializing," he said, looking out at the lake. His cologne brushed past me, and I breathed it in. His charm and good scent was probably the way he won most girls over.

"I don't know about socializing," I said, looking down at the glass of juice. He looked to the side watching me. "I just don't want any pictures taken of me. I don't trust anyone anymore," I said softly because saying it out loud made me feel more insecure. He stretched out his arm and placed it over my shoulders pulling me into him. I gave a small smile and it felt good to be nestled in his arm. He tightened the embrace a bit to keep me close to him.

"I know. I think for Cole it's second nature just to snap the camera at anything. I don't think he thought about the consequences it was going to have. He did it innocently and, yes, it was strange, but he found a beautiful moment and wanted to capture it," he spoke softly, and every word seemed to reassure me.

"I guess you're right. Did everyone on the boat hear the commotion?" I asked, looking up at him. There were only inches of space between our faces and, if I had been a person on the outside looking at us, I would have said that we were about to kiss. I look at his lips, which looked soft. I thought back to the moment we were alone in the bedroom and how his lips traced mine and how he confidently was able to move me from one spot to the next. He was confident. In every breath, I had forgotten what a man he had become. That he wasn't a little boy anymore. He knew what he wanted when he wanted it and that was quite something to think about. Butterflies spread through my stomach, and I looked away and I closed my eyes, trying to think of something other than him.

"Don't worry about what those people think, Amelia. You limit yourself if you constantly think of what other people are thinking," he said, looking away from me and taking in another sip of his drink. He didn't let go of me and I enjoyed being so close to him again. He was right.

"Thanks for coming to get me today. I think I was starting to go stir-crazy," I said, resting my head softly on his chest.

"I couldn't handle the silence anymore, so I had to come and rescue you. Just in time, anyways. When I saw Tyron was there, I could only imagine how you felt," he said.

I smiled. "Yeah, he is something else," I said looking down at my juice again.

"Guys, enough flirting. Would you please come over here and play a game with us," Skylar said loudly.

I could feel my cheeks flush, and Alex let go of me. I moved away from him and looked up. He stood up and gestured for me to take his hand. I took it and let go the moment we were standing.

"What kind of game?" Alex asked, and Skylar gave a smirk.

"Truth or dare."

I shook my head. "No," I said quietly.

The last time we'd played that game, Sebastian and I had kissed. I looked down and followed Alex. He walked inside to where everyone was sitting. There was a mat on the floor and Sebastian was already sitting down, same as Ruby and Cole. I didn't want to sit next to Cole or Sebastian. So, the moment I could grab a seat I sat down next to Sky as she sat down next to Cole.

Cole laughed and shook his head. "No, there has to be a girl in between every man," Cole said, pointing at Skylar and me, sitting next to each other. I looked at Sebastian. I would have to sit next to him. He looked at me and then looked away as quickly as our eyes connected.

I sighed. "Listen, isn't this game old? Can't we play something less predictable?" I asked, feeling annoyed about how we always had to play a stupid spin the bottle game at a gathering. We all knew how it was going to play out. We were going to kiss each man in the room, some girls were going to get jealous. I was over the whole drama scene. Besides, the stalker didn't even want me to see Alex and Sebastian. I was breaking all the stupid rules, defying the threats and allegations that this person was giving me. I can only imagine how upset they would become if I had to kiss one of them again.

"Spoil sport," Skylar said, booing me.

"We can play something else if you're uncomfortable with this game, but the catch to this truth or dare is that we take out cards that are in a box. Either you take a truth card, or you take a dare card. It's nothing like the original game, where everyone makes everyone kiss each other and do stupid shit," Cole said, looking past Skylar at me, and I squinted my eyes at him. It was still very debatable. I nodded my head and that made him smile.

"Do you want to play?" Alex asked from behind me, waiting for me to scooch over so that I could sit next to Sebastian. I looked up at him and his eyes were glowing. This was his game. His prime time.

"Yes, I'll play, but don't judge me if I keep going for truth instead of dare," I said, moving over so Alex could sit.

I moved just enough so that there were three hand spaces between Sebastian and me. Being so close to him reminded me of the night we kissed. I couldn't believe how different everything was now. I tried to act calm and oblivious to his closeness. Alex sat next to me, and he didn't care about space. Our arms were rubbing and I was sure he'd done it deliberately. Right in front of us were two boxes. One was pink for dare and the other was blue for truth.

"On a scale of one to ten, how bad are these truth or dare questions?" Ruby asked curiously, folding her legs, looking eager, as though she were about to finish a puzzle that had taken her forever to complete.

"You'll see," Cole said, smirking at her, and we all groaned. I was curious, but only to a certain extent. "Let's just say, even if you choose truth, you'll want to rather do dare," he said and I frowned, pulling my legs up to my chest. "Okay, so rules apply. Please don't be a party pooper and not tell the truth or refuse to do a dare, otherwise you might as well not play the game," Cole said, looking at each one of us in the room. I looked around and I watched as everyone nodded their heads. He smiled, nodding his own head. "Right, so then I'll go first and after me we'll go clockwise," After him was Ruby and then Sebastian. I felt butterflies rushing in my stomach when I thought of my turn.

Cole leaned forward and picked up a blue card, truth. He smiled while reading it aloud. *"Who is the sexiest person in this room?"* He held down the card and looked around the room at each of us. Cole looked at Sebastian and winked and we all started laughing.

"This is a tough one, hey? Okay, and I'm sorry, baby, I'm going to have to go with..." He grinned, looking at Skylar and then he leaned forward gave her a small kiss. He then looked up at Alex and said, "I'm going to have to go with Alex." Alex laughed and so did the rest of the group. He blew Alex a kiss and I smiled. He was full of games.

Skylar shook her head, smiling at him. "Babe, I said you mustn't lie," Sky said, looking at him, smiling. Alex held his chest in such a way as to say that he was offended, and he smiled.

"Wow, thanks Skylar," he said sarcastically, and we all snickered a bit.

"But it's true," she said, laughing. Cole wrapped his arm around her and squeezed her shoulders tightly.

"Okay, Rubes, you're next," Cole said, putting the truth card at the back of the stack.

I watched intently as she looked at each box, deciding which one to take. She placed her hands together and smiled nervously and looked up. "Gosh, I can't choose." She looked down again and took a truth card. I watched as she bit her pretty dark lips and she read the card out loud to us. *"Who do you most want to sleep with, out of everyone here?"* I watched her cheeks redden. I would honestly hate that question. The worst part is that she actually had to answer it. I placed my chin on my knees, and I hugged my legs a little tighter. I think it was inevitable who she'd rather sleep with.

"Gosh these questions aren't very nice," she said, putting the card at the back of the stack. Everyone was waiting to hear her answer. "Okay, Sebastian, you're up," she said, smiling. I didn't know if I'd missed it or what, but I could have sworn she hadn't answered the question.

"No, you have to answer, sweetie," Skylar said, and the boys laughed.

Ruby didn't look up at anyone and I could only imagine how embarrassing it must have been for her. "Okay, fine, I'll sleep with Sebastian." She practically whispered his name. Everyone whooed, except me. I watched how Sebastian wrapped his arm around her and then pulled her in, giving her a side hug. Jealousy enfolded me and all I could think of was how he had told me that he didn't date. Had he been lying or was he just using her as a hook up, like the other women? I had to tear my eyes away from them.

"Yeah, you will," he whispered to her.

Everyone heard it. I didn't want to make it obvious that it bothered me so much. I looked over at Alex, who gave Cole a high five behind Skylar's back, as though they had just planned something. He had a big grin on his face.

"What was that?' I asked and he smiled, shaking his head.

"Don't worry about it, Em," he replied, being mysterious.

"Let's choose dare," Sebastian said leaning forward picking a card from the pink box. His cologne swept past me, and I was left with feelings of regret. I never should have kissed Alex. I bet Bas thought Alex and I slept together. He held the card up and read it aloud.

"Have someone blindfold you, and then have everyone in the group kiss you on the cheek. You must say which one is your partner and then kiss them on the lips."

"That's easy enough," he said, leaning forward and putting the card at the back of the pink stack.

"Here's a blindfold," Cole said, appearing from behind a small hatch that led further under the boat. He approached Sebastian and I could see that Sebastian felt slightly uncomfortable, despite the smirk on his face.

"No one must do crazy shit," Bas said, as his eyes were being covered. I gave a small laugh. I watched as Cole tightened the blindfold around his head. "Damn, Cole, seems like you've had practice at this kind of thing," Bas said, teasing, and Cole smiled.

"Don't tell them everything, my love," Sky said confidently. I couldn't help but give a small laugh. We all watched as Bas stood there, blindfolded. His lips looked so irresistible as they were the only thing that was exposed.

"Alright, everyone line up and start the kissing. Remember, the aim is to try see which one is your partner," Cole said smiling. "No kissing on the lips, ladies. I know you want to," Cole added, holding his hips and pointing at us and then his eyes fell on me, and he smiled. We all laughed, even me. I shook my head at him, and Sebastian sat there with a grin on his face.

First up was Cole. He gave Sebastian a big wet kiss on the cheek. "Mwah," he said pulling away.

"Alright," Sebastian said uncomfortably, wiping the kiss from his cheek.

I laughed. Next was Sky. She held his chin and kissed his cheek and walked away quietly, trying to not make it obvious that it was her. Next was Alex. He gave him a quick kiss on the cheek and walked away.

"Damn, you can tell which kisses are the girls' and which ones are the men," Sebastian said, slightly disgusted.

The room giggled. I was next. I took a step forward and softly placed my hand on the other side of his face and I placed a soft kiss on his cheek. His skin was warm and I so desperately wanted to place one kiss on his lips. I moved away as quickly as I had placed the kiss on his cheek. I walked over to Alex, and he gave me a weak smile. I knew he hated it. I looked down and watched as Ruby kissed Bas on his cheek and I looked away because it just annoyed me.

"Alright, everyone, go and sit down again and then Sebastian can take off his blindfold and tell us who he thinks his partner was," Cole said, and we all made our way to our seats and I leaned back with my legs crossed. The blindfold was removed, and Sebastian smiled.

"Gosh, I don't think I've ever been so loved as I was a couple of minutes ago," Bas smirked. His sense of humor was coming out and it was very attractive. "Ruby's kiss was last. I'd like Ruby to give me a kiss," he said, looking at her. This game was getting old, and I just wanted to go home. He leaned over and placed a kiss on her lips, and it was more than just a kiss. I rolled my eyes without even noticing.

"Get a room," Skylar teased.

When they were done with their scene, I leaned forward and took a pink card.

"Wow, you're brave," Alex said, impressed that I hadn't chosen truth.

"I'd rather take a dare at this point than be asked an embarrassing question," I said, looking at Alex, with the pink card in my hand. I could feel everyone's eyes on me as I read aloud.

"If there's a pool, you have to go skinny dipping and you can choose a buddy to go with you." I looked down, shaking my head. "Thank goodness there's no pool, and besides it's freezing outside so there's no way I'm jumping in that water," I said smiling, placing the card back in the pink box.

"Yeah, but rules are rules," Alex said, pulling a face. I smacked his leg softly, hoping he would get the message that he wasn't supposed to encourage this kind of behavior. He chuckled at my reaction, and I shook my head.

"Rules may be rules, but I'm not skinny dipping. There's no way." I folded my arms over my chest, and I watched as Sebastian looked at Cole. I could see he wanted to say something, but he kept quiet.

"Do it in your underwear, then," Cole said, and I looked at him and rolled my eyes. Of course, he would suggest that. I looked at Skylar and then at Ruby.

"There's no way I'm letting any of you see me in my underwear," I said, slightly annoyed.

"Well," Alex said, and I got annoyed by his comment. I shot him a look, and everyone knew exactly what he meant. I could feel the air getting thick. He shrugged his shoulders.

"Okay, babe, I'll do it with you," Skylar said, and I looked at her. She smiled at me, and I felt a little better now.

"Yeah, I'll even do it with you guys, if you want?" Ruby said, trying to make me feel better. I could only imagine how she looked in her underwear. I looked down and I could basically feel the men holding their breaths.

"I still don't feel comfortable doing it in my underwear," I said folding my arms over my chest.

"At least it's not skinny dipping," Alex said, and I shook my head.

"Okay, let's just get this over with," I said annoyed by the dare. I could swear the men were getting excited by the situation.

"You guys better have warm blankets waiting for us when we come out and some hot cocoa," Skylar said, pointing at Cole.

He eagerly nodded his head. I hadn't even thought of that. All I could think of was how cold it was outside and how cold and dark the water was.

Skylar was the first to get up and walk outside and both Ruby and I looked at each other.

"I guess that's our cue," I said to her, and she smiled, standing up. I followed her and we both walked outside. We could hear the boys getting excited behind us as they followed us outside.

"It's going to be freezing," Ruby said, hugging her arms.

We walked to the nose of the boat to where Skylar and I had been sitting earlier. Skylar started taking off her jacket. She looked at us and gestured for us to do the same. I looked at my jacket and pulled it over my head. I could already feel my skin sting with the cold. Before taking off my top, I turned around and looked at all three men staring gleefully at us.

"No pictures, alright," I shot a look at Cole, and he held his hands up in surrender, smiling.

At that I turned and looked at Ruby and Sky, whose shirts were already off. Ruby had on a pink bra and panties set, and

Skylar wore a nice gray and blue laced bra, which looked very seductive. I could only imagine that the boys were enjoying every moment.

I pulled my shirt over my head, and I felt as though everything was going in slow motion. I wore a black lace bra and thank goodness that today out of all days I was wearing the matching panties. I pulled my boots off and next were my jeans. I was well aware that I was being watched, especially since I was the last one to get undressed. I felt the insecurity flowing over me. I hated this game. It was stupid.

"Didn't they say skinny dipping?" Alex asked, teasing again. I shot him a look as I climbed on the edge, where Skylar and Ruby were waiting.

"You wish." I practically spat the words out. I was getting cranky because of how cold it was.

"Why did we agree to do this again?" Skylar said, panicking as she looked out to the dark water.

"Sorry, ladies, I'm afraid of the dark water. I can't do it alone," I said, staring down at the icy water.

"Let's get this over with, ladies. Don't want to give the men any more time to stare at us," Ruby said, grabbing my and Skylar's hands. It felt strange, but I didn't pull away.

"Wait. If you guys are going to go in, before attempting to jump at least put life jackets on. You guys could go into shock because of how cold it is. The life jackets will keep you from drowning," Alex said, pointing to our practically naked bodies.

"Right," Cole said, and he turned around and went and fetched life jackets from inside the boat. He walked up to me first and handed me the life jacket and then he passed me and went to Ruby and Skylar. I placed it around my body and didn't really have a good feeling about what we were about to do. I clipped the life jacket and looked up at Alex and Sebastian. They were looking my way, and I gave an awkward smile before I turned away from them.

"You know what, girls? You also need to exercise before you go inside, so I think you should do some jumping jacks before you go inside," Alex said, very seriously. I laughed and so did the other girls.

"Stop playing with us, Alex," Skylar said. I shook my head and turned away again. Sebastian was standing next to Alex.

"I'm not, so don't tell me I didn't tell you so," he said, shrugging his shoulders. "Amelia, even if they don't listen, I think you should at least do it for safety reasons," Alex added, and I shook my head, smiling. I could feel my cheeks burn from the embarrassment. I watched as he folded his arms over his chest out of frustration.

"Good luck, ladies," Sebastian said, smiling.

We all joined hands. I took a deep breath and I overheard Alex telling Cole to get the blankets so long.

"Alright, on the count of three. One, two, three," Skylar said and on three, we all leaped forward. I couldn't help but join in the united scream. We all let go of each other's hands before we hit the water.

I felt the water engulf me and I swear I lost my breath. The water was so cold, it felt as though my body was being cut by sharp razors. I inhaled out of reflex, and I swallowed some water. Every limb in my body felt as though it were cramping up. I opened my eyes underwater and instantly regretted it. It was so dark that I couldn't see anything in front of me. Panic kicked in. I swam to the surface of the water, and gasped, coughing as I was trying to get rid of the water I had just swallowed. Alex and Sebastian were at the edge of the boat, watching us all moan in pain. I looked over to my left and saw the girls complaining. Skylar seemed to be taking short breaths.

"My legs feel numb," Ruby whimpered as she neared the boat.

"Just make your way to the boat and we'll get you guys out," Sebastian said, raising his voice so we could hear him. Skylar was taking short breaths. Alex and Sebastian easily pulled her up out of the water. Her lips were turning blue. I felt as though there was something heavy pushing against my chest, making it hard for me to breathe. I couldn't help but moan in pain. It was the coldest I had ever felt in my life. Not to mention that all I wanted to do was get out of this dark water. We didn't even know what was under there.

"I feel like I'm going to pass out," I said, feeling nauseous, I took short breaths to help calm myself down.

Skylar was pulled up next and knowing I was the last one in the water made me panic but, before I knew it, I was pulled out of the water by Sebastian and Alex.

"Shit, you guys, this was a bad idea," Sebastian said, looking at how all three of us girls were blue in the lips, and were shivering uncontrollably. I took off the life jacket the moment I was out of the water. Alex placed the blanket around me and wrapped his arms around me.

"No shit." Skylar stuttered the words sarcastically.

"Let's get you girls inside," Alex said, and at that we all headed inside. Alex held onto me while we walked inside, and I felt so much better knowing he was by my side. We were the last to enter and Cole had already made each of us hot cocoa. I think it was the first time I had ever been so grateful for a cup of cocoa in my life.

"Thanks," I said quietly to Cole as we sat down on the floor again.

I drank the warm cocoa greedily and sat against Alex. His arm was around me, making me feel warm. I could feel the warmth flow through my body. I closed my eyes and rested my head on Alex's chest. I opened my eyes and looked around the room. We were all quiet, even the men. Ruby was nestled in close to Sebastian and Skylar was practically sitting in Cole's lap, while his arms were around her. Their lips looked much better, and I was grateful for that. Their cheeks started coloring, which was a good sign.

"I think it's safe to say that no one should try that dare in winter," Cole said, and Sky groaned. "Do you guys want to continue?" Cole asked, and I shook my head.

"I think that's enough for one day," I said, feeling exhausted by the dare. Ruby nodded her head and so did Sky.

"Okay, how about us just doing truth for now? No dares," Sebastian asked.

I looked at him and he looked at Cole and then he looked to the side and his eyes fell on me. His green eyes were bright. I watched how he looked a little longer than he had wanted to and then his eyes fell on Alex's hand around my neck, and I could have sworn I saw a slight twitch in his eye and then he looked back at Cole. He was hiding something.

"Okay," Cole said, nodding his head.

It was then that I realized that none of us had gotten dressed in our clothes and that we were still in our underwear. That realization made me pull the blanket around me a lot tighter than before.

"Are you okay with it?" Alex asked, looking down at me. I looked up and our faces were only inches away. I looked at his lips and nodded my head. I watched how his mouth curled up at the corners, into a small smile. "Alright," he softly whispered back, and I watched how the words left his lips so gracefully. I was mesmerized.

"Are you two love birds ready?" Cole interrupted us. I looked away quickly, feeling embarrassed that we'd got caught in the moment. I didn't dare to look up. Why did everyone have to be so childish. We were just speaking, not doing anything else. It made me feel annoyed.

"Right, next in line is Alexander," Sebastian said, and it was the first time I'd heard Bas say his full name. I was used to calling him Alex, so hearing his full name made me feel strange.

"Alright," Alex said, sighing slightly.

He tapped me lightly and I got the message. I moved away from him slightly, so that he could reach forward and take a card. I watched how he held the card in his hand so softly. The card basically disappeared in his one hand. It was intimidating to see. He held the card up and everyone's eyes were on him. He read out aloud: "*How many people have you slept with?*"

Everyone in the room made a noise. I looked at him and he held his hand in a fist to his mouth. He didn't want to answer it. I was curious, but I afraid to know as well.

"Shit," he said putting the card back. I sat aside slightly, watching him as he moved back into his seat. He looked up at Cole, who was amused, and he smiled back. "Where did you get these cards, man?" Cole laughed and shrugged his shoulders.

"Don't avoid the question, Alex," Skylar said, curious as well. I smiled as I watched him rub his hands through his hair.

He looked down at the floor. "I don't know. I don't keep count," he said, leaning back and putting his weight on his arms while his legs were outstretched and crossed. He was lying.

"Smooth, man," Sebastian said, chuckling, and I watched these two players. They did this on a regular basis. The thought made me look down.

"Come on now, Alex, if you could put a number on it?" Skylar said, challenging him.

He shrugged his shoulders. "I don't know, man, about twenty?" he said uncertainly.

I couldn't help but silently open my mouth in disbelief. I quickly placed my mouth against the blanket when I realized I was making my disbelief obvious. I faded out everyone's conversations for a minute and thought back to the night I'd almost had sex with him. I loved Alex, but knowing how many women he'd slept with, and knowing that my virginity would have just been added to that list, made me feel so disgusted. I didn't even want to know how many women Sebastian had slept with. I wondered if Alex even remembered all the names. That is, if he were telling the truth about sleeping with twenty women. I wouldn't have been surprised if it had been more. When Alex put a number on it, it made it more unbelievable. I frowned at the thought.

I looked up and realized that Ruby wasn't anywhere to be seen; nor was Skylar. Cole was making something for us to drink again in the small kitchen and I had not realized that I had been left alone with Alex and Sebastian in one room.

Alex's phone rang and he looked down and then looked back up at me. "Listen, I'm going to quickly take this call," Alex said, and I nodded my head at him.

Alex stood up and went outside to take the call. How much had I missed in the time that I'd zoned out? I looked at Sebastian.

He was quietly sitting by himself until he turned his head to look at me. My heart skipped a beat.

"So, you and Alex?" he asked as calmly as he could in a situation like this. I shook my head and looked down. Here we go.

Chapter 19

UNEXPECTED

I heard voices speaking outside. I rubbed my eyes as I sat up. I looked around and started piecing together the area I was in. I saw Skylar and Ruby asleep on the bed next to me. I yawned, trying to remember all the things that had happened last night. We were in Alex's hideout place. I guessed that everyone had crashed there the night before. I didn't even remember saying I was going to stay the night. I felt a slight pain at my temples. Headache. I must have drunk too much last night. I closed my eyes again, groaning as I got out of bed. I felt the cold air hit my bare legs. What on earth? Where were my jeans? Had we stayed in our underwear all night? I was wearing an oversized white T-shirt, which I was guessing was Alex's.

I stood up and felt my head throb and I closed my eyes, standing still in one spot for a second. I remember us all doing some more truth questions after everyone came back from wherever they had disappeared to. I also remember Sebastian asking me about Alex and me. I denied being in a relationship with him. I also did say that I was sorry about how everything turned out. He had just shrugged the matter off. I remembered Cole bringing out some more shooters after we had all warmed up, and I remember snuggling warmly into my blanket.

I didn't remember putting on my clothes, or even the shirt for that matter.

I walked over to the bathroom door and closed it behind me. There was no mirror in this bathroom, and I couldn't help but hate the designer of the house. I walked over to the shower and switched the warm water tap on. I pulled the shirt off. I opened the shower door and climbed in. The warm water made my skin burn.

I closed my eyes and tried to think about the events that had taken place last night. I placed my head against the wall and let the water run down my body. I remembered Alex being there. He was always close by. I think I remembered us all agreeing to come here last night. I didn't know how Alex had convinced my parents to let me stay the night. I remembered Sebastian and Ruby making out a lot last night. I think Alex and I even kissed. I groaned as I started getting frustrated by the fact that I couldn't remember. I finished showering and covered my body with the towel. I slowly opened the door and didn't see any of the men standing outside. I was grateful. Ruby and Skylar were still sleeping. I slowly opened the door a bit more and walked into the room, and I saw movement to my far left. I cocked my head in the direction and jumped as I saw Alex standing by the kitchen. He looked up and smiled when he saw that he had startled me.

"Morning, sunshine," he whispered. I crossed my arms over my chest, feeling insecure about the fact that I had nothing on under the towel.

"Hey, do you know where my clothes are?" I asked, looking from him to behind me at Skylar and Ruby, making sure I didn't wake them by speaking. I watched how Skylar softly snored. I can't even remember what time she went to bed.

"Here you go," Alex said softly, startling me again as he was only two feet away from me. He had my clothes neatly folded in a pile. I looked up at him and gave a small laugh.

"You keep startling me," I said, looking down at the clothes and taking them out of his hands.

His blue eyes were clear and soft this morning. His hair was spiked, and he looked as though he had gotten up much earlier than any of us. He wore a dark blue jacket today, with black jeans. I watched as his eyes moved over my face. He didn't hide the fact that he was moving his eyes from my face to the rest of my body.

I looked down and shook my head slightly. "Stop, Alex," I whispered, holding the clothes against my chest.

The cold was unbearable, and I didn't even wait for him to reply. I just kept my eyes down and walked back towards the bathroom. He didn't say anything, but I could feel his eyes on me. I closed the door behind me and put my clothes on. I dried my hair with the towel and pulled it up in a pony, to keep it from wetting my neck. When I knew I was warm and not exposed anymore, I softly opened the door again and walked out. I held Alex's shirt in my hand and, when I looked to the left, by the kitchen where he had stood a couple of minutes ago, I saw that he wasn't there.

Sky and Ruby were still fast asleep. I heard the boys speaking quietly outside. I made my way past the bed and towards the outside. I peeked my head around the corner, nervous to see the three men. To my surprise, Alex and Cole were the only ones outside. Sebastian was nowhere to be seen. My heart sank a bit. I opened the door and closed it behind me, stepping outside. They were sitting down on the chairs drinking coffee. Alex looked my way and smiled, and so did Cole.

I gave an awkward smile back. "Morning, Cole," I said softly. He returned the greeting and I looked at the table next to them. There was a third cup with warm tea in it. I smiled, knowing Alex had made me some.

"I made you something to drink," Alex said, lifting the cup. I walked over and took the cup from him. I placed his shirt down next to him and gave a small smile.

"Thanks for the tea and thanks for letting me sleep in your shirt last night," I said placing both my hands on the warm cup and letting my fingers sting from the warmth. I looked out at the trees. It was a peaceful day. No wind and no noise, just the sound of birds in the distance. The water was calm, and the view looked beautiful.

"Ahh, Amelia, this isn't my shirt," I heard Alex say. I looked at him and frowned. His expression was serious, and I felt completely confused.

"What do you mean it isn't your shirt? Whose is it then?" I asked, looking from him to Cole. Cole shook his head, holding his hands up in surrender. I could sense he felt uncomfortable. I looked at the shirt again and shook my head. I watched as Alex tensed his jawline.

"I'm guessing it's Sebastian's, Em," he said, taking a sip of his coffee and not looking at me. I was speechless. How on earth could it be Sebastian's shirt? I felt the warmth of guilt rush through me.

"Where is Sebastian anyways?" I asked, looking to the right again, making sure he didn't magically appear.

"He had to go to work," Cole replied. I looked at him.

"What time did we go to sleep last night?" I asked, confused by the night. Cole shrugged his shoulders.

"Ruby and Sebastian disappeared for the night and then Skylar and I decided to go next," Cole said. He frowned slightly. "Don't you remember?" he asked.

I looked at him vaguely and shook my head. "No, I don't really remember much from last night," I said, looking back to

Alex. "If it was you and me awake last night, why on earth would I have had Sebastian's shirt on?" I asked, confused by the whole situation.

"You tell me, Amelia," Alex said calmly, not looking up at me.

"Look, we were all drunk last night. I think it's fair to say that no one can be upset with anyone if anything happened," Cole said, and both Alex and I looked at him, upset. "Alright, I'm going to go and check up on Skylar and see if she's awake and give you two some space," he said, uncomfortable. He stood up and cleared his throat as he passed by me. I watched as he opened and closed the door, walking inside.

"What time is it, Alex?" I asked.

He pulled his phone out his pocket and looked at the time. "It's thirty-five minutes past twelve," he replied and placed his phone back in his pocket. I remembered the lunch that I had promised I would attend at my mother's house.

"Alex, we need to go. I promised my mom that I'd have lunch with Tyron," I said a little louder than I would have liked.

Alex looked up at me and sighed. "Alright, let's go," he said plainly. He stood up and walked towards the door. I heard him say a few words inside to Cole. I presumed Skylar and Ruby were awake. I took another sip of my tea before setting it down on the table outside. I headed towards the door.

...

Alex wasn't up for conversation during the drive home. I kept looking over at him and making sure he was okay. His eyes were dark, and he seemed quite upset. Everything about his mood made him look more attractive.

"Alex, look, I'm sorry that I was wearing his shirt," I said, watching his jawline tense the moment I said the sentence.

"Don't be sorry, Amelia. You have every right to do whatever you want," he said softly. We pulled up in front of my house and he switched the engine off. I didn't know what to do or say.

"Look, can we just pretend that what happened earlier didn't happen?" I asked, reaching my hand out and touching his leg. I didn't like him being upset. I could only imagine how upset my mom was that it had taken me this long to show up for the lunch.

Alex turned his face to look at me. His eyes moved all the way down to my neck, and I saw a slight pain in his eyes. I frowned and held my neck, uncertain why he would react that way. He quickly covered it up and looked ahead out the window. "Do you like him, Amelia?" Alex asked, keeping his eyes ahead. I could see he was bracing for the worst. I shook my head, uncertain of what to say.

I looked down at my hand and thought about the question. "Why are you asking this question Alex?"

"It's a simple yes or no answer," he said plainly. I could see in my peripheral vision that he'd turned his head and his eyes were on me.

"Gosh, Alex," I said softly. I started fiddling with my nails.

I heard Alex sigh heavily and he leaned back in his seat. "So, you do then?" he said more aggressively than before.

I looked up to him and there weren't many times in my life when I had seen Alex like this. His hair was a mess. I guessed he had just run his fingers through it because he was upset, and his eyes were dark. His emotions were being revealed and I felt bad that I was the one to bring this side out in him. I nodded my head, feeling the warmth of guilt run through me. He grimaced at my response, and he turned away.

"Alex, yes, I like him, but I like you too," I said reaching out to touch his arm. He pulled away and I felt like a child. I looked down and sighed. I felt defeated. I couldn't help my emotions.

"You can't like us both, Amelia. You have to choose one," he said coldly, still staring ahead.

"I know. I'm sorry. This isn't easy for me either. I don't know what you expect from me. You never wanted me and now that I'm finally interested in another man, you show interest?" I said the words and the instant they left my mouth, I regretted them. He cocked his head around and looked at me, frowning.

"Are you really that ignorant? I've had feelings for you for many years, Amelia. I've left hints and, yes, I may have not always acted on my feelings, but I was doing it to protect you and obviously because your brother would have kicked my ass," he said, raising his voice. I couldn't stand the eye contact, so I kept my eyes low. "I've always loved you," he said, sounding almost like he was pleading with me.

I looked up to him and I was lost for words. "I always knew there was something. I guess I just didn't want to get my hopes up," I said quietly. I felt so vulnerable and insecure about how much we were sharing with one another.

"I don't want you to be insecure. I want you to know that, from today onwards I choose you and only you. I want you to be mine." He said the words and I felt as though I were radiating warmth. I nodded my head and Alex grabbed my hand and squeezed it, making my heartbeat race slightly. I gave him a small smile. I found myself staring at his lips. He let go of my hand. His eyes changed from anger to vulnerability. His eyes softened and his eyes were searching for mine, until they too fell on my lips. I could feel the energy between us intensifying. I moved forward, taking the lead, and I watched as his hand softly played on my cheek. Our lips were only inches away when he slowly rubbed his thumb over my bottom lip.

"I've been waiting for this moment, for so long," he said moving his hand back to my cheek. In one motion he leaned forward, and our lips crashed upon each other. I had forgotten how soft his were. His breath brushed past me, making me want to kiss him further. I opened my mouth, allowing my tongue to find his. His hand moved down to my hips, and I could feel that he wanted me to climb over onto his lap. I ran my hands through his hair, and I felt him softly tug at my lower lip with his teeth. I smiled. I looked up at him and he looked at me. His eyes were dark. His pupils were dilated. I closed my eyes again and closed my mouth, finishing the kiss off.

I heard a bang in front of us. Both Alex and I pulled away and looked in front of us. I moved off of him and sat onto the seat. We watched as the car in front of us started up. I could see Tyron staring at us through his rearview mirror. His engine revved and then he spun away, making dust and stones fly everywhere. I felt guilt all over my body. I placed my hand over my mouth, feeling like a fool.

"I wonder what's got into him," Alex said, annoyed. I looked at him and I moved my hand away from my mouth.

"I wonder," I said, and I pointed at Alex.

We both smiled at each other and then for some reason we both chuckled. A part of me felt guilty for missing the lunch but another part of me didn't care. I looked at Alex and smiled and he did the same. He reached over and played with a strand of my hair.

"If you want to, later I can come pick you up and we can have some fun at my place? Go for a walk and maybe make a nice homemade burgers?" Alex asked, running his finger up and down my cheek. I found it hard to concentrate.

"Okay. Let me first see what my parents say. Especially since I missed lunch and I'm guessing my parents heard how he sped away. So, I'm sure I'll get an earful when I get inside," I said, letting out a big sigh.

He put his hand to his side and nodded his head. "Okay. I'll call you later to find out what the verdict is," he said smiling, and I looked down and nodded my head.

"Okay, hopefully I'll see you later then," I said, smiling at him and he leaned forward. He rested his hand behind my neck. His confidence was so attractive.

"Definitely," he replied, and he moved forward, placing a soft kiss on my lips and, as quickly as it was there, it was removed. He only left me wanting more. I opened my eyes after a small while and looked down. I turned around while smiling and I reached for the door.

"See you later," I said, and I opened the door and shut it behind me. I didn't look back because I didn't want to make it awkward. I could feel him watching me. I made it all the way up to the door but, before I opened it, I turned to look at him and I waved and so did he. He started his engine, and I opened the door and shut it.

Here comes the grief.

I walked in and an aroma of food filled the air. I couldn't see anyone. There was soft acoustic music playing and the fire was on. I looked to the right and saw no one sitting by the island in the kitchen. I decided to head straight up to my room. I didn't feel like dealing with all the negativity after the butterfly sensation I still had bubbling in my stomach. I took one step up the staircase.

"Not so fast, missy," I heard my father say behind me. I jumped at the sound of his voice. I looked to the right and followed his voice. He was standing behind the island by the kitchen.

"Where on earth did you come from?" I asked, startled.

"I was packing some things away in the shelf below," he said, pointing below the island.

I nodded my head. "Oh, I see," I said smiling, and then I turned and tried to head back up the stairs.

"Amelia, get back here," he said in a stern voice. I stopped in my tracks. Dad was usually the calmer one. He didn't get upset, so when he was upset you knew you were in trouble. I turned around again.

"Where were you? Tyron came and prepared a lovely lunch for us. Mom suggested that we eat without you, but he didn't want to. So, eventually when you didn't pitch up, he said that he would reschedule with us." My father looked so mad. Or perhaps more disappointed than mad. I looked down out of shame.

"I'm sorry. I woke up late. The moment I realized what time it was, I promise I told Alex to drop me off. I'm sorry I missed the lunch," I said sincerely. I honestly felt bad for Tyron.

I watched as my father shook his head and looked down at the table. He gave a big sigh. "Don't say sorry to me, Amelia. You need to apologize to Tyron. He is the one who went to all of this effort, only to be let down. I think you need to phone him and tell him that you're sorry and that you want to have him over for supper. We can save all this food for then," my father said, looking up at me.

I nodded my head slowly and remembered what Alex had promised me. How was I going to get out of this one? My father held up his hand and waved me off. "Well, go on then," he said and turned his back on me. I nodded my head and turned to head up the staircase. "Mom is resting, so don't wake her," he added as I was halfway up the stairs.

" Alright, I wasn't planning on it," I said and, as I got to the top of the stairs, I took a right.

I headed to my room and closed the door behind me. What an unexpected turn of events. I didn't want to call Tyron and reschedule, but I knew that for the family's sanity I had to do it. I gave a big sigh and started walking towards my bed. I pulled my phone out of my back pocket and dialed Tyron's number. His phone rang. My room looked so neat and tidy. There were no more boxes in sight and my floor was swept. The windows looked cleaner than usual. I moved my hand over the covers on my bed and they felt different. My mother must have come in here and she must have cleaned everything. She liked cleaning when she was overthinking or when she was stressing too much about something. I didn't mind because I knew my room needed it, but I wondered when she had done all the cleaning.

The phone stopped ringing. He hadn't answered. I decided to give him another call. This time it didn't even take long before the call was disconnected. He'd declined the call. A feeling of guilt spread through me. I could only imagine how upset Tyron must have been with me, to decline my call. I put my phone down on my bed and shook my head. "I tried anyways," I said out loud to myself.

I pulled my shoes off and turned to lie down on my covers. I looked up at the ceiling and replayed the last hour in my head. I thought back to how jealous Alex was of Sebastian. I didn't think I'd ever seen another man bother him as much as Sebastian had. I squeezed the bridge of my nose as the embarrassment engulfed me as I thought of how I was wearing Sebastian's shirt. He must have thought I was some desperate little girl, obsessing over him. Thank goodness Ruby hadn't seen anything. I wondered how on earth I'd managed to find his shirt anyway, especially if he and Ruby had gone to bed first.

So many things happened last night that I didn't quite remember. The overwhelming feeling came over me and I started to feel nauseous. I quickly jumped up and made my way over to the bathroom. I made it to the toilet just in time before everything I had drunk last night came up. I didn't want to drink so much again. I wiped my mouth and flushed the toilet, making my way over to the sink. I was a light drinker, I couldn't handle a lot of alcohol. I looked terrible. I reached into the drawer and took an elastic out and tied my hair up so it could be out my face. I saw a dark mark on the left side of my neck. I quickly moved my neck closer to the mirror. It was a love bite. I gasped. It was huge. That explained why Alex had looked pained when he'd looked at my neck. How was I going to hide this massive thing from my parents? I could only imagine what they'd think when they saw it and I'm sure it wasn't Alex who had given it to me. So how was I going to explain to them that it's a love bite and it was not from Alex? I covered my eyes with my hand and sighed, thinking of the next hours that lay ahead.

"You always know how to put the cherry on the cake, Amelia," I said, removing my hand to look at it once more.

It was purple and blue and in the shape of a perfect oval. Very obvious. I quickly opened my drawer again and searched for my foundation. Maybe if I covered it with foundation it wouldn't be so obvious? I rubbed the moisture on my neck and watched how it slightly covered the mark. I was really starting to build a reputation for myself. I frowned. I would have to wear my hair down for most of the day and night.

I heard my phone ringing in the bedroom. I put the foundation down and made my way back to the room. It was Tyron. I answered.

"Hey, Tyron," I said.

"Hey, Amelia," he said, sounding out of breath. I frowned at the thought.

"Are you okay? Why do you sound out of breath?" I asked.

"I, uh, I went for a jog. Had a lot on my mind," he said.

I sat down on the bed. "Oh, okay. Listen, I just want to say that I'm sorry for missing the lunch with you guys."

"That's fine, Amelia, it's no big deal," he said simply, and I knew he was lying because the way he had acted earlier told me everything was not okay.

"Great, so then will you come over tonight and we can eat the food you made?" I asked, and he sighed in the background.

"Amelia, I don't want to force you to have to spend time with me. I know you don't want to" he said sounding exhausted.

"No, I want to, I promise" I said lying a little bit. I felt sorry for being so horrible to him.

"Amelia, it's fine. I'll come over, but please don't run off again,," he said, as if he were my father. I rolled my eyes at his comment but to keep the peace I bit my tongue.

"Yes, I won't, don't worry. I'll see you later then?"

"Alright," he answered and then we said our goodbyes and I ended the call.

I looked outside at my balcony and thought about how strange he was. I was going to take Skylar's advice. When he arrived, I'd get his DNA and keep it safe. I'd ask Sebastian to run it through forensics if he could, since he worked in the police force. The thought of doing something so secretive made my stomach churn.

I went into Alex's chat and sent him a message saying I couldn't make it that night, even though I really wanted to see him again. I locked my screen after the message was sent and I lay back down on my covers. There was so much happening. The best thing right now to do was to take a nap, especially if I was going to steal some of my "half-brother's" DNA. My eyes grew heavy and, before I knew it, I had blanked and fallen into a deep sleep.

Chapter 20

THE DISCOMFORT

I awoke to a knock on my door. I looked around the room, uncertain of where I was and of what time it was. Dusk had started to settle in, and I couldn't quite place the day. I heard the knock again and I sat up rubbing my eyes.

"Come in," I called. The door opened and standing in the doorway was Tyron. I looked up and frowned at the thought of him standing there watching me.

"Sorry, I didn't realize you were sleeping," he said, turning around, getting ready to walk away.

I rubbed my head, shaking it at the same time. "Don't worry, I fell asleep and forgot about the dinner. I didn't think I'd be out this long," I said, looking outside at the dim lighting.

"You obviously needed the sleep," he said, putting his hands into his pockets.

He wore light jeans, white sneakers and a navy blue button-up shirt. It was then that I realized he wasn't wearing the glasses that he always had on. It made him look better than he'd looked before. His face was clean shaven, and I could see his cheekbones more clearly now. His dark eyebrows were more prominent with the glasses gone. He looked very different than before, and I didn't know how to feel about it. He even looked like he had been working out, but I wouldn't dare ask him. I tore my eyes away from him and focused on the main goal of the evening: his DNA.

"Sorry about this afternoon," I said once again, and I didn't look up at him and I could only imagine him shaking his head.

"That's okay; you're here now. That's all that matters," he said calmly.

I looked at him and I could smell the food downstairs. My stomach grumbled and I remembered that I hadn't eaten anything all day. I was famished. I slipped off the bed and I caught him staring at me as I walked to my desk and slipped my night slippers on.

"Sorry, I'm not going to dress all fancy for the dinner. I hope you don't mind," I said, not asking for his permission.

He smiled and looked away. "You don't have to try, just be yourself. That's all I ever want from people," he said, and I walked towards him, not even thinking of going to check on how I looked.

"Is everyone downstairs already?" I asked, standing in front of him.

He still didn't move from the doorway, and I wasn't going to squeeze past him. His eyes were pitch black and he stood a whole two heads taller than me. He was pretty intimidating, but I didn't want to show him I was afraid, so instead I kept eye contact.

"Yes, shall we?" he asked, stepping aside and gesturing for me to pass him. I nodded my head and moved past him.

"Thank you," I whispered, and I headed towards the staircase.

"Did you have fun last night?" he asked, the words sounding almost sour in his mouth.

I quickly stopped in my tracks and turned around and looked at him, curious. "Why do you ask?" I asked, wide-eyed. He tapped the side of his neck with his finger, and I immediately grabbed the left side of my neck where the love bite was. "Oh no, I forgot about that," I said, pushing past him to go back into my room.

I walked through the closet and entered my bathroom. It was so obvious, and I could only imagine what Tyron must have thought. I scrambled through my drawer, looking for the foundation again. He stood at the bathroom door watching me apply it to my neck.

"It's not what it looks like," I said, feeling judged. He watched me intently and shook his head slightly.

"What is it then?" he asked.

I covered it nicely and pulled my hair out of the pony it was in. When my hair was neatly placed to the sides of my neck, I looked at him and sighed. His arms were crossed over his chest, and he really looked like an over-protective older brother. I looked down because I felt embarrassed. It's not really the kind of impression I wanted to give to him.

"We were just all having fun last night, and I guess I drank way too much. I don't remember much that happened and when I awoke this morning I was wearing another guy's shirt and I had this thing on my neck," I said, shaking my head and putting my hands over my eyes, feeling ashamed.

"Look, I'm not judging you. I just think you need to be careful. You are young and beautiful. Men will take advantage of that. I know you've probably heard this before, but it's true. You need to watch how much you drink. At least mix it up; have one drink, then the next have a glass of water. There's nothing fun about waking up the next morning feeling as disorientated as you feel right now," he said calmly.

I nodded my head and looked down. "You probably think I've been around the block," I said, looking down.

"Don't ever say that." His words came out harshly. I looked up at him and I watched how his jawline tensed and then he looked away from me.

"Sorry," I said, looking at him, curious about how quickly his mood could change.

"Don't be, it's okay. Look, from what I've seen, I just think you have bad people around you, influencing your actions," he said, looking back at me. I gave him a small smile.

"You sound like my parents."

"Guys, are you coming down anytime soon?" My father's voice reached us through the bedroom door. I looked at Tyron and placed my finger on my lips, indicating that he kept it between me and him. I didn't need my parents to ground me. He nodded his head, with a serious expression.

"Yeah, we're on our way," I said, raising my voice.

I walked past him, smelling his cologne. It was strong and musky, not really my cup of tea. He was family anyways, so it didn't have to be. He followed behind me. We exited my room and made our way down the staircase. The smell was strong, and I could have sworn everyone could hear my stomach grumble. I couldn't wait to eat.

My mom looked up from the table that was set. She was seated at the far right, in the corner of the house, by the dining room table. We almost never used the table. Only when guests came over and ate. The curtains were all drawn. She looked down and fixed her napkin neatly on her lap. "I'm surprised to see you here, Amelia," my mother said sarcastically, without looking up.

I didn't know how to answer, so I didn't. I picked the seat furthest from her. I watched my father sit next to her and Tyron picked the seat next to mine. There was so much to choose from. Tyron had made a lamb roast, with green beans, pumpkin and mixed vegetables. There were baked potatoes and some bread on the table. There was a saucer filled with sauce for the lamb.

My mouth was practically watering, and I couldn't wait any longer.

"Would you like to say grace, Tyron?" my father asked, and Tyron stiffened at the offer.

He moved uncomfortably and then, before he was about to respond, my mother offered to say it. We closed our eyes, and she said grace. Everyone started dishing up, except for Tyron. He watched as everyone helped themselves and only when everyone was done dishing up did he lean forward and start to dish up for himself.

"So," my mother said, taking a bite of her vegetables. Here it came. She looked up at me and moved her fork in a circular motion towards me. "Did you have fun last night?" She looked down at her plate, taking another bite of the food. I shrugged my shoulders and looked down at my own plate.

"Uhm, yeah, I guess," I responded.

"What did you guys do?" my father asked curiously. I looked up and frowned at them both.

"What do you mean? We went back to Alex's place, and we all had a good evening, drank some hot chocolate. Nothing special," I responded, and I could feel the tension slowly starting to build.

"Why did you miss lunch earlier today?" my mother asked, looking at me skeptically.

I looked down and sighed. "Really Mom, you want to do this now. In front of Tyron?" I said, holding my hand out towards him.

He didn't look up once from his meal. I saw how the napkin was placed neatly on his lap. He ate very neatly, and he was very quiet. I didn't blame him though, considering the situation.

"Don't try to make excuses, young lady. Why weren't you here? That was your one and only rule remember? If you go out you have to be back by lunch and you weren't, so what was the big hold up?" She was staring at me now, not even eating.

"Sorry about this, Tyron," my father said, sighing because he didn't want to have this conversation now. I also stopped eating and looked at her. Tyron waved my father off.

"I overslept. I forgot about it. The moment I realized, I told Alex to drop me off," I said, defeated.

She looked away from me and continued eating. "Next time, put an alarm on," my mother said, irritated by my irresponsible behavior. I looked down at my food and I realized that I had just lost my appetite.

"It's alright, really. I'm glad we are all here now," Tyron said softly, giving a small smile and trying to lighten the mood.

"That's right," my father agreed with him.

After that, everyone ate quietly. Mom and Dad would ask some questions now and then and Tyron would answer. Just the occasional chit-chat. I offered to take the plates after everyone was finished eating, but Tyron refused. I didn't know how I was going to manage to get a DNA sample from him without making it look obvious. Even so, him being so polite made me feel worse because I felt like I was betraying him and my family in a way. If his DNA did match my father's, Tyron would feel so offended that I had gone and got DNA testing done behind his back. The whole situation was messed up.

I held my breath and watched as he walked away with the plates to the sink. My father followed him. They had gotten into a gripping story about the Switzerland kidnappings. Apparently, Tyron knew some people down in Switzerland and somehow, somewhere, the story had been passed down. It was everything my father lived for, stories like this. Talking about kidnappers, I had been expecting a letter from my stalker when I'd arrived this morning, but there had been nothing. Neither had there been a letter two days ago, or even a week ago. Maybe us going to the cops had spooked him or he'd finally found someone else to obsess over. Either way, I wasn't going to complain. It felt nice to not have to constantly look over my shoulder.

"Penny for your thoughts," Tyron asked, sitting down at the table. I was so lost in thought I hadn't realized that I was the last one left at the table.

I shook my head and gave a small smile. "Oh, nothing," I said, looking down at the table, and then I fiddled with the white tablecloth. I could feel him staring.

"How is everything going? How is your love life?" he asked, and at the mention of a love life I practically scoffed at him.

"Curious, are we?" I said, watching him. I didn't trust him yet and I felt like if I opened up to him it would make us closer, and I didn't like the idea just yet. I wanted to know the results of the DNA test before I confided in him. I watched as he gave a small smile and kept eye contact with me.

He shrugged his shoulders lightly. "Just want to get to know you, that's all," he said softly. I broke the eye contact and looked to the left. I watched how the fire burnt.

"What job do you do?" I turned back to him and asked.

He folded his arms across his chest. "Well, since I moved here just the other day, I'm currently unemployed. I used to be in the special forces, though," he said simply. It was as though a whole new light shone upon him and I couldn't unsee him in the army.

"What was it like?" I asked curiously, not breaking eye contact. He looked down and cleared his throat.

"Tough," he replied.

"Wow, I must say I didn't think you were the special forces kind," I said, leaning back and observing him.

"You don't seem like a girl who goes out partying and gets drunk and loses all her sense of responsibility, yet here you are," he said, leaning slightly forward.

I squinted my eyes at his comment. "Don't be rude," I snorted.

He didn't really seem to be the violent type, or at least he didn't portray himself that way. He held his hands up in surrender and kept his dark eyes on mine. Just as he was about to say something, my phone started to ring in my pocket. I looked down and pulled it out, seeing what the caller ID showed. Skylar. I answered.

"Hey, babe. Listen, please come with to Sebastian's party tonight. I'm not accepting any excuses." She sounded as though she had had too much to drink.

I looked up at Tyron who was staring intently. "I can't, Sky. Tyron's over and we are having family time," I said, looking away from him.

"Bring him with, then. I guess he needs to meet everyone one way or another and that way your parents will let you leave," she said, and I looked back up at him.

"Okay, I'll ask him and then I'll call you back," I said.

"Alright, don't be too long," she replied and finished the call before I could even answer her.

I looked to Tyron. He was still looking at me. "That was Skylar. She wants to know if you'd like to join us to go to Sebastian's party tonight?" I said, curious about what his answer would be.

He looked to the side and his eyes squinted in a way of disinterest and then he looked back at me. "Look, I appreciate the invite, but I'm not interested in going out and getting drunk," he said, not looking me in the eyes.

I shook my head and leaned forward. "C'mon. You say you want to get to know me better. What better way to get to know me than to meet my friends? Besides, Mom won't allow me to leave unless you come with me," I said quietly as I watched my mom and dad talking in the kitchen. I looked back at him, and he turned his head to look straight into my eyes.

He stared for a while, pinching his lips together, contemplating whether it was a good idea or not. "Alright," he said quietly. My smile grew. I watched as he gave a small smile back.

"Could you please tell my parents that?" I asked, looking from him to them. He turned slightly in his seat and looked at them as they were cleaning up and packing the leftovers away.

He turned back to me. "You want me to take the brunt of things if we are late or if something happens to you?" he said, watching me, and I simply nodded my head.

"Don't worry. Where we are going is safe. Besides, I think the stalker has given up on me. He hasn't sent me a letter in days. I think he has moved on," I said hopefully. "So, it should be safe. I mean, after all you do know how to kill someone with your bare hands so, if I were to say anything I would say that you are probably the safest person I could be with." Just saying the words felt foreign in my mouth. I didn't want to admit it, especially when I saw what joy it brought to him.

He sighed and stood up. "You should still be wary, even if your stalker hasn't sent letters recently," he said looking down on me, making me think twice. "I'll go and speak to your parents," he said, turning to leave.

I grabbed the glass that he had been drinking from and hid it inside my jacket. I quickly gathered all the dishes so as not to look as suspicious as I felt. I walked over to the kitchen and smiled awkwardly at my parents, who looked annoyed.

"Amelia, you can't use Tyron to get out of the house," my mother said, placing her hands on her hips.

Unveiling Secrets

I put the dishes down and looked at her. I shook my head. "I'm not. He was also invited," I said, looking at him.

She sighed and looked at my father. "What do you think?" she asked. I smiled and my father looked at Tyron.

"Not later than midnight, alright?" my father said, and Tyron nodded his head sternly.

"Yes, sir," he replied, and I felt uncomfortable.

I packed the dishes in the dishwasher and tried my utmost best to keep calm and not look suspicious at the same time. "Okay, awesome. Thanks, Dad. We'll be back before then, I promise," I said, turning around with my hands folding over my chest. I could see Tyron watching me carefully. He had beady eyes.

"Okay, so I'll be going upstairs to get dressed. I'll meet you downstairs in ten minutes," I said, turning to Tyron, and he gave a small nod.

I hurried away with my arms still folded. If I didn't know better, I would say that he knew that I was hiding something. I headed upstairs and found my way to my bedroom and closed the door behind me. I could feel my heart racing. I felt so guilty. I moved over to my bed and found my bag. I wrapped the glass in my gray sweater and placed it inside my bag. I placed the bag down on my bed so that I wouldn't forget about it. I took a deep breath and walked over to the closet. I found the black polo neck hanging in my closet. I pulled it out and pulled it over my head. It definitely made me feel more comfortable. I pulled my black jacket over my shoulders and put on my navy blue jeans and black boots and I walked to the mirror in my bathroom. I liked how I looked.

I let my hair down and I pulled my fingers through the waves. I opened my makeup bag and applied mascara to my eye lashes. I then put a liquid eye liner on my eyes, to make a pretty cat-eye look. I then applied clear lip gloss and gave one big smile in the mirror to see how I would look if I smiled. I liked it. More importantly, I was sure Alex would too. The thought of him brought butterflies to my stomach. I was sure he was going to be at Sebastian's party. Or maybe he wasn't, considering the turn of events. I'm sure Skylar would have called him too, if she knew how he felt about me and everything. I couldn't wait to see him again. I was so happy my parents were letting me go.

"You ready?" I heard a voice from inside my room.

I jumped. I had been so lost in thought that I hadn't realized that Tyron had walked up the stairs and entered my room. I walked out my bathroom and entered into my closet's walkway. Tyron looked up at me and I saw a quick flash of emotion in his eyes. Awe-struck.

He covered it up with a smile and cleared his throat in the process. "You look nice." He forced the words out and I gave a small smile as he looked away uncomfortably.

"Thanks," I said. "We can go now," I walked over to my bag and placed my perfume inside after I had sprayed some on my clothing. I pulled the strap over my shoulder and headed for the door. Tyron let me walk first. I passed by him as he stood at the door, and I could smell his cologne. We made our way down the stairs, and I waved goodbye to my parents. Both stared at me as I was about to exit the house.

"Please be careful, Amelia," my father said before I opened the door.

I nodded my head gently. "I will," I said and turned around.

"And responsible," my mother added sternly.

I didn't turn around. "Okay, I'll see you guys later," I said, looking at the door.

Tyron greeted my parents and at that I opened the door and we walked out onto the pathway. The cold hit me like a ton of bricks. I shivered. I didn't feel very comfortable driving alone with Tyron, but I had to at least put my crazy ideas aside for a change and maybe just give him a chance. I held onto my bag tightly, to prevent it from falling open and spilling everything. I opened the gate and stood in front of the passenger door. I watched as he leaned forward and opened it for me.

"After you," he said, and I gave a weak smile.

"You don't have to open for me. You know that, right? I have hands. I just thought the car was locked," I said.

"I know. I'm just being polite," he said as he closed the door behind me.

I watched as he walked around the car and scanned the area before climbing in. I frowned. He climbed in.

"Why were you looking around?" I asked curiously.

"You can never be too safe. You don't know where your stalker is, or even who is watching. I was just making sure," he said, looking at me with his dark eyes.

My discomfort grew. I hadn't even thought to look around. Maybe it was a good thing. It showed that I wasn't afraid of the stalker anymore because it felt as though he had officially left me alone.

"Okay," I said, looking away and checking my phone. No texts from Alex and it was starting to get late. Strange of him not to call me back. I hoped he had a reasonable explanation for why he wasn't answering his phone. Maybe it was because he was already at the party and couldn't hear it ringing. I gave a sigh.

"What are you worrying about?" I heard Tyron say as he pulled into the road and started driving forward.

"Alex," I said.

Chapter 21

ALEXANDER

Pain. I opened and closed my eyes, but I could see nothing. Confusion settled in and I couldn't quite recall where I was. I rubbed my eyes. It was pitch black. Darkness enfolded me and I could feel fear creeping in. I couldn't see anything. My head was throbbing from pain. I touched the spot that felt the most sensitive. It was wet. I couldn't tell whether it was blood or just sweat. I reached my hands out around me to see if I could feel anything, but there was nothing.

"Hello? Is anybody out there?" I shouted out into the darkness. My voice echoed. My heart dropped when I realized that I was stuck or trapped somehow. I felt on my body for my phone but didn't feel it anywhere.

"Help!" I tried to scream again, which only made my head throb more.

I slowly started crawling along the ground. I could feel soil. I could smell earth around me, but I couldn't see a thing. Either I was trapped inside a room, or the sun had gone down, and night was upon us. Panic started setting in. Where was I? Who would do this to me? I moved along the ground and before I could get any further, I felt my leg jerk. I stopped and turned, moving my hands down my leg. I could feel metal around my ankle. A chain. Shit. I was trapped. I couldn't go anywhere, nor could I see anything. My heart started racing in my chest. Had I been kidnapped?

I could feel myself hyperventilating. There was a breeze in this place. Goosebumps started prickling at my skin. I was cold and afraid. I moved back to my old spot. I felt safer there as I could feel a bulky wall behind my back. So, I knew I was secured from anything attacking me from behind. I couldn't hear anything but silence and the soft buzzing in my ear from no sound. I hugged my legs to try to generate some kind of warmth. I closed my eyes and thought back on how I had got into this situation.

I remember seeing Amelia. I remember telling her that we'd see one another later. Damn it. She probably thought I was avoiding her. I wondered if she'd even noticed that I was gone. *Her stalker*, I thought. This is honestly the only explanation I have to what has happened to me. I remember Amelia and I were kissing, and the stalker must have seen. He knew Amelia wanted to start a relationship with me, so it makes sense that he didn't want that to happen.

My heart started throbbing again. I remember going home, wanting to take a nap when there was a knock on the door. I thought it was Amelia. But sadly, it wasn't. Ingrid stood in front of me. She was dressed up, her hair pulled back nicely. She wore a shirt that was extremely revealing. Her lips were cherry red, and her eyes were wild. I remember thinking what a bad idea it was that she was there in that moment. Guilt flowed over me as I thought of the next moments. I remember asking her what she wanted, and she said, "You". I told her it was over between us, but she wouldn't take no for an answer.

She grabbed my shirt and pulled me forward. I pulled away before our lips touched and I told her I wasn't interested. That was until she opened up her winter coat, which she had on, and she was naked underneath. All my senses fell away. I remember her ridiculous smirk because she knew she had me. She closed the door and my whole body filled with lust. I dare not say more. All I know is that I regretted it. I regret being with her. If

Amelia found out I slept with Ingrid, right after we said we'd be together, I know she'd never forgive me.

The frustration and anger boiled up inside me. I had been stupid. I remember telling her to leave after the deed was done and I remember how hurt she looked, but I didn't care. She hadn't listened and now I had to sit with the consequences. I remember her leaving and that was that. What followed after that was quite blurry. I didn't remember much. I just remembered waking up here.

"Alexander," a masked voice came through. It echoed and it made me shiver. Who was this person? "Not so strong anymore now, are you?" the voice taunted me. The person must have been speaking through a microphone, to mask their voice. It only made the situation worse. Fear engulfed me and I felt very helpless.

"What do you want from me?" I asked, trying to sound undaunted.

"I wanted *her*, and you always got in the way of things." The voice sounded angry. I struggled to swallow. It was him, the stalker.

"Listen man, I think you and I both know that she doesn't want you. So, save yourself the bulls–"

I felt a blow to my head and then darkness followed.

Chapter 22

SET ALIGHT

The drive had been quiet most of the way. My nerves were building up as I thought about seeing Sebastian. He'd obviously had seen me sleeping in his shirt because I'm sure he couldn't find it when he wanted to leave in the morning. It was honestly embarrassing. I thought of Alex and how we had shared our kiss only a couple of hours ago. I could still taste his kiss. It brought butterflies to my stomach. I really think he meant what he said. I knew Alex was serious when he put his mind to something. Besides that, I felt as though the whole Ingrid thing was over; he'd made sure of it.

I thought that between the two of them, Sebastian and Alex, Alex was the one who seemed to have kept an interest in me. So, maybe it would be a good thing if I stopped giving Sebastian attention and focused on Alex. I could understand why Sebastian had decided to move on, but yeah, it showed that he wasn't willing to fight. But what was I even saying? If I'd found out that Alex had kissed another girl, just after he'd kissed me... Never mind kissing. If I'd found out that he'd slept with another woman, right after we'd said we'd like to see each other, I would also be upset, and I'd probably also move on. Not probably: definitely.

"What's on your mind," I heard Tyron say.

I looked over to him. His eyes were fixed on the road. His glasses fitted perfectly on his nose, and he had a small smile fixed on his face. There was soft acoustic music playing over the radio so that it wouldn't be too quiet in the car. I felt awkward at the question, as I was thinking not only of Alex but of Sebastian too. I looked away from him and looked out at the road.

"Nothing really," I simply replied.

I watched as we drove past all the pedestrians on the sidewalk. So many different characters out there. The streets were busy, and the cars were moving in and out of many different locations, until we turned down a quieter road.

"Strange how quiet the road is now," I added.

"Yeah, because we're leaving town," he said.

It gave me a slight feeling of discomfort. He noticed as I shifted in my seat.

"You're safe with me Amelia. You can trust me. I know I haven't given you motive to, since I appeared out of nowhere and called myself your brother, but I promise you that I only have pure intentions. Ever since I was little, I always dreamed of what it would be like to meet my father. I didn't think it would ever happen. Little did I know I had siblings. It was such a dream come true to meet your father and you. I'm sorry if it's brought you discomfort and confusion. I don't blame you for feeling that way. I promise, I will try my best to bring you joy and I'll make sure to protect you when needs be," he said sincerely.

His dark eyes moved from the road to me many times, and they were vulnerable. I felt guilt settle in as I thought of how I was prepared to get DNA testing done because I didn't trust him. I looked down and gripped my bag more tightly as I was afraid that he would find out what was inside.

I looked up at him and gave a small smile, a sympathetic smile. "I guess you're right." I thought for a moment how it must have felt to have lived without a father his whole life. "Didn't your mother ever marry?" I asked, and watched his emotions change quickly to stone.

"Yes, but he never really was my father. He was corrupt and he made me want to join the Special Forces so I could sort men like him out," he said bitterly. I watched as he gripped the steering wheel tighter. I got the idea that his stepfather must have been abusive. I didn't ask any more questions. There were balloons on a pole to our left. We turned down that road.

"Looks fancy," I said, without thinking.

We stopped in front of a big wooden gate which had beautiful flowers and branches carved on it. There was a buzzer. Tyron pulled down his window and before we'd even pushed the button, the gate slid open. There were trees on both sides of the road leading all the way down. Up ahead, you could see the house. It was a big white double-story house. There were lights on all over the garden, lighting it up so that we could see where we were walking. Where the lights stopped was where my vision became blurry. It was too dark to see without the lights, but I could make out that we were surrounded by a forest.

Tyron stopped the car, and we climbed out. There was a massive bonfire lit in the distance. Most people sat around it. I could see some people were dancing. I felt my nerves kick in as I thought of all the people I didn't know. We could hear the music blaring. I heard my feet crushing the snow beneath me. I pulled the bag over my shoulder and closed the door behind me. There were many cars parked outside. I even saw some police vehicles in the parking lot, which made me nervous. Skylar had told me before not to trust the police. She had told me it was a story for another day.

Tyron walked around and waited for me to join him. We started walking towards the house. Must be nice to be friends with cops. I could only imagine the secrets that you'd know mixing with them. I looked at Tyron as I started to feel uneasy.

He walked tall. He seemed as though he was never afraid of anything. He seemed proud, as a matter of fact. We walked past some people smoking in the corner. I wondered if Sebastian even knew all these people, or if they were just people who'd rocked up out of nowhere. Tyron was much taller than I was and definitely built well. So, when he walked in front, I couldn't see past him.

"Tyron and Amelia!" I heard a familiar voice.

I looked past Tyron and there was Skylar, standing close to the bonfire. I smiled at her. She gave Tyron a quick hug and complimented his look. I could see he felt uncomfortable. I felt strange coming to the party with him. I'm sure everyone thought that we were together and that was the very last thing that we were. Skylar's hair was in a bun, and she had a cream-colored coat on with her light jeans and brown boots. Her makeup was applied thickly, and she wore red lipstick for a change. She looked striking. She saw me and stepped aside to give me a good look. I laughed and stepped forward to avoid the analyzing.

"Wow, babe, you look beautiful," she said and pulled me in for a hug. I laughed into her shoulder.

"You too. The red lipstick really suits you," I said, and she pulled away, smiling at me.

"Felt like shocking people tonight," she said with a small chuckle.

"You achieved that goal, for sure," I responded, smiling at her.

"Do you want some?" she asked, and I gave a small smile while shaking my head. Red was quite a shocking color, and I wasn't looking for any attention tonight. She frowned and reached into her bag, pulling the lipstick out.

"No, come on. It will look great, and I know Alex will love it. Not to mention Sebastian too," she said, winking at me while opening it up. Peer pressure. I leaned forward, wiping the clear lipstick off and stood still. Tyron walked away from us and walked over to Cole.

"Okay, but not too much. I don't want to draw too much attention," I said and felt her applying the lipstick. I looked past her and saw Tyron and Cole speaking. Tyron had a beer in his hand already, which I presumed Cole had given to him. They were looking around and mumbling things. The music was anyways too loud to make out what they were saying. Tyron caught me looking and then he looked away and continued talking to Cole. I hadn't known that they knew each other.

"There, now you look sexy. The black outfit looks amazing with the red lipstick," she said, admiring the look. I looked down and felt shy.

"Thank you," I said and looked up. "Big party, huh? I wonder if Sebastian even knows all these people?" I said, looking around.

She followed my gaze. "Maybe. I know that his buddies organized the whole thing. So, he probably knows everyone, or probably doesn't," she said, looking back at me.

"Speaking of people who are attending, have you seen Alex yet?" I asked, feeling excited to see him. She frowned and then looked around again.

"No, not yet. But I'm sure he will pitch up sometime. Why do you ask?" she said, and I gave her a big smile and she gave one back. "What? What is it? Just tell me already," she said, holding my arms in excitement.

"Nothing much. Just that when he dropped me off earlier, he said to me that he was done with Ingrid and everything and that he wanted me and only me. We had a really great make out session and then he said that he wanted to take me out on a date later, that was if I wasn't grounded. But then you invited me to this thing, and I never heard from him again. So, I don't know. Maybe he has just fallen asleep, or maybe he knows we're here and he's going to pitch up? I did try to call but he never answered his phone." I said, looking around to see if I could see him. She grabbed my hand out of excitement and beamed at me.

"Well congratulations man! I'm so happy for you and that he finally grew a pair and asked you!" she said, making me laugh.

"I know, right. Took him like five to six years to finally admit that he had feelings for me. Just happy that Marcus isn't against us anymore. I also think that's why he finally decided to give us a try," I said, looking down and thinking back to the kiss. The way his hands held me so close and the way everything spiraled so quickly. I couldn't help but smile.

"Gosh, but you are in love!" she said, and I snapped out of my gaze and started to giggle.

"Just a little," I said. "I hope he comes, though, because all of this is for him," I said, pointing towards my outfit. She looked to the side.

"Don't worry, I'm sure he'll make a turn," she said, and I nodded my head.

I touched my bag and leaned in towards her. "I got the glass and I'm going to ask Sebastian if he won't mind getting a DNA test done for me," I said quietly. Her eyes grew serious. She looked at my bag and nodded her head.

"Does he know?" she whispered, indicating to Tyron, and I shook my head.

"No, and he can't find out because I'll get into so much trouble," I said quietly, looking around to make sure Tyron stayed where he was.

Unveiling Secrets

"Listen, I wanted to tell you I did also tell Cole about what you were doing, and he completely agrees with me," she said quietly, and I frowned.

"Why did you do that? What if he talks?" I asked annoyed.

She shook her head. "Don't worry. He won't speak. I can assure you of that," she said, grabbing my hand again to calm me down. I looked away.

"I hope you're right," I said, looking back at her.

"Don't worry. Anyways, let's go get you a drink," she said, grabbing my hand and moving me towards the staircase. "Listen, I can see the love bite on your neck" she said trying to not look suspicious. I stopped in my tracks. "You can?" I asked holding my neck and turned to look at her. She smiled.

"Yes, but it's not obvious" she said trying to reassure me. I placed my hair in front of it.

"I don't know who gave it to me. Last night is such a blur," I said feeling confused. She turned to me and gave a small chuckle.

"It was me silly. We kissed, just to turn the men on and then I gave you the bite" Skylar said giving me clarity. I smiled.

"What? Okay, but then why did Alex looked so pained when he saw it this morning?" I asked and she shook her head.

"He wasn't there when it happened. I don't know. He's a sensitive one, but don't worry, it wasn't just anyone who did it, it was me," she said and I smiled, feeling oddly uncomfortable and happy knowing that I hadn't just kissed everyone.

"Well, thank you for clarifying, because I was really confused," I said, chuckling. She nodded her head and pointed towards the house.

"No problem, babe, let's go get something to drink," she said.

I followed her and walked up the beautiful stairs. There were people also sitting out on the deck and I heard a familiar voice. It was Sebastian. He sat with his friends, and he was talking while they were turning meat on the barbecue. He had a drink in his hand, and he looked as though he was actually having a good time. He seemed so relaxed compared to his usual self. His hair was spiked up. He wore his earrings. His skin looked darker than usual, but maybe that was just the lighting. He had a deep blue hoodie on, with dark jeans and sneakers. He was leaning against the wall, next to the barbecue, while his friends were looking at him, sitting down on the chairs which were on the deck. They were chirping him stuff, which made him smile. I had forgotten how good he looked when he smiled.

I made it to the top of the stairs, and it was as though time slowed. He caught my eye and he just stared. His green eyes softened, and he gave me a smile. I felt so flattered by the gesture. It didn't take long for his friends to notice that he was taking too long to reply. They looked my way. I returned the smile and looked away. Skylar opened the door and walked in, and I followed. Gosh, that moment had given me a rush of adrenaline. I could only imagine what he was telling his friends. Men are so curious. I couldn't help but smile at the moment. He definitely had more than one drink in him, because he was much more relaxed than the Sebastian that I knew.

Right in front of us was a spiral staircase that led to the second floor. There were fairy lights leading all the way up the staircase, making it look quite magical. To the far right was a room in which there were bookshelves. There were couches in the room and there was a fireplace. As I walked further into the house, I marveled at the design. There were ferns hanging from the ceiling of the room to the right. There were so many books that I would have loved to have gotten my hands on. To the right, in the corner, was a door that opened and closed often. People walked in and out quite often. The kitchen maybe? I thought. To my left was a guest bathroom and I presume a guest bedroom next to it, as the door was closed. I looked up at the staircase as Skylar lead me past it and I could see an open plan area, but that was all. My curiosity grew. We walked towards the white door that opened and closed the whole time. She pushed it open, and I followed her.

"Wow, this house looks beautiful," I said to her as we entered into the kitchen.

There wasn't anyone inside it. Thank goodness. There was a white island in the center of the kitchen, on which a set of knives and forks stood. There was a small sink in the middle of it. The fridge was to the left and dishwasher next to it. The walls were a cream color and there was a nice fruit basket on the table, making the place look homey. There were more than thirty bottles of alcohol stacked on the table to our right. I sighed as I thought of what a bad idea this would be.

"I know, right. Wish I had grown up in a home like this," she said, looking around at the glass cabinets. She took two glasses out and I smiled at her.

"I know, right?" I said. She poured us both a drink. It was colorful, almost like a cocktail but not exactly. "Thank you," I said looking at it and deciding to take a sip. Sweet, with a slight burn. She smiled at me as my eyes closed at the burn.

"Come on, let's go and have some fun," she said, putting her arm through mine.

I smiled and walked with her. We walked out of the kitchen and there were more people who seemed to have entered the house. A couple walked past us into the kitchen. I looked to my left, at the room with all the books. It looked so cozy. The fire was also lit, and I could see people smoking more hubbly by the couch.

"Can I go look there first?" I asked Skylar, and she stopped and looked at the room.

"Alright. Can I meet you outside?" she asked, and I nodded my head.

It gave me a chance to look around. I watched as she headed towards the door. I walked up the step towards the room. I could practically smell the books. The light was dim, but I could make out all the books' names. Most of the books were non-fiction. I wondered if his parents read as much as mine did. My father raised us up on reading, especially since he was a journalist. I moved my finger along the books and looked at the different authors.

"How did I know I'd find you here?" a voice said. I cocked my head in the direction and saw Sebastian leaning against the door frame. I smiled and looked away. Why was he so intrigued? Where was Ruby? He wasn't my friend just a day ago and now he wanted to talk?

"I guess you would find any reader in this place," I replied quietly. I heard the crowd behind us snicker. I turned to look at them, but they were in their own world. They weren't even acknowledging us. I turned back.

"What's your favorite book?" he asked, and I couldn't help but smile as I skimmed over the titles.

"What's *your* favorite book?" I turned the question around, to avoid replying. I looked at him and his green eyes were on me, watching me closely.

He gave me a smirk. "You won't know the author," he said quietly as he watched me.

I smiled and turned towards him. "Try me."

A small part of me felt as though we had entered into flirtation mode. I didn't want to overthink it, but I was certain that was what we were doing. He looked down and walked over to me. I couldn't help but feel nervous. When I noticed, he was only one foot away from me and I took a step back. My back touched the bookcase and now I was trapped, in a way. He finally stopped in front of me and looked at me. He scanned my face. I could feel my heart pounding in my chest. What was happening? His green eyes were so clear, I felt as though I could dive straight into them.

He broke the eye contact and I watched in slow motion as he reached up above me and got a book out from the bookshelf. He was very close to me, and I could smell his cologne. I scanned over his face and so desperately wanted to place my lips on his. I felt as though I had forgotten how to breathe when he was so close to me. *Ron McLarty, The Memory of Running.* I read the words on the front cover as he handed the book to me. Our fingers touched slightly as he handed the book down to me and I couldn't help but feel flustered. I cleared my throat as he took a step back. He smiled at me, and I looked at the book, forgetting that that had been our conversation before he'd started walking up to me and seducing me with his good looks.

"Interesting," I said, as I blankly looked at the book, finding it hard to concentrate with him a few feet away from me. Not to mention, with him staring the way that he was.

"Your turn," he simply said.

"I don't have a favorite," I said hugging the book to my chest, looking up at him. He gave a small smile.

"There must be one that you like in particular," he said, and I shook my head.

"Too many good novels out there. I can't choose which one is good enough to make the cut," I said, handing his book back to him. He took it from me, and his green eyes never left mine for one second. I couldn't take the energy between us. Alex would be livid if he could see how close Sebastian had got to me. I looked down. "Anyways, where is Ruby?" I asked. I could see the question bothered him as he immediately turned away from me and placed the book randomly down on the table, closest to the couch.

"I wouldn't know. We aren't a thing," he said, and I gaped at him. Shocked is the word.

"What do you mean? You were all over her last night?" I asked, confused. Or was I the only one who had seen that?

He looked up at me and gave me a small smile. "Jealous much?" he teased, but all I did was roll my eyes at him.

"No!" I practically spat the word out.

I was lying to him. I had been jealous. It had been the first time seeing him in so long and to see him throw himself at another women in front of me did sting. So, yes, I was jealous. But was I going to admit it? No.

He had a stupid grin on his face. "Alright," he said putting his hands up in the air. "Ruby and I didn't work out," he said simply, and I felt a slight pain in my chest.

He had looked as though he had been in love with her, and now they were not meant to be. He was just like the other men. Got what he wanted and then he left. I looked away from him and stared at the fire, which was lit. The more I got to know each one of these men, the more I realized that they just used women as their pawns, in their games. I felt sick to my stomach.

"Sorry to hear that," I said, looking away from the fire and back at him. His eyes seemed darker.

"I'm not," he simply said. It left me speechless as his eyes looked into mine. What was he trying?

"Don't you think you've maybe had one too many?" I asked him, breaking the eye contact to look down at the drink in my hands.

"I'm sober. I've been having sodas all this time. I don't want to get drunk tonight," he said, folding his arms over his chest. I smiled. That was a wise decision. I didn't know if I believed him, though.

"Good choice, especially after last night," I said, feeling guilty.

He gave a smirk and looked away. "Yeah, was my shirt comfortable?," he asked, looking back at me with a ridiculous smile. I couldn't help but laugh. My cheeks were burning, and I looked away from him as he watched me in fascination.

I shook my head. "Gosh, I'm sorry. I didn't realize I had done that. I thought it was mine. I guess I must have just found a random shirt lying on the ground and was like, okay, this will do," I said, holding up the imaginary shirt in front of me. Sebastian laughed and I loved how he looked. So relaxed. I needed to stop talking to him. He always made my emotions confused.

"Yeah, imagine my confusion when I woke up this morning, looking for my shirt and there you were, sleeping in it," he said smiling, and I didn't even want to look at him. I could feel my cheeks burning and I was so embarrassed by my actions.

I put one hand over my eyes and giggled. "Sorry, gosh. It's so embarrassing," I said, and I uncovered my eyes.

"Don't worry, I thought it was cute, actually," he said, flirting again.

I could see he was looking down at my lips as I smiled. Gosh, the room felt quite small again and I felt as though, if I didn't change the subject, he was going to maybe make a move on me.

I looked away from him. I remembered taking his shirt with me, so that I could give it back to him.

"Thank you." I then cleared my throat again and moved my hair behind my ear. "Here is your shirt back, by the way," I said reaching for my bag. He waved me off.

"No, it's fine, keep it," he said, giving me a smile. I hated it. Why was he being so nice? I held the shirt in front of me and wanted him to take it, but he just shook his head.

"Please, I insist," I told him, but he shook his head again.

"No, you keep it for when you can't find your shirt and you need something to sleep in," he said with a smirk, and I thought he was being downright cheesy. I giggled and thought of what Alex would do if he knew I had it.

"Alex would hate it, Sebastian," I said, and I watched as his jawline twitched and he took a step closer to me. He looked down at me and I felt so small.

"Alex doesn't own you. You do what you want. Keep the shirt, don't keep it, it's up to you. But don't let a man make your decisions," he said, and I was quite impressed by what he'd said. I smiled and nodded my head. I looked down at the shirt and placed it into my bag.

"Thanks, I guess," I said and as I said that I saw the glass in my bag. "Oh, yes, before I forget. Can I ask you a favor?"

The conversation went from flirting to immediate seriousness. His eyes focused on mine, and he nodded his head. "Sure, what do you need?" he asked calmly.

I brought the bag forward and showed him the glass inside. He looked confused by the gesture. "Could you maybe get a DNA test done for me, on this glass? Tyron drank from it, and I don't know. I placed a hair brush of mine inside the bag, so you can compare the two DNA's together to see if it's a match. If he says he is my half-brother, then I at least want the paper to prove it. Would you be able to do this for me, quietly? Because if anyone found out, I would be in so much trouble," I quietly said.

He nodded his head, and it was crazy to see how relaxed he had looked earlier compared to how he looked now. His green eyes had grown dark, and he seemed quite intimidating, if you asked me. "I'll even pay you to do it. I just don't want him to find out because he is quite scary, and I don't want him to hurt me or anything." That seemed to have triggered Sebastian a little. His jaw line twitched.

"No, don't pay me. I will gladly do it. You need to know if the man who claims to be your half-brother is really your half-brother. I won't tell anyone. And Amelia, if you ever feel threatened by him, don't drive alone with him or be alone with him. You can ask me, or Alex if you want. We will help you out. You shouldn't have to feel forced to put up with him just because he says he is your half-brother," he said sternly. I nodded my head.

"Thank you," I said gratefully. He gave a small smile. "But what do I do if my parents want us to drive together?" I asked.

He shrugged his shoulders, and he thought for a second. "Then get Skylar to drive with or something," he said, and I nodded my head.

I didn't know what next to say, so I said the obvious. "Happy birthday, by the way" I said smiling handing him the bag. He looked at it. He gave me a smirk and looked up at me. "Must be nice to have cop friends, who can arrange this for you. To be quite honest with you, I'm afraid to even drink in front of them," I said pointing at the wall, where they were. He chuckled and I loved it.

"Don't be silly. You can be yourself here. They are off duty tonight," he said confidently. I nodded my head smiling at him.

"I didn't bring anything for you, I'm sorry," I said shamefully.

He shook his head and rested his hip against the door frame. "You being here is good enough," he said, and it only made me feel more confused. His eyes were burning into mine and he was flirting with me. I wanted to get out of the situation, just in case Alex showed up. Sebastian was getting too comfortable. I smiled at him.

"Amelia?" I heard a voice speak from behind Sebastian. Sebastian turned around and behind him stood Ingrid. Gosh, was she the last person I wanted to see? Immediately my temper changed, and I felt my body tense up. What did she want?

"Hello, Ingrid," I said, annoyed because I didn't like her and I knew she didn't like me. What was she even doing here?

She gave a small smile and nodded her head. "Hey, Bas, I brought you a gift and I put it in the kitchen. I hope that's okay," she said, looking at Sebastian and smiling at him. I hated her. I felt like rolling my eyes, but I didn't want her to notice that I was challenged by her.

He smiled and nodded his head, clearly picking up the vibe in the room. "Thank you, Ingrid. You didn't have to, but I appreciate it," he said smiling. She nodded her head, and I watched as she rubbed his shoulder, looking back at me.

"It's only a pleasure," she said, and I felt like I wanted to hit her. Gosh, what game was she playing?

"Look, I know you don't like me, and I don't like you, but I need to ask you a question," she said simply and I was glad she'd stated the obvious. I shrugged my shoulders at her so she could continue speaking. "Okay. Well, earlier when I was at Alex's place, I left one of my things behind and..." she said, and my heart dropped. I couldn't even concentrate on whatever else she was saying. Why had she gone to his place? I looked down and tried to calm myself.

I put my hand up in the air to shut her up. "Wait a minute, did you say you were by his place earlier?" I looked at her and focused on her lips. She frowned and nodded her head, clearly confused by my question.

"Yes, I was there. What's the problem?" she said confused.

I looked away and took a deep breath. "Why were you there? What did you leave behind?" I asked, getting frustrated. I found it quite hard to calm myself at this point.

She put on the best snotty face she could find and looked at me. "What is it to you, why I was there? I was dropping something of his off when he asked me to come inside. I refused but I mean, look at him. So, we did our usual love making," she said with a smug look on her face. I hated her. Everything inside me burned. Everything he had said and told me was a lie. I tried to hold back the lump in my throat, but it was growing fast.

"You're lying," I said, feeling so humiliated. I'd got all dressed up for him, only to find out that he had been doing this behind my back. Couldn't he at least have waited a day? Why do it on the same day that he promised that he was done with her? Did he want one last go at it before he called it quits?

She shook her head at me. "I wish I was," and she revealed the love bite on her neck.

It wasn't even small. He must have enjoyed it. I felt my heart set alight. He had lied to me, and he had broken our promise. I didn't want anything to do with him, or any man for that matter. The tears streamed down my face, and I felt like a loser. I watched as she smiled at me slightly, knowing that I had feelings for him. The anger inside me grew.

"I'm sorry, I didn't realize it would make you react like this," Ingrid said. She was such a liar. She knew exactly how I felt about him, and she knew how I would react. I took a step forward and smacked her straight across the face as hard as I could. Sebastian called my name and tried to step between us. Ingrid turned back to look at me and she looked angry.

"You knew exactly how it would make me feel, you whore." I spat the words out and I watched as she held her cheek. I didn't care anymore. Tears started streaming down my face. I just wanted to get out of there. I pushed past Sebastian and walked past her. She didn't do anything to me, I think maybe because she was quite stunned that I had hit her.

"Amelia." I felt Sebastian grab my hand as I moved past him. Gosh, the room was just caving in. I hated that he had to see me like this as well.

I looked at him and pulled my hand out of his. "Please stop. I'm sorry to have ruined your party," I said painfully. The tears were streaming, and I could see he looked hurt.

"Amelia, you didn't ruin it. I'm sorry Alex hurt you," I heard Sebastian say. I wiped the tears that kept streaming and I shook my head. I wanted to get out of here. I turned away from him, leaving him there and I headed towards the door. So much for I love you and only you Amelia. I put my drink down on the table that was closest to the door,

"Why did you have to do that?" I overheard Sebastian saying, to Ingrid, I supposed. It was nice that he was standing up for me, but so embarrassing that he had seen me like this. I wiped my eyes and I stepped outside, hiding my face. I probably looked like such a mess. I scanned the crowd for Tyron.

"Amelia." It wasn't even seconds and Tyron had found me. "What's wrong?" He was serious.

I looked to the ground and felt so overwhelmed by the story. "Can you take me home, please? I don't want to be here, especially looking like this." The last thing I wanted to do was cause a scene, especially on Sebastian's birthday.

Tyron nodded his head and didn't even think twice. "Okay, let's go," he said.

I walked ahead and kept my face down. Before I knew it, we were in the parking lot. I heard Skylar calling me, but Tyron waved her off. I felt as though I was making a big scene over it when it was probably not so big. I climbed into the car and felt my heart shatter. I put my hands over my face, and I cried. Alex didn't deserve me. He was only a player, and he didn't care about my feelings or me. He only wanted to have sex with me and then he was probably going to leave me.

When Tyron climbed into the car, I took a deep breath and gathered myself. I didn't want to do this in front of him. I let him drive us home and I looked out the window and cried silently.

"You don't have to talk to me about it, but whatever it is, I'm sorry, Amelia," Tyron said as he pulled onto the road. I sniffed and wiped the tears as they fell.

"Yeah, me too," I said bitterly. The rest of the drive home was quiet, for which I was grateful.

Chapter 23

ALEXANDER

"Alexander." I heard a voice say my name. Pain. My head was throbbing. I touched the side of my head and groaned. I opened my eyes and still couldn't see anything.

"Alexander, would you like to discuss why you're here?" the voice said.

"Where am I?" I asked, knowing I was still in the same place I had been before the person hit me unconscious.

"Far away from civilization, if that's what you want to know," the voice replied.

"What do you want from me?" I asked, feeling frustrated.

"What I want is you out of the equation," the voice said. "I want you to know that while you sit here and miss her, I will be there getting closer to her," the voice said, tormenting me. The anger inside me started growing.

"You wish, you coward. You think sending her messages in a letter will win her over?" I practically spat the words out at the voice. He snickered, which only annoyed me more.

"Silly boy, you don't realize how big this goes," he said.

"Enlighten me," I demanded.

"She doesn't know it, but I'm one of the closest people she knows. I've been invited into her home. I've been in her room, in her head. I'm surprised she hasn't told me that she loves me yet. She is gullible and she believes anything you tell her. And right now, because of the stunt you pulled with Ingrid, she is more vulnerable now than she has ever been. She will be like

Unveiling Secrets

putty in my hands," he said, and instantly my heart pulled. I had forgotten what I had done with Ingrid.

"How does she know?" I asked, feeling ashamed of what I had done. My heart started to ache.

"How do you think? Ingrid couldn't wait to spill the news to her, and you should have seen it. Oh man, the way she broke. Like you had shattered her heart into a thousand pieces," the voice said.

I was so angry about what I had done. I had so much regret. If I wanted to change it, I wouldn't be able to because I knew her. I had promised her that I'd look after her and I'd never go back to Ingrid and there I was. She would never take me back and I did love her. I wanted to get to know that intimate side of her. I wanted to explore all those beautiful moments with her. My heart pulled at the opportunity I knew I had lost. Why was I so stupid? Why had I let Ingrid seduce me?

"I will now leave you to your guilt and shame. You will hurt the way you've hurt her," the voice said, and fear gripped my heart.

"Don't! Let me go. I will make it better. Don't leave me in here," I pleaded with the voice, but the voice never replied again, no matter how many times I screamed and shouted. The voice had fallen silent and I was all by myself again. My anger burst up and I slammed my fists into the ground beneath me. The pain shot through my knuckles and my wrist, but it felt better than the pain I was feeling inside. I wished I weren't alive. Maybe if her stalker took my life, it would be better than sitting here and knowing she was in pain because of me. I was such an idiot. I felt the lump in my throat and, for the first time in a long time, I felt tears of shame and regret stream down my face. I'm sorry, Amelia, I really am.

Chapter 24

THE SHOCK

I awoke with heavy eyes. I had been crying all night and I'd switched off my phone. I guessed I knew now how Sebastian had felt after everything I'd put him through. My room was darker than I would have liked. I moaned as I sat up in my bed and I rubbed my eyes. I climbed out my bed and moved towards my curtains and opened them up. The day was dark, as the clouds in the sky seemed to have picked up my emotions. They were a dark gray and I knew they were pregnant with rain. I opened the sliding door and felt the cold sting my cheeks. I didn't mind. I sat down on the chair that was closest to me and looked out into the trees. So dark and ominous.

I wondered what Alex was up to at that moment. If he was even thinking of me or if he was thinking of how he was going to lie his way into my heart. I closed my eyes, as there was a slight breeze that blew in the air. After all these years of knowing him, I had really thought he loved me. The pain in my chest grew. I thought of how he had kissed me and how he had gone home and placed those same lips on the girl I despised. I took in a deep breath. I wanted to make sure he would never be able to contact me again. I wanted to hurt him like he'd hurt me. I stood up and walked back over to my bed. I opened the covers again and climbed inside. I felt numb and I didn't want to see anyone. I closed my eyes and drifted off to sleep.

I jumped at the sound of a knock at my door. I groaned and turned away from the door, covering my head with the covers.

"Amelia, it's Mom. I'm coming in," I heard her voice gently saying from the other side of the door. I kept still as I heard her open the door. She sat down on the bed and placed her hand on my leg. "When are you going to get up? It's one in the afternoon," she asked, but I remained silent. "Do you at least want to talk about it?" she asked, and I could hear the rain pouring down outside.

"No," I quietly replied as I felt the lump in my throat. My eyes started to burn again, and I shut them to stop the burn.

"Alright. I need to tell you something," she said in a weary voice. I kept quiet, so she would just continue. "Alexander has been reported missing." The words left her mouth and I felt my heart skip a beat. I pulled the covers down from my face. My mom's eyes widened at how I looked. I didn't know what I looked like but could tell from her expression that it wasn't good.

I sat up immediately. "What do you mean? I just saw him yesterday?" I said, panic in my voice.

My mother cleared her voice and looked away. "Honey, I don't know all the details, I just know I was called by Deborah, and she asked me when you had spoken to him last," my mother said.

I looked away and fear gripped my heart. "Mom," I held my chest as I could feel a lump in my throat, "please tell me you're joking." My voice started to break. I looked up into her eyes and she shook her head.

"Sorry, dear, I wish I were. Did you not see him last night at the party?" she asked. I shook my head as the shock started settling in. Ingrid was the last one to be with him. Did that mean that he'd disappeared right after she'd left? Had he left because he couldn't handle what he had done with her or was it...? I thought about my stalker and how he had threatened that he would get rid of Alex if I didn't stay away. I covered my eyes and pulled my legs up, resting my head on my knees.

"Oh no, Mom! It's all my fault. He got kidnapped because of me," I pleaded.

She gripped my arm gently. "Don't say that, Amelia," she said, worried.

I looked up to her and I could see her face was filled with concern. "It is, Mom. The stalker told me to stay away from Alex and I didn't and now he has been kidnapped," I said, the words breaking under my voice. The tears streamed and my mother pulled me in for a hug. It felt good to be held in this moment. She patted my back softly.

I pulled away and wiped my eyes, sniffing at the same time. I looked at her and she looked at me. "How do we know he didn't just run away? What if he decided to take a break?" I asked, hoping there could be another explanation for his disappearance, instead of blaming the stalker.

She shook her head. "Deborah said that she went to his place, only to find his car still parked in the garage," she said quietly, sending goosebumps down my spine. Something was wrong.

"Mom, what if my stalker took him?" I said, panicking, and my mom shook her head and moved a little closer to me. I could feel my eyes well up with tears again.

"No, honey. I don't think we should jump to conclusions. The police have been notified about the situation and they will get to the bottom of it. Hopefully in our case he just decided to take a taxi and take a small break from reality. For now, I want you to please stay home, where it is safe. I can't let anything happen to you too," my mother said sternly.

"Mom, I'm scared. What if I get blamed for his disappearance and go to prison?" I asked, afraid of what would happen to me. I thought of him and how he was probably so afraid. "Oh, my gosh." I couldn't help but feel so overwhelmed. I wiped at the tears as they streamed down my face. I looked over at my bedside and grabbed my phone. I switched it on and immediately messages started binging on my phone. I never should have left it off. What if he'd tried to get hold of me?

"Amelia, I don't think you should go on social media either, until we know what the truth is," my mother said.

I saw messages from Skylar asking if I was okay. I looked at the next message. It was from Deborah, Alexander's mother. She had given me three missed calls and two messages asking if I had heard from Alexander because he hadn't gotten back to her in a while. Then I saw it.

I did it for you – Anonymous.

The shock gripped my body, and I couldn't help but let out a panicked cry. "Mom, look!" I turned the phone and showed her. It was the stalker. I was sure of it. He had taken Alexander and I was sure the stalker was going to kill him because of me.

Chapter 25

INVESTIGATION

I had answered as many questions as I could handle later in the day. Mom had taken me to the police station, to help give evidence for Alex's case. It didn't prove that he had been taken by the stalker, but we all pretty much assumed that it was the stalker who had taken Alex. I showed them the letter where the stalker had threatened me not to see Alex and Sebastian anymore. I was sure that this case put Sebastian in a pretty uncomfortable position, as he was also seen as a potential next victim.

My eyes were burning from the lack of sleep and the crying I had done the previous night. My heart still stung when I thought of Alex and how everything had changed so drastically in a couple of hours, for both of us. My mother didn't want me to stay any longer, especially considering how she had seen me behave last night, when I had come home.

I had seen Sebastian coming into the building once to get something and then he was out again. He looked very smart and neat in his uniform. Very attractive. His hair had stuck out from underneath his hat. His expression had been stern, and I could only wish that I knew what was going on in his head. His eyes found mine as he was walking past to get some forms from the next room, and he gave me a small nod. I gave him a small smile back, although it still didn't seem as though it took the stern look off his face. The FBI agent had already asked me questions about my relations with Sebastian. It was uncomfortable. I didn't tell them much, just the fact that we kissed and that was as far as the relationship went.

They had told me a whole bunch of things like I wasn't allowed to speak out on the investigation, to anyone, until they got down to figuring out who the stalker was. Skylar had been called in for questioning, Cole was next. Even Tyron was called in, surprisingly, even though those two never hung out together. I was told that Sebastian wouldn't be a part of the investigation, so no matter how much I wanted to know about it from his point of view, he wouldn't be able to tell me.

The very next step was the security. The FBI agents didn't believe I was safe anymore on my own. They believed that I was a target and that I could be the next missing case. So, they had assigned an officer to my protection, to keep guard outside my house at all times.

How quickly my life had turned, from being completely normal a couple of months ago, to being completely messed up overnight. I was told that I would have two officers looking out for me. They would be doing shifts. One would patrol during the day and the other one would do night-time duty.

As we left the station, I was escorted by a cop. Michael was his name. He was African American. He had pitch black eyes, a little stubble and his uniform was neat. He looked as though he was well into his late thirties. He was polite most of the time and always kept his eyes on our surrounding. We climbed into our car, and he climbed into his. The whole time I kept thinking of Alex. Even though a small part of me hated what he had done to me, I still didn't want anything bad to happen to him. I thought of where the stalker could have taken him and how he was feeling now.

When we got to the house, Tyron had called my father and asked if he could stop by. He was already waiting inside as my father accompanied him. Mom and I climbed out the car and walked to the house. I'll be honest, I was all talked out for the day. I didn't have much conversation left in me.

"Alright, you guys have a safe night now. I will be sitting out here until 6PM and then Angus will take over the night shift. If there is any trouble, let us know right away. You have us on speed dial, and we are parked right outside anyways," the cop said, looking at my mother and me sternly.

"Alright, thank you, officer," my mother said as I nodded in agreement. He turned to look at the car parked in the parking lot.

"Who is accompanying you guys in the house?" the cop asked, looking at Tyron's vehicle. I frowned as I looked at the light from the sun ray reflecting off his windshield.

"That's Tyron, my husband's son," my mother said.

We heard the door open and out walked my father.

"Alright, thank you. I just need to keep tabs on who comes in and out of your property," he said sternly, and he watched as my father came closer to us.

"Everything alright?" my father asked, as he stood beside us.

My mother gave a small smile and nodded. "Yes, Officer Michael was just briefing us on everything," my mother said, looking at my father.

My father nodded his head and looked at the officer. "Alright. Thank you. Officer, we will go inside now," he said, and Michael nodded his head and headed down to his car and climbed in. We all turned around and walked up to the house. This was one tiring day. I walked in after my mother, and my father closed the door behind us.

"Amelia, I'm sorry you have to go through all of this right now," my father said as I walked over to the kitchen table.

I saw Tyron coming downstairs. I gave him a weak smile as he waved at me.

"It is what it is, Dad," I said, defeated. I pulled the chair back and sat down. I couldn't help but yawn. Being investigated all day long was so taxing, not to mention the little sleep I had got the previous night. I put my head down on my arms. Sleep would be good now.

"Come on, Em, how about we watch a good movie in front of the fire, to take your mind off of things," Tyron suggested. My heart jumped at the word "Em", and it made my stomach churn. Only Alex called me Em. I didn't want anyone else calling me that.

I sighed and lifted my head. "No, you guys go ahead. I'm beat. I need rest. I'm going to go and take a nap," I said, standing up pushing my chair back. I could see Tyron was disappointed in my answer, but I didn't care. I didn't really want to be around him, especially in times like these. Who knows? He could be the stalker.

My mother nodded her head. "I think that's a great idea. Go and rest. Go and rejuvenate. Let us know if you need anything. We will all be here when you come down," my mother said, rubbing my shoulder. I gave a weak smile and turned towards the stairs. I was greeted with a big bear hug from my father. I smiled and let him hug me. I guess I needed it. It made me feel emotional. My mother joined the hug, hugging me from behind.

"Family hug," she whispered.

"Come join in, Tyron," my father said and soon Tyron has also joined the hug. It was seconds and then they left me.

I smiled and gave a small laugh. "Thanks," I said, and I headed up the steps, feeling everyone stare at me.

I couldn't wait to get into my room and close the door. The moment the door shut, I rested my back against it and just exhaled. I felt so vulnerable and alone. I felt my throat burn as I walked over to my bed. I couldn't help the tears from falling as I thought of how trapped I felt. Everything was different now and my best friend, whom I loved, was also gone because of me. So much for the stalker won't get to you as long as I'm around. Alex was way in over his head. The tears streamed more, and I rested my head on my pillow. I closed my eyes and let the sorrow overwhelm me. Before I knew it, I had fallen into a deep sleep.

Chapter 26

NIGHT SHIFT

I awoke from a dream. I dreamed that Alex had been tied up in a warehouse and that he kept asking me to come and save him. I kept trying to walk towards him so that I could free him, but my legs felt like lead, and I just couldn't get to him. A very frustrating dream. I felt my temples ache from the crying and I'm sure the other reason was the dream. My room was dark, and the house sounded quiet. I looked over at my phone and saw it was one in the morning. I had slept many hours. They were many hours that I had needed.

I switched my bedside light on and felt instantly better with the presence of light. I sat up in my bed. I wondered what time Tyron had left for the night. I got up out of my bed and walked over to the door. I opened it and I could feel my stomach grumble. Food would be satisfying. I walked down the hallway, and the house was very quiet. I hated the sound of it. I held my phone close to me as I walked down the stairs. The stairs creaked under my weight. I hated making a noise. I didn't want to wake my parents.

The room was dark and luckily the moment I got downstairs I reached the light. I switched it on and walked over to the kitchen. I opened the fridge and saw that my mother had left a plate of food covered in the fridge for me. I smiled. I took it out and put it in the microwave. Chicken and veg. I could smell the food and it only made me hungrier. My phone beeped, which made me jump. The microwave stopped and I took the food out.

I sat down at the table and grabbed a fork that was on the table. I unlocked my phone's screen as I took a bite of my food. Heaven.

"You awake?" I frowned as I saw the message from Sebastian.

"Yeah, why are you?" I couldn't help but ask.

"Couldn't sleep much and you?" he replied. Shame, my heart went out to him. He was probably as stressed as I was about everything. Especially now that the police force was involved.

"I was hungry," I replied. Nothing but the truth, I thought. I couldn't help but smile a little.

"Have you managed to sleep?" he asked.

I couldn't help but feel strange that he had taken so much interest in me. "I couldn't help but sleep when I left the station earlier today. I actually just woke up now," I replied.

"I saw your light go on," he replied. My heart skipped a beat. I stopped eating immediately.

"What do you mean?" I asked.

"Angus couldn't attend his shift."

I practically leaped within. I couldn't help but smile. That meant he was guarding my house. Pretty stupid if you ask me, since he was part of the victim list.

"What are you so excited about?" I heard a voice in front of me. I jumped in my seat and felt the cold run through my body. It was Tyron.

I held my heart and looked away. "What the hell, Tyron, you scared me," I said, annoyed.

I looked back up at him and his hair was a bit of a mess. He didn't have his glasses on, which made him look completely different. His jacket that he had been wearing earlier was gone and he had a dark blue long-sleeved shirt on.. He looked as though he were wearing black sweatpants. He definitely hadn't gone home for the night.

His black eyes were softened by my reaction, and he smiled at me. "Sorry, I didn't mean to startle you. I was sleeping and you woke me up. I was just making sure no one was breaking in," he said, shrugging his shoulders and pointing his thumb behind him, towards the door. I looked at the door and got annoyed.

"That's why the cops are here, Tyron. To make sure no one breaks in," I said, only realizing after it was said how cold it sounded.

His eyes twitched a bit and he looked down, clearly hurt by my response. "You're right, I suppose," he said quietly.

"Why did you sleep over?" I asked and still it sounded cold. I couldn't help it, though. I watched as he rubbed the back of his head.

"Well, your life is at risk. But, if I tell you that I slept over to make sure everyone else stayed safe, you're just going to tell me that the cops will handle it," he said with a forced smile on his face. I looked away.

"Sorry, you just startled me, that's all. I guess it's fine if you sleep over. I can understand why you would want to, especially knowing all the skills you know about fighting," I said, giving a small smile.

He smiled and nodded his head. "So, why are you up anyway?" he asked curiously.

I pointed to my food. "I was hungry," I said, smiling. And he gave a small laugh.

"Okay, makes sense," he said, putting his hands back in his pockets. "So why were you smiling earlier?" he asked curiously. I looked at my phone and remembered that Sebastian was sitting in the cop car outside. I smiled and shook my head.

"No, nothing. Just that Sebastian's on shift now looking after our house instead of that Angus guy," I replied, and Tyron frowned.

"Isn't that illegal?" he asked.

I shrugged my shoulders. "Maybe it is, maybe it isn't," I said standing up to walk to the curtain. I pulled it aside slightly so I could see the car. It was there, but it was too dark outside to see him inside the car. I closed the curtains and thought that maybe I should go outside.

"Don't even think about it. It's a bad idea," Tyron said looking at me and reading my mind.

I shook my head and gave a small smile. "I wasn't going to but now I really want to," I said, curious.

His dark eyes grew darker. "What about the stalker? What if he takes you the moment you step outside?" he asked, and I shook my head.

"I have both you and Sebastian at my side. I'm sure I'll be okay," I said. I could see my words comforted him. "Just cover me, if my parents come down, okay?" I asked nicely, and he shook his head slowly and gave a sigh.

"You'd better be quick," he said and at that I grabbed my phone and walked over to the door and opened it, stepping outside.

The cold air hit me, and I covered my arms as I looked at my surroundings before stepping down. I hoped the stalker was asleep. I took my first step and felt slightly afraid of being alone in the dark, so I hurried the last steps up, practically running towards the car. Before I even got to the car, I could see Sebastian had seen me. I smiled and he popped the passenger door open. I climbed in gleefully.

"Hello," he said in a cheerful tone.

"Hi, so much for couldn't sleep," I said playfully, smacking him on the shoulder. He smiled and I loved the way he looked. He was dressed in his uniform, and it suited him so well. His hat was off. His hair was messed up. It looked good on him. His pupils were dilated, and I couldn't explain how irresistible he was in this moment. I had to look away.

"Yeah, well, I can't sleep, I'm on duty. So, in a way, I wasn't lying," he said quietly, and I smiled.

"Okay, true. Aren't you going to get in trouble for looking after my house?" I asked, looking at him, while he looked outside. His hands were resting on the steering wheel, and they looked so powerful. I remembered when they had held me close to him. So strong, so amazing. Gosh, I couldn't be alone with him. Not now, not when I was so vulnerable.

"I won't as long as we don't interact," he said and then he slowly turned his head towards me. His smile had disappeared, and his face looked sad. The words stung a bit, but I understood why.

I put my hand on the door handle. I didn't want him to get into trouble. "Oh, okay. Sorry. Let me go before anyone sees us together. You know how this stalker can be," I said quietly. I opened the door and lightly moved off my seat. I felt his hand rest on my leg, stopping me from climbing out.

He sighed. "Don't go. It's fine. I volunteered to look after your house. I wasn't allowed to, but I managed to twist Angus's arm," he said with his head down, looking away from me. Almost as if he wanted to hide his emotions. A small flame burned inside me. I thought that he still cared about me, but I didn't want to get ahead of myself.

"Okay, but I don't want you to get into trouble," I said, closing the door slowly.

He shook his head. "It's okay. I insist," he said quietly, and I gave a small smile and looked away. "I would rather be here and know that I can at least stop the stalker from taking you, than wake up one morning and hear that you've been taken," he said softly.

My heart swelled. So, he did care about me. 'Thank you for sacrificing your job to watch out for me," I said, touching his knee in a friendly way.

Although it felt everything but that. Electricity flowed through me while my hand was on his knee, and I watched how his eyes looked to where my hand rested. I pulled away, realizing it was maybe too intimate to do something like that.

He cleared his throat. "So, what's the real reason you couldn't sleep?" he asked, and I looked away thinking of the dream of Alex. I'm sure he didn't want to hear that right now.

"I get night terrors. I always dream of the stalker either taking me away or taking someone I love," I said painfully, as I thought of where Alex was. My heart pained as I hoped nothing bad was happening to him and he was still alive.

"Like Alex." He said the words as thought they were difficult to say. I nodded my head and he sighed.

"I just hope he is okay and isn't dead or anything. I wouldn't be able to forgive myself," I said, my voice beginning to break.

"Hey, if anything, none of this is your fault. So, please don't ever blame yourself for something the stalker decided to do," he said, touching my arm gently, reassuring me. I tried with everything inside me not to cry. Thank goodness it was working.

"Okay. I just feel that everyone who knows me is going to get taken away from me and that's my biggest fear. I don't want to lose anyone," I said softly. He moved his hand, and I felt the cold replace the place where his hand had rested.

"If I know the FBI unit we have, they will find this man and they will make sure he stays behind bars for a very long time," he said.

"I hope so," I said, looking out the window into the dark surroundings. My father had installed some lights around the house but, if anything, they only made us stand out more than anyone out in the woods. "Doesn't it frighten you to sit here by yourself?" I asked. I knew I wouldn't be fit for this job. I looked at him and he shook his head.

"No, this is nothing compared to certain parts of town that are really scaly. This is still good. Do I get nervous when the suspect comes at me? Yes, but it's just like instinct that kicks in. I always defend myself," he said, his hands folded over his chest.

When he spoke, vapor flowed from his lips, so gracefully. Even the vapor danced when it touched his lips. I didn't blame it. His eyes fell on me when he realized that I was staring at him. His pupils were still dilated, and his eyes were darker because of the lighting.

"I wouldn't be able to do what you do," I said, looking at him, and he gave me a small smile and shook his head.

"You'll be surprised what you can and can't do. You just have to train in it, and you'll blow yourself away," he said positively.

I beamed at him and, for the first time since yesterday, I was actually happy. I wasn't sad. "Yeah, I suppose," I said. I looked at my surroundings and thought of the stalker again. "Am I not distracting you from your duty?" I asked him, and he chuckled.

"No, you're just making it better, actually. Sitting in a car by yourself for hours on end is taxing, not to mention lonely," he said. I nodded my head.

"I can imagine," I replied.

He reached for his rearview mirror and adjusted it. "So, I heard from Michael that Tyron is still here?" He asked sounding like an inquisitive child. I nodded my head.

"Yeah, he slept over," I replied. Sebastian's jaw flinched and I know that if I had not been looking at him, I never would have picked it up.

"Why though?" he asked, and I shrugged my shoulders.

"He said something about wanting to protect us if the stalker enters the house. I mean, I understand what he is talking about, but it's honestly not necessary. I told him that the cops were patrolling outside. He didn't care, so yeah. That's the reason," I said.

Sebastian shook his head as he listened to my story. He was looking at his steering wheel. His mind looked busy. "Speaking of him, I haven't gotten the DNA test results back. They said at least another week, especially since I'm asking them to do it secretively," he said as he reached to put the heater one notch up.

It felt cozy in his car. Sebastian always seemed to be doing things for me that he wasn't allowed to do. Like breaking the law. It sent a warmth through my heart, making me feel special.

"That's not a problem. Right now I have more important things to worry about, like Alex and my safety," I said, thinking of Alex again. It was silent in the car for a couple of minutes. "Have you heard anything about him?" I asked Sebastian.

His face was stern. He shook his head. "No, not really. I know they sent the troops out to look for him in the woods. Maybe the stalker went there? They're checking neighborhoods. Especially in his neighborhood. Someone must have seen something. Other than that, there isn't much I can tell you," he said. He looked up at me. "They've kept me out of the case, especially because it's too personal for me. They don't want me to even work at the station anymore, because they consider me a suspect. Due to the fact that we both had interests in you, and there's a stalker out there who has taken Alexander. So, they were weighing their options. They wanted to suspend me until further notice. I will only find out the answer tomorrow," he said, and his eyes looked defeated. I'm sure all of this was taxing on him too. All because of me, he was going to be suspended. I frowned and shook my head.

"They can't possibly think it's you. Is it you?" I asked, doubting my own judgment for a second, and he looked at me.

"Yes, Amelia. I'm your stalker and I took Alex away from you. I'm madly in love with you and will do anything to have you to myself," he said sarcastically.

I felt a little hurt. I looked away from him and shrugged. "You could have said it with a bit more enthusiasm," I said, feeling down. This man has got me feeling hot and cold all the time. I heard him chuckle and I liked it. I gave him a small smile. "Listen, I just want to say that I'm sorry how everything went down yesterday at your party." I said the words very quietly as I felt embarrassed.

"Don't be. I completely understand why you reacted the way that you did. Nice smack, though. I'm sure you'd been holding that one in for a while," he said amused, and I laughed a little.

"You have no idea," I said, smiling, thinking back on how great that smack was. I was sure Ingrid hated me now, forever but I didn't care. "I was disappointed in Alex. He told me that I was the one and that he wasn't going to go back to her, but he did." I said the words and they felt so bitter in my mouth.

He reached his hand over and squeezed my hand. "I'm sorry, Amelia," he said quietly.

I looked at him and he turned from looking outside, to me. "I'm sorry for what I did to you. I guess it's a taste of my own medicine," I said, and he kept his eyes on me.

He nodded his head slowly and he looked away. "Can't say it didn't hurt, but I guess it's one of those things, hey," he said, looking out the window.

So, I was right. He was hurt and so was I. What a bad combination we were at this point.

We heard a knock on Sebastian's window. We both jumped. I could see the figure. It was Tyron. Sebastian cursed while opening his window.

"Good evening, officer. May I ask you to please release my sister? It is late and I don't want her to be out here any longer where she could be in danger," he said, clearly annoyed that I had stayed out longer than he had wanted.

"Shit, you're right. She isn't safe with me, an officer. She ought to go back inside that house where she is much safer, without an officer," Bas replied sarcastically.

Tyron gave a nervous laugh and I didn't want to be a part of this conversation anymore. "I'm coming, Tyron. Go wait in the house. I'll be right behind you," I said, annoyed.

He cleared his throat and drummed his fingers on the door. "Alright," he said looking away. Then he looked down at Sebastian. "You be careful now. There's a lot of crazy people out here. Don't really know who you can trust in these present days," Tyron said, staring Sebastian dead in the eyes.

"Ditto," Sebastian said back.

"You have a good night shift now," Tyron said.

His words sounded spiteful. I didn't know if I was over analyzing the story but I felt uncomfortable at what had just happened, and I didn't know what to say, quite frankly.

We watched him turn around and head back into the house. Sebastian didn't take his eyes off him until he couldn't see him anymore. The moment he closed the door, he turned to me in an instant.

"I don't trust him, Amelia. I have a gut feeling about him and I don't know why, but I don't trust him one bit." Sebastian's words were stern and serious. His eyes were dark. His words only put more fear in me. He had made my eyes widen a bit from seriousness.

"Okay, I understand. What can I do, though? He is my half-brother," I said, worried.

He shook his head the moment I said half-brother. "I don't give a shit. He can be the prime minster, for all I care. I want you to try your best to stay clear of him, until we know the DNA testing has told us that he is your brother," he said.

"What do I do now? I have to go in there and pretend to be okay?" I asked, confused by the whole situation.

"Yes, fake it," he said.

I felt so confused and overwhelmed by all the uncertainty in my life. "Sebastian, I don't know if I can anymore. All of this is just too much. I don't want to go inside there. Every time I think about everything, I'm reminded of how trapped I feel. How I can do this and can't do this. I don't know who I can trust anymore, and it makes me feel so dysfunctional. I want to be normal again. I want to go back to Switzerland where everything was okay. Where there was no stalker, no boys and zero drama," I said a little too loudly. I could feel I was getting all worked up. His eyes were on me, watching my every move. "I mean, I made a man disappear because of me," I said as my voice started to break again. I could feel the lump in my throat.

"Amelia, I know it's uncertain times at the moment. I want you to know that in all of this you can trust me. You can ask me for help. I'll be here, waiting outside your house. I will make sure you don't get harmed, even if it's the last thing I do," he said, looking into my eyes very seriously. I nodded my head quietly. He was being too kind. "We will find Alex and we will find the stalker and then your life can go back to normal," he said, his eyes not leaving mine.

I nodded my head again. I looked away and picked my phone up. "Okay. Thank you," I said quietly, and I looked back up at him.

He wasn't far from me, because the conversation had gotten us excited and we were only inches away. I watched as his eyes moved down to my lips and I couldn't agree more on maybe sharing a kiss in this vulnerable moment of ours. It was a second longer than it was meant to be and then he broke the eye contact before anything could even happen. Disappointment followed. Maybe he wasn't as interested in me as I had thought.

He looked out the window again. "Okay, so you should probably go, before he comes to fetch you again," he said, giving me a small smile. I chuckled.

"Okay, but really stay safe and thanks for listening to my story," I said, smiling at him before I climbed out the car. He smiled and nodded his head. I climbed out and closed the door behind me. Knowing he was looking after my house made me feel much safer. Now it was only down to finding Alex and finding out who the stalker was. I opened the front door and walked inside, closing it behind me.

Chapter 27

TRUTH

Two days had gone by. In those two days Alexander had still not been found. I had a bad feeling about the whole thing. It was cold at night. So, if he were out somewhere in the woods, without a blanket, I was sure he would die of hypothermia. My thoughts always tended towards him and what he could be doing. If he were alive. His mother and father had become bitter towards me. They were upset that he had been kidnapped, and they blamed me for it. I could understand why they would resent me. I wanted to help look, but the detectives had everything under control, apparently. They didn't want me to get into more danger. So, they told my family to stay indoors until they caught the stalker and found Alexander.

Because of the whole ordeal, I had lost my appetite. I didn't really feel hungry anymore. Skylar had visited once in the two days. She wasn't as happy as she usually always was. Me being in lockdown made her feel nervous about coming to visit. She mentioned that Cole was also very distant and acting strangely. And then to top it off Alexander is still gone. We were all in a sad mood. I guess we all just didn't know whom we could trust anymore.

Sebastian had looked after the house again the one evening, but the next night he did not show up. I supposed he was tired from the night duties, and he just needed the rest. It made me worry about him too. I wondered if he was okay or not. I had sent him a message but he still had not read it.

Tyron had slept over every night since the kidnapping. He said it was to keep a close eye on us. Mom and Dad appreciated it. With him in the house, he started looking more like a permanent fixture. He kept to himself more and more and stayed in my brother Marcus's room. He would leave occasionally, to run some errands, but other than that he was always there.

I sat up in my bed and stretched. I got up and walked towards my balcony door. I heard a slight rumble outside. Rain? I opened the curtain and saw how the rain was softly coming down. There was something about rain that always humbled everything. The rain started coming down harder. Please be okay, Alex, I thought. With the rain coming down, it made the temperatures much colder than normal. My heart went out towards Alex.

I turned around and walked over to my bathroom. Since Tyron was here all the time, I didn't feel comfortable going downstairs in my PJs. I quickly brushed my teeth and walked over to my closet. I pulled on my red sweater and dark jeans. I left my slippers on as I knew we were not going to go anywhere. I left my hair down. The weather made it extra wavy. I didn't even bother to put makeup on.

I opened my door and walked down the hallway to the stairs. I climbed the staircase and felt the warmth downstairs from the fire that was burning. As I reached the bottom of the stairs, Tyron was moving one or two logs around in the fire. He turned around and caught my eyes. His smile grew and I gave him a small wave and looked away.

"Good morning. How did you sleep?" he asked as he walked over to the kitchen island, where I was standing.

I shrugged my shoulders. "Okay, I guess. I didn't have any bad dreams last night. I don't actually think I dreamed at all. Just kind of closed my eyes and opened them," I said, looking down at the table so I wouldn't have to look into his dark eyes.

"It's good that you didn't have another night terror. At least you are okay and you're feeling better. Listen, I thought maybe, to take your mind off things, we could watch a movie today in front of the fire. Have a little bit of bonding time?" he asked quietly. I felt uncomfortable at the idea, but I nodded my head slowly. Maybe watching a movie would help a little, especially because he did ask about it the other day.

"Okay, I guess," I said, and he beamed at me.

"Okay, awesome. I'll get the popcorn going and you can choose the movie," he said eagerly. I hated that he was always pretending as though nothing was happening in our lives. Like the fact that Alex was missing, and they still couldn't find him. I felt nauseous as I thought of that.

I walked over to the TV and switched it on. I switched through a couple of channels but didn't see anything I liked. I was over it. Maybe it was because I was missing Alex so much. My heart began to ache as I started to imagine life without him. He had always been there, whether I wanted him to be or not. He had become a part of the furniture. Always at our house every weekend. I remembered how I used to fantasize about the idea of us getting together one day. He had become my obsession. I remembered when he would sleep over. I think I was happier than my own brother was, that he was sleeping over. Marcus always knew I had a crush on him, so he would deliberately speak of other girls in front of me to Alex, just to irritate me. Then we became closer as I got older. I wasn't as annoying as I always used to be. I slowly got over the whole Alex and Amelia together forever thing.

I don't know why, but ever since then he'd started to notice that I wasn't a little girl anymore and we just grew close. He became very protective over me, and I always knew there was something between us, but I didn't want to ever mention it, in case I was wrong. So, I kept it secret and enjoyed all the "what if's" in my mind. To the point where we moved, and I actually saw his true feelings towards me. The feelings that seemed stronger than just being friends, or best friends for that matter.

He always knew how to cheer me up. Always knew how to make me laugh when I really didn't want to. He always knew how to protect me, and this year I seemed to have let him down in that regard. I let him get kidnapped. He gave me his love and then he got kidnapped for it. Who knew my life would become so complicated. I thought of all the precious memories we had shared. Our kiss, his tongue, his arms, his body, the warmth, and the connection. I could feel the butterflies in my tummy flying around. But what if I would never ever see or feel him again? My heart began to ache and, as quickly as the butterflies came, they died. I was a big mess. I felt a tear trickle down my face, and I wiped it away quickly.

"Is everything okay, Amelia?" Tyron asked as he reached my side and I quickly snapped out of the trance I was in and sniffed, looking up.

"Ahh, yes. Sorry. I was just caught in a thought, that's all," I said, clearing my throat. Alexander, I hope you make it home safely, I thought to myself. I could feel Tyron staring at me. I turned to look at him. "Yes?" I asked, feeling insecure.

He shook his head. "No, nothing. It's just that if you need to talk, I'm here," he said quietly. His dark eyes looked vulnerable.

I looked away from him. "I just miss Alexander. I find it strange that the cops haven't found him yet. It's been days. He could be dead." Saying the words aloud made me want to cry again. He could be dead. That was the honest truth.

"I understand how you feel, but listen to me," he said sternly. I looked up and was quite shocked at his response. "The stalker won't kill him. He needs him as bait. Think about it. He wants you and only you. Yes, sure, Alexander is a threat, but he will deal with him later. What he'll do is use him to get to you. So, you need to be careful," he said. His words ran down my spine and made my hairs stand up. His eyes were black and cold, which made what he said even creepier.

"He is going to use Alexander?" I asked. He was right. I sat up and moved slightly back so I could look at him properly. I frowned. "How do you know all of this?" I asked suspiciously.

"Because," he said quietly, "we trained in knowing the suspect's mind. What they do, why they do it. How to prevent it from happening again. How to cover up. All of that. We train, we fight, and we learn to observe," he said, not taking his eyes off me.

"So, you think Alex is fine?" I asked hopefully.

He shrugged his shoulders. "If the stalker is smart enough, he wouldn't kill the bait. I know I wouldn't, but that's my opinion," he said, folding his hands over his chest. I looked away from him and at the TV screen. He was right. I had to be careful of my next moves. "That is why I tell you to be careful of who you see and who you get close to. He could be anyone, Amelia." His words were like ice. So cold they left goosebumps in their place.

"Don't say that," I said, afraid. I couldn't help but look around me.

"Don't worry. As long as you are here, with us, your family, I'm sure you'll be safe. Where the stalker can't get to you. I'll make sure of that," Tyron said, holding the popcorn bowl in front of him. He sat beside me, and a small sense of comfort formed. Alexander was alive.

But I thought that I needed to give myself up, to ensure his safety. I was certain of my decision. I was going to pretend to sleep and then I was going to sneak out and maybe let the stalker find me, so that he would let Alex go. That's if he was going to let him go.

There was a big knock at the door. I jumped as I snapped out of my thoughts about the stalker finding me. What if it was the stalker? What if he was coming to take me now?

Tyron got up and was about to answer the door when I held my hand out in fear. "No, wait. Don't open it, please. Check the peephole first," I said, and he cocked his head to look at me.

He gave me a small reassuring wave. "Don't worry. I'll make sure it's not a threat," he said quietly, as he looked through the peephole. I watched in anticipation. His emotions changed from calm to stiff in a moment.

"Who is it?" I asked curiously.

"It's Sebastian," he said, sounding exhausted. I jumped up from the couch as the second knock came and then Tyron opened the door.

"Hey, man, do you live here now?" Sebastian asked as Tyron watched him.

Tyron nodded his head. "You can say that, I guess," he said simply.

"Is Amelia around?" he asked, stepping inside. "There is some important news I need to share with her," he said, and his eyes found mine.

My curiosity grew. I wondered if they had found Alex.

Sebastian's hair was wet from the rain, making it look darker than ever. His green eyes stood out with the black hooded leather jacket he had on. His face lit up when he saw me, and I knew that Tyron saw it. I smiled at Bas, and he did the same back. I was happy to see that he was doing well and that he hadn't been taken by the stalker.

"Did they find Alex?" I asked as I stepped closer to them. I forgot to breathe as I waited for his answer.

He shook his head. "No, I'm sorry. It's something else," he said sadly.

I looked down and exhaled. Gosh, this was starting to get very depressing. I missed Alex. I missed his smell and his dimples when he smiled. I missed his stupid humor. I wanted him back. I watched as Sebastian stepped forward and touched my arm out of sympathy. It felt strange but nice at the same time, that he cared about my emotions. I looked up and his eyes were a mixture between sadness and something else. I couldn't place my finger on it. His eyes looked more intriguing than they had ever been. His lips looked soft and slightly darker, due to the cold outside. He moved his hand off my arm as we both heard Tyron say something.

"Would you like something to drink? We were just about to watch a movie?" Tyron interrupted my gaze.

Sebastian looked at Tyron and gave a weak smile and shook his head. "No, thank you. I was actually hoping to take Amelia out," he said, and then turned to look at me. I thought back on what the cop had said about me staying indoors, due to the stalker.

"I would love to, but the FBI told me to stay indoors," I said, looking at him just in case he had another option.

He shook his head and semi rolled his eyes. This rebellion. "I know, but you'll be okay. I am like the FBI," he said confidently. He gave a small smile, and I couldn't help but smile back.

"I don't know, I don't like this idea. I think you should consult your parents first before you go anywhere," Tyron interrupted our gaze.

I looked at him and nodded my head. "Okay, I'll quickly go and call my mother," I said, looking from Tyron to Sebastian. Tyron looked so bothered.

"Okay," Sebastian said calmly. I walked away and went to the end of the living room to give my mother a call.

I pulled my phone out and dialed my mother's number. My parents had gone to the store, a cop accompanying them while they were on their journey. The cop had tried to insist that he would do the shopping for them, but my mom was going crazy. So, she told the cop to follow them instead. I listened as the call dialed and my mother answered.

"Yes, dear?" my mother said.

"Hey, Mom. Listen, Sebastian's here and he wants to know if he can take me out. Is that alright?" I asked her. A small part of me was excited about it and another part of me felt guilty for even wanting to have fun while Alex was out there somewhere in pain.

"No, I don't think so. It's unsafe and I don't want anyone else to get hurt or disappear, my girl. You are a target. Remember that. You should be the one to stay indoors." The words my mother said spoke deeply to me. I felt so afraid after she had said I was a target. She was right. I couldn't go anywhere. "Let Sebastian just stay there with you. Why go out when our house is perfectly fine?" Mom asked.

I gave a big sigh. "Mom, Tyron is here *all the time*. I would have let Sebastian stay, but Tyron is so nosy," I whispered to her. I looked over my shoulder just in case they were listening. Tyron was sitting on the couch, eating the popcorn he had just made, and Sebastian was waiting, leaning against the wall. Looking very attractive, I might just add.

"Listen, let me ask your father first. I'll call you back now," she said, and we both said our goodbyes.

Once I was off the phone, both boys looked up at me. I felt guilty as I thought about what I had just said about Tyron. He'd probably heard it.

"What's the verdict?" Sebastian asked.

I gave a small smile. "I have to wait for her to call back. She's asking my father first," I said, looking at both Tyron and Sebastian.

"Okay," Sebastian replied and looked away from me.

"I'm going to make something to drink while I wait. Are you sure you don't want anything?" I asked, looking at Sebastian.

He smirked and shook his head. I looked at Tyron and he also shook his head. I think he was upset with me. He wanted so badly to do the whole bonding thing and then, of course, Sebastian shows up.

"So, Tyron, how's work going?" I heard Sebastian ask as I walked away from them.

I got some juice out of the fridge and poured myself a glass. I made myself look busy as the two of them spoke. I noticed that Tyron was again not wearing his glasses. He looked better without them on. I took a sip and watched as Sebastian rested his hand firmly on the couch, while he was speaking to Tyron. A small part of me got excited as I thought of this man being interested in me again. I looked down at my orange juice and tried to change my mind; otherwise I was going to screw things up if I over thought.

My phone rang and I picked it up when I saw my mother's name was on the caller ID. "Hey, Mom," I said.

"Yes. So, your father says it's fine as long as you tell the officers outside to accompany you wherever you are going," she said, and the excitement boiled inside me. I tried to remain calm.

"Thank you. You do know that Sebastian is a cop, right?" I said.

"I know. But it doesn't matter what he is, he will be too occupied with you. It's always better to have someone else keeping an eye out while you are busy," she said, and I understood.

"Okay. Thank you, Mom. I appreciate it," I said gleefully.

"Don't thank me, thank your father," she said,

I smiled. "Thank him for me, then. Okay, I love you, bye," I said and at that she said her greetings and we ended the call.

I looked up at Sebastian and smiled, nodding my head. He also returned the smile and rubbed his hands together. "Okay, then. Get something warm because it's cold outside," he said joyfully.

"Okay. My mom asked you just to ask the cop to follow us as we go places. She doesn't want anything happening," I said, and he nodded his head.

"Alright, I'll ask Damen outside," he said, and I smiled. It was very appealing how he knew every cop. He gave me a sense of security. I felt as though I was a cool girl, hanging out with a cop who knew everyone in town. I watched him walk outside and I left to go upstairs to put warm boots and a jacket on.

...

The rain outside was a beautiful soft fall. We had the one officer follow us all the way. Sebastian had given three options on where we could go.

1. His house
2. His cottage house
3. Or any place in town.

I chose his house. It brought back so many memories. I remembered how Sebastian and I had been making out on the couch and how Alex had knocked on the door, very annoyed. The thought made me smile and feel sad at the same time. I was seated on that exact couch as the memories came flooding in. The fire was on, and it felt so nice against my damp skin. The rain didn't stop, and I could imagine how the lake was filling and the streams were overflowing. Sebastian was in the kitchen, making us some hot cocoa.

"So, I wanted to take you somewhere, where it wasn't home, and you didn't feel like you were being watched," he said as he brought the hot cocoa over and handed me a cup. The scent of his cologne brushed past my face, and I calmly breathed it in.

I smiled at him and took the cup. "Thank you," I said, taking the cup and taking a sip. It was the best decision on a rainy cold day. He sat beside me, and my heart skipped a beat and I remembered the last time this had happened. I felt nervous having him so close to me. I tried to distract myself. "So, what was it that you wanted to tell me?" I asked him, and I turned to look at him. He set his cup down and looked past me to the table in the kitchen. I followed his gaze, and then I felt him shift off the couch.

He walked over to the table and picked up documents that I hadn't seen him put there before. "These are the results of Tyron's DNA test," he said as he walked over.

My attention sharpened and I sat up straight. "Yes," I said as he handed me the papers.

"It matches with your DNA," he said, and his words left me speechless. Wow, I guess I hadn't known what to expect exactly. I guess I just felt sorry for judging him so much. I looked up at Sebastian and he watched my emotions carefully.

"I don't know what to say," I said, holding the papers in my hands. I just kept quiet, and he didn't take his eyes off me. "I mean, I feel bad, I guess, for not believing him and also now I hate the fact that it's true because it means that my father did have another woman in his past who he had a child with and I think that hurts me a little, especially knowing that we weren't the only family he has or had," I said, putting the papers down. Sebastian moved in next to me and I sighed.

"Look, like you said, it was in his past. He didn't know about Tyron until this year. I think you've got to give him the benefit of the doubt. I know it isn't nice and it might sting a little, but at least you know the truth now," he said so sincerely.

I looked up at him and nodded my head slowly. "Thank you for going to all this effort to help me out," I said, and he nodded his head.

"Not a problem at all," he said simply.

I kept looking at him and thought about the past nights we had been spending together in his cop car. "Where were you last night? I waited and you never came," I said, feeling a little ashamed that I had revealed so much.

He broke eye contact with me and looked away and I could see he looked sad. "Ahh, nothing. I couldn't make it in the end," he said sadly. I didn't take my eyes off him. He was hiding something.

"Was it family?" I pried. He shook his head and looked at me. His green eyes were dark, and in a way, I found it very alluring.

Unveiling Secrets

"I was suspended until further developments. This whole case has made it difficult for me at my job. They don't want me to spend time with you at all or to see you. I got into trouble for telling the other cops who were looking after your house to go. They said I was being insubordinate. They said it was very irresponsible of me because I was also a target, and I could have risked both your life and mine. So, they suspended me from duty until this whole thing blows over," he said, breaking eye contact with me eventually. I felt so bad for being the reason that he'd got suspended.

"Oh no, I'm so sorry," I said, feeling so sad.

He shook his head. "No, don't be. I wanted to see you," he said quietly. I looked at him and couldn't believe he was saying that.

"But why? It's not worth losing your job over," I said, feeling annoyed with myself and him.

He shook his head. "I didn't lose my job. I'm only not working until they say I can come back. So, it's okay," he said defending himself. "And I don't want anything happening to you, especially after they've taken Alex," he said, looking down and frowning. He still cared about me. It made me smile.

"Don't you think that I'm the problem?" I asked painfully.

He looked up and shook his head. "Why would you think that you're the problem?" he asked.

I looked away from him. "Because, if I just gave myself up, none of you would get hurt," I said looking back at him and his eyes were searching for mine. He had a lot on his mind, I could see it.

"And then you get hurt? It doesn't make sense. The problem is the stalker, and he needs to be dealt with," he said. He sat up and turned away. "Look, I know what you're thinking. You probably want to run away and let the stalker catch you. But let me tell you why I don't think it's a good idea," he said very sternly. I listened as he closed his hands into one another.

"We have no idea what kind of stalker we are dealing with here. He sounds dangerous, as he has taken Alex, and we still haven't been able to recover him. He's been making threats for so long and we did nothing about it. I think you should count your blessings that you are still here with us and, for as long as I can, I'll make sure that he or she does not lay a finger on you," he said, turning his head to look at me. I was intimidated by this serious side of him. He didn't even blink when he said it.

"But what if he takes you too?" I asked sadly.

He gave a small smile. "Don't worry. I can defend myself well enough," he said confidently, and I liked that he was so confident.

"Did you know that on the last day I saw Alex, he said that we were going to be together and that he didn't want anyone else but me," I said painfully, as I thought back to the moment. "We kissed and then next thing I know Ingrid is telling me that they slept together after we'd had that conversation and then he was taken," I said looking down. I could feel my throat burn. "I have so many emotions regarding him. He has always uplifted me and then he has always found a way to make me come crashing down," I rubbed my hands together to try to distract myself from crying.

"I'm sorry, I don't mean to bring him up. It's just that he means so much to me, and the day he said he loved me and that he wanted to start a relationship with me, the stalker kidnapped him, because I didn't listen. I don't want to get close to you and then he takes you too," I said, just imagining the pain.

"Amelia, I have many things I'd like to say about Alexander, but I won't. I think he is an idiot, but that's just my opinion. I can understand why the stalker wanted him out of the picture. If I got annoyed with how Alex treated you at times, I can understand why an obsessed person would too. Look. Like I said before, I am capable of looking after myself. We trained to protect ourselves against anyone who wanted to harm us. We were trained for times like this. Can I just say, I would never treat you the way he did." His eyes were still dark, but they never left mine. So sad, knowing I treated him the way Alex treated me. I felt strange knowing how much he had shared with me.

"But I thought you didn't care about me anymore," I protested, confused by his behavior in the past.

He shook his head and looked away. "I didn't want to show how I felt because I knew you would anyways have chosen Alex," he said with his head down.

I felt sorry for him. He was jealous of Alex, and it was because he knew we had a stronger connection. "That's not true. You should have just kept trying. I did like you," I said, and he looked at me and I could see his eyes were vulnerable.

"I did, and then *he* came and took over, just like he always has. He slept with you and just like that, in one go, he won the battle," he said, and I sat there feeling so bad.

"He didn't win. He kept trying and that's why I leaned more towards him," I said.

He shook his head and looked at me. "You know how it felt when you found out that Alex slept with someone else after you had told him that you loved him? It's a similar feeling to how I felt, after I found out about you two," he said, and I knew he was still bitter about it.

I looked down and felt so ashamed of myself. "I'm truly sorry for that night," I said slowly, making my way over to him. I wanted to touch him in reassurance, but I didn't.

"It's fine. It was a long time ago," he said, not even looking at me anymore. The air felt thick, and I wish we'd never brought the topic up. "Besides, I didn't call you here to speak about this," he said, trying to lighten the mood. I felt happier that he wanted to move past it.

I looked down and had to say it. "Listen, just so you know. I'm so sorry for the way I treated you. It wasn't fair on you, and I know now how it feels. It's horrible and I definitely deserved it. I never should have played you both at once. It's just Alex always had this way of twisting things. I meant what I told you that night, I really did. Alex just didn't want to take no for an answer," I said, shaking my head and looking down.

"You don't have to explain yourself. You chose him and that's fine," he said spitefully.

I frowned and stood up. I felt very frustrated. "Listen, I didn't choose anyone. You are right! I don't need to explain myself. I don't need to explain what actually happened in those photos and that there's more to it than meets the eyes. I just know that I am sorry. I am sorry that I disappointed you. You two anyways needed to stop treating me like I was some kind of prize you could win." I couldn't help but spit the words out in frustration.

I wanted to tell him that I hadn't slept with Alex, but I didn't want to tell him that and find that he then started wanting to have sex with me because I was still a virgin. He looked startled by my behavior. I turned around and wanted to just get out of there. I didn't need this and maybe it was better that we stopped talking. I grabbed my coat that was on the table but, before I could even take two steps towards the door, I felt Sebastian's strong grasp around my wrist. He stopped me and I turned around.

"Amelia, wait," he said, sounding nervous and exhausted. I turned to look up at him and he looked down at me. "I didn't mean to upset you," he said, more softly this time. He let go of my hand. I stood only inches away from him. "I don't want you to go anywhere. I want you to stay," he said again, just more vulnerable.

"Why?" I asked, and he looked away, trying to hide his eyes from me. "Tell me why I should stay, and then maybe I will," I said, feeling a boost of confidence.

He sighed and looked back up at me. "Because, despite everything that has happened, I still care about you. I still want to hear your stories and see you smile every day. I want to know what has bothered you throughout the day and, most importantly, I would like to know that you are safe every day. That would make me happy." He said the words and I felt baffled. I hadn't thought that after all this time and after everything I had said, he would still want me.

"But I don't understand. You looked so happy with Ruby the other day, and she was amazing. Why didn't you want her?" I asked, and he looked as though he was getting frustrated with my questions.

He looked away from me. "Because she wasn't you. None of them have really made an impression on me the way you have," he said, and he was gazing into my eyes. I couldn't help but smile. I felt so honored. I looked to his lips and felt as though this would be the perfect time to give him a kiss. I saw Alex in the back of my mind and felt distracted. I looked down and I felt Sebastian brush his fingers down the side of my face. He moved one of the strands of my hair behind my ear. I smiled at this kind gesture, and I knew he was watching my every move. I placed my hand on his chest and felt my heart burst with warmth. I could feel his muscles underneath his shirt, and I could just imagine running my fingers along his chest. I inhaled deeply and then I looked up. He was smiling down at me, and I returned the gesture.

"Look, I'm trying my best to not kiss you right now," I said, as I felt he put his hand around my waist, and he pulled me in. His breath brushed past my cheeks and I watched as he observed all my facial features. I smiled, closing my eyes as he took his index finger and brushed the other side of my cheek.

"Why not?" he whispered, and I couldn't help but giggle.

Gosh, all my senses screamed yes, but Alex kept popping up in my mind. I opened my eyes and watched how his green eyes were glowing. His eyes were soft on the edges, and he had such an adorable smirk on his face. His finger brushed gently over my lips and then his eyes, in one swift motion, looked into mine. Fire burnt within me and all the reasons to not kiss him right now went out the window. I looked at him with desire and I was certain that all I wanted right now in this moment was his lips.

I looked at his lips and leaned forward. It wasn't even a second and then our lips touched. His lips were so soft against mine. He kissed me with so much passion. His mouth opened gently and closed gently over mine. He pulled me in and there was no space between us now. Every inch of my body felt as though it was vibrating. His kiss felt so complete and full. I didn't want to stop. Our tongues found each other. Electricity coursed through my body. Gosh, how I'd missed his lips. I ran my fingers through his hair. His cologne danced on my skin. I wanted more from him and so did he as his hands loosened from around my waist, and moved up my back. I closed my mouth over his and pulled away. I looked down and placed my forehead on his chest.

"We need to stop. I want to continue, but I want us to take our time," I said into his chest and his hands fell to my hips.

I looked up at him and he nodded his head, while he smiled down at me. He was so beautiful. His lips were so irresistible. I stood on my tippy toes and gave him one last kiss. I made sure to make it a long one, so that I would have something to cherish. It felt so good to know the truth about his feelings. I pulled away from him and placed my head on his chest. He placed his arms around me and in that moment, we stood silently holding each other. It was golden, it was safe.

Chapter 28

ALEXANDER

The cold was unbearable. I had been given one thin blanket to sleep under. The captor gave me something to drink now and again. They wanted me to stay alive, but not let me go. My ankle had scabs from where it was chained. It felt like hell in there. There was never light, just eternal darkness. My body ached from being on the floor for so long. I thought I was in a cave. It would explain the darkness, the sand, the pebbles and the big rock behind me. That was, of course, what I had felt with my hands.

Fear would course through my body when I heard footsteps. I didn't know whether it was the captor or an animal that had just entered into the cave. When the captor visited, he would stay silent, and I always felt as though he were watching me. I would ask questions, but he would hardly reply. Then some days he would ask me about my childhood. I didn't tell him much. Didn't want to involve my family in any other way. He would leave again.

The cave wasn't always so quiet. Sometimes, I could hear bats chirping their way through the cave. I could hear a dripping of water somewhere. I just prayed and hoped that I would never be found by an animal. So, in the time that the captor was away, I moved my hands along the ground and looked for anything sharp. There was mostly sand and small pebbles, which wouldn't help me in this situation. I needed to get myself out of there.

Every time the captor left, I would listen to the steps. He walked forward and then it sounded as though his steps took him left. I needed to remember that for when I was going to escape. The captor hadn't come for what felt like a whole day. I needed something strong to break the chain off and I needed to make it quick before the captor came back.

I moved my hands along the walls and tried to feel for any loose rocks. I tugged and tugged and didn't succeed. I moved myself to the far right and felt for anything that was loose on the ground. I found nothing but small stones again. I felt so defeated and as though I would never see my family again. I stretched a little more forward and found nothing. Just as I was about to give up hope, my fingers moved across something large. The excitement grew inside me. I forced myself forward and felt the pain shoot up my leg. I couldn't help but groan as I clasped the thing on the floor. I managed to grab it. It was heavy and sharp. It felt like a rock.

I groaned some more as I brought it closer to me. I held it close to my body as I felt for the chain on the floor. I moved my hands over it and the cold metal under my hands. I had to be careful not to bash my fingers open. I crossed the leg that was chained, and I tucked the foot away so that only the chain was exposed. I moved the remaining chain so it would be in the middle, in front of me. I held the rock above me and made sure to tuck my fingers in a bit, so I wouldn't hit them in the process. I brought the rock down hard and hit the ground. I didn't hear the metal. I felt again for the metal and felt it was in one piece.

I felt frustrated and I wished that there were a light. Making so much noise put me on edge. I felt as though anything could come and sneak up on me in this moment. I repositioned the chain and lifted the rock and brought it down again, hard. I felt it hit the chain. Relief. I placed the rock down and yanked the chain. It was still attached. I felt along the chain and felt the small dent in the one piece. The frustration followed again as I would have to hit it in exactly the same spot to break the chain. I repositioned it and brought the rock down on it again and felt it yank. I felt the chain and it was still attached. The anger boiled inside me, and I couldn't help but scream out of frustration. Using all this energy was making me tired. I sat there, feeling defeated and exhausted.

Images of my mom reading me my favorite bedtime story flashed through my head. She had always done it, even though she needed to finish a hundred other chores in the house. She always made sure I was well fed. She always listened to all my boring stories. Dad had always played ball with me, and he'd always supported all my dreams and success. I remembered us going on fishing trips. I remembered how proud he was of me when I caught my first fish. I smiled and remembered how good it had felt.

I remembered going out with all my friends and enjoying the best of life. I remembered how Marcus was always there when the women would stuff me around. I remembered Amelia. She was so innocent, so curious. She always had a smile on her face. She always wanted to be involved in our games. She always cared, even when it didn't involve her. She was always beautiful, inside and out.

I missed them all. I missed my mother's chicken and how good it tasted. I missed the barbecues on Saturdays we would have with the family. I felt a tear run down my face. I exhaled and took a deep breath. If I wanted to see them again, I had to try to get out of there. I repositioned the chain again and this time I held the rock up in the air and brought it down and hit it with all the strength I had left it me. I felt the chain yank, and I placed the rock down. I pulled at the chain and felt it was loose. Joy swept through me. I had broken it. I was free.

Chapter 29

HEROIC

I listened to soft acoustic hollow coves music early in the morning. It helped my mind relax. I had no idea where I was and how to feel about life at this point. Sebastian had kissed me last night, which I never thought would happen again, and Alexander was still missing. Guilt swept over my body as I thought of how he would feel knowing I was kissing Sebastian while he was gone. I felt so cheap. I felt as though I had been throwing myself at every man who made himself available to me. I hated it. I hated that Sebastian and I had made up. We weren't supposed to be in this phase. We were supposed to only be friends. Now, all I keep finding myself doing was thinking of him. Thinking of what he was doing.

I would find myself thinking of how we walked up to his room and how we cuddled on the bed, while rain was playing in the background. I had told him my fears and he'd reassured me. Everything was great, but it still felt bad. I still felt guilty, as though I was cheating. I wanted to know that Alexander was safe. That he was alive. My heart ached at the thought.

My mother showed me the news on the TV and how his face was up everywhere. Seeing his face brought tears to my eyes. I missed my best friend. I missed him playing with me and joking around. I missed everything about him. It had been a couple of days now since he had disappeared. He was gone and I was here. I was here in my bed, sleeping under warm covers. I was with my family, while he wasn't. I was okay and, who knows? Maybe he wasn't. I was not held captive, yet he was.

I looked out at my balcony window. I thought of how I could escape without them knowing. The thought petrified me, but I needed Alex back. I needed him to know that I hadn't forgotten about him. I didn't want to be the reason that he was gone, or hurt, yet I was. Maybe, if I offered myself up, the stalker would appear out of nowhere and come and get me. Maybe it would be a fair trade. I didn't want my parents to know. Seeing Alex's face on the news only made it more real to me than ever. He needed my help. I was going to leave my phone just in case they tried to stop me. Sebastian flashed in my mind, and I could only imagine how disappointed he'd be.

Thank goodness Tyron wasn't there. When I had gotten back last night, my mother had said that he had left. I told her I thought he was upset because he'd wanted to spend time with me, and I'd ended up leaving with Sebastian. He hadn't been back since. Maybe it's for the best, so he couldn't stop me when I escaped.

I walked over to my closet and pulled on a jacket. I placed my warmest tights on and slipped on my boots. I tied my hair up in a pony and I felt the rush of butterflies make its way through my tummy. I was nervous about what I was about to do, but maybe I could be the hero this time.

I walked to the balcony window and looked over to make sure there was no one in sight. I climbed over the railing and held on and did another quick check. My heart was beating rapidly. I looked at the distance I had to fall. I had learned that if you had to jump from a high distance, you would have to bend your knees as you hit the ground, to ensure that you didn't break your legs. I knelt down and decided to jump. I had to bite down to make sure I didn't scream. I bent my knees in the process and

I hit the ground like a heavy bag of concrete. My legs pained and I groaned. Maybe this wasn't such a great idea after all.

I had fallen next to the bushes, so I was sure that no one had seen me, except possibly the stalker. Maybe he was too busy with Alex. I sat up and slowly stood up, dusting off my clothes, which were now slightly damp from the wet ground. At least it wasn't raining. I made sure to move my way to the one small tree we had in the garden, and I peered around the corner, making sure there was no one in sight.

I heard as the two cops were talking between themselves, while leaning against the car. The one was smoking, and the other one's back was towards me. So much for looking out for our house. If I were to run towards the forest, the one smoking would see me. I decided to make a diversion. I looked around for a small stone. I found one under the small bush. It was a smooth pebble. I picked it up and walked to the opposite side from where I was standing. I threw it as hard as I could, but it only went as far as the middle of the house. I watched in the distance as I saw a car pull up to the front lawn. I quickly sat down to disguise myself. I didn't recognize the car. Maybe it was one of Tyron's new vehicles. This was my opportunity.

I quickly stood up and ran to the other end of the house. I looked around the corner and saw how the cops weren't standing by the car anymore. I made a run for it. My blood was pumping. I ran as fast as I could. I watched as the trees got nearer and, before I knew it, I had entered into the forest. I hoped they had not seen me. I slowed down and stood against a tree to catch my breath. The air felt thick and humid from yesterday's rain. I watched how the bugs floated around in the air, from the morning light that was breaking through the trees. If it weren't for the light, the forest would be dark, because it was dense.

I decided to think of Alex and how happy he would be if he knew I'd tried to save him. I started walking again. I walked past another tree and over fallen-down logs. I found a pathway, which was nice. I continued and heard the birds tweeting in the background. It was peaceful. The pathway sloped up and then became steep. Thank goodness it wasn't bear season yet. They were in hibernation. I could only imagine how bad it would be if I ran into one. I continued walking and started feeling my nerves kick in. I knew I was alone, and I knew that I was vulnerable. I decided to run so that I knew I wouldn't look like any bait for any animal that was lurking around the forest. I ran as fast as I could and before I knew it the pathway curved sharply around the corner. I took it and came to a halt when I saw that there was a big rock that ended the road. It was like a dead end unless I climbed it.

I presumed that that was what other people had done. I turned around and I could see dark figures in the distance. I didn't feel as confident as I had before. I started to panic as I thought of what a stupid idea this was and how dangerous the situation could get. I was alone and I was the stalker's prey. I wanted to save Alex, but I thought that doing it this way wasn't the best way. I could only imagine how frantic my family would be if they saw I wasn't home and that the cops who were supposed to be looking after me hadn't done their job.

I heard a twig break in the distance and that was enough to send me into a panic. I quickly turned around and started reaching out for the rock. I grabbed any hold I could find, and I started climbing. The rock went high up, and I was intimidated by the height, but I knew that it was better going up than staying down there and being cornered. I thought that the stalker was there with me. Maybe I was wrong, but if he was who he said he was, maybe he was there, watching my every move waiting for me to fail so that he could snatch me up. I kept a good pace and kept gripping different spots on the rock and pulled myself up carefully.

My wrists started aching as I pulled myself up. I put my hand on another rock, and it came loose. I let out a scream and, as my hand slipped, I felt my arm being scratched as I fell down and hit the ground. It was a two-meter fall. A good enough fall to knock the wind out my chest. I gasped for air, but it was difficult to breathe. I took short breaths. My ears were ringing, and I just lay there until I knew I was okay.

My hip hurt, and I reached underneath me and found a small rock underneath me. I closed my eyes and groaned as the pain throbbed in my side. I couldn't help but let out a small cry. I tried to sit up. It hurt. I lifted my shirt and looked underneath it. I could see a big bruise where I had hit it. I could feel my eyes sting as the tears threatened to surface. Luckily, there was no bone sticking out.

I felt my arm burn and realized that my jacket had torn. I looked at it and saw blood. I must have scratched it as my arm slipped. This had been such a bad idea. I wiped my tears and pushed myself up, holding my breath. I couldn't go up the rock. It wasn't safe, so I decided that maybe it was a good idea to try to go back home. Even if it meant I had to fight whatever was out there. I picked up the rock that I had fallen on and held it in my hand for protection.

I heard voices as I was about to walk around the corner. My body tensed up and I looked around to hide away. I quickly made my way behind the tree that was covering the side of the wall. I stood as still as I possibly could. I could feel my heart hammering in my chest. I had not really thought this one through.

The figures appeared from around the corner. I saw the face and recognized the face immediately. It was Lincoln. The man who had harassed Skylar and me at the cottage. I remembered how close he was to me and how I didn't want anything to do with him. He was with another man; I didn't recognize him. They both wore dark pants, with running shoes and long-sleeved jackets. I didn't want to move a muscle. It looked as though Lincoln had let his hair grow out, making it look like a mop of dark brown hair. They were talking to each other about a race that they soon wanted to join. Lincoln challenged his friend, to see who would be the first to climb up the wall. I watched as they approached the wall, and I could feel my breath escaping very slowly from my lips as I remained silent.

"Alright, wait you little shit, let me first tie my shoes. Then we can start," Lincoln said. He knelt and started tying his shoe. I watched as he stopped the process and frowned. Did he know I was there? My body started going cold. He moved a bit closer to the ground and looked up at his friend.

"What is it, bro?" he asked, confused by Lincoln's behavior.

Lincoln pointed to the ground. "Look, it's blood," he said and then I watched as he touched it with his finger. "And it's fresh."

I started to panic. Everything inside me wished I hadn't made this stupid decision. I should have looked when I fell. I hadn't realized that I had dropped some blood from my wound. I tried to slowly move myself further into the tree. I watched as Lincoln scanned the area, and so did his friend. He looked the other way slowly and then back again. He scanned over the tree quickly and he looked away. Just when I thought I was safe, I watched as he looked back at the tree, the one where I was standing, and I thought that he had seen something that triggered his attention. He kept looking at the tree and I was paralyzed with fear.

He took a step closer and squinted his eyes. "Well, well, if it isn't the pretty girl," he said, giving me a smirk as he edged closer.

I knew nothing else but to run. I turned around quickly and squeezed myself past the branch. I came out the other side and I tried my best to get away, but he was faster. He grabbed my arm and yanked me towards him. I couldn't help but give out a pain-filled moan as I knocked into him.

"What are you doing out here, all by yourself?" he asked, looking down at me. By now he had both my hands in his grasp and I couldn't get free.

"Let me go, or I will scream," I demanded.

"Lincoln, come on man. Just let her go. We don't need this drama," his friend said. The friend started stepping closer.

"Stay away, Teagan. Don't get involved," Lincoln said angrily. He looked down at me and I could see his eyes filled with lust. Fear gripped my heart. I tried to yank my arms out of his grip, but I was too weak, and my arm hurt when I did it. I couldn't help but feel overwhelmed.

"Don't cry, I won't hurt you," Lincoln said, but I could feel tears burning my eyes.

"Let me go!" I screamed it as loudly as I could. There was only one thing to do to get out of the grip. I bent down and bit his arm. He screamed and let go of my hands immediately. I fell back and turned around and tried to scramble away.

"You bitch! You're going to pay for that!" he shouted. I tried to stand up, but it wasn't long before he had reached me. I knew I was in trouble. He had pinned me to the ground on my tummy and I couldn't move anywhere. I screamed.

"Get off of her, now!" I heard a familiar voice saying. I felt Lincoln let go of me.

"Alright man, take it easy," I heard Lincoln saying as he stepped off me.

I managed to push myself off the ground and I turned to look to see who was there. Sebastian. Relief came over me. I ran over to him. He was standing in the middle of the pathway with his gun in hand, and it was pointed at Lincoln. His eyes fell on me as I ran over, and I could see how angry he had become. I felt ashamed. I stood behind him and felt so secure. He was like a pillar. I looked around the corner to see Lincoln holding his hands up in the air.

"Look man, I wasn't going to hurt her," Lincoln said, a small smile forming on his face.

"Yeah, shut up. I know exactly what you wanted. Get down on your knees. I'm placing you under arrest for assault and harassment," he said to Lincoln. Lincoln gasped and shook his head.

"Like shit I'm doing that, I didn't even do anything. She's fine," he said, not even lifting his hands anymore.

"I'm not asking you. I'm telling, get down or I will shoot you down," Sebastian said with so much authority. It was very intimidating. Lincoln refused to listen, and Sebastian shot the ground next to him. It gave all of us a fright. I jumped. I could feel the tears forming again. I was afraid, and all I wanted to do was go home.

Lincoln didn't take any more chances. He knelt down to the ground, and so did his friend. "Stay here," Sebastian said sternly to me, and he walked over to Lincoln. He walked around Lincoln's back and pushed him to the ground with his foot.

Lincoln crashed into the ground and cussed some more. "So uncalled for," he said angrily as he lay on the floor. Sebastian knelt down and pushed his knee into Lincoln's back. Lincoln moaned and groaned. "I don't deserve this. I'm going to report you," Lincoln shouted in frustration.

"Do what you like, buddy. I've wanted a reason to lock you up and now I have two," he said as he held his head against the ground.

Sebastian didn't have cuffs with him. The friend just watched as his friend was being arrested. Sebastian took his gun and moved it closer to his head. I was worried at this point. He raised the gun, I watched in slow-motion as he said, "If you ever lay your hands on Amelia again, this will be the last thing you hear," and with that he hit him with the bottom of his gun, and I watched how Lincoln's body fell still and he became unconscious. His friend held up his hands as Sebastian stepped off Lincoln. I was made uncomfortable by the situation. Sebastian looked at the friend and told the friend to also get on his knees.

"What's going on here?" I heard the officers running from around the corner.

Sebastian pointed to Lincoln and then to me. "This man was assaulting and harassing Amelia. There has been more than one occasion when he has done this to women," he said and I saw his jaw tense. The two officers looked at me and they were both frowning. The blond officer looked back at Sebastian.

"Did you fire your firearm?" he asked concerned.

Sebastian nodded his head. "Yes, as a warning shot. He didn't want to listen to me. So, I had to do what had to be done. I didn't shoot him. I knocked him out. He was resisting, so it's better this way," he said shrugging his shoulders. "You should take Lincoln to the cell for the night and file the charges against him. He needs to be locked up. Who knows what would have happened to Amelia if I hadn't followed her," he said, forcing the words out his mouth like they were hard to say. He didn't look at me once. I looked down and felt ashamed.

"Are you alright?" the officer who was standing next to the blond officer asked me. I looked up and nodded my head. How had this turned so bad? I wanted to hide away. "Did he do *that*?" he asked, pointing at my blood-stained sleeve.

I looked down and saw how it had torn from the fall. "No. That happened as I was climbing the cliff. There was a loose rock and I fell," I said, remembering how painful it had been when I'd hit the ground and had lost my breath.

"Right, okay. Why didn't you let us know that you were going for a walk?" The blond officer asked.

I looked down as all four men looked at me. Here goes nothing. "I don't know, I thought maybe if I took myself away from everyone I loved, they would be safe. And if I went where the stalker could find me, he would bring back Alexander and take me instead," I said, ashamed.

I watched as Sebastian looked away and shook his head slightly. He was angry at me.

"Very heroic, but very foolish. You shouldn't risk your life. We could lose two people, while we're trying to gain one. Don't do that again," I heard the blond officer say. I just nodded my head quietly.

"Take her back home, Sebastian. We'll take care of Lincoln and his friend," the other cop said.

"False alarm. All clear, we found Amelia. She is fine and Sebastian will be taking her back home," I heard one of the officers saying into his radio, which was attached his uniform. I hadn't realized I would cause such a scene.

"I didn't do anything, I swear," Lincoln's friend said, panicking.

"His not lying; he tried to stop Lincoln," I said in his defense.

The two officers quietly looked at him and nodded their heads. "All the same, he was part of the incident, so he at least has to sign as a witness," said one of the officers. I nodded my head.

Sebastian walked up to me, not making much eye contact with me. I could see he was upset. "Come, let's go." His voice sounded exhausted. I didn't protest. I followed, as he took the lead. If I had known it was going to escalate in this manner, I would have thought twice about it.

Sebastian was very quiet. The birds that had once sounded peaceful, didn't anymore. The whole mood had shifted. I was just very grateful that he had followed me and saved me. He always seemed to be doing that. He occasionally turned his head, to make sure I was still following him. He was mad at me, and I didn't blame him. We walked and walked. We passed many trees and stumps on our way. I couldn't even remember having passed so many. The earth was damp, and the air was humid. I couldn't wait to get out of the forest and get back home. We saw the opening, which led its way to my house. As we reached it, I pushed past branches and stepped over the log that was in the way. I could feel my hip ache as I lifted my leg. I sucked in my breath. I didn't realize I had done it louder than I would have wanted. Sebastian stopped and turned to see what I was doing. I tried to cover it up.

"What's the matter?" he asked sternly. I shook my head. His green eyes were dark. He frowned at me and looked away. He continued walking and I followed him like a lost puppy. We crossed the street, and we started onto my back lawn.

"How did you know I was gone?" I asked him curiously.

He gave a sigh. "I came to visit, and I saw that you weren't there. I saw that your balcony door was left open. When I went outside to look, I could see the evidence, where either you were pushed or you had jumped onto the soil. So, I decided to follow the tracks, which wasn't easy, and eventually, when I entered the forest I walked further in. I heard voices," he said, walking past my house, to his car. I looked from my house to the car.

"So, now what? You're just going to leave me here?" I asked, feeling defeated and upset. He reached his car. It was the car I hadn't recognized earlier.

He turned and looked at me. "Not just yet. I'll wait for the other back up to come and then I'll leave," he said. His hair was washed and combed straight. He had a brown jacket on with his dark jeans. His eye color stood out more with the brown jacket.

I nodded my head and crossed my arms over my chest in frustration. "Why? Why are you going to leave me here?" I said the words desperately. I'm sure I must have looked vulnerable because he looked away and sighed.

"You've really done it, Amelia, risking your life to save Alexander. What kind of bullshit is that? He isn't with the stalker anymore. They have found him; he is safe. So, you doing your heroic scene would have caused us to go on another man hunt, just because you wanted to save the day." He spat the words out but all I could hear was that they had found him, and Alex was safe.

"Did you just say that Alex is safe?" I asked him despite everything else he had said. He looked at me and I could see he was getting even more upset because I was joyful over Alex.

His jawline tensed and it looked so attractive. "Yes, he is safe. We can't see him. He is in protective custody at the moment, and the family asked that no one visits until he has properly recovered," he said, watching my every emotion. I couldn't help but smile.

"Thank God. What about the stalker? Did they find him?" I asked, dropping my smile and instantly becoming serious.

He shook his head and looked away from me. He leaned his body against his car, and he folded his arms across his chest. "No, I don't know all the details. I just know that my one buddy phoned me to tell me the good news. He said we needed to keep you safe," he said, finally looking back at me. His eyes were hazy. I couldn't read them.

"So, are you sure they won't allow us to go and see him?" I asked, feeling hopeful. I wondered what had happened to him. How he had gotten out. If he had seen the stalker's face. If he had got hurt. I wanted to know the whole story and, most importantly, I wanted to say I was sorry. I watched as Sebastian pushed himself off his car and shook his head.

"No, they said no visitors. So, I guess you can wait for him to say when he wants to talk to you," he said, turning away from me and opening his door. I could sense that he was jealous again. I walked over to Sebastian. I grabbed his hand before he was about to climb into his car. He turned to me, and he looked down at me, making me feel so small. This Sebastian reminded me of the very first time I met him, when he was so self-guarded and not open and welcoming.

"I'm sorry. I didn't think how this would upset you. I don't mean anything by wanting to see him. I'm just happy that I wasn't the reason he was killed or anything. I'm happy he is safe and sound. I just wanted to know what he experienced, that's all. I don't want him like that. I just wanted to hear his story," I said quietly, reassuring him.

He looked up and watched our surroundings and sighed. "I know, I'm sorry. It's a lot, Amelia. You don't understand what we're dealing with. We don't even know yet. You can't just run off into the forest and want to be kidnapped, while there are people who care about you," he said, trying to be calm. I nodded my head as I tried to avoid eye contact with him, while playing with a piece of his jacket.

"I'm sorry," I said softly and this time I decided to look up and his eyes were a lot calmer than before. He didn't say anything but just kept staring at me. I watched as he lifted his hand and touched my cheek where my face had been pushed into the ground by Lincoln.

"I'm sorry you had to deal with Lincoln," he tried to reassure me.

I looked down and sighed. "I'm just glad you came when you did," I said, remembering how trapped I felt and scared.

"How did *he* even find you?" Sebastian asked curiously. I shrugged my shoulders.

"It's like Alexander said, the darkness always finds its way to me somehow. It's just my luck that I had bumped into him at the forest" I said shaking my head.

"What bullshit is Alexander telling you? You are not what you attract. Darkness doesn't follow you, it's just bad timing. That's my opinion," he said, frowning and shaking his head.

I wished in a way that I had never come back. Everything would have been so much better. I never would have had to deal with all of this drama. I remembered how Lincoln had looked at me with so much desire and all I could feel was violated. I was tired of always being the target. I felt so overwhelmed and, before I knew it, I could feel a tear drop running down my cheek. Sebastian wiped it away before I could. He pulled me into a hug, and it felt good. It felt full and secure, like no one could break us apart. I could hear voices in the distance behind us. The officers were coming back from the forest. I didn't look; I just kept holding onto Sebastian.

"You deserve so much better than this, Amelia." He whispered the words to me, while he rested his head on mine. I breathed in his cologne and held on to the moment a little longer. He pulled away from me and looked into my eyes. "Let's go to my place to get you cleaned up. I don't want your parents to see you like this. I'll phone your dad with the news and tell him not to worry, that I'll bring you back. I'll get one of the officers to follow us back to my place, just so that it's a little safer," he said as he let go of me.

I nodded my head. Anything to get me away from this place and my situation. Alex was safe and I knew that he wasn't in harm's way anymore. I felt a hundred times lighter. I held onto Sebastian's hand as he walked around the car to the passenger door. He opened it and I climbed in. What a turn of events.

Chapter 30

BOUND
———————

Sebastian had spoken to my father. He had explained the matter in a good way. He'd explained to him that he would take me to his house and keep an eye on me for the day and he would bring me home later. My father seemed to trust him. I could understand why.

Dad had to go into the office that day; Thursdays were those kinds of days. Mom was somewhere, and I had no idea where Tyron was. He was still quiet. Marcus was still away, studying like he should be. Mom and Dad had told him to stay and focus on that and not to worry about what was happening at home. I was sure that they had not told him everything, though, because if I knew Marcus he wouldn't have taken the situation lightly. Especially knowing that his best friend Alexander had been kidnapped. He would have been on the next flight out this way. Mom and Dad didn't want to worry him, so they kept it secret from him.

We had been at Sebastian's house for about fifteen minutes. Sebastian had made me hot tea, to help calm my nerves and emotions down. He had packed wood in the fireplace, and he had lit it. I watched as the wood slowly started catching alight. There was soft music playing in the background. He had taken his brown jacket off. He had on a white long-sleeved V-neck shirt on. He had pulled up his sleeves when he was handling the wood. I admired every twirl of tattoo that was sticking out from beneath his shirt. His silence always made me feel so uneasy, but also very intrigued. I never knew what he was thinking. He was a man full of thoughts.

"Alright, now that the fire's done, let's get your arm checked and everything," he said, stepping up and moving away from the fire and dusting his hands off.

He said it simply and I set my cup down on the table in front of me. I sat up and pushed myself off the couch that I was sitting on. The pain in my hip pulsed at my movement. Since the fall, I hadn't looked at it to see how bad it was. Sebastian was with me, and I didn't want to upset him anymore. I tried to calm my face. His eyes were back to the forest green color I knew them to be. He watched me as I walked towards him, and I looked down out of nervousness.

"We can go upstairs. That's where everything is," he said pointing at the staircase.

I got nervous thinking about me lifting my legs and using stomach muscles, which would affect my hip. "Okay," I said softly.

He looked away and took my hands in his, which sent butterflies to my stomach. He moved his way gracefully to the staircase and stopped before he went up and he gestured for me to go first. I gave a weak smile. Standing so close to him as he towered over me made me feel intimidated and so attracted to him at the same time. I looked away from him and touched the railing. I pulled myself up the first step and felt the sting in my hip. I kept quiet. Good, he hadn't noticed. I went up another step and then another. Before I knew it, I was almost at the top. I watched how the other floor started to appear.

"Did you hurt yourself somewhere else?' Sebastian asked from behind me.

I tried to pull myself up another step. "Just a little, on my hip," I said quietly.

He remained quiet for a few seconds. "Did you hurt it in the fall?" he asked curiously.

I reached the top of the staircase, and I couldn't have been happier. I turned around to face him when we were both upstairs. "Yes, I fell on the rock that made me slip in the first place. It came out of the wall while I was climbing up and I fell," I said, looking at him.

He looked down at my hip. "Can I see?" he asked, and I nodded, nervous to see myself. He lifted my shirt and he frowned.

He bent down to look further at it. "Amelia, this bad," he said, reaching his fingers out to touch it.

"Careful, it's sensitive," I said. His fingers grazed over my skin lightly and I tensed at his touch. It felt good to show him my skin. It was the second time now that he had seen my stomach and where he was touching me felt so intimate. I looked down at my hip and it was already bruised and red. The skin was a little grazed, where the rock hit it, but it wasn't a big cut. He stood up and looked down at me.

"Thank goodness you didn't hit your head on the rock," he said, worried. I nodded my head and pulled my shirt down. He looked at his bathroom and then back at me. "I think you should shower, to get everything clean, and then we'll disinfect the wounds afterwards," he said, pointing at his shower.

I nodded my head. It was a very personal thing to do. One thing I could say about Sebastian was that I trusted him. I knew that he wouldn't just barge in while I was showering. He was a gentleman and he always wanted the best thing for me.

"Okay, but no peeking, okay?" I said playfully, and he gave me a small smile. He shook his head at me and walked over to the bathroom. I followed.

"I won't peek, don't worry," he said, looking under the bathroom sink for more towels. He gave me a clean pair and I smiled at him.

"Thank you," I said, and he nodded his head.

"I'll be downstairs. You can take as long as you want. You are safe here," he said again, especially emphasizing the words "you are safe here".

I smiled at him. "Thank you," I said, smiling at him again.

"I'll leave a clean set of clothes outside for you. So, when you're done showering you can just put the clean clothes on," he said, and I nodded my head. I closed the door as I watched him turn away.

I had never thought that I'd be here, showering in his shower. I honestly hadn't thought that we would ever get into a relationship again after what had happened between us. I locked the door just in case something dramatic happened, like Sebastian got shot and I was up there naked, being live bait for my stalker.

I walked over to the shower and turned it on, closing the door while I waited for the water to get warm. I lifted my arms, feeling my body ache as I pulled the jacket off, and then the shirt, and then the rest of my clothes. I climbed into the shower and felt the wounds burn as the warm water hit them. I groaned in pain and closed my eyes and waited for the sting to subside. I washed my body and, after I was done, I turned the water off.

I climbed out and wrapped the towel around me. I walked over to the mirror and wiped it, so I could see how I looked. I could see a small bruise on my face from where Lincoln must have pushed my face into the ground. Gosh, what a day. I slipped my underwear on and kept the towel on over the underwear. Hopefully, he wouldn't think I was weird. A part of me felt slightly okay with the idea of us sleeping together. I opened the door and felt the cold hit me. It was way too cold for this.

"Sebastian, I'm done," I said a little too loudly.

"On my way," I heard him saying from downstairs.

I quickly went back into the bathroom to pick my clothes up and I could hear him walking back up. He was standing by the bed when I walked out. His eyes immediately fell to my body, and he tried to look away.

"Uhm, there are the clothes," he said nervously, pointing to the neatly folded outfit.

I couldn't help but giggle. "I thought it would be easier to put the ointment on first and then I would get dressed. Don't worry, it's okay," I said as I set my clothes down on the side of the bed. I walked over to him, and he still didn't look at me. "Sebastian, really. It's fine," I said smiling. I was standing in front of him, and he had the medical kit in his hand. He turned to me, and I couldn't hide the smile on my face. Such a big guy, being such a gentleman. His eyes fell to the towel that was around my body and he closed his eyes again.

I laughed. "Stop being so silly. I'm not the first woman you're seeing half naked," I said playfully, and he opened his eyes, looking to the side.

"Yes, but that's not the point. I don't think you know how beautiful you actually are," he said. Butterflies fluttered around my stomach.

I reached forward and lifted his chin and made him look at me. "It's okay, you can look. I won't bite," I said smiling, and he gave a smile back. I felt very drawn to him, especially knowing the circumstances we were in.

I could see how nervous he was becoming. He gestured for me to sit on the bed. So, I walked over to it and sat down, making sure nothing opened up. He sat next to me, and I watched how nicely he dipped the ointment onto the cotton wool. I lifted my arm for him, so that he could dab it on for me. I was completely capable of doing this on my own, but I liked knowing that he wanted to help me. He dabbed the cotton onto my wound, and I tensed.

"I'm sorry," he said, as he looked up to me and continued dabbing. I shook my head.

"It's okay."

It was burning, but it was a good burn. It was a small scrape but enough to bleed out onto my sleeve. I was sure that if I had not had long sleeves on, it would have been worse. He held my hand to help lift it. I felt so intimate in this moment.

"So, why did you want to climb the rock?" he asked curiously.

Out of shame I rubbed my face with my free hand and sighed. "Gosh, I don't know. I heard a noise, and I thought the stalker was close, so last minute I changed my mind and tried to make an escape, and the only escape was to climb up the cliff," I said, thinking about it.

I didn't even notice how he had stopped dabbing to listen to my story. His eyes were soft on the edges, and he was calm. His eyes seemed to have changed to a slightly warmer green. I don't know if it was because he was comfortable, or happy. I couldn't tell. I hadn't seen all his sides yet. I caught myself staring for a bit too long into his eyes and I was the first one to break eye contact. I couldn't help but smile.

"Uhm," he said, clearing his throat, "I'm sorry you got hurt. I'm thankful it wasn't worse," he said again, letting my hand go. I could feel the absence as I rested it back on my lap.

"It's fine. I'm just glad you were there. Thank you," I said again, playing with the material of the towel. "I probably look like such a mess. I don't know why you'd want to be involved with this chaotic life of mine," I said, feeling vulnerable.

"I like chaotic. That's why I became a cop," he said, giving me a small smirk. He was damn attractive, and all I wanted to do was kiss him. He had the typical bad boy smirk with the eyes that could easily make you feel weak with one look.

"Watching you operate today was quite interesting," I said, watching him. He rolled his eyes and smiled looking away.

"I'm sorry you had to see that. I know that you don't like violence, but if I could have I would have done worse to Lincoln. He had it coming," he said, not looking at me. I could see he was thinking of something.

"I know, but he will get his punishment," I said, trying to help get the mood back to where it had been before. "You surprise me because when I met you, you were calm and collected and didn't want to talk to me and the next minute you were protecting me and caring about me. You're a ball full of emotions," I said, watching how he was listening but not saying much.

He looked down and shook his head lightly. "Well, the only reason why I didn't want to talk to you was because you are so beautiful, and you already had so much attention on you. Alex liked you, another man liked you, your stalker, all of the above. I didn't want to feel the feelings I felt for you. But I couldn't stop them from coming anyways," he said, finally looking at me. I could feel my cheeks flush a little.

"I didn't want to like you either, because you are a player. Just like Alex. That's why I didn't want to give into Alex and his tricks," I said, and I could see I had said something wrong.

He shook his head and frowned. "I'm nothing like him," he said, offended.

I hadn't meant it like that. "No, you aren't. You're right. You are much better and kinder. You are very attractive and you're a gentleman. You accept it when I feel uncomfortable, and you will try to make me happy. Most importantly, you make me feel safe and I like that. I feel safe with you, and I feel like I can trust. I don't always feel like that with Alex," I said, and it felt good to admit.

I watched how his eyes had softened again and he looked at me. He smiled and damn, his smile was beautiful. It was pure. I looked at his lips and I knew that he knew what I wanted to do. I leaned forward and he did the same. My heart was beating faster. His face was only inches away from mine. I pressed my lips softly against his. It felt so smooth and comforting. I kissed him softly and held the kiss and then I pulled away, leaving him wanting more.

"Come here," he said quietly. He reached his hand out and hooked it behind my neck and he gently pulled me in for another kiss. He opened his mouth over mine, and the instant our tongues met I could feel the fire burning in my stomach. My butterflies weren't flying anymore; they were on fire from the electricity that was pulsing through my body. I could feel he had missed me. His kisses became stronger as they went on. His lips crashed upon mine, and I love it. I wanted to explore more of him. I moved my hand under his shirt, and I could feel his muscles tense.

He pulled away. "Amelia," he said with a small chuckle. "You are very irresistible at this moment..." he said, looking down and trying to catch his breath. I smiled and wanted to tempt him more. "But I think it's better if we stop. I don't want to make you uncomfortable, and right now you're very vulnerable. So, to save us both, I think we should stop, and you should put some clothes on, because I can't..." he said, holding up his hands and smiling at me. His eyes fell to my towel again and I couldn't help but giggle. He wanted me, just like I wanted him. I pushed myself off the bed and stood in front of him. He knew what I wanted to do. My heart was pounding in my chest, but I so badly wanted to know what "it" felt like. He was looking and me.

"Sebastian, I am comfortable with you and if I were to give any man my innocence, it would be you." I said it confidently, hoping he wouldn't break my confidence. I stepped forward, trying to get closer to him and I watched as he pieced the pieces together in his mind.

"So, you didn't sleep with..." I interrupted him, by shaking my head, still smiling. I've never seen a man as happy as he was at that moment.

"I didn't want to. He didn't deserve it," I said.

Before I knew it, Sebastian had stood up and was smiling at me. He leaned down and placed his lips on mine again. I moved my hands under his shirt. Feeling how soft his skin was under my touch was so blissful. I moved my hands higher, and he pulled away and in one swift motion he pulled his shirt off over his head. I stood in awe at how beautiful his skin looked and how attractive the tattoos made it look. He was much fitter than the last time we had been together. Everything was nicely shaped. He let me run my finger over his chest and I could feel him watching me. He was irresistible. I leaned forward and placed a kiss on his chest, and I slowly moved it up his neck, breathing every bit of him while I did it.

"What about your hip?" he asked, as I placed another kiss on his neck. His cologne made me want to devour him.

"Don't worry about it. We should just be careful," I said, pulling away from him, smiling.

Unveiling Secrets

He nodded his head. "Okay, I'll try," he said.

He moved me gently towards the bed and I understood what he meant. I climbed on, ignoring the sting on my side. When I was completely on the bed, he smiled at me and joined me, kneeling in front of me. He reached for the towel and looked up at my eyes, to sense any judgment or insecurity, and when he saw I wasn't showing any uncomfortable emotions, he opened the towel slowly. I had my pink underwear on. It wasn't lace or anything, but it did at least match. He gracefully slipped his hand under me and lifted me gently higher up the bed so that I could rest my head on the pillows. I watched how he admired my body. He took his finger and, starting from the bottom of my leg, he ran it all the way up to my thigh. I felt goosebumps rise everywhere on my skin and I couldn't help but smile and feel weak with desire.

"I love your smile," he said, as he leaned down to give me a kiss. He pulled away and kissed me on the cheek and then on my jaw and then he moved down to my neck, which made me giggle and I could hear that he loved it.

"It's ticklish," I said, holding onto his broad shoulders.

He moved his kiss down to my collarbone and I could feel my heart racing. I was actually going to do this. He moved his hand under my back and unclipped my bra, slowly pulling it off. I was impressed. I didn't let the thought linger too long; I didn't want to think about how he did it so easily. I watched as he looked at me with so much love and desire. I didn't know whether to hide my breasts from him or to let him look.

"You're so beautiful," he said, making eye contact with me, and I gave him a shy smile.

"Thank you."

At that, he leaned down and kissed my breasts, sending warmth through my body. He handled me with such care and gentleness. I missed his lips, so I pulled his face back up and our lips crashed upon one another. Our tongues intertwined. He pulled away, removed all his clothing and I felt my cheeks flush as I admired him. He leaned forward and pulled my underwear gently off, so he wouldn't hurt my hip. This was it. The big moment everyone always spoke about. I could feel the adrenaline pulling through me at this moment. His pupils were dilated, which only made his eyes more alluring. He moved in between my legs and, before he did anything, our faces were inches away and he looked me in the eyes.

"Are you sure, you are okay with this?" he asked, trying to comfort me. I nodded my head.

He moved further between my legs. I gripped his shoulders, and he planted a kiss on my neck. I felt the pain spread and I moaned. He moved his face above mine and kissed my lips, trying to comfort me. Even though it was painful, it still felt gentle. I knew now that this moment we shared was something beautiful and special. He was gentle and caring. Feelings of love burst inside me, and I don't think I have ever felt so passionate about anyone. The more he moved back and forth, the easier it felt and the more comfortable I started feeling. I thought I loved him. He placed another kiss on my neck as his whole body tensed up. I was more attracted to him now than I had ever been. I trusted him with everything inside me.

We were bound together and I couldn't have been happier.

Chapter 31

SKYLAR

It was late at night and Cole still hadn't come home. He'd left early that morning and told me that he needed to get something done. I was worried about him. I could see something was bothering him and to top it off he didn't really want to talk about it. He was acting very strangely. His temper had become short and he always seemed to be distracted when we were together. Maybe he was beginning to feel like he needed a break from me? I had been sleeping at his place for the past month already. He'd allowed me to use everything in the house, which was nice. I didn't really want to go back home to my mother. She was always so controlling.

Cole would have nightmares at night, where he would ask the person to stop, and would say that he didn't want to hurt anyone. I would wake him, and he would be very disorientated. I'd ask him what it was about, and he'd say he didn't remember, but I knew he was lying. He was keeping secrets from me, and I knew because he told me one day that, if he were to share all his secrets with me, I would never look at him the same again. He was a case that I couldn't quite solve. It always made me insecure about everything. About whether he still loved me, or if he had cheated on me. Some days, I just didn't want to think about it. That day was one of those days, especially since he had been gone for so long and had still not come home. Where was he?

I tried to distract myself by thinking of Amelia. I hadn't spoken to Amelia in a while. She was on my mind, but I didn't really want to get involved. I didn't want to also get kidnapped by the stalker for getting close to her and I also just didn't know how to handle the situation with Alex being gone. All of it was too much and, call me a bad friend if you want, I was just too afraid of the unknown.

Last time I had seen her, she'd told me that she had gotten closer to Sebastian. She'd said that he was looking after her house at night, making sure the stalker wouldn't come over. To be honest, I had always envied her for always getting all the attention. She was beautiful, but I hated how the men practically died over her. I'm glad she never knew about Sebastian and me. We had hooked up once, and I'd wanted to start something with him, but he was definitely not interested. Kind a sucks when you see your best friend has him falling for her. I'm sure he hadn't told her either, but to be honest it was more of a one-night stand kind of thing and he just pretended like it never happened, so I guess I did the same thing. It isn't awkward unless you make it awkward, right?

Don't even get me started on Alex. Alex had always been this hot mess. He always messed every girl around and always, of course, Amelia was his favorite. There were many times that I wanted to be like her. Her mysterious personality. She always looked like a plain Jane, but she rocked the plain Jane look. She was different and didn't want the attention, like all the other girls wanted.

I was happy when I found Cole. He was attractive, and he was mine and I was so glad that she never caught his attention. That was why I didn't want to get involved. It would be better if I was just not in the picture, especially since we didn't even know if the stalker would be knocking on our doors at night or not. The whole story was just messed up.

It was night-time and the stars were nowhere to be seen. I was sitting outside in the hot tub. Cole had a cat, called Daisy. She was a ginger cat, and she liked being around people and keeping them company. She sat with me as I sipped a glass of wine and now and again she would meow, to let me know that she was still there. I looked around the patio and started to feel uneasy. I didn't like always being home by myself when Cole was gone.

My phone pinged. I put down my glass of wine and I picked my phone up. It was a message from Amelia. *I slept with Sebastian!* I read. It was enough to get me to sit up and squeal. Yes, I was happy for her in the end, because now finally she had lost her virginity.

I replied: *Gurl, well done! I'm happy for you! Where did it happen and when?*

It wasn't long before she responded: *At his house, today. It's definitely nothing like the movies show you. But it was still nice. I trust him with my whole heart, especially now.*

I didn't know what to say about that. I remembered how I felt after sleeping with him and sharing a couple of kisses. He was great, but he was only interested in one thing at the time. Maybe it had been different this time round with her?

She sent another message: *Oh, and they found Alexander. He is safe and sound. I'm so relieved.*

Joy filled my heart. That was good news at least. I replied: *What about the stalker? Did they find him?*

No, unfortunately not. He is still on the loose...

That message sent a cold shiver down my back. I looked around me and didn't feel safe outside anymore. Before standing up, I sent her a message: *Amelia, stay safe. Until he is caught, you are still vulnerable. You need to stay safe!*

At that I stood up and called Daisy inside with me. I was so cold. I wrapped the towel around my body and walked inside, closing the door behind me. Inside, the house was warmer. Cole's housekeeper had made a fire for us.

"Bethany, would you please make me some hot cocoa?" I shouted as I dried myself off.

She came around the corner and smiled. "Yes, dear," she said in her strong British accent. And off she went to the kitchen.

She was older than me for sure. Maybe late forties? She wore her brown hair up in a bun, to be more productive. She had gloves on at all times; I don't think I ever saw her hands. Her eyes were gray and her skin was pale. I was sure that she had been stunning, once upon a time. She wore red lipstick and a coat to keep warm, while she tidied the house. I made sure to lock the door behind me, just in case I was next on the stalker's list.

I pulled on my robe and walked over to the piano, which was in the living room. I opened it up and ran my fingers along the keys, remembering how my father had taught me all that he knew. I pressed a key and felt the instant pull to play more keys. I started playing at the keys and I felt how everything inside me, the stress and anxiety, started easing up. There was something about music that really helped people escape. Something out of this world.

"Very beautiful," her strong accent, made me jump. I held my heart and gave a small laugh. "Sorry, I didn't mean to scare you."

I looked away from her and waved my hand. "No, no. When I play, I get into this trance, and you just startled me. It's okay," I said smiling, and she handed me the hot cocoa.

"Okay, here you go, dear," she said smiling and I took the cup from her.

"Thank you." I gave her a small smile.

"Only a pleasure. Let me not disturb you. I'll be heading to the back now, okay? If you need anything, just shout and I'll be here," she said, smiling as she looked me in the eyes. I nodded my head.

"I understand. Thank you for everything," I said, taking a sip of the cocoa. She squeezed my arm and turned around.

I watched as she walked through the passage and turned down the hall. I didn't hear her footsteps anymore and I figured she had walked outside to her small cottage. I heard a ding in the distance and picked my phone up, just to make sure it wasn't that. There were no notifications on my phone. I looked up, frowning. Unless it was Bethany's phone that had gone off? I looked for Daisy, but she wasn't anywhere to be seen.

I stood up. "Bethany, was that your phone?" I raised my voice, hoping she'd answer, but she didn't.

I decided to walk down the step leading to the piano. I walked to the middle of the living room. Cole had an open plan bottom floor. I heard the ping again and decided to build enough confidence to check it out. It sounded as though it was coming from the study. I walked down the dark hall. I felt on edge, as I thought, what if the stalker was there? I came to the door to the left, which was slightly open. I pushed it further open slowly and switched the light on. I jumped when I saw Cole sitting in the dark at his laptop. He squeezed his eyes shut from the bright light. When had he gotten home?

"Babe, the light," he said, shielding his eyes from the light.

I folded my arms over my chest and shook my head at him. "When did you get home? Why didn't you come and say hello? Here I was thinking Amelia's stalker was here to come and get me next," I said, annoyed. He gave a small chuckle and shut his laptop. "Who were you talking to anyways?" I asked, pointing at his laptop. He looked over at his laptop and shook his head, quickly looking away. There was something he was hiding, and I needed to find out.

"Why all the questions? I did say hello, you just didn't hear me. I came in about a half an hour ago," he said, looking at me. He gestured for me to come over to him.

I rolled my eyes. "No thank you. I'm not interested," I said with my arms crossed and looking away.

He gave a small chuckle. I hated it. He always thought everything I did was a joke. I watched as he stood up from his desk and he came over to me. I looked at him and watched how damn attractive he looked when his hair was pulled back the way it was. He smirked at me as he came close to me. I rolled my eyes again. "Cut the bull, Cole. What did you do today? Where did you go for so long?"

He pulled me against him. I let him. His breath brushed past my cheeks. He always did this. He always tried to seduce me when I asked him questions that he didn't want to answer. "Enough with the questions. Let's go to the room instead and I can show you how much I missed you today," he said, whispering it into my ear, making goosebumps run down my body.

The anger inside me subsided and I gave in. Every time. I smiled and pulled away from him, holding his hand. He followed. I walked into the living room and I made him sit down on the couch. If anything, I wanted him to think that I didn't care where he had been. I wanted him to forget that I had seen him on his laptop. I wanted to know what was on there and if it meant that I had to seduce him to sleep, then so be it. I took my robe off and, as he sat on the couch, he eagerly zipped down my costume. Two could play at this game. I let him have his fun. He pulled me in for a kiss and before I knew it, we were making love in front of the fireplace.

...

When I felt his body go limp, I knew that he had fallen into a deep sleep. I wiggled my way out from under him and put my robe on again. The fire was burning low, and it was well past midnight. I tip-toed my way down the hall, feeling on edge. I didn't want him to catch me doing this, but if he wasn't going to tell me anything then I was going to find out for myself. Daisy meowed next to me, making me jump. I shooed her away. I looked back to make sure that he hadn't woken up. He hadn't.

I reached the door and opened it quietly. The suspicions were making my heart beat very fast. I didn't want to do this. I closed the door slightly behind me as Daisy joined me in the room. It was better that she was with me; she helped me feel less on edge. I switched my phone's light on so that I could see what I was doing. His laptop was placed neatly on the table. I walked over to it and opened it up. Yes! Thank God it hadn't locked the screen. It had just gone to sleep.

His main screen was a photo of him and me, which made me feel a whole lot better. Maybe I was overthinking all of this. I started feeling guilty and almost decided to close the laptop when I thought of how many times he had been keeping things from me. I saw a folder that said "work". I went into it. It was just a whole lot of boring pictures of landscapes and strangers posing. I then decided to go into his emails. There was nothing but emails between clients, asking him to take pictures of them. I went out and decided to go into his recycling bin. Maybe that would be full? It wasn't; it was empty. There had to be some dirt.

I went into his documents and pictures, but there was absolutely nothing.

I exited everything and I looked at the screen. Each folder was normal things. Games, pictures, work, Word documents, exams, family, and the list went on. I hovered my finger over the scroller and decided to check out the games that he liked. I went into the folder and there was a whole list. Call of Duty, Assassins Creed, God of War, WW1 and Captured. The icon for the last one even looked a little different from the other games. I was intrigued by it. I clicked on it. It opened up and a whole bunch of photos fell out.

My heart dropped and I forgot to breathe. There were hundreds and hundreds of photos of Amelia. My heart ached at the sight of this. There were pictures while she was taking a shower; there were pictures of her sleeping; pictures of her kissing Alex and Sebastian. There were pictures of her hands and feet. There were pictures of her mouth and eyes, while she was sleeping. Pictures of her crying. Some more nudes. He had taken all of these. My heart was racing, and I didn't know what to do with the information. I felt as though my whole world had just been pulled upside down.

I hated her. She always got everything. Even Cole was obsessed with her. And then it clicked. He must be the stalker. Cole *was* the stalker. It makes sense of why he had all those pictures of her. Fear fell over me, and I put the laptop down and scrambled for my phone. I had to get evidence of this. I took a picture of the screen with all the pictures and sent it to Amelia. I looked up at the door, making sure he wasn't coming. *He* was the dangerous stalker, and I was sleeping with him. He had been using me all this time, just to get close to Amelia. It all made sense now. My heart ached and my throat tightened. Tears started streaming down my face, as I sent Amelia the message.

Cole is the stalker. He used me to get close to you. I found a folder on his laptop, which had hundreds of photos of you on it. Cole is the stalker!

I couldn't stop myself from crying. I felt my whole body shake as the tears just kept streaming. How stupid I had been to think he loved me. All this time, right under our noses, there he was. He had always been there. The realization kicked in when I thought about it all. Cole was with me on the night that Alexander disappeared, though. It didn't make sense. Unless he had a helper? A second party?

I jumped as I saw the door swing open, and the light got switched on. Cole was frowning and I watched as he looked from me to the laptop and his whole body tensed. "What have you done?" he asked cautiously.

I wiped the tears from my eyes and turned the laptop towards him. "I think I should be asking you that question. What have you done, Cole?" I said, raising my voice.

I watched as his whole face changed and he took a step forward. "Let me explain. I know it looks bad," he said quietly. I took a step back and even Daisy decided to run out the room. I was alone now.

I shook my head at him. "How are you going to explain that?" I asked, shouting it at him.

He held up his hands and tried to think for a moment. "You didn't tell anyone did you?" he asked, searching my face and a cold sweat ran over my body.

"I did. I told Amelia," I said slowly.

"Why would you do that?" he shouted, and I jumped.

He stepped towards me, and I decided to make a run for it. I ran around the table, and he followed. I tried to make it out the door, but he grabbed my robe. He pulled me around and everything inside me panicked. Was this going to be my ending too?

He managed to knock me off my feet, making me hit the floor. I groaned and he sat on top of me, restraining me from moving. I tried to scream but he immediately placed his hands over my mouth, muffling it. His eyes were vulnerable, and they looked panicked.

"I did love you, Skylar, I did. Things just got complicated. There's more to the story than you know. I told him I didn't want to do it, but he wouldn't listen," he said, shaking his head and I wondered who else was helping him. "I'm sorry it had to end this way, but I can't let you get away now, without me fixing it first," he said nervously.

Fear engulfed me and I tried screaming through his hands. I watched as he scrambled around the room to get something and eventually he gave up. I was making too much noise for him.

He held up his hand. "I'm sorry, I didn't want to hurt you," he said sympathetically, and at that he swung his hand down and smacked me right across the face. Darkness folded in. He had knocked me unconscious.

Chapter 32

UNVEILING SECRETS

Dreams are a funny thing. You either dream something that's about to happen, like an omen, or you dream about the past. At times you dream about things you've seen without even realizing that you've taken note of them subconsciously. It's a funny thing. It always amazes me when you dream of things that feel vivid. Like winning the lottery or watching someone you love die. So much emotion placed in something that's not even real, yet it feels real.

That was the kind of dream I was having; a rather good kind of dream. I dreamed of Sebastian, and how he'd kissed me. I dreamed of a life with him that was stress-free. A life where we went on adventures, and where he stopped being a cop. Where we moved away and lived somewhere far away, across a lake. With the glass house so beautifully lit with fairy lights that it looked like a fairy tale. I dreamed that he kissed me and made love to me every night, and that our souls danced blissfully together when we did. Everything about him was magical and I saw through that cold demeanor he always tried to show. I saw through all those hurt threads that he had, and through time I slowly helped him knit it all back together. It was a dream where there was no stalker, and no competition. Alexander was nowhere to be seen, and maybe that was for the best. My life with Sebastian seemed like an endless love story, and I was lucky to be the main character. But in the end, I had to wake up.

I gave a small jerk as I awoke and saw the ceiling in my room. It had all been a dream. A lovely, but sad dream. I felt a teardrop run down from my eye as I was reminded that my life couldn't be so simple and easy. I gave a small sigh and turned to look beside me. There he was, Sebastian. Lying beside me so peacefully, as though nothing in life had ever gone wrong for him. His eyes were shut but they were moving slightly. He must have been in a deep sleep. A part of me wondered what he was dreaming about.

I placed my hands under my head as I looked at him. His dark eyelashes looked so perfect, in the lighting. I looked at his nose, which had the slightest touch of sun freckles on them. His skin was a golden brown and his lips had the lightest plum touch to them. I stared at him in awe. How had I managed to get such a good-looking man? Why did he find me interesting? I thought back to the night before when he'd kissed me to sleep and whispered something only I would ever hear. My heart raced at the memory of our soul tie when we made love. For once in my life, I had felt completely certain that I was making the right decision.

I looked at the tattoo that was peeking its way out of his shirt and thought back to how I'd brushed my lips against every single one, devouring everything that was him. I had wanted to do that for such a long time. Maybe it was okay that my dream was only a dream. Maybe reality was going to be far better than that, because one thing was for certain now: I had him and he was here. He was sleeping in my bed, and I knew that he was in love with me. That was good enough for me now. I looked away from him, just so he wouldn't wake up to me staring at him.

I thought of how my parents had let him sleep here because I had told them that it made me feel safer and more comfortable. They liked him because he was a cop, so they definitely knew he would take care of me if anything happened.

We hadn't come home late the night before. After we'd made love, we had showered together, which took a lot longer than it needed to. Then, we'd made lunch and after lunch I'd asked him to come back to my place. My parents appreciated it. They liked that I hadn't broken the rules again. Now that Alexander had been found, maybe it was better to be surrounded by as many cops as possible, until they found out who the stalker was. I thought of Alex and thought about how I wanted to see him again.

"Good morning, beautiful," Sebastian said softly, breaking into my thoughts. I looked to the side and smiled. His eyes looked as though they had a deep-green glow to them. His smile was soft, and his eyes had softened on the edges. He was calm. I liked seeing him like this.

"Good morning," I said softly back, and I moved closer to him.

"I'm happy to see you are okay, and that you slept well," he said, watching me as I edged my way closer to him.

He lifted himself slightly off the bed, to lean on his elbow. His muscles tensed under his weight. I nodded my head gently, not wanting to tell him what I had dreamed about. I didn't want him to think that I was some obsessed girl. I watched as he leaned closer to me, and he placed his body on mine. I smiled at the gesture. I loved how dominant he looked when he towered over me. It's almost as if every single muscle in my body wanted to weaken. I placed my hands on his arms and could feel his warmth beneath his shirt. I could feel my hip sting a little under the weight, but I tried to ignore it.

He ran his fingers past my cheek, tickling it in the process. I closed my eyes and giggled as he moved his mouth down onto my neck, making me shiver. The stubble of his beard tickled my neck. He planted a kiss on my collarbone, and he chuckled when he heard me squeal slightly. I loved hearing him happy. His laughter was like a melody to my ears. I placed my hands on his face and tugged it slightly higher. He got the message and lifted his face and he looked into my eyes. With my hands behind his neck, I pulled his face closer to mine and closed my eyes as our lips softly pressed upon one another. So blissful. It reminded me of the dream, and it only brought joy to my heart. It was like my own happy little secret.

He pulled away from me and just looked at me, and I saw so much emotion in his eyes. "Thank you for trusting me," he said, and I felt very sympathetic at that moment.

I smiled at him. "Of course. Thank you for showing me that you are actually decent, despite what the others say," I said, saying the last bit of the sentence a little softer. He gave a small chuckle and he looked at my lips again. "I wish I had met you a whole lot sooner. Like, I mean, if you grew up here everything would be so different now," I said again, looking at him. He smirked at my comment and his eyes seemed to glow. My fingers had nestled themselves comfortably in his hair. His morning look was even better than his neat self. Messy suited him, especially because I always saw him neat.

"Everything happens for a reason," he said quietly. I smiled at him and at that he planted another soft kiss on my lips. I held the kiss for as long as I could. I moved my hands further down, until they slipped beneath his shirt. He tensed and pulled himself away from me, chuckling.

"No. As much as I would love to do this right now, we can't. Not here, and definitely not while your parents are in the same house," he said, looking around the room, as though they were in the room with us.

I chuckled. "Oh, come on," I said, looking down at his shirt and trying to run my hands further up his tummy. It felt so good to feel his torso and to be allowed to do this. He chuckled more and tried to stop my hands. His smile was so beautiful. I loved every bit of it.

"No, I'm serious," he said playfully. His eyes looked at mine. We both jumped as there was a knock at the door.

"Yes?" I said a little louder than normal.

"I'm going to go to the bathroom," Sebastian said quickly, as he jumped off the bed to hide in the bathroom. He closed the bathroom door as the bedroom door opened. I smiled at it.

"Amelia, dear?" my mother said as she opened the door. She looked around the room.

"Yes?" I asked, knowing she was looking for Sebastian.

"You have a visitor," she said, giving me a weary smile.

I frowned at her. "What do you mean, a visitor?" I said carefully.

She looked at me. "It's Alexander. He knocked on the door this morning, asking to see you. He brought a couple more police officers with, as he is supposed to be in protective custody, but he didn't want to listen. So, they brought him here," she said, watching my every move.

I nodded my head slowly. "Okay, thank you. I will be down shortly," I said quietly. I watched her nod her head and she turned around and closed the door behind her.

I sat there in the bed feeling quite displaced. I didn't know whether to be happy or worried. I quickly climbed off the bed and walked over to my closet. I pulled out a red jacket and slipped it on. I pulled on my blue jeans. I put my brown slippers on, as I knew I wasn't going to go outside. I walked away from my closet and over to my table. I picked up my brush and brushed my hair. My nerves were getting the better of me. I thought of how Sebastian would feel about the whole situation. I thought of how Alex would feel, seeing Sebastian coming down the stairs with me. Gosh, I wanted to hide away at this point. When Alex and I had last seen each other, we'd confessed our feelings for each other, and we were certain we were going to get together. I didn't know how on earth this was going to look in his eyes.

I walked over to the bathroom and sighed as I knocked on the door. I didn't hear anything, but the shower's water was going. I knocked again. I heard a faint voice saying that I could come in. I opened it slowly.

"Are you covered up?" I asked.

He chuckled. "Yes, don't worry," he said as I heard him closing the shower door.

I pushed the door open more, and I walked in. I looked up and I saw him standing in a shower towel. His body was damp, and his tattoos looked darker. When he stood there, I could properly look at how fit his body was. His arms weren't too big for his posture. His hair looked almost black when wet and it was spiked up from how he'd tried to dry it. He looked like a hot mess, and I was definitely finding it hard to concentrate. He smiled at me because he knew I was admiring him.

I shook my head and turned around. "I can't concentrate when you look like that," I said, and I folded my arms over my chest.

I could feel him staring. Before he could say anything more, I had to tell him about Alex. Maybe it wasn't such a good idea, while he was naked. I turned back to him, and I tried to be as serious as I could, and I could see he sensed it because his smile disappeared and it went stern.

"I need to tell you something, when you are ready and dressed. I'll tell you outside," I said, looking at him, and he frowned.

I could see his eyes were searching my face, to see if he would get any hint out of me. I gave him a weak smile and turned around after he'd nodded his head at me. I opened and closed the door behind me. I went over to my bed and picked up the covers and dusted them off. I made it nice and neat and puffed out my pillows. I drew open my curtains and saw how the clouds covered most of the sky. I walked away from the curtains and wanted to check to see if Alex had maybe sent me a message on my phone. Maybe it would explain why he'd pitched up here. Maybe he'd sent me a message and I hadn't seen it.

I looked next to my bed and found it. There was a text from Alex, saying *I need to see you.* That was all. He had sent it early that morning. I watched as the bathroom door opened. I put down my phone and I straightened out my covers.

Sebastian wore dark colors, which always made me more attracted to him. His skin tone suited the dark colors. He wore a black hoodie and blue jeans with his sneakers. His hair was spiked up from being dried with the towel. He looked very handsome. His eyes were dark, and I knew that he was worried.

"What did you want to talk about?" he asked.

I moved closer to him. "The knock at the door was my mom. She told me that Alex is here and that he wants to see me," I said as I watched his expression.

He kept frowning, not changing his face one bit. He nodded his head. "Okay, that's fine, I guess. I can imagine why he would be here," Sebastian said, forcing the words out of his mouth. He crossed his arms over his chest, and I could see he was in a very dark space.

"There's more. I think you need to let me talk to him alone," I said nervously, and I watched as he scoffed and looked away.

"And what if he makes a move on you and you choose him?" he asked. He was very vulnerable, and I could see he was jealous.

I sympathetically moved over to him and touched his arms with my hands, to try to reassure him. "I promise you this, I chose you for a reason. I won't let Alex do anything. I just think it's better for him to process the information once he knows it from me. If you tell him, there might be a fight and I can just see it being bad," I said and I watched as Sebastian sighed and unfolded his arms and we held hands as we looked into each other's eyes. It felt good. I knew it was hard for him, but at least we were compromising. "You don't have to leave. Just let me talk to him and hear what he has to say and then we can maybe go out for something later," I said, and he nodded his head, but I could see his eyes had darkened.

Just the very fact that he hadn't said much made me nervous. I turned away from him and looked at the door and gestured for us to go. He held onto my hand and walked to the door. He opened the door and let me walk out first and then he followed afterwards, closing the door behind him. I could feel the butterflies rushing around my tummy. I was so nervous I even felt nauseous. I could see the staircase up ahead. I turned left and went down the first step. Sebastian was right behind me. I could hear Alex talking in the distance.

I got to the bottom of the staircase. I was actually too afraid to look up and see him. As we turned right, I looked up and saw him sitting there with my mom. She was making small talk with him. They were sitting in front of the fire while they had a cup of something to drink in their hands. He looked worn down and tired. He had definitely lost weight and it pained me to see him that way.

He looked up as he saw us approaching and his eyes locked on mine. I could see he had cuts all over his face and that his one cheekbone was still badly bruised. His knuckles had been cut open. I couldn't even imagine what the rest of him looked like. I held my hand to my mouth in shock when he looked properly at me. I felt a kick in my stomach. I don't know what kind of emotion I was feeling, but it wasn't the good kind. I walked around to meet him, and I couldn't help but frown in sadness.

"Alex, I'm so sorry that this has happened to you," I said as I saw his one eye had a little bit of red close to the iris. Gosh, he looked terrible. I couldn't even imagine what he had been through.

He shook his head. "Don't be sad or sorry. I'm just glad that I made it out alive," he said, trying to lighten the mood.

I moved in and stretched out my arms and he welcomed the hug, and I held him tightly. Feeling his hug again made me feel so happy, although the hug felt very different. I was so grateful that he was okay. I was so happy that I could hug him again. I couldn't even remember how many times I'd wanted to hear his voice and feel his hug. His hug was a little weaker than it used to be, and he didn't have the usual comfort that he always had, but I didn't blame him. I could smell his cologne and it brought back memories. Many happy memories that made me sad now because I knew that those memories were long gone.

He didn't let go until I eventually did because I could feel Sebastian staring at us. I wished I could have done this alone. He looked at me and I could see lots of pain in his eyes. I thought that he knew that I wasn't the same anymore. He looked away from me and looked at Sebastian, who was standing only a few feet away from us. I turned to look at Sebastian. His jawline seemed to be more defined now. His eyes had darkened, and I knew he wasn't happy. I watched as he stretched out his arm and gave Alex a handshake and a side hug at the same time.

"Glad you are okay, man," he said. It almost sounded as though the words were hard to say. I was so nervous that one of them was going to break and start throwing their fists about.

"Yeah, thanks man. You should actually thank Amelia; she was what kept me going," Alex said, and he looked away from Sebastian to me. I didn't know how to react to the comment. Sebastian looked down and I watched as he tensed his jaw. Gosh, I decided that I needed to quickly defuse the situation.

"Alex, let's go and speak somewhere, where it's more private," I said sternly, and I watched as my mother got the message.

"Sebastian, would you please help me here in the kitchen?" My mother raised her voice over us, just to make sure we heard her loud and clear.

He looked up and I could see his mind was completely fogged over. He looked like he had the very first time I had met him. Very guarded and cold. He nodded his head and turned away from us and didn't even dare to look at me. I didn't want this for us. I really did like him a lot and I didn't want him to think anything of it. I felt guilty as I knew that Sebastian felt hurt. I looked to Alex, and we moved to the furthest point in the room. We sat at our dining room table, and I couldn't even see Sebastian and my mother anymore because we had turned the corner to sit down.

"I'm surprised you even wanted to see me," I said quietly as he sat down across from me. He looked at me and it pained me to look at him, so instead I kept my eyes on the table.

"I wanted to see you every day. I kept telling myself that when I got out that I would come and see you," he said, trying to look at me.

"What happened?" I asked him, trying to avoid his statement. I heard him sigh.

"I was snatched at my house. The day we last saw each other. I never saw who hit me, and I never saw who my kidnapper was. I was in a dark cave. Very far away from here. They even had auto-tune so that I wouldn't hear the voice. So, whoever they are they knew exactly what they were doing."

By then I was staring at him, captivated by his story. "How did you escape?" I asked curiously, and he shook his head. You could see it pained him to say all these things.

"I was chained to the wall, and I looked for a rock to hit the chain free. Eventually, after the third hit I managed to break the chain. I felt along the path until I saw a light ahead and escaped. I'm so glad that they didn't come back when I had escaped, as I'm sure they would have killed me," he said, and he looked up at me.

I was shaken. I didn't know what to say. "I'm so sorry. It's because of me that you were in there," I said, and I could feel my throat burning again. I tried my utmost best to keep the tears at bay, but it was difficult. He could see I wanted to cry, and he reached his hand out for me and I don't know why, but I took it and he squeezed it.

"Amelia, we will find this person whoever they are and, when we do, they will surely pay," he said, trying to reassure me. I nodded my head, and I could feel the lump in my throat easing up. I let go of his hand and I knew he noticed. "I'm sorry I couldn't be here to protect you," he said quietly, and I shook my head.

"Don't be silly. That should have been the last thing on your mind. Besides, Sebastian would do night shifts when he was still working as a cop. So, in a way he looked after me and made sure nothing happened." I said the words, even though I knew they would hurt him.

"I'm glad he could be here for you, when I couldn't." I could hear that the words felt sour in his mouth. It was quiet between us for a couple of seconds and then he broke the silence. "Amelia, I never intended for you to find out about Ingrid the way that you did," he said, and I felt as though it was a year ago since that happened, but when he had said it, it seemed to rip open an old wound. I looked up at him and I felt like smacking him for how he had hurt me. I had so much to say that instead I just sat there and looked at him in bitterness. "I'm sorry, I did love you and I did want to start a new chapter with you," he said again.

"Why did you sleep with her then? You just couldn't help yourself, could you?" I spat the words out and he tightened his jaw and looked down.

"Look, I didn't want to sleep with her, but she wouldn't stop. She begged me to take her back and I kept saying no, and eventually I thought she would leave me alone if I gave her one last taste."

The words turned my insides inside out. I couldn't believe I had trusted him. "I trusted you with my heart. How could you do that to me? I really thought you meant it and then I found out from her later that evening that you had slept with her. Do you know how that hurt me?" I felt the lump in my throat burn. I could feel the tears stream down my face. I watched as his face broke at the sight of my tears.

"I'm truly so, so sorry, Amelia. If I could take it back, I would," he said, trying to reach out for my hand, but it only made me pull my hands off the table.

I looked at him and shook my head. I wiped the tears from my face. "You can be sorry, but it will never be the same again, Alex. You can be my friend if you want, but I will never trust you again with my heart. You lost that. I do still love you, but I have to let that fantasy go now," I said bitterly.

He stood up and he knelt down next to me, wanting to hold my hand. I could see his eyes were watery, but I only shook my head. "Amelia, please," he begged, and I let him take my hand. All I wanted to do was hug him, but I had to stop everything inside me from doing so. He kissed my hand, and I shook my head. I pulled my hand away from him and looked away. He was making this more difficult than anything.

"Alex, when I said you were too late, I also meant that Sebastian and I are an item now. I trust him. I trust him with everything of me. I know he won't do anything like that to me. I'm sorry," I said looking down, too afraid to look up at him.

"Have you slept with him?" he asked quietly as he stood up and looked at me. He obviously had added all the dots in his head.

I looked away from him. "Is that all you care about?" I said coldly, and I felt everything inside me crush. I heard him sigh and I knew that he knew. He was my childhood love. My whole life I had wanted him to be my everything and slowly I was watching those dreams crumble away.

"Well, Amelia, I may never get your forgiveness again, but I want you to know that I still love you. I always have and always will. No matter how many men you see in the future. I will always love you, even if I showed it to you poorly. Please know I am sorry for what I did, and I hope you can forgive me one day. All I ever want for you in life is happiness, even if it means that it isn't with me. I know I will forever regret what I did." I could hear his voice break. The tears were streaming now and all I could do was hold my hands in front of my eyes to shield them. "I didn't intend to leave you like this today. I will always be here for you. I'm sorry that I've hurt you so. I think it's best if I go now," he said and at that I looked up at him and all I wanted to do was hug him and hold him close.

It felt as though I was losing a lifetime best friend. I grabbed his hand and held on to it. Don't ask me why I did it; I think maybe it was the fear of losing someone I loved. And then I watched how he gave me one last kiss on my hand and then he let go of it and I felt so sad. I watched as he walked away and he greeted my mom and then he opened the door and then he was gone. Just like that. How quickly life can change.

I watched as Sebastian walked over to me. I heard my father walk through the door. Sebastian reached me and he didn't say anything, but he did open his arms and allowed me to hug him. I appreciated it. I stood up and wrapped my arms around him and I let the last couple of tears and regret run down my face. He held me tightly, and I felt so much better once I was done. My heart felt numb.

"I'm sorry," I said to him as I was holding him. I could feel him rest his chin on my head.

"Don't be sorry. I'm here for you," he said quietly.

I smiled a little. I wiped my eyes and pulled away from him, so I could look at him. "I'm sorry that Alex and me hugged for so long," I said quietly, and I could see a small smile form on his mouth.

He shook his head. "Look, it was tough, but it's okay," he said, trying to be positive. I smiled at him, and he looked down on me with sympathy.

"So, we said goodbye then. I guess I'm just sad because I've lost a childhood best friend as well," I said, feeling the tears build up.

His whole face was stern. He gestured for me to come in for another hug, and I did. It felt good to hug him and to be comforted in a time like this. I eventually took deep breaths and just stood there, listening to his heartbeat. I pulled away from him and looked past him, at my mother and my father talking in the distance. I looked up at Sebastian.

"Let's go, before my parents start to get worried," I said quietly, and Sebastian nodded his head. Before I could walk away, he pulled my hand and I turned to him, and he planted a quick kiss on my mouth. He pulled away and it did manage to make me smile, although I didn't really feel like any kisses right now.

"Do you want to go and get an ice-cream afterwards?" he asked, and I shook my head at him.

I looked at him and his eyes were still slightly darker. "If it's okay, can we go to your place?" I asked him, and he gave a small smile and nodded his head.

"Of course, we can," he said, and he placed his arm around me and gave me another squeeze before we pulled apart and walked over to my parents.

The fire felt perfect, and I tried to not look at my parents. I walked over to the kitchen island, which was filled with food.

My mother looked at me and gave me a sympathetic smile. "Are you okay, dear?" she asked, and I nodded my head. I didn't want to talk about it, otherwise I'd be a mess again. My father didn't say anything, although I know it did bother him. "Alright, dig in," my mother said, and I picked up a plate and gave another plate to Sebastian. We dished some food up on the plates. I took very little as I had lost my appetite. We sat down and began to eat. My dad asked Sebastian some questions, but I zoned out. I looked at Sebastian, who was already staring at me. I smiled at him, and he gave me a small smile as well. His eyes looked brighter than before.

Everyone else was munching away, but I didn't want to eat. I looked at Sebastian as he had asked my father a question about the journalism. I thought of Alex and felt the pain in my chest. I pushed the thought out of my mind.

"Oh, I forgot, Tyron sends his love," my mother said as she looked at me. I looked up at her and felt confused.

"Okay. When did you see him?" I asked, confused.

She took another bite of her food and finished chewing it first before answering. "Last night, after you two went to bed, I heard a knock on the door and found Tyron there. He said he missed us and wanted to have a quick cup of coffee. Dad was with us. He said he was in the neighborhood. I told him that you two were upstairs and I asked him if I should call you and he refused. He just said I should send his love to you," she said.

I nodded my head. "He has been very busy lately. I remember there was a stage where he refused to leave the house, and now he is gone all the time," I said, looking at my mom.

She shrugged her shoulders. "He said he was doing small jobs in town, here and there. He did go upstairs to get something out of Marcus's room. He said that he had lost one of his cables and wanted to see if we didn't maybe have it. So, he did go upstairs. I'm surprised you didn't hear him," she said, looking at me, and I also shrugged my shoulders.

"I guess I was really tired," I said.

Before I knew it, I had finished everything on my plate. Everyone thanked each other for the effort and for the company. My dad asked us what we were going to do for the day, and I told them I wanted to go to Sebastian's place. My mother asked if we didn't rather want to stay at home with her and bake some cookies and watch a movie. Have a relaxing day instead. I did thank her for the idea, but I told her I wanted to have some time with Sebastian as we didn't always get time together. I'm sure she didn't believe me when I said that. After what had happened with Alex, I'm sure she understood what I meant. She nodded her head. She told us not to stay away too late. She told us she would make a very nice meal for the night and that we should promise not to eat too much before then. She told me she would also make my favorite strawberry pie puddy and that she would be waiting for us. We all laughed at how much care and effort my mother was putting into everything.

We stayed for one last cup of hot cocoa and then I greeted my parents. Mom gave me an extra-long hug; I supposed it was because of what happened to Alex and me. She knew how much I cared about him. My dad kissed me on the head, and I felt as though they were being a bit much. I tried not to push them away, even though I felt it was very strange.

"Okay, guys, we'll see you later. I love you. Thank you for letting me go," I said one last time. My parents put their arms around each other and watched Sebastian and me.

"It's fine, my dear. Please just be safe. I don't want anything happening to you," my mother said, and she looked worried. It felt strange.

"Yeah, maybe ask Michael to escort you guys to Sebastian's house. That way you have extra protection," my father said, and Sebastian nodded his head.

"Of course, sir," he said, and I shook my head.

"Sebastian is a cop. I don't think the stalker will try anything on him, even if he wanted to," I said confidently.

"You'll be surprised at what criminals do," Sebastian said, looking down at me. I felt small.

"Take the extra protection. If you want to go to his house, that is our one rule," my father said sternly.

"Yes, sir," Sebastian said.

"Take your phone with you as well, please, so that we can contact you," my mother said.

I nodded my head. "Okay," I said.

We waved goodbye to my family one last time. Sebastian opened the door for me, and we walked out. Bas held my hand as we walked down the pathway. He opened the small little gate and let me go first. We walked over to the car, and he unlocked it and opened my door for me. He gestured for me to climb in.

"Let me just go and speak to Michael and then he can follow us," Sebastian said, and I nodded.

He closed my door. After speaking to Michael, he climbed into the car and locked the door. He started the engine and drove onto the road. We drove down the road and Sebastian switched on the radio. A song came across the radio, and it sounded good. He tried to skip it and I skipped it back.

"No, please, I want to listen to this song," I said, and he smiled and left it to play. It was called *The Feels* by *Labrinth*. The song had a very sad tune to it. I loved it. It was maybe because I did feel sad.

"Gosh, I wish I could talk to the Author of my life and ask them to take it easy. There's only so much I can handle," I said, looking at Sebastian and he smiled. He reached over and gently squeezed my hand. He kept his eyes on the road as we passed many trees and he looked at me at one point and looked back at the road. He placed his hand on my thigh. It sent warmth all over my body.

"This song is so intense. I love how atmospheric it can be and how chaotic at the same time. This song reminds me of you sometimes, especially the verse where the woman speaks about how she's lost in emotion and that she's intoxicated with the person. It's how I feel about you," he said with a smile on his face as he looked ahead. My heart warmed. It was like the dream I'd had in the morning. I leaned over and kissed him on the cheek, and he smiled. I sat back into my seat, and we stopped at a T-junction. The roads were quiet, which was nice. I could see Michael put on his hazards behind us and then he pulled off the road. I turned around and looked at him.

"Sebastian, Michael has put on his hazards," I said, feeling wary of the situation.

Sebastian frowned and looked back. He reversed the car and stopped next to him. "Michael, are you okay? What's up?" he asked.

Michael climbed out of the car and looked around the car. The tires were flat. He looked up at us and he shook his head. "Listen, I think you should continue driving. You never know if this is a diversion. It's safer if you drive on. I'll call the rest of the buds to come and help me," he said, looking around him. I started to get a bad feeling inside. I looked at Sebastian and his face was stern.

"Are you sure?" he asked, and Michael nodded his head.

"I'll send another unit out to you guys. Let me know if you get there safely," Michael said, and he looked away from Sebastian and looked around again.

"Alright, bud, see you," Sebastian said, and he turned back onto the road. We came to the T-Junction.

I looked at Sebastian. "Do you think it's a set up?" I asked, worried. I saw a car on the road to our right. Sebastian waited for him to pass. I wanted to go home.

Sebastian looked and I watched as he his lips parted to say something. "I have no id..."

There was a big smash, as a car drove into the side of our car. The car swerved and spun around, making me hit my head on the side window. I heard someone scream and realized it was me. The car stood still, and I opened my eyes and looked over at Sebastian. He was okay. There was a cut on his head from the blow, but he was okay.

He looked at me and I could see blood running down his face. "Are you okay?" he asked. I nodded my head. He looked at my head and reached his hand out to touch me.

"You're cut," he said, and I touched my forehead and felt moisture. I look at my fingers. It was blood. I felt so confused.

"What happened?" I asked, looking around.

There was glass all over the dashboard and both mine and Sebastian's windows had been hit out. I unclipped myself and so did Sebastian. I watched as Sebastian's whole face changed to shock. He quickly tried to reach for something under his chair, and he was staring behind me. Before I knew it my car door opened, and a figure appeared beside me. I looked up.

"Hello, Amelia," Cole said, standing next to me. I frowned at him, and I watched as he reached inside his jacket and drew out a gun. Fear. Sebastian didn't think twice; he shot at Cole. I screamed. He shot Cole in the shoulder and then in the neck. Blood splashed across my face and all I could see was Cole choking, he held his neck as blood started streaming down his neck. I began to cry. I watched as Cole fell to the ground. I looked at Sebastian in fear. What on earth was happening?

"Amelia, you need to listen to me now. This isn't a game. This is a setup. I think they are here to kidnap you. You need to run, even if I don't follow. Run until you reach home," Sebastian shouted, and I felt as though my whole body was stuck to the seat. I was so afraid and shocked. I didn't know how to handle the situation. The tears kept streaming down my face.

"Sebastian, I'm scared," I screamed out to him, and he tried to remain calm.

He touched my leg, which helped me look at him. "I understand, but you need to think of your life. You need to run and hide. Try to calm down. I'm sure Michael has already heard the shots and will have already alerted the rest of the cops," he said, and I nodded my head.

"Okay," I said, and I looked around the corner and it looked clear. Except for Cole's body, which was laying in the road. There was so much blood. I could feel my body shake. "Come with me please," I asked him, and he nodded his head.

"I'm right behind you," he said, and he opened his door.

I climbed out the car and turned to Sebastian. I watched it all in slow-motion. Sebastian climbed out the car and I heard a gunshot go off. I stood there as I watched Tyron walk towards him. He had shot Sebastian in the shoulder. I screamed.

"I think you've done enough," he said to Sebastian. Sebastian raised his gun. "You've been lying to her this whole time," Tyron shouted, and I watched as Sebastian shot him in the shoulder and then he shot him again, I didn't see where, but I all I could see was Tyron drop. Lifeless.

"No, Sebastian! Wait," I screamed as I saw Tyron lying on the floor. My heart ached. He was my brother after all. I felt so confused. Sebastian sighed and looked up at me. I just stared at him blankly, trying to piece everything together. Why he had just killed Cole and Tyron, who seemed to be protecting me.

"Put your hands up, Sebastian," I heard Michael say from behind me. I had forgotten that he was just down the road from where we were. He must have heard the shots. Michael had raised his gun, and it was pointed at Sebastian. I didn't understand what was going on. I felt so disorientated. I looked at Bas, whose face was so stern and serious. He held his gun in his hand, and it looked as though he was plotting something in his mind.

"Sebastian, what going on?" I asked, shaking from the shock.

"Put your gun down now! You are under arrest for second degree murder, for kidnapping and for attempted kidnapping. Put your gun down and your hands up where I can see them!" Michael shouted, as he held the gun directly at Sebastian. I heard as the radio on Michael's shoulder asked Michael if he had found Sebastian.

Was all of this true? I started feeling so sick to my stomach.

"Look, Michael, I can explain," Sebastian said, still holding his gun but putting his hands in the air.

"Don't worry, you will have your chance to explain how you managed to pull this all off," Michael said, disgust in his voice.

I slowly started piecing everything together. I thought about what Tyron had said, that Sebastian had lied to me. I looked up at him, and his eyes were already glued to mine. They were dark and unrecognizable from the normal green eyes I had grown to love.

"Are you the stalker?" I asked, afraid of saying the words too loudly.

"Yes, he is." Michael spoke for him before he could even answer.

Sebastian didn't say a word. His jaw stiffened. My heart felt like it ripped apart. Everything inside me felt so confused and used. I looked down and saw small spots of Cole's blood on my hand.

"Is this a joke?" I asked hoping it was. Sebastian looked at me sternly and shook his head. How didn't I see it?

"Why, Sebastian?" I asked, shattered.

He looked back at Michael and then at me.

"The cops are on their way, Sebastian, so put your gun down and we can put an end to all of this," Michael said once more. I held my hand up to my mouth and took a breath. I started stepping back and I knew he was watching me. How had I been so blinded all this time? It actually made sense. He had always been around, always with us. I felt everything inside of me cave. How could I have been so stupid? He had been the stalker all this time. *He* was the creep. He had wiggled his way into my life, and he had seduced me.

I watched as he tried to take steps closer to me, which only made me back away. I heard a gunshot go off. I jumped and screamed as it frightened me. It was Michael warning Sebastian. I needed to get out of here. I looked at Sebastian, who was still assessing the situation. I turned around and decided to get out of harm's way. He wasn't who I had grown to love. He was dangerous and a killer. I didn't want to be in the environment anymore. I wanted to hide and run like he had told me to.

I took a step, and I heard another gunshot go off. I screamed. I watched as Michael screamed in pain. Sebastian had shot his leg. He knelt in pain as he held his thigh.

"Michael," I called. I stood there and watched as blood started streaming slowly down his pants.

"I'm sorry, man. It's nothing personal," I heard Sebastian say as he walked up from behind me, walked past me and stood in front of Michael, who reached up and tried to aim his gun at Sebastian. Sebastian was faster. He hit him on the side of the head, with the butt of the gun. I watched as Michael groaned and fell to the ground. Game time. It was as if everything in life had just stopped, and this was the most dangerous moment of all. Sebastian looked at me and I felt paralyzed.

"Amelia, I know it looks bad, but I have a good reason for everything. Come with me now and I can take us somewhere safe, and we can be together." He said the words very quickly.

I shook my head. "No," I said the words firmly.

I watched as his expression went cold. He looked down and then I knew it was now or never.

I stood still for a second. I built up all my energy and darted. I ran as fast as I could in the opposite direction across the snow, but that too wasn't good enough. He tackled me to the ground. I groaned as my body crashed into the ground. I screamed as loudly as I could. I made sure that whoever was near would hear me.

"Shhh, Amelia, I'm not the enemy here. I want to protect you and love you from all these crazy people. Why are you making this more difficult than it has to be? Remember, it's me, Sebastian. You love me, I'm not the enemy," he shouted at me. I felt him pin me to the floor.

I cried out into the cold snow. "Sebastian, please. I don't want this. Just let me go," I sobbed and, before I knew it, he placed a cloth over my mouth and nose. I started to suffocate.

"I thought you would understand why I did all of this. I can't lose you again. I won't let them take you away from me. We will go to a safe place," he said as I moaned and cried. The chemicals burnt my nose and I started to lose consciousness. Blackout.

The day had finally come, and he had finally caught me. I had thought he wasn't real, but little did I know that he was the man I had been kissing all this time. He'd tricked me so well, making me think that he wasn't involved. Making someone take photos of us, so that I would think that the stalker hated him, yet he was the stalker. He had been with me all this time and my family didn't even know it. I couldn't believe that I had slept with my stalker. Oh, how bitter the unveiling secrets…

ACKNOWLEDGMENTS

Thank you, Lord, for blessing me with this talent to write and for allowing me to make a book. I love You.

Thank you to my husband for always listening to all my stories. I know it was tough. Thank you for being my best friend. Thank you for helping me get through the book with many ideas and tips. Thank you for helping me never give up on the story. I love you dearly.

Thank you to my mom for always encouraging me to never give up on my dreams and myself and for supporting me and my book. Thank you to my dad for always being proud of me and my goals, and to my family for being there for me. I love you.

To all the Haigs who have put all their love and kindness into me and my dreams, thank you for pushing me to succeed. I love you.

To my friends, who have been there since the beginning and heard this story when it wasn't even this mature. I love you all so dearly. Thank you for always being so motivating and supportive in wanting to read my story. You guys are the best!

Thank you for all the pre-orders that the book received; because of you, the printing of my book is possible. Thank you to everyone who put so much sponsorship towards the book and for everyone who supported me. I appreciate you from the bottom of my heart. May you enjoy this book as much as I enjoyed writing it! And to many more copies that get sold and printed. Thank you to everyone who wants to read my story. I love you all and may God bless you all!

Hugo Herbst
Kayla Walters
Dean Lunderstedt
Scarlette Cummings
Dennis Haig
Natasja Haig
Megan Menin
Tersia Illingworth
Tracy De Vries
Vivean Appelgryn
Modikwe Malema
Verve College
Cheryl Haig
Amber Beeton
Yvonne Haig
Hestia Elmes
Ricky Lunderstedt
Andrea Enslin
Karina Matthee
Regina Tlou
Remo Bartel

Kirsten Gibbon
Roger Haig
Idali Haig
Crystall Barnard
Hayley Louw
Vanessa Klincharska
Dylan Tupper
Virginia Klincharska-Quirk
Suzanne Klincharska
Alzander and Jeanine Gouws
Cassandra Moss
Martin and Paula Lunderstedt
Devan Welgemoed
William and Anne-Marie Haig
Nicole Vermaak
Gerhard Klonus
Caitlin Gelderblom
Chloe Jordt
Madelein Terblanche
Phillip Janse van Rensburg

COMING SOON...

Torn
BETWEEN

Tennille Haig

Printed in Great Britain
by Amazon

48331049R00219